CW00872214

The Queen of Carleon

The Queen of Carleon

Legends of Avalyne Book 1

Linda Thackeray

Contents

Prologue

The Veil was breached.

Her home was ablaze. The fires turning the forest into ash were no longer cackling but roaring in triumph as they continued to ravage the Wanderer's Wood. She could feel the intense heat prickling across her skin as she staggered blindly through the thick smoke, the hem of her dress greying with ash.

Under normal circumstances, her gift of Sight would be of use, but today it only added to the confusion. Already disorientated by the fire's victorious sound, adding to the confusion were the cries of her people around her. She could not just hear their terror, she could also feel it. She saw their fate rushing towards them and was unable to prevent any of it.

The protective shield keeping the realm of the elves separate from the world of men was torn asunder, and her city lay exposed, like the weeping wound from a picked scab. Berserkers warriors swarmed through the Veil, setting the forest alight. Fire raged through the undergrowth, engorging the trees, and enclosing the city built in the heart of the wood in a ring of fire. It was a prelude to a more direct assault.

Invaders rushed in through the inferno so quickly, and with numbers so large, it made her head spin. One minute, Lylea had been in her bed, and the next, she was overlooking the carnage from her keep in the Whispering Oak. Her people were taken by surprise, and she watched with horror as they rallied to save the forest, and their loved ones, despite being outnumbered by the heavily armed troops

Lylea's eyes glistened when she descended the keep and saw the world before her burning. Screams of terror whistled through the blaze from the trees that were ancient when she was young. In anguish, she watched them be consumed in columns of flame, hearing their wizened voices screaming in agony. Tears scalded her cheeks, as the forewarning of all she knew was about to befall her realm.

She turned away in time to see a berserker coming towards her where she stood. He rushed at her, this monstrous beast standing taller than most men, clad in heavy armour that bore the crest of the simurgh. Her heart sank each time she saw the crest because it had once signified hope, and now, it was the symbol of everything wrong in Avalyne. The beast swung his blade at her, and she raised her own to fight back. In her lifetime, she had prevailed against much fouler things than this soldier trying to end her life.

Although he was strong, she was skilled. She parried his attacks with vigour and determination, pushing him away with enough strength to send him staggering back a step or two. Giving him no time to recover, she immediately reacted in riposte by burying her sword in his neck. Dark blood, oily in its texture, spurted out of the wound as the beast uttered a strangled cry.

Through the smoke, another berserker emerged from the chaos, followed by more of his unit, until her world became engulfed in a clash of swords. The enemy's bodies lay strewn around her, and although she knew she was holding her own against them, they had kept her trapped and confined, unable to reach the others and soothe their panic.

When yet another soldier advanced upon her, she raised her stained sword to fight, ignoring the ache in her limbs and the minor wounds sustained during her battle. Five thousand years of rule had not dulled her skill, but no warrior could continue battle indefinitely without some injuries.

"Stand down!"

The voice was familiar, and when she discerned who it was, she understood how the Veil was breached. From the day of his birth, he was immune to her Sight. He was the one person in the whole of Avalyne whose future she could not see.

The berserker halted its advance and retreated, lowering his blade to allow his master to approach. Watching him step through the smoke, clad in his father's armour, the father whom he murdered to acquire the throne, was like a knife to her heart. Handsome and strong, he was Dare's son, but when she looked at his face, she also saw her daughter's eyes.

This was Arianne's boy, and her grandson. "Grandmother, will you yield?" His sword was drawn, and surrounding her were dozens of his servants, preparing to overwhelm her in sheer numbers.

"No," she hissed in anger, knowing her refusal meant death, "I will not." There was no mercy in his eyes only callous indifference. His answer was expected.

"Then die."

* * *

It was the points of many blades piercing her skin that woke Lylea, High Queen of the elves from her bed in a cold sweat.

For a moment, she lay against the sheets, dazed. It took a few seconds for her mind to settle, and when it did, she found herself shrouded in the silence of night. Beyond her room, the city of Eden Taryn remained in its customary tranquillity. The Wandering Woods were intact, and the blaze haunting her in her dreams was little more than fragments fading from her mind.

Yet, Lylea knew this was not merely a nightmare. What she saw, like most of her dreams, often came to pass. This would be no exception.

Without understanding how, Lylea instinctively knew her daughter would soon be pregnant.

And the child she bore, would be a monster.

Chapter One

Unexpected Expectation

When Calfax confirmed the news, Arianne could scarcely believe it.

She had worked herself into vexation fighting the desire to place more importance on the symptoms she experienced. Until she knew for certain, she would not accept the signs of impending joy. She moved through her day, trapped in a state of limbo. Her mood drove her poor husband to distraction because he could not fathom what was at the heart of her temperamental state. She longed to tell him what was in her mind, but held back at the thought of disappointing him. That, and the possibility that he might become so terrified by the idea that he could take the first horse out of the kingdom and hide in Tamsyn's remote tower in the forgotten corners of the Jagged Teeth.

What was it with men of courage and strength, who could ride forth and slay a thousand beserker warriors without a flinch, but went into complete and utter ruin when confronted with the possibility of becoming a father? Arianne suspected not even the Gods could answer that question, and as a result, she chose not to torment her king with the possibility that he might have an heir before she herself knew without doubt.

Besides, there were other matters to occupy Dare's mind.

As the High King of the newly unified Carleon, the War Dragon was working hard to rebuild the kingdom in the wake of the destruction wrought by Balfure's war. Any person who thought being king was about power and glory would be shocked to learn how arduous it was to be architect of a country's restoration. Too many times Arianne stepped into the Great Hall to see him working tirelessly in consultation with his ministers to the late hours of the night.

When he paused to catch his breath, Arianne saw the glimmer in his eyes, longing for simpler days, when he was simply Dare—the exiled Prince of Carleon. Yet, he was a good man, the one she loved beyond reason or thought. He would carry the burden because his people needed him, and because he was the last of his house, at least until now. He alone left Eden Halas and stepped out into the world, with the courage and the will to see Balfure driven away from Avalyne for all time. Arianne would be at his side forever, carrying that burden with him, to fill his life with the simple pleasures, such as the news she was now about to impart.

Today, there was no longer any doubt in her mind once Calfax, the royal physician, confirmed her suspicions—she was with child. She drifted, if it was possible for a flesh and blood being to drift, through the halls of the palace, with her hands on her belly in secret delight. What a sight she must have been to the palace staff—the queen of Carleon sweeping about the place wearing the smile of a happy fool.

She knew they were probably grateful for her good mood, since she had been difficult of late. Arianne resolved to make it up to those who bore the brunt of her temper, especially Dare, who was a devoted and attentive husband as any woman could ask. After all, being queen did not excuse bad behaviour in any shape or form. Her mother taught her that.

Thinking of Queen Lylea made Arianne's smile widen, knowing how thrilled she would be at the news. Despite her sometimes aloof manner and her adherence to ensuring all forms were observed, Arianne knew her mother would like nothing better than to be a grandmother allowed to spoil her grandchildren shameless. It was a right after all.

* * *

As always, when he was with taking counsel with his counsellors and advisors, Dare was in the Great Hall when Arianne found him a short time after she had received her news. He spent a great deal of time in this room, attempting to portion out men and resources to the few lands still being plagued by scattered remains of Balfure's army. The beserkers, without their master, were even more dangerous than ever, as their rampage was now without purpose or direction. They were mindless beasts, driven by instinct and need, making their behaviour difficult to predict, and even harder to defend.

She watched him a moment, circling the large wooden table covered with maps, engaged in serious discussion with Aeron and Ronen, his most trusted advisers, while she stood there being so very proud of him.

* * *

Arianne remembered the day Dare first arrived at her mother's court in Eden Taryn.

He was but twenty-five, having spent much of his life in the court of Eden Halas. Arianne had heard the gossip of a human child being adopted by Queen Syanne, and how this action had caused much disquiet between her and her king. Naturally, she was curious as to what reason this human could possess to seek an audience with her mother—the High Queen of all the elves in all of Avalyne. He was taken through the Veil by Syanne's youngest child, Prince Aeron. Even so, Arianne was astonished that her mother allowed the incursion by a human into their lands, even if he was accompanied by an elf.

Lylea, who possessed the gift of the Sight, claimed this audience was one of importance. It could change everything.

Arianne found this difficult to believe at her first sight of him. He looked like a ruffian, with threadbare clothes, dusty from too much travel, and the leather of his boots were scuffed and worn. Sporting a day's growth on his face, his dark brown hair was unruly, and hung about his shoulders, like it had never known a brush. Still, he was beautiful despite the pains he took to conceal it. She wondered if he simply did not care enough to exploit his looks, or whether this was a guise he wore to disarm people into believing he was nothing more than a vagabond. Overall, it was *not* a good first impression.

At least, until he spoke in that soft spoken voice of his, revealing words that were remarkably eloquent, possessing a tone of humility and awe at being in their presence. Even without the gift of her mother's Sight, Arianne was capable of recognising liars, and she knew every word he uttered was issued with sincerity and reverence. When he addressed them, he did not bandy about words to flatter or posture. He spoke from the heart, and told them what he dreamed.

He dreamed of uniting Carleon to drive Balfure from Avalyne forever.

He was the last son of House Icara, and it was his duty to honour the kings before him by restoring Carleon to its people once more. Such dreams were nothing new from the race of men, Arianne thought. They were always quick to anger and easily prodded into war, which was why the elves wanted nothing to do with them in the past and remained hidden behind the Veil. It was what he said next that made everyone in the court sit up and pay attention.

None of them could defeat Balfure alone.

Prejudice and tradition prevented the races of Avalyne from standing as one, thus allowing their kingdoms to fall. All the people of Avalyne needed to work together, not just men and elves, but the dwarves too, and any race that felt their liberty threatened by Balfure's hunger for conquest. How much longer were they prepared to put all their faith in the Veil? What was to stop him from breaching the protection of Eden Taryn, if he set his mind to it? And, if he chose to come, were they certain they could stop him?

If we do not stand united, we will fall divided.

Arianne remembered how those words resonated with her, even after the conclusion of the audience. Dismissed until Lylea made her decision, Dare respected the lady's need for deliberation, and retreated to the woods where his circle awaited him. Before departing their presence, he paused long enough to cast a shy gaze at Arianne. When their eyes touched, he pulled away, embarrassed, as if he was caught spying upon something he had no business in seeing.

Intrigued, Arianne found him at his campsite later that day, and when she spoke to him, he was barely able to meet her gaze. She found it utterly endearing that he, who was so strong and determined before her mother, appeared flustered and uncertain in her presence. When he did look at her, Arianne found herself staring into eyes so blue, it was like staring into drops of sky. His spoke to her with the wonder of a man who could scarcely believe he was in the company of one such as her.

Arianne was a thousand years old, but no elf she met in all that time ever touched her heart the way Dare did when she finally got him to smile.

* * *

She hated to interrupt him when he was in counsel with Ronen, the Bân of Carleon, and Aeron, representing the elves, because Dare wanted the relationship forged by the Alliance against Balfure to endure beyond the war. They must be maintained, Dare told her, or each race would fall back into its old practices of isolation, and they would be in the same vulnerable place that Balfure found them.

Arianne did not have to hear what was being discussed to know the subject of greatest concern at this time was the rorting of the beserkers across Northern Province. Dare told her the night before he would have to dispatch soldiers to clear out the infested lands so the business of farming and industry could resume once more. They needed to feed and build to forge a new future, and this could not be done if towns were constantly besieged by the remains of Balfure's monstrous armies.

It was Aeron, with his keen elven senses, who first noticed her arrival. The others followed his gaze and stopped immediately what they were doing to face her. She stifled a laugh when she saw Dare's pained expression, as he wondered what sin he had committed to warrant an unexpected visit to call him out.

Poor Dare, she thought, and knew that she had many amends to make to her husband, who could not conceive of her unhappiness if there were something he could do to change it.

"Your highness," Ronen, the second highest authority in the kingdom, greeted her. She always found that he was such a physical contrast to Dare. Ronen wore his dark blond hair worn loose, as was the fashion for men of Carleon and appeared well-groomed, unlike Dare's perpetually unruly locks.

"Ronen," she answered with a slight bow of her head.

Ronen was the first captain to follow Dare, when the exiled prince returned to Sandrine, and rallied the forces needed to fight Balfure. By the time Dare arrived, Ronen's spirit was near exhausted from having to uphold Balfure's occupation of his homeland. A soldier with a good heart, he was not much older than Dare, and enforcing Balfure's law was driving him to breaking point. The arrival of the king renewed his sense of hope, and his loyalty became the basis of their deep friendship.

There was no need for such formality when she regarded Aeron. He was fair, like all her people were fair. Tall and lean, his brown, almost black hair, was worn loose, and always seemed wild and tousled even though it was braided in places to keep it from being untidy. Only the tips of his elven ears were exposed through the dark strands. Even though he walked Avalyne for a thousand years, he bore the appearance of a thirty year old.

"My *queen*." He said, his dark blue eyes dancing with mischief while a small smile crossed his lips.

Arianne rolled her eyes at the formal greeting, wondering how it was that Aeron, with whom she spent many summers as a child during Lylea's visits to Eden Halas, could still remain as vexing to her as he was in those days. It was she who gave him his first kiss when they were eight years old and witnessed his first fall out of a tree. They were friends for most of their lives, too long for him to ever need to call her by any title. No matter how many times she reminded him of this, he continued to ignore her. Arianne was convinced he was doing it to be annoying, just like when they were children.

Dolt.

"Arianne, is something wrong?" Dare asked his wife gingerly, as she was easier to provoke these days than an ogre with a bad tooth.

"Nothing, my love." Arianne assured him, and disarmed his anxiety with a smile he'd know was meant just for him. "I would just like a moment alone with my king, if my lords do not mind?" She glanced at the two men.

"Of course." Ronen answered without hesitation, and he glanced at Dare for the King's leave to depart.

"I will send for you when we are done." Dare replied, thinking absurdly that she wanted privacy so there would be no witnesses when she slaughtered him.

Both man and elf obeyed and left the room.

"If this is about where I left my boots again, I swear that affairs of state occupied my mind and I forgot…" Dare started to apologise before Arianne closed the distance between them, and silenced him with a kiss.

Caught by surprise, he stared at her with puzzlement for a moment, before the pleasure of it made him slide his arms around her waist and kiss her back with equal affection. She was the love of his life, and being King would mean nothing if she were not at his side. Her love had given him the strength to take back his kingdom, save his people, and be the man he was today. If he became a great king, it was because she had made him so.

"I am confused," he finally admitted when they parted.

"Of course you are," she said smiling, "I come here on an entirely new matter. However, now that you have made mention of it, is it so hard to put them away?"

"You are teasing me," he retorted, a brow cocked over one eye in playful accusation.

"Yes, I am," she confessed, smirking.

Dare drew her to him and kissed her again. He was glad to see that she was in a better mood than she had been during the past few days. In truth, his desire for self-preservation was superseded by his love for her, and so he worried what could have bothered her so greatly that she was lashing out so uncharacteristically. Arianne's nature was playful and spirited, but she was never biting in her manner. Her behaviour of late was a new experience for him.

Yet, it took only a kiss for him to fall in love with her all over again.

Her effect on him was always the same. Since the very first moment he laid eyes upon her at Lylea's court, Dare was lost. She was a vision of loveliness that almost made him forget everything he came to say to Lylea. Arianne took after her father, with shimmering dark brown hair framing her oval face with high cheek bones, full lips and eyes like the richness of the earth. Her skin, like all elven ladies, was pale, but to his eyes it was almost luminescent. She did not seem quite real, like something wandering out of a dream. Seeing her for the first time made his heart pounded in his chest like a boy.

To this day, Dare never understood why she loved him enough to give up her immortality.

"And what can the king do for his queen today?" he asked, considerably more at ease.

"I came to apologize for how I have been these past few weeks," Arianne admitted first, and foremost. "I know I have been difficult."

That was an understatement, but he wisely chose to remain silent.

"What troubled you, my love?" he asked, grateful at last she was talking to him about this. They always shared everything, and not knowing the reason for her foul mood had provoked his worst fears about their relationship. "I was starting to fear that you might have regretted the choice to give up your immortality for me."

Arianne stared at him with disbelief at the mere suggestion.

"Fool!" She snapped, and swatted him on the arm for still harbouring such foolish insecurities. Did he still not grasp, even now, that he was her life? "You men can be so frightfully wrong at times," Arianne chided.

"I warn you lady, striking the king is a mortal offense," he returned playfully.

"I will take my chances," she snorted dismissively. "I will tell you this once more, but if I have to do it again, I will call upon all the powers at my disposal to show you my displeasure. I *love* you and I always will. Immortal or not, you are my soul mate. If one lifetime with you is all there is, I will never regret it. You hold my heart, my king. Be secure in that fact, if no other."

Properly admonished, Dare nodded in silence and knew that it was foolishness that allowed his mind to travel such dark roads. She proved her love for him on more occasions than he could count, and he had faith in her. Still, he could not help but wonder what in the name of Celestial Gods she saw in him to abandon her immortal existence and share a very mortal one with him.

"All right," he conceded defeat, "but you must admit you were rather frightening these past weeks, and fear is not something I succumb to easily. I've fought *monsters*."

"I have my reasons," she said dryly, disappointed the surprise she intended to give him was waylaid by this old argument. Then again, what in life ever took place according to plan? "Something has been preying upon my mind of which I could not speak to you until I had confirmation of it. I am afraid waiting for an answer frayed at my nerves more than my disposition could endure."

"What, Rian?" he demanded, a little alarmed she kept something so worrying from him. Theirs was a relationship that turned on their ability to confide everything to each other. It worried him what she might think too much for him to bear. "Did something happen? Are you alright?"

"I am fine," she stilled him again her finger. "Dare, we are going to have a baby."

The expression of stunned silence crossing his face was so acute, there was an instant she thought this news was not to his liking. All men wanted sons, did they not? She wanted to give him an heir, to consolidate his claim to the throne, and show him he was not the last son of his house. His astonishment was but brief, and her fears were dispelled when a great light flickered into being behind his eyes. Soon, it encompassed his face with a brilliant, and happy, grin.

"A baby!" he exclaimed, with the eagerness of a boy given a wondrous gift. "Are you sure?"

"Yes," she nodded, relieved to be finally able to tell him and sharing in the joy of it by his reaction to her news. "I suspected weeks ago I might be quickened, but I could not be certain until today. It is why I seemed so out of sorts. I am sorry I was upsetting but I so wanted to be certain before I told you."

"And you are now?" he asked, staring at her in wonder before his gaze dropped to her stomach where his child, no, *their* child was growing within.

"Yes. Calfax confirmed it for me today. We are going to have a baby in the spring."

"Oh, Rian!" he exclaimed, and he lifted her up by the waist and twirled her around in an uncharacteristic show of exhilaration. "I love you, and I will love our son!"

"Your son?" She gazed down at him with an imperious stare. "Are you so sure it's going to be a boy? It could be a girl."

"I don't care what it is," he admitted, immediately. "I do not care if we have a boy or a girl. I will love it either way. You have already made me happier than I ever thought possible but now, knowing that we have created this together—there are no words to describe it."

"Oh, Dare," Her voice was choked with emotion at the delight she saw in his face. Resting her head against his chest, she took comfort in the sound of his heart beating so close to her ear and wondered if her baby was listening to hers in the same fashion. "We are going to have a baby! Keeping this to myself has been so hard, I've wanted to shout it out from the roof tops ever since I first thought I might be with child. I am so glad I no longer have to keep this from you!"

"I wish you had told me," he brushed to top of her dark hair with a light kiss. "You should not have to keep such a thing to yourself. It's no wonder you were so disagreeable."

"I did not want to plant false hopes, my love. You have so much to worry your mind already, I didn't wish to see you disappointed if I was wrong."

"Nothing that you do could ever disappoint me, my love." Dare stared into her face, wanting her to see it was the truth." Still, he could not deny he was delighted they were going to have a child. He truly meant it when he said that he cared little if it were a boy or a girl. "Now that we know for sure, I feel as you do. I want everyone to know!"

"Everyone?" She gave him a look, wondering what devilry he was conjuring in his mind.

"Yes," he grinned, "I think it is time that the King and Queen of Carleon hold court with their friends again. How about we have a little party and we can make the announcement to the whole city?"

Arianne thought of her mother Lylea, the wizard Tamsyn, Kyou the dwarf, Celene, Tully and Keira of the Green. The last time they were all been gathered, it was during Dare's coronation and wedding. She would dearly love to see them again, and knew that Dare would also be pleased to spend time with the people who knew him before he became King.

"I think that would be most acceptable, my lord." She showed her agreement with another kiss.

"Well then run along and arrange it." He smirked, dismissing her with a wave of his hand.

"This was your idea!" She exclaimed, with mock outrage. "How is it the duty falls to me?"

"Well, celebrations are strictly your responsibility, my queen. I only deal with the running of the kingdom, fighting the wars and killing of the occasional insect in our chambers. If you wished the arrangement changed, I have no objection." He winked at her.

"Really?" Arianne snorted and pulled away from him. In truth, her duties amounted to more than that. As his queen, it was her responsibility to ensure well-being of their people by seeing to the creation of schools, houses of healing and other public works. Nevertheless, her mind whirling already with all the things had to be done for such a celebration to take place. "I will do your bidding this once, my king," she teased. "But only because it suits me."

"Well *thank you*, my queen," he returned, smiling as he watched her sauntering towards away. Knowing he was soon to be a father, by a woman he never thought could love him back, made the day's duty a little less tedious. Arianne was able to lift his spirit like no one else alive, and he still marvelled at the discovery someone so beautiful could also be as equally kind.

"Rian," he called out before she left the hall.

"Yes, Dare?" She cast those magnificent blue eyes back at him with a quizzical expression.

"I love you," he said softly.

"As you should, my love," she replied as she left.

Chapter Two

Invitation

Visitors to the Green were rare.

Nestled in the western shadow of the great Baffin Range, the village was hidden away in the middle of Barrenjuck Green, the oldest forest in Avalyne. It was also the only community of size before one reached the distant fishing town of Lenkworth. Shielded by the mountains and flanked by the Brittle Sea, the people of the village were of human stock, but managed to remain untouched by Balfure and his armies. Mostly farmers, the folk of the Green found no reason to venture beyond their borders, particularly when they heard the tales of travellers who spoke of trouble happening in the rest of Avalyne.

Everyone noticed the rider from Carleon.

Garnering curious stares from the locals as he rode through the small community to deliver his message, the messenger knew his instructions. Deliver the news, wait for a response, if there was one to be received, and then leave *immediately*. He was to disturb nothing in this small community, beyond the duty he needed to perform. Once he left the Green, the town of Tumbur, which sat at the foothills of the Baffin Range, would be the only place he could stop for rest before crossing the mountain and returning to Carleon.

Although the presence of the visitor drew much interest, the locals knew for whom the messenger had come. There was not one person in the village who did not know the high king's connection to the occupants of Furnsby Farm. The couple was deemed foolish by most of the village for becoming involved in the whole business when they gave the future king of Carleon refuge from Balfure's Disciples. The consequences to Keira Furnsby were terrible indeed, but there was no denying the lady's courage or the admiration she earned for saving the king.

The messenger gave his news to Keira as soon as he was met at the door to their home. Keira gave her response immediately, aware it was a long ride to Tumbur, and he would have to make it again if she made him wait for an answer. It was more than a year since she and Tully last travelled, and she knew he would very much like to accept the king's invitation. Despite the fact Tully enjoyed his life in the Green, he liked to travel and would be thrilled to see what had become of the world since Dare was crowned king.

Sending the messenger on his way, after telling him the Furnsbys would be in attendance at the King's celebration, she left the house in search of her husband. Putting on her boots and her cloak, because the air was cool this morning, she went to the east paddock where she knew Tully was working. Today the spring calves were finally old enough to leave their pens, and she knew Tully would like to keep an eye on them as they took their first tentative steps into the world.

"Tully!" She called out to him as she neared the paddock, her red hair escaping the hood of her cloak and blowing over her face. Tully Furnsby was watching carefully the calves sniffing at each other in interest, trying to make sense of the world outside their confinement, when he heard his wife's call. Leaning against the fence, he glanced over his shoulder to see her approach, wondering what she was doing here. She was a small woman, petite in her stature, with freckles across her nose and brown eyes. Life on a farm had made her strong, although not even to withstand torture by Disciples, he thought sourly.

"Is everything alright, Keira?" He asked, as soon as she was near "You're not feeling poorly, are you?" He had launched into the familiar tirade of questions that was sure to annoy her, he realised belatedly.

"Tully," Keira's expression darkened, wishing he would not treat her as if she were made of glass, "I'm fine. I would tell you if I wasn't."

"No, you wouldn't." Tully countered, perfectly aware that she'd keep silent him because she didn't want to worry him. He knew he shouldn't be so over-protective. Ever since the Disciples, Tully blamed himself for what happened to her, though he would never admit it out loud. Whenever she had a bout of sickness or woke up screaming in the night from a nightmare, he cursed himself again for letting this happen to her. He wished he could show her how much he admired her for withstanding the torture, and how strong she was but all that ever came out was his worry.

"We are pair, aren't we?" He smiled at her.

"We are." Keira agreed, leaning over the fence to kiss him on the cheek. "So, what's happened? Did you need me for something?" He guessed whatever the reason for her presence here, it wasn't urgent.

"I do." Keira nodded, reaching into the folds of her cloak to produce the invitation delivered to by the man of Carleon.

The envelope was very fine and did not appear to be stationery common to the village. Farmers were very sensible with their parchment, preferring function over ostentation, and they certainly wouldn't use one gilt with gold, if they even used it at all. In the Green, the fastest way to pass news was to go to the market and tell Mrs Birdweather about it. After that, *everyone* in village would know.

"What's this?" he asked.

"This," Keira said, smiling, "is an invitation from Dare to visit him and the queen in Sandrine. It appears he is having a party and wants us to attend."

As always, Tully's first thought, when considering such a trip, was how Keira would manage. Sandrine was quite a ways away. Despite the fact it was seven years in the past, Keira did not recover as she ought, and occasionally she had strange turns, but he also knew a change of scenery might also help the situation.

"I told the messenger we would go." Keira declared in case his hesitation was due to his usual concerns about her.

"You did?" He asked with some surprise, and he felt himself relax in light of that revelation. If she felt well enough to go, she'd only get cross with him if he did. Keira didn't like being reminded she wasn't as well as she should be. "Then we'll go." He grinned. "It would be nice to see Dare and that lot again."

It still felt odd though, calling the king of Carleon by name, or to think of him as the War Dragon. To Tully, he would always be Dare, who appeared on their doorstep needing help, and showed them there was no such thing as hiding from evil if evil was determined to seek them out.

"Yes, it would," Keira agreed, grateful he offered no protest.

"I wonder what the celebration is about," he mused, not expecting an answer.

Keira knew, but she kept it to herself for now.

"I suppose we'll find out when we get to Sandrine. The 'why' doesn't matter much as long as we get to see our friends."

"You're right as always, Tully," Keira agreed, glad to be going on a trip to see everyone again.

* * *

Unlike the messenger, who was required to cross the Baffin Range to deliver the invitation to the Furnsbys, the invitation sent to Kyou, the Weapons Master of Carleon, did not have far to travel. At that very moment, the dwarf of Iridia was in the city, helping to reinforce the fortifications after years of neglect and damage from Balfure's attacks.

During the occupation of Balfure's forces across Avalyne, Kyou, like most of his people, was forced to flee to the other parts of Avalyne or fall under the yoke of the Aeth Lord. Balfure invaded their ancestral home of Iridia, in the Starfall Mountains, with his beserkers army to enslave Avalyne's greatest craftsmen so they would build him his weapons of war.

Years later, Dare sought out his people in the Jagged Mountains because, to unite the scattered dwarf clans of Iridia, he needed support from the son of their most respected chieftain. Kyou joined Dare because more than he wanted revenge, he wanted what his father had died for—the freedom of his people. When Dare left the Jagged Mountains, Kyou accompanied him while the rest of his people set to work giving the future king exactly what he wanted: the greatest weapons every forged.

* * *

"Master Builder!"

Kyou glanced up from the parchments laid out on the table before him. They were the plans of the work needed to be conducted to the western wall of the city; the one that was hit the worst during the siege of the city when Balfure first attacked Sandrine. During the occupation, the Aeth Lord neglected the city and did not bother to make repairs. Reconstructing these now would allow him to conduct the rest of the improvements he was asked to carry out by Dare.

Only the elf would be so bold to call him by the title. In truth, there were a number of rituals he needed to perform in the traditions of Iridia before any dwarf could assume the title of Master Builder. Kyou never completed them. He was too busy fighting a war at Dare's side.

"Must you persist in using that infernal title?" Kyou glared at Aeron with hazel eyes.

"Yes, *Master Builder*," Aeron replied, amused by the grimace that crossed the dwarf's face. "I bring you tidings from the king."

Kyou snorted in annoyance and turned back to his plans. "You may tell his Royal Highness that the wall must be rebuilt before I will add any weapons to it. If it cannot take the weight, it will be of little use to him. We are working as quickly as we can, and if he persists in hounding me, I shall return home and he can finish it himself!"

"I will tell him that if you like." Aeron rolled his eyes sarcastically. "But he did not send me here to request an update about the progress of the work. I offered to come here in place of one of his riders."

"Oh?" Kyou stared at him. "And what would he want of me, if not to know how his fortifications fare?"

"To invite you to a *celebration*," the elf declared, always amused at how Kyou's temper could make him jump to foolish assumptions. After all these years of friendship and camaraderie between them, Aeron wondered if 'disgruntled' was the dwarf's natural state. "It appears that there is an important announcement forthcoming. The queen has summoned her mother, and mine, to attend. Meanwhile, the king has sent riders to the Green and the Jagged Teeth."

"Interesting." Kyou absorbed the news, and scratched the stubble on his cheek at what the announcement could be. "Do you have any idea what this news might be?"

"Not really," Aeron confessed. "I know Arianne required an audience alone with Dare while we were in discussion about the trouble in the Northern Province."

"Ah!" Kyou exclaimed, with a note of triumph in his voice. "It's a baby then."

"A baby!" Aeron retorted, wondering how the dwarf made *that* leap. "What makes you say that?"

"Let us examine the evidence—a celebration involving the queen's kin, and the gathering of their friends, the closest that the king has to family, not to mention that we are speaking about the most serious man in creation, choosing to celebrate some grand news? What else could it be?" He gave Aeron a look of amusement, wondering how a thousand year old elf could be so naïve at times.

"Well, I suppose he did seem rather cheery after the fact, grinning from ear-to-ear as a matter of fact. It was rather unnerving."

Kyou rolled his eyes once again, and muttered, "Aeron, you are in *sore* need of female company."

* * *

If an invitation was sent to the tower in the mountains of the Jagged Teeth, there would have been no one to receive it.

A week before, the first of the riders set off Tamsyn, the last mage of the ancient Order of the Enphilim, departed his secluded domicile. He rode with all haste to the Wanderer's Wood to take counsel with Queen Lylea of Eden Taryn. The journey was long but the urgency of the situation demanded nothing less.

What he had seen in his Scrying Pool was convincing enough.

The city of Eden Taryn was not as lavish as Eden Ardhen, which had stood for thousands of years before its destruction by Balfure's beserkers. It was an infant, thirty-five years old, and although the elves constructed a beautiful city among the woods, it did not possess the grandeur of its predecessor. The city was built upon the branches of the great Whispering Oak, nurtured by the elves to reach its immense size, so it could take the weight required to bear it.

Tamsyn ascended the great winding staircase coiled around the tree, leaving behind the forest floor. Its branches were thicker than most tree trunks, and it spread across the sky until only a single stream of light could penetrate the dense canopy of leaves. He was greeted at the curtain separating the world from the Veil by the queen's guard, and suspected by now, Lylea would be awaiting him. This would be the first time they had seen each other since the wedding of the queen's only daughter, Arianne.

He wasn't sure how he would be received, now they would be facing each other alone.

* * *

Tamsyn first met Lylea when her father died fighting in the Primordial Wars, almost three thousand years ago. The young woman was called upon to lead her people as High Queen, and it was a role she did not expect to take so soon. Not even betrothed, Lylea was required to lead a war where the elves were the foot soldiers to the gods. Their immortality given so they could continue to serve in the war for as long as possible.

It was longevity that came with a bloody price.

The war against Mael and his Primordials already raged for two thousand years by the time Lylea became queen. Even with her gift of the Sight, she was young and unsure, certainly impressionable enough to accept the guidance of a mage, who as was as new to his role as liaison as she was to being queen. While he was far older than she, he bore the appearance of a man in his fiftieth year, with dark hair and equally dark eyes and, while he never considered it, he might be thought of as handsome.

Certainly Lylea found him so, and while he should have known better, he indulged the attraction, even consummating it. By the time he realised the folly of what he had done, she was deeply in love with him. While Tamsyn cared for her deeply, he was conscious she was a young woman, even for an elf, and probably would be better off sharing a life with her own kind, as opposed to a mage, who could be called on to serve his masters at any given time.

Instead of telling her any of his fears, he retreated to the mountains of the Jagged Teeth, and there he had remained, in a deep sleep lost to the world.

When he was awakened by the intrusion of the dwarves some two thousand years later, he learned that Lylea never took an elven husband. Her consorts were always human, and the marriage usually provided a child, the last being Arianne. Although proposals were made to her by her own kind, she accepted none of them, and Tamsyn feared his betrayal soured her on the experience of finding a soul mate for all time.

At the wedding of Dare and Arianne, they regarded each other for the first time two millennia, even though news of his return must have reached her ears before that. He could have tried explaining himself, but she treated their past association as little more than an old friendship from long ago. Not once did she acknowledge once upon a time, they made each other burn beneath the light of the stars.

* * *

"Mage." Lylea gazed down at him from her single throne, elevated on a raised platform, resting atop the wooden floor upon which he was presently standing. While she now had the appearance of a woman in forties, she was still no less dazzling than she had been as a young woman. Possessing a lighter shade of hair than Arianne, Lylea wore it up with delicate strands brushing her long slender neck. Her cheek bones were high, and gave pronouncement to her elfin features, as she stared at him with blue eyes lacking their usual warmth.

Although her personal guards were present, the absence of everyone else in the hall made him uneasy. There was too much unspoken between them, and the substances of it lingered in the air, waiting to choke them at any moment. Choosing to remind himself he was here for a reason, he ignored memories of their turbulent history.

"My Queen," he replied with a bow. "I am sorry to impose upon your realm but…"

"I have seen it too. I know that my daughter's life is in danger." She cut him off abruptly, her voice hard, and he knew it was not usual for her to speak this way. He noted one of her guards shifting his gaze subtly in their direction, surprised by her response.

"Then, you have seen the portents," he said grimly, ignoring her aloofness when he knew she had cause for her hostility.

"It came to me in a dream," Lylea explained, thinking of the impending doom hurtling towards her youngest, and perhaps most beloved, child. "Since then, I have felt the growing malice coming from the north, but what causes it is unclear. It does not please me to tell my daughter her happiest day may soon be her darkest."

"Nor does it please me," Tamsyn spoke in sympathy. "Both she and her husband are dear to me, and this news will surely send them both into panic. But we must make haste to Sandrine and tell her while we still have time."

"We have less time than you think," she declared, rising from her throne and descending the steps to the floor. Approaching him, she held up her hand revealing a letter gilt in gold. "The announcement has gone throughout kingdoms. It is what the enemy has been waiting to hear."

"I feared this," Tamsyn grimaced. "He has been waiting since Balfure's end for this moment, when the people of Avalyne have grown complacent with peace."

"And nothing puts anyone more at ease than the arrival of a new prince," the high queen reminded. "A mother to be should not be embarking on any quest, not so soon," she said unhappily.

"This is no mere quest," Tamsyn pointed out quickly. "To strike at the most vulnerable place there can be is evil of the foulest kind."

"I know." Lylea turned away from him, not wishing to see just how much this pained her. With a human for her father, Arianne made the choice to give up her immortality, something none of her other children had done. While Lylea understood her daughter's reasoning, she would never come to terms with the inevitable end Arianne could face. This evil could usher that end all the sooner. "I wish this did not have to be Arianne's burden alone. She should share it with Dare."

Her pain made Tamsyn wish to offer her comfort, but painfully aware any gesture he made towards the high queen would not be well received, he remained content to simply agree with her. "I wish the same too. He loves her more than anything in this world and would allow nothing to harm her or his unborn child, but he is just a man. The enemy has no reason to keep him alive if he becomes inconvenient. Arianne is an elf with powers of her own and because the enemy needs her child, he cannot risk harming her. If Dare knew, he will be determined to protect Arianne by going himself and that is something we *cannot* allow."

"Perhaps, we do not have the right to make that choice for them. Perhaps, assuming what is best for them is wrong." She turned around and stared at him directly.

Tamsyn swallowed thickly, aware that her question was not merely statement, but a barb at an old grievance. He ignored it for now, because it was too big a subject to delve into at the moment when there were real matters of urgency to contend with. As it was, he felt guilty keeping secrets from Dare. The young king looked to him for counsel, had come to him for help to restore order to the world. Through those shared trials, they had become friends.

After a moment, he answered her. "I love them both dearly too, and my heart aches in fear at the danger that Arianne will face, but it must be done this way. If she were to fail in the undertaking, we would face a danger far worse than any we could possibly imagine. This could mean the resurrection of powers so dark no army in Avalyne can withstand it. No race will survive."

"So is she to go alone in this peril? When we dealt with Balfure, we had an army. Is Arianne not allowed to have such support?"

"She will find her own way. There are allies for her in the strangest of places and she will find them. Dare shall not be completely forgotten in this either, but it must be his queen that paves the way for him to act."

At least that was something, Lylea thought. Still, she could not help feeling as if she were abandoning Arianne to a questionable fate. It was necessary her carry out this quest, but Lylea could not say for certain whether or not she ought to do it alone.

"I guess it is time to visit Sandrine," Lylea said with a heavy sigh. "It appears that we have a celebration to attend."

Chapter Three

Celebration

When the announcement was made at the opening of the celebration the queen was with child, jubilation swept throughout the city, like the rising swell of an ocean wave. It moved outwards from Sandrine to the rest of the kingdom like wildfire. Messengers departed the instant the news was revealed, riding to the four corners of Carleon, to deliver the announcement an heir was coming, finally marking the successful ascension of King Dare to his throne.

Days before the celebration, Sandrine was transformed into a magical version of itself, full of lights and coloured banners, streamers and ribbons hanging from windows and awnings on every street. Merchants were commissioned to provide food and ale for all the guests in and out of the palace. City workers were soon erecting tents, assembling tables in squares where the feast for the commonfolk would be held. Stages were erected for the performers entertaining the masses and fireworks readied for the night A steady stream of cooks, performers and guests began arriving into the city to take part in the celebration.

The inhabitants of Sandrine lined the streets, watching the procession of guests, fascinated to see folk they only heard about in legend, such as the mage Tamsyn and the High Queen of the elves—the very beautiful Lylea who was mother to their own queen. The alliance made elves known to the people of Sandrine, but even the most jaded were dazzled as Lylea rode by in her robes of white. They gaped in wonder as she passed them, thinking she could be one of the Celestials walking in their midst.

Once the announcement was made, the festivities truly began and continued into the night. The setting of the sun only brought more revels to the already exciting event, as fireworks were launched into the night sky and magic tricks were performed by skilled, if powerless magicians. Gasps of excitement swept through the crowds as each explosion of colour and light superseded the last spectacle. Fireworks of giant dragons trailed sparkles of glittering embers as they flew overhead in the night air, followed by horses thundering across the sky and butterflies streaking past the audience like clusters of falling stars.

The merriment was no less spectacular within the palace of the king. Guests were received with much warmth while friends were reunited, regaling each other with tales of their homeland and their adventures, since parting company. Keira related to Dare all the gossip in the Green while Celene, once a member of his Circle during the war, told Aeron and Arianne how things faired in Gislaine, the city she and Ronen now ruled in the Southern Provinces. Meanwhile, Kyou explained to Tully the tremendous undertaking that was the refortification of Sandrine's defences, and how fared his family who returned to Iridia and was awaiting his return upon its completion.

Neither Tamsyn nor Lylea made any mention of the enemy for the moment.

* * *

It always amused Celene just how nervous the king seemed to get whenever she, Keira, and Arianne wandered off to talk privately away from the hearing of their men. She had no idea what secrets Dare thought she might impart upon Arianne, or Keira for that matter, but Celene took great delight in making the king of the realm a little anxious whenever she made the suggestion. It was truly ludicrous when one considered how highly she held Dare in regard, and obviously, she would never dream of embarrassing him before his queen.

Well, not much anyway. Besides, the only stories she had of him were of their adventures when they crossed Avalyne to create the alliance needed to launch his campaign against Balfure.

In a houseful of sons, Celene was the only daughter to Yalen, Angarad's king. Her mother Celene, for whom she was named, died in childbirth, leaving her to be raised by her father, who saw no reason to treat her any differently than a boy. While certain aspects of her upbringing were handled by her nurse Ilsa, for most part Celene was educated and raised side by side with her brothers.

Like all women of Angarad, Celene was required to wield a sword. Angarad could not be expected to defend its borders against Balfure if all her people were not schooled in the art of war. Despite their dedication to combat, the Angarad were not mindless warmongers thirsty for blood. Learning to wield a weapon was paramount, but the mind was an instrument too, and it had to be honed as sharply as the blade.

When Iridia fell, the dwarves suffered the worst of it. Hunted for their expertise, they were scattered throughout Avalyne, seeking refuge with anyone who would give them shelter. Some came to Angarad offering their skills as master craftsmen in exchange for a home. For the next two decades, both peoples worked to keep Angarad free of Balfure. By the time Dare arrived at the capital, the dwarves were such a large part of Angarad life, it was difficult to remember what it was like before.

It was Celene who convinced Yalen to let her join Dare's circle—to travel with him and see if he did indeed have the support he claimed to possess from the elves and the other races of Avalyne. Her father was reluctant to let her go, but he had sons to defend the realm, and he could not deny a daughter who was trained but untested, the chance to prove herself. He understood her need to find her own destiny, to blood her sword, and be the warrior he moulded her into.

Celene was nineteen years old when she joined Dare. The exiled king accepted her presence with some ambivalence, as he was unaccustomed to a woman with a sword. Unlike Angarad, the women of Carleon were not warriors. In time, experience would soon make him appreciate her skills as they faced many evils over the years. From fighting beserkers, goblins and ogres, to hiding from the Disciples, she was at his side as the Aeth Lord hurled all the darkness he could muster at Dare to prevent the unification of Avalyne.

It was during the siege of Astaroth, deep in the heart of Balfure's kingdom, Celene was almost killed by an ogre. She had faced them before, but this one was of a breed she had not seen, with a serpent's tongue and clawed feet. It resembled a lizard more than an ogre. She fought it as best she could, but there came a moment when Celene realised the thing was going to kill her.

No sooner had the thought crossed her mind, a soldier of Carleon drove a spike through the creature's side, taking advantage of its single-minded pursuit of the warrior maiden at the expense of all else.

In its death throes, the beast swung its large mace one last time, but it was enough to sweep the soldier off his feet with a blow that should have killed him. Celene heard his bones crack against the boulder when he landed making a chilling sound that would follow her to the grave. Stunned by the sudden rescue, she recovered her senses and rushed to his side, refusing to abandon this man who came out of nowhere to save her.

She found him where he landed, his head bleeding and his body limp. There was still enough breath left in him for Celene to drag him off the field and place him on a cart bound for the healers' tent. Then, she returned to the battle.

Days later, she sought him out to learn he did survive, despite the severity of his wounds. He was not conscious when she happened upon him because his skull was almost been split open from landing against the rocks. It was many days after she found him that he finally regained consciousness, and introductions were made. His name was Ronen, Captain of Carleon.

She knew the name.

While Celene had not met him in person, Dare spoke highly of the captain, who was tired of enforcing Balfure's will. After Balfure was vanquished for good and the army recovered its wounds, she visited him at the healer's tent. They would talk, exchanging tales about their homeland. He was surprisingly educated for a soldier with the mind of scholar. Like her, he lost family to Balfure's forces and, in their shared grief, they formed a deep understanding of each other.

When it was time for him to return to Carleon with the rest of wounded, the ache she felt at his departure was like nothing she'd ever known. She missed talking to him and how he made her laugh. She even missed how he pointed out she was far too serious for a maid, especially one who wielded a sword. She did not know if Dare had any ulterior motive when the king asked her to accompany the wounded soldier out of the war zone, but for once she did not mind being sent off the field.

She was in love with Ronen before they even got halfway to Sandrine.

* * *

"So tell me, Arianne," Celene asked as she, Keira, and the queen, walked the gardens of the palace, away from the noise of the celebration taking place in the Great Hall. "How does it feel to have the House of Icara's newest heir growing inside you?"

34

Since her marriage to Ronen, Celene spent four months out of the year at Sandrine. This was required for Ronen to fulfil his duties as Bân. During the sojourn, Celene become a trusted friend to the terribly homesick Arianne, who missed Eden Taryn, and was still finding her way among humans after being sheltered behind the Veil for so long.

As two friends, they could not have been more different. While Arianne was elven grace personified, Celene's hair was like the gold of a sandy shore and her disposition just as breezy. She had hazel eyes and preferred breeches to dresses. However, they both shared a liking for the absurd and, as Dare and Ronen often remarked beyond their hearing, they shared the same stubborn streak capable of bending iron.

"Nicely put, Celene," Arianne replied with a smile, accustomed to Celene's teasing. Celene had a mischievous wit, and Arianne knew that much of the reason why she enjoyed her company was because the daughter of Angarad could make her laugh.

"I agree," Keira said giving Celene a look of amusement. Comma after "said" "You sound like Tully when he's describing one of the sheep after quickening!"

"Fine, fine," Celene said, as she rolled her eyes. "Your Highness, is your heart all aquiver and your soul warm with the joy of delivering to your lord and master his first heir?" She smirked.

"I think I preferred the first way," Arianne returned, making her face at Celene's amendment. "However, to answer your question, I feel well. I am told this will change as the child grows, but I suppose it's the same for *all* women, human or elf."

"Tully is looking at me strangely," Keira frowned. "I think your situation has made him wonder why we aren't like everyone in the village, saddled with a dozen children. Although, it isn't for the lack of trying."

Although she was smiling as she spoke, it did not reach her eyes. Both Arianne and Celene understood this would bother

Keira, because the people of the Green tended to have large families, and lack of children at Furnsby Farm would not have gone unnoticed by their neighbours. Yet she had to be concerned if there was the possibility the Disciples' torture might have made her incapable of bearing children at all.

"I think a child will only form when it is ready, but there is nothing wrong with enjoying each other before a third party arrives. Dare and I waited to be with each other for so long we have no wish to delay starting a family. We have only one lifetime to share together and so we must fill every moment, as soon as possible. It feels right for us that a child should come sooner, rather than later."

Arianne smiled to herself, remembering the searing night of passion that followed after she told him about the baby. "Do not worry about children just yet," she said to Keira, trying to put the woman's mind at ease. "Let it happen as it will. If I were you, I'd enjoy the time while it is just the two of you because once the children come, the whole world changes. I know it has already for Dare and me."

"That's true," Celene agreed, giving Keira a look of sympathy, realising what Arianne was about. "Still, I think all men feel they have failed in some fashion if they do not produce a strapping son to follow them. I came from a house of five brothers. When the time comes for me, I want a *girl.*"

"You would say that," Arianne retorted. "You just want someone to teach the sword."

"I know I could teach a boy too, but it won't be nearly as interesting." Celene winked at her two friends.

"Honestly, Celene," Keira declared, "I don't know if I would have had the courage to do what you did—fighting at Astaroth and then leading your father's army into battle."

"Nonsense," Celene dismissed such talk immediately. "You saved Dare from the Disciples. We all know what you went through, and I cannot say if I would have prevailed in the face of the Blinding Curse. I can fight against things I can raise a sword to. What you endured, that was different."

"Strength does not require a person to be a great swordsman," Arianne said, squeezing Keira's shoulder. "Sometimes it's just having the will to endure."

"Thank you," Keira said gratefully. "Poor Tully seems to think I'm so fragile, and I want to show him I'm not."

"He's a man," Celene snorted. "They never know anything until you hit them on the head with it. I never had to prove myself in Angarad. It was only after I left, I was treated differently. Men always seem to think you need special consideration."

"Tully loves you, Keira," Arianna said kindly. "I think he has been so worried about you healing that he has forgotten to do it himself."

"I suppose." The mistress of Furnsby Farm sighed, before deciding that a return to a happier subject was in order. "So, I suppose this means that if we have daughters, they too, will be headstrong, determined and thoroughly capable of getting into trouble?"

"I prefer the word self-sufficient as opposed to headstrong," Celene quipped.

"Self-sufficient—I do believe I like the sound of that," Arianne nodded with agreement, before the three women exchanged glances and burst out into another round of laughter.

Suddenly, a beam of moonlight slipped past the clouds and struck the pond in the centre of the garden. The reflection of the moon shimmered across the surface and its light caught Arianne in the eye. For a moment, she felt her mind empty, and the voices of Keira and Celene seemed like distant echoes. Without warning, she heard her mother's soft voice speak inside her mind.

Come, Arianne. We need to speak.

* * *

The summons by Lylea left Arianne with such a feeling of anxiety, both Celene and Keira insisting on following her to her audience with her mother. None of them spoke as they approached Lylea because they could feel the weight of something terrible awaiting revelation in Arianne's eyes. There was a sense of ominous foreboding in the air when they found themselves standing next to Lylea at another part of the palace grounds. This space was more isolated, with a tall hedge allowing no one to see them as they stood in its boundaries waiting for Lylea to speak.

Oddly enough, Lylea did not object to either Keira or her being present. Celene noticed this and wondered why. The elves were not known for their ability to take other races into their confidence, and while Arianne was different from most, Celene did not expect her mother the queen to be similarly disposed.

"Thank you for accompanying my daughter," Lylea said to Celene and Keira upon receiving them. "She will need your strength."

Celene suddenly felt terribly afraid for Arianne.

"My daughter." Lylea turned to Arianne, and spoke softly, reaching forward to brush her hand over her daughter's hair like she had done for most of Arianne's life. "There is something you must see, something I must show you."

"What is it, mother?" Arianne asked, more than a little afraid. All her life, she had seen Lylea's Sight at work and, though she did not have her mother's talent, she believed in its power. Her mother was standing in front of a smaller pond, holding the urn Arianne knew she used when there was a vision Lylea wanted to share with someone who did not have her gift.

"I think you know," Lylea replied, and poured the contents of the urn into the pool. The water trickled forth lightly, gurgles against the broken surface, sending ripples outward.

"I don't know," Celene blurted out, feeling the same fear, and reacting in the only manner in which she knew against such anxiety. "Tell me."

"All in good time," Lylea said smoothly, accustomed to such impatience from humans.

Arianne swallowed thickly, looking to Celene and Keira before turning to Lylea once more, her innards twisting with growing anxiety. Her mother's Sight showed many things—the past, the present, and the future. It was a window into infinite possibilities, and yet, as Lylea asked her to look she felt uncommonly afraid, more than was usual for her. She was not a woman who cowered in fear at the first sign of danger. She faced evil before and prevailed. But this thing Lylea would have her do frightened her in a way she could not explain and could not refuse either.

Deciding the fear would only have more power over her mind if she continued to delay, Arianne neared the edge and cast her gaze into the pool, seeing what it was Lylea needed her to witness. As Celene and Keira took a step closer, she wondered whether they would see the same.

At first, Arianne saw nothing except water becoming stilled after its earlier turbulence. The ripples disappeared into a smooth reflective surface once more. Arianne could see the stars twinkling from the sky in the reflection and drew comfort from that. It was short-lived.

The twinkles of lights coalesced on the surface of the dark water into a raging inferno, turning the pool amber with flame. Arianne's breath caught, and she wanted to recoil, but the images forming before her were mesmerizing. They ensnared her mind in their trap so she was unable to look away.

And it showed Arianne her son.

She knew he could be no one else. He had the look of his father except perhaps his hair was darker and his chin more set.

He wore the armour of the king about to ride into battle, and though she did not know him, she loved him immediately. He was as beautiful as she always imagined a child of hers and Dare's would be. She saw him riding into the night, with Carleon's banner held high and his armies behind him. There was something strange about the soldiers—they did not appear as they should. For a brief instant, Arianne tried hard to discern what was so strange about them, when the glow of the flames illuminated one of their faces and she understood why.

They were beserkers!

Her son was the leader of an army of beserkers! How was this possible? There was little time to question this as the image changed again, and this time it was not of a handsome king leading his troops into battle. It was the image of a madman waging war, and presiding over the slaughter of innocents in a ruined city. She knew, without a doubt, it was the city of Gislaine. Its tall spires were ablaze, like candles burning in the night. She could not hear the screams, but she could see them in faces of the people fleeing, and by the Orean River running through Gislaine, filled with bloated bodies.

And, in the centre of all this carnage, was her son!

She knew without seeing the scope of it all, he was bringing war to the cities of Carleon, claiming his lordship over them by violence. Her child—the one slumbering even now in her womb as she watched this nightmare unfold—was going to be monster! She and Dare's child would be an evil more terrifying than even Balfure! The horror of it was beyond her comprehension. She could not believe the Celestials would allow an act of love between two parents to culminate in the birth of such a creature!

"WHAT IS THIS OBSCENITY?" Arianne demanded screaming, stepping back from the pool, too horrified to think.

"Arianne!" Keira immediately came to her friend's side as Arianne sank to her knees shaking in disgust and horror at what she had witnessed.

"What has she seen?" the Lady of Gislaine demanded vehemently of Lylea. She and Keira did not see what Arianne had, but the horror on her face told Celene it was terrible indeed.

"She has seen what could be," Lylea revealed, her face showing the pain of forcing her child to witness the dark future lying before her and all of Avalyne. Lylea stood here now, not as the mother of Arianne but as the high queen of the elves.

"What *could* be?" Arianne cried out, looking up at her mother with tears running down her face. "You turn this happy day into a nightmare, and speak in riddles? My son cannot be this creature! I will not believe it!"

Lylea, finally, went to her daughter and lowered herself unto the grass next to Arianne, taking the hand that Keira had been holding and spoke gently. "You must believe it, little one," Lylea said, using her nickname from childhood. "You must believe it, because it will come to pass unless *you* stop it."

"Me?" Arianne stammered, her mind reeling still from the images. "I do not understand!"

"There is an evil afoot—an ancient one we have not seen hiding because we were too preoccupied with the threat of Balfure and his war. For many years this enemy has been watching and waiting for one thing—the conception of your child."

"What is this enemy?" Celene demanded, furious there was still evil capable of bringing darkness to Avalyne after their hard won battles against Balfure. Enough brave men died to prevent such a thing. How many more needed to die? How much more was needed before they could be truly free? "What is this new evil?"

"It is not new," Lylea continued, and turned her attention back to Arianne. "My sweet Arianne, trust me when I say to you all is not lost. What you have seen is indeed your son in the flesh, but his soul was vanquished before he was born, and replaced by another."

"Replaced?" Keira exclaimed in shock.

Arianne was growing confused and stared at her mother. "Who then has possession of his life?"

"Mael." Lylea's voice was barely a whisper.

Neither Celene nor Keira recognised the name immediately, but Arianne certainly did.

"That's impossible!" she declared. "He was destroyed! The Celestials chained him in the Verse! He was vanquished!"

"Mael is one of the Celestial Gods," Lylea replied. "He was made by Cera the Creator and is equal to any one of them. He may have been bound to Avalyne when he chose to come here, but like the Celestials, he does *not* die. His spirit lives. The enemy has decided with Balfure gone, it is time for the return of his former master, Mael. Unfortunately, Mael cannot be resurrected without a vessel, and so the enemy has chosen your child for this purpose."

"No!" Arianne's cry was almost on the verge of hysteria. "I will not allow this! There must be a way to stop this abomination!"

"There is," Lylea nodded. "The enemy cannot perform the ritual to resurrect Mael until your babe is strong enough to accept such a spirit. It is too young and fragile inside you to make such an attempt now. You must stop him before two full moons have passed. Arianne only you can do this because, as much as the enemy hates us all, it cannot allow any harm to come to you. You are the mother of its future master, and while it may kill all others around you, you are beyond its reach."

"Dare cannot know then," Arianne declared, meeting the eyes of the other women in the garden. "If he learns of this danger, he will insist on fighting it and the enemy will destroy him."

"Yes," her mother nodded gravely. "This is your quest, Arianne. The fate of your child lies is in your hands alone."

"No," Celene stated, not understanding all of it, but enough to know her friend was not embarking on a terrible quest alone. "I will go with you, Arianne. I pledge my sword as the Lady of Gislaine, and as a princess of Angarad, to the service of my friend and my queen."

"And I'll come too…" Keira started to say, when Arianne cut her off.

"I can't ask you both to do that," Arianne spoke, her voice very small in her ears. "This is my doom."

"All the more reason for you to have help," Celene retorted, her tone indicating that she would tolerate no argument on the matter.

Arianne closed her eyes, feeling tears of anguish rising up within her. She wanted to scream and shout at the unfairness of this, but she could not waste time with such displays. Inside her body, her son needed her to be strong for him, stronger than she had ever been in her entire life. She could not falter now, not when his soul was at stake. She would accept their help because she was not foolish enough to think she could do this without her friends at her side.

"Tell me then, mother," Arianne said finally, "What must I do?"

Chapter Four

Quiet Partings

Upon returning to the Great Hall, where her friends and invited guests were presently continuing their revelry into the night, Arianne realised it was no easy thing for a queen to preside over a celebration that gave her no joy. How could she, after glimpsing the terrible future awaiting her son?

Even as she took her place next to her king, her heart was pounding so hard beneath her breast she feared Dare might hear it through the din of chattering voices around them. Try as she might, she could not force away the terrible memory of what her mother showed her. Surrounded by a sea of voices belonging to the people she cared most for in the world, Arianne felt like an island of loneliness, forced to endure her despair in secret.

To their credit, Celene and Keira attempted to support her, wherever they could, throughout the course of the evening. They interjected when she could not think of a thing to say, and offered her pregnant state as an excuse when she lapsed into her own thoughts. If not for them, Arianne did not think she would have been able to maintain the gracious mask she wore for the benefit of those around her.

Lylea chose to withdraw for the evening, perhaps realising her continued presence at the banquet was only adding to her daughter's melancholic state. It was she who had brought this doom upon Arianne, and she could well understand if Carleon's queen chose to look at her with resentment for spoiling what should have been a day of celebration and rejoicing. Tamsyn watched Lylea depart, wanting to speak to her and learn how Arianne took the news, though it seemed obvious by Arianne's sedate manner it was not received well. As if it ever could be received any other way.

Arianne was glad Dare was not paying her close attention, because he might have noticed her troubled disposition. Fortunately, the king was occupied with the company of his old friends as they spoke of their adventuring days. Under any other circumstance, she knew if he had asked, Arianne would not able to hide her anguish from him. They could read other too easily for anything of this magnitude to be concealed from each other indefinitely.

She longed to tell him the danger threatening their child, to feel his strong arms about her, and to hear him say nothing would harm either her or the babe while there was breath in his body. He would be true to his word. He would put their lives before his, and as surely as she had seen it come to pass in Lylea's pool—Arianne knew he would die because of it.

The thought of his existence being cut short, taken from her too soon before they even had a chance to live one lifetime together, was more than she could stand. It stabbed at the heart of her deepest fears now that she chose to live a mortal life with him. Forever was now a few decades when time was once unlimited. Her mother warned her about the hazards of mortal existence. Her own father was human, and it had nearly killed Arianne to watch him wither and die as his mortal existence reached completion. She vowed she would never do it again. It made the choice to surrender her immortality so much easier when Dare came into her life.

Her mother preferred to take men as her consorts largely because of their finite lifespan. Lylea had no desire to be tethered to anyone for thousands of years, but on occasion, even the high queen required company. Once they were gone, she mourned them quickly. Then she continued on as she always had, until the need for company overtook her again and she ventured out of the Veil for a temporary salve. Arianne did not blame her for it. She understood Lylea saw these men as transitory elements in her life.

Arianne knew she could never feel the same way about Dare. To face all of eternity without him was unimaginable, and so she accepted the price—to live one short span of life with a man she loved more than anything. It made Lylea's demand to keep this from Dare all the more reasonable. If the enemy required her child for its dark purpose, then Arianne was the only person it could not harm. Any force capable of drawing a god from the Verse was more than capable of killing the king of Carleon.

She would not risk Dare for anything.

The voice of Imogen, one of the fairest singers in Sandrine, carried through the hall, as she performed her song for the king and his guests. She sang a sweet melody of love and courage, of great deeds and tragic losses. The audience listened in rapt attention, and Arianne studied Dare unnoticed because he was too mesmerised by the enchanting music. When he did catch her gaze, he turned to her, favouring Arianne with a smile as he covered her hand with his.

In that moment, she knew he was happy.

Becoming the king was difficult for Dare. For years, his only goal was to free Carleon and Avalyne from Balfure, but she realised he thought little as to what came after. He was so accustomed to moving about freely, going on adventures, and sleeping under the stars with his companions. For so long, he drove the mechanism towards their liberation from Balfure, and now peace had come, he was finding the adjustment from warrior to king difficult to make.

Right now though, he appeared finally at peace with his life in a way she had not seen since before his coronation. Her heart soared at this knowledge, but also plunged because she knew how much of this happiness stood on a knife's edge. Her course was now clear. This quest was hers to fulfil.

Whatever the outcome.

* * *

"It was good to see everyone again," Dare sighed happily, as he lay contented against the cool sheets of their bed, his wife's warm body encircled in his arms.

It was in the small hours of the night and their guests had turned in or were still sprawled under tables where they had drunk themselves to a merry stupor. When Arianne spirited Dare away to their bed chamber, the king was certain he saw a pair feet protruding from beneath the table, either belonging to either Ronen or Aeron. He was not certain which. Even if the folk of the Green did not think much of interacting with the other races, they certainly knew how to drink. Tully showed a remarkably lusty appetite for ale, and held is own quite impressively against Kyou and Ronen in a drinking contest.

The king himself indulged, and as he rested his head against his pillow, he knew he was going suffer tomorrow. He prayed his wife had some elven remedy to spare him some the torture. Then again, she might just as well let him suffer to teach him a lesson.

"Yes, it was," Arianne agreed, savouring the feeling of lying in his arms and in their bed, secretly aware it was going to be the last night they would share together until her quest was done. "I forgot how much I missed them all."

"So had I," Dare breathed in the heady scent of her hair into his lungs. "Sometimes I think everything before the war happened to some other man. It seems like a lifetime away from where I now stand."

"The world changes, my love," Arianne smiled, her fingers tracing small circles against the bare skin of his chest with her finger. "You have simply changed with it."

"Until tonight I did not know I could be happy as I once was, although I wonder if I was ever truly content. I always had the dream of the alliance to drive me, and I do not think I gave any thought to what I wanted for myself, other than us being together. I had so much freedom as an exile and none now that I am king. I have yet to decide which is better. Still, I have you and soon our child, so I think I can be happy as king," he admitted.

"I am glad," she said softly, her eyes fixed on his. "I want to see you happy, Dare. You deserve it. You brought pride to the House of Icara and its line of kings. When our son is born, he will have a father he can look up to."

Dare looked at her with mischief and remarked, with a brow raised. "How is it so that you are so sure it's going to be a boy? It could be a girl," he teased, mimicking her taunt.

"It will be a boy," Arianne replied softly, saddened by how she had come to know this fact. "I *know* it."

"I did not lie when I said I did not care what it is, Rian." He raised her chin so that he could look into her eyes. "Any child that comes from you will fill me with joy, no matter if it is a girl or boy."

"I know," she smiled, and leaned forward so she could kiss him.

There was no terrible darkness waiting on the edge of her consciousness when her lips touched his. As always, they were two creatures perfectly attuned to each other's needs as he rolled over and covered her body with his, taking charge of their intimate exchange. Their intimacy as husband and wife always felt deeper than flesh. Arianne did not care what tomorrow would bring. All she knew was she loved him, and this was possibly their last night together if she failed in what she intended to do.

Shrouded in each other's heat, their need for one another became an agonizing game of pleasure and pain, of touching and tasting, of animal lust, wrapped within the complexity of deep, abiding love. When they were both complete and he lay against her breast with the air soaked with the scent of their lovemaking, she watched him sleep. There was no trace of Alasdare Icara, the king of Carleon, but just that scruffy young man who appeared at her mother's court and stole her heart away.

* * *

Celene's farewell to Ronen was nowhere near as passionate as Arianne's, but she did not mind it terribly.

Unlike the queen, Celene did not believe their quest would fail. She considered her parting with her husband a temporary thing, for she fully intended to see him again. He won her heart because he understood, even if she was warrior born, there was still a woman beneath the armour who wanted the same things as her mother before her. Wanting a home and children of her own did not make her any less of soldier, and his realisation of this simple truth was what made her love him so.

Of course, their love was love sometimes tested, particularly when he was in the company of his friends.

She watched him snoring in their bed, dead to the world, certain to suffer spectacularly for the excesses of the evening. Even if she could rouse him from his drunken slumber, she doubted she would get any sense from him at all. Accustomed to brothers who loved their ale, Celene could not fault him for enjoying himself in the company of Tully, Aeron, and Kyou. It was not often he could forget his station and be himself amongst people he could truly call friends.

Celene stayed at his side all night, if only to make sure he did not drown in his own vomit should his body revolt against all the ale he imbibed. Fortunately, Celene was spared the indignity, and when dawn's first light finally peeked over the horizon, she left his bed to embark on the journey ahead. The previous night's revels ensured he did not notice her departure with Arianne and Keira.

Even though she was now the Lady of Gislaine, she was still, at heart, a daughter of Angarad, and her travel garments reflected that past. She wore a dark red leather jerkin, with a belt at the waist to hold her scabbard, and breeches of a similar colour. Wearing the same boots she donned when she followed Dare's Circle across Avalyne, Celene strapped on her vambraces and took up her sword, a blade of the falchion design favoured by the Angarad, and she was ready to go.

She returned to the bed where Ronen continued to snore in deep slumber, and she found a little smile crossing her lips as she took in the sight of him. Leaning forward, she kissed him lightly on the lips and then frowned because his black sleep made him oblivious to it. With a sigh, she drew away, and hoped he would not be too upset at her when he awoke to learn what she had done.

Whatever his reaction, she knew it mattered little. Arianne needed her, and Celene would not fail her queen.

* * *

If Tully knew what Keira was about to do, he would have thought her mad.

To him, she wasn't an elf princess like Arianne, nor was she a soldier like Celene. She was a farmer's wife whose days were spent cooking, cleaning, growing vegetables on their farm, and occasionally going into the village to hear the latest gossip. She had no doubt he would have considered none of these skills terribly useful, if one was embarking on a quest to fight an opponent planning on hijacking an infant's soul, and replacing it with the spirit of a god.

This moment was what she had been waiting for. The words had escaped her lips before there was any time to consider how she would embark upon the quest with Arianne without Tully protesting her participation. Fortunately, the urgency of the situation required secrecy, and they would have to be away from Sandrine without revealing their plans to anyone, which suited Keira fine. The less Tully knew, the better.

Keira knew Arianne and Celene probably expected her to turn back and return to Sandrine. *They may even be relieved*, she thought silently. After all, what was she but a provincial woman of the Green, who spent her days growing things and looking after the needs of her husband? She stood on the periphery of world changing events while they had been in the thick of it. Save for that one incident with the Disciples, Keira had little to do with the defeat of Balfure. She was certain they expected her to turn back before they were even half way there. Except she wouldn't. She joined this quest for a reason.

Like Celene, Keira had no chance to say goodbye to Tully, or even give him some semblance of a veiled farewell the night before. He was properly drunk by the time she'd dragged him from under a table in the Great Hall, having intoxicated himself into a stupor with Ronen, Kyou, and Aeron. Fortunately, the mage Tamsyn, who was also retiring for the evening, came to her aid in helping her take her almost unconscious husband back to their chambers.

Tully fell face first into the clean sheet of the enormous mattress, his legs dangling over the side, muffled snores escaping him, and completely oblivious to the two people staring at him.

"If his head feels like the inside of a drum tomorrow, he'll have no sympathy from me," Keira snorted as she turned to Tamsyn, ready to thank him for his help.

"Will you be here for that?" he asked, his dark eyes boring into her.

Keira's voice caught in her throat, and she glanced anxiously over her shoulder at Tully, even though he was in no state to have overhead anything. Facing the mage once more, she tried to recover her composure and respond, but it was he who spoke again.

"Are you sure this is what you want to do?" Tamsyn asked, staring at her hard, like he could see something inside her like no one else could.

Tamsyn caught her off guard, and Keira was still uncertain how to respond. She did not wish to betray Arianne's plan to the mage, but she realised it was because he was a mage he knew what they were intending.

Collecting herself, Keira finally replied. "Yes, I need to do this. I'm not getting better, and if I leave it any longer, I never will be."

"I suppose there is no changing your mind from this course." He continued to give her a hard stare. "I can sense the shadow inside you—it is thick and blinds me somewhat. You prevailed against the Disciples, I am told, and that is not easily done. Perhaps there is darkness in your soul, but you most certainly are not weak as people believe."

Keira did not speak to that. She was considering his words, trying to determine what he could really see, and what he was merely assuming.

Whatever his intention, his words stayed with her for many hours that night.

* * *

When they left Sandrine, the city was bathed in the amber glow of dawn from the sun beginning its ascent into the morning sky. On their way out, they noted the silence as they rode along the cobblestoned streets. Most of Sandrine's inhabitants were still lost in the slumber following the previous days' celebration. Every street and square seemed to bear the signs of the revelry. The remains of food, crushed streamers, and flags mingled with the litter on the ground, to say nothing of the unconscious people passed out on benches, beneath porticos or inside doorways.

It surprised Arianne just how much she had come to love this city in the last year. The city and its people, even in their presently undignified condition, were now as dear to her as her former home of Eden Taryn. Dare did not lie when he described the beauty of the place to her so many years ago. Even before his return to the city as king, he and his friend Braedan, also of Sandrine, were frequent visitors, moving through it anonymously, and getting to know its people on a more intimate level.

In truth, she was dubious about his description because the elves considered the architecture of men to be a crude and clumsy affair, lacking the elegance and grace of their own cities. Still, Sandrine was not constructed from mud and brick. It was paved with marble, adorned with sculptures and frescos of ancient kings, green with manicured gardens, and filled with paved courtyards allowing its people to enjoy the sun shining past the tall spires and domed ceilings. Its beauty survived, despite the ugliness of Balfure's occupation, as if maintaining it was a connection to the kingdom of the past.

As the city was left behind her, Arianne hoped the quest would ensure Sandrine, like the rest of Carleon, did not know the shadow of another oppressor.

Even one who may be her son.

* * *

Celene nudged her grey steed alongside of Keira's smaller chestnut pony after they'd passed through the gates. Once next to the woman of the Green, Celene leaned over to her saddle bags and gripped the handle of a sword she had tucked away, presenting it to Keira.

"This is for you," Celene announced as she waited for Keira to take it.

"For me?" Keira stared at the woman in dumbfounded as she took the weapon, a short sword sheathed in a leather scabbard mounted with brass at the point and mouth. The blade was surprisingly light, with a ribbed grip that sat comfortably in her hand with the intricate design of a small bird on each finial of its cross guard.

"Yes," Celene said proudly, oblivious to the discomfort Arianne could see on Keira's face a mile away. "It's my first blade, actually. It was gift from my father for my fifteenth summer. It's not terribly heavy, but it is still sharp. I thought it would be a good weapon for you, since you're joining us on this quest."

"But I have no idea how to use such a thing!" Keira protested, even though she was pleased to be armed if they were going to be facing dangers along the way. "I'll probably cut myself!"

"No, you won't," Celene grumbled impatiently, trying not to feel peevish her gift was rejected so. "I'll show you how to use it, because if we fall into peril, I will not have you completely defenceless."

Arianne could appreciate Keira's hesitation, even if Celene could not. Celene came from a people who could not conceive of any existence where they did not have a sword in their hand, while Keira came from one that could not conceive of any reason why they would need one in the first place.

"You will be fine," Arianne assured her. "And it is just for the sake of safety. If we have to fight, Celene and I are capable, but we will not leave you unarmed either."

Keira nodded, accepting the reasoning behind it. "If Tully could see me now," she sighed.

"If our husbands could see *any* of us," Arianne remarked with a smile, "they would lock us away and never let us out."

"That will be the day," Celene snorted derisively. "I would like to see Dare try."

"It would be amusing to see," Keira laughed, and then added, "Alright then, teach me how to use this, but I don't think I'll be any good at it."

"Don't you worry," Celene said confidently, happy at Keira's agreement to take some instruction. She refused to believe any woman was incapable of wielding a sword, even if the rest of the world beyond Angarad had a rather narrow view of what one could do. "I'll teach you as I was taught by my father with a houseful of brothers."

Keira gave Celene a look of scepticism, but as she held up the sword she admired its craftsmanship, and the idea of being able to fight back was reassuring. It was time to show them her worth, starting with this.

Arianne, who had experience with an older brother and sparring, did not know if this would be of any comfort to Keira, but said nothing. The woman of the Green was driven by more than just the need to help her, and the queen did not fault her for that. They all had their reasons for joining this quest. Hers was to protect her son, while Celene's was to defend her queen. Who was to say that Keira's reasons were any less important?

Amidst the rolling hills of pastoral land, they could see the fork in the mighty Yantra River that ran throughout the length of Carleon. It began its life in highest peak of the Jagged Teeth and was the main waterway for the northern and central provinces. It also ran through Aeron's home of Eden Halas and of course Angarad. At the fork, the great river split into two smaller tributaries, the Orean and the Risselle.

"So, where are we going?" Keira asked, as they travelled northwards along the river. Arianne had hoped not to answer this question too soon, but she could not avoid Keira's direct approach. During the previous evening, Lylea told her many things—where they had to go, what they would encounter, and what she needed to find before she arrived there. The high queen's Sight determined from where the danger would come, and Lylea also reminded Arianne she had the blood of Celestial in her lineage. She had power capable of being drawn upon if she believed in it.

Arianne never found the courage to try.

Lylea did reveal, for the sake of her companions, details of the quest should be meted out sparingly. The enemy would not hesitate to torture them for information if he required it, and after what had happened to Keira at the hands of the Disciples, Arianne was risking none of her friends to that kind of danger again. Unfortunately, the notoriety of where they had to go would not be lost on Celene even if Keira did not recognise it.

"Sanhael."

"Sanhael?" Celene twisted sharply in her saddle to stare at Arianne in astonishment. "*That* is where we must go?"

"What's wrong with that?" Keira's gaze shifted between the two women, as she saw Celene's shock and Arianne's reluctance. "What is Sanhael?"

"Sanhael is the ancient stronghold of Mael," Arianne explained, feeling a chill run through her, just describing the place. "It was thought to have been destroyed when the Celestials finally banished him from Avalyne."

"Except they destroyed it by driving it into the earth," Celene pointed out. "The Celestials wanted it wiped off the face of the world, to be removed from Avalyne for all time."

"Then, how...?" Keira started to ask.

"My mother tells me that is where the enemy now resides. We must cross the Frozen Mountains and descend into Mael's Pit. The way into Sanhael lies through the foot of it."

"The Frozen Mountains," Keira's mused, taking in their destination. She knew of the mountains of ice that sat on the edge of the known world, facing the Brittle Sea. "The enemy is there?"

"It is as a good a place as any for an ancient evil to hide unnoticed," Celene stated. "There are stories of dragons, shape shifters, and other foul things residing there."

Celene wondered what else Arianne knew about the enemy. What had Queen Lylea told her the night before? Her experience with elves taught Celene they could be annoyingly cryptic at times, and as much as she loved Arianne, the queen of Carleon was apparently no different. Celene suspected she was holding back the whole truth to both spare and protect them. She had little doubt Lylea provided Arianne with a good deal more intelligence than she and Keira were privy to, and Arianne would dispense it as needed.

With a sigh, she decided there was nothing to be done now, except to continue on as they had planned.

"If our course is the Frozen Mountains, so be it," Celene turned to Keira, aware that the mistress of Furnsby Farm must surely be fearful now their destination was revealed. "We knew this would not be an easy journey to make, but we are both resolved to stay at Arianne's side, are we not?"

"We are," Keira confirmed, as she gave Celene a nod of confidence before turning to Arianne. "We are with your Arianne, wherever you must go."

"Thank you." Arianne extended her reach towards Keira, who took her fingers and gave them a gentle squeeze.

With the agreement to go on reached, Celene spoke up. "If our destination is the Frozen Mountains, then I suggest we take the river route. We will find a boat at the docks at Naiad and continue down the river, until we reach the Winter Keep for fresh supplies."

Grateful Celene was moving onto more practical matters, Arianne agreed with the route mapped by the warrior of Angarad "We could also disembark at Eden Halas and gain fresh horses for the ride into Angarad."

Even if relations between Dare and Halion were chilled, Arianne knew they would be afforded every courtesy by his wife, Queen Syanne, Dare's adopted mother. The lady had not attended the celebration at Sandrine but Arianne suspected it was because of Halion's dislike of his queen leaving the safety of Eden Halas and travelling so far from home to a city of men.

Despite the importance of the quest before them, Celene could help feeling some pleasure knowing Angarad was on the way to the Frozen Mountains. It would be good to see her father and brothers again. She had not seen them since she led their army away from their capital Wyndfyre to join the Alliance in the march towards Abraxes and their final showdown with Balfure.

"You will get to see your family," Keira declared, fascinated to know what kind of people had spawned such a fearless creature as Celene.

"Yes," Celene nodded. "Although, there will not be much time for reunions. We need to make haste to reach our destination."

"We are in your hands, Celene," Arianne replied. "You know the Northern Province far better than I."

"Thank you, Arianne," Celene said, grateful for the faith being given to her. Still, there were some things she needed know about their quest. "Arianne, we know you have your reasons for telling us little, but we must know something of what is happening, if we are to be of any use to you."

"Yes, Arianne," Keira added her voice to lend weight to Celene's entreaty. "Please tell us what you can. You don't have to reveal everything."

Of course they had a right to know, even if her reasons for keeping silent were good ones. The enemy's resources were unknown to them. They knew he was powerful and could call resurrect Mael, but could he see the past, present, and future as Queen Lylea could? If so, was he looking at her now? Watching her with a reptilian third eye, carefully charting her flight from Sandrine?

Lylea told her there was a task to complete before they reached Mael's Pit, and for the sake of her friends it was best to keep it silent. If the enemy knew what she going, he would also know what it was she sought. Arianne asked for more detail, but her mother was as cryptic as always, and being her daughter did not allow Arianne any special consideration. She wondered if this was her own good or simply because it was Lylea's way. One thing did stand out above all the warnings and instructions given by the high queen although Arianne did not fully understand it.

"Your blood is more than just human or elf. Your grandfather was sired by a Celestial and that, too, runs through your veins. You will do well to remember that."

Arianne knew her family line was descended from the Celestial Enphilim, but she had no idea how it manifested itself in her. If there was power in her, Arianne had never seen it.

"I will tell you what I can," she said after a moment. "The enemy is not known to my mother. She cannot see him, but she knows he is powerful indeed. Perhaps not strong enough to strike directly at Dare while he surrounded by an army, but more than capable of killing him were they to come face-to-face. We do not know if he can see us, and so we must take precautions."

"Is that why we had to leave in such secret?" Keira ventured to guess.

"Yes," Arianne nodded sombrely. "Because I want the enemy to think that I am still in Sandrine, not coming for him. If I am unseen by most in the city, it can be explained. I am, after all, with child—a difficult pregnancy might warrant the need to be sequestered until the baby is born. Better yet, if Dare pursues us, the enemy might think the king is the one who is going to confront him in the Frozen Mountains, not us."

"So, he will not realise we are actually on our way before Dare leaves Sandrine, because he thinks you are still in the city." Celene nodded in understanding.

"If he is using an agent to watch over me, yes," Arianne nodded. "I can get to him before he realises I am no longer at Sandrine. We must reach him before the second full moon."

"We will have to ride hard," Celene said, with a sigh. They would have to remain hidden from the enemy but also keep one step ahead of the king. As someone who was accustomed to riding with Dare, this would not be easy to do.

"We must," Arianne whispered. "I have to reach the enemy before I give birth to a demon."

Arianne closed her eyes in anguish, unable to speak any further because the horror of it was more than she could bear. Her body shook with emotion and her hands tightened around the reins of her steed with such intensity her knuckles became white. Tears wanted to spill from her eyes at the unfairness of her lot, but she knew it would avail her nothing. It would not change the reality of the enemy harming her baby unless she prevented it.

"It will not happen," Keira assured her, her hand still in the queen's and she squeezed tighter because her anguish was so exposed, there was nothing else left to say assuage her fright.

Arianne looked up and met Keira's gaze, grateful for the support.

"I swear to you Arianne, not only as your friend, but as your loyal subject, I will die before I allow my future king to be blighted with an obscenity. We will stop him Arianne, I promise. We *will* stop him," Celene said firmly.

Despite Celene's confidence, Arianne knew the quest ahead, was nowhere near as easy to accomplish as her words implied. There was real danger ahead and every chance they could lose their lives in the process. Nevertheless, it meant a great deal to her friends to be at her side and Arianne was grateful she was not totally alone with what awaited her in the Frozen Mountains.

"Thank you," she replied, her voice filled with emotion. "I do not deserve friends such as you."

"Well," Keira declared with a hint of mischief, intending to bring a smile to her friend's face, and dispel the heavy mood of the moment. "That goes without saying, of course."

Chapter Five

Discovery

When Dare awoke the next morning, he found himself alone.

His aching head reminded him painfully the evils of drink should never be underestimated. Grimacing at the throbbing inside his skull, he sat up in his bed and stared for a moment at the empty space beside him, wondering where Arianne had gone. Slightly disappointed by her absence, he was not so drunk the night before to forget the heat of their lovemaking. It would have been much nicer to suffer the drumbeat inside his head, if he could lie in bed with her.

No doubt she was somewhere in the palace, attending to her own duties, most likely conferring with the seneschal regarding the comfort of their guests this morning. He supposed she would appear soon enough.

Still, when he climbed out of bed, a feeling of uneasiness came over him he could not explain.

Ignoring it, he went about the rituals of morning, dressing and making himself ready to move about his court and appear kingly as he did so. Still, the odd sensation of something being a missed continued to dog him. These were instincts he relied upon for much of his life, saving him more times than he could count. Experiencing them now, in a place he should have felt the safest, made him tense. When he emerged from the royal chambers, he remained gripped by the feeling of something lurking in the periphery, waiting for an opportunity to ambush.

Making his way to the Great Hall, cleared of the previous evening's decadence and readied for breakfast, Dare was certain that the others would be awake by now, headache or not. Their long friendship taught him one thing about his former travelling companions—not even Balfure could keep them from a good breakfast. Indeed, before he even reached the large doors that emptied into the room, he could hear the chatter emanating into the corridor. The sound of their animated voices brought a heartfelt smile to Dare's face, for it felt like old times again.

Before he could join them, he heard a familiar voice call.

"Dare."

Dare glanced over his shoulder to see Aeron. *Of course it was*, he thought silently. Aeron was still the only person capable of sneaking up on him. As the elf approached, Dare stifled the smirk threatening steal across his face. He noted the prince did not have the usual spring in his step Dare had become accustomed to seeing. In fact, for someone so light on his feet, it was safe to say at the moment, the expression on Aeron's face was positively grim.

Elves were notoriously bad drinkers, but when Aeron and Kyou challenged each other to be the last man standing, all good sense left them both. Their competition was eventually joined by Tully, Ronen, and himself to a lesser degree. Still, they were accustomed to drinking; Aeron was not.

"How do you fare this morning, Aeron?"

"I think I'm going to be ill," Aeron complained.

"The nearest window is that direction," Dare pointed helpfully.

The elf glared at him through narrowed eyes. "If you were truly my friend you would kill me and end my misery."

"I thought elves were known for their ability to endure. I am certain that your suffering will pass."

"Not soon enough," Aeron grumbled as they resumed their journey into the hall, where the smell of food was wafting down the hallway.

"Tell me," Dare asked, as they approached the entrance. "Did you see Arianne anywhere?"

"No." Aeron shook his head. "I have not. Why?"

"It's just I have not seen her this morning," Dare replied, feeling once again uneasy. "I wonder where she is."

"She is probably seeing to your guests," Aeron responded, noticing the concern in Dare's face as real worry.

Dare supposed he was being ridiculous. After all, they were presently host to some of the most prominent people in Avalyne. Aside from her mother and their friends, there were lords from other cities in Carleon in attendance, and he could appreciate Arianne feeling a little self-conscious while playing hostess to such a prestigious collection. She was queen as long as he had been king, and while he had numerous chances to prove himself since beginning his rule, Arianne's opportunity to shine in her position was limited to occasions such as this. Prior to the arrival of their guests, she was a flurry of action, moving across the castle, determined to ensure everything was perfect.

"I am sure that you are right, my friend." Dare patted Aeron on the back and grinned. "Come along, Aeron. Let us get some food into you. I am certain some meat off the bone, tender and red, covered in thick gravy, and a couple of eggs bubbling with fat will make you feel much better. All that food churning in your belly, bubbling with last night's spirits..."

Aeron scowled at him and muttered under his breath, "And they thought Balfure was the evil one."

* * *

If there was one thing Dare knew he would never become accustomed to since becoming king, it was the practice of everyone rising to their feet when he entered a room.

While he resigned himself to his fate in the company of his subjects, it was even more disconcerting when he saw it being performed by his friends. These were the people with whom he had travelled the wilds of Avalyne, shared a campfire, and gotten drunk with in taverns. They'd fought together and bled together. They even mourned as one. Their friendship was far too deep for this formality to ever feel appropriate.

Nevertheless, it was a burden of his station, and he bade them to sit once he entered the room. Beside him, Dare heard his best friend snigger in discomfort, and felt some vindication for his earlier teasing, because Aeron knew just how much he loathed all the royal ceremony and pomp.

At the long dining table in the Great Hall, the servants were working busily to see to the needs of his guests. They walked up and down the large room, filling up goblets and setting down trays of food. Directing this activity, with the expertise of a battlefield general, was a thin, hollow cheeked man with an aquiline nose and an impeccably groomed beard named Esau.

Esau came into Dare's service when the king had finally regained control of Sandrine Keep. Esau's family served the Keep and the kings within it for five generations, and with the return of the rightful heir, he wanted to serve House Icara again. Dare, who knew nothing about maintaining a castle, was more than happy to appoint Esau his seneschal, and the man never gave Dare cause to regret it.

As he approached his seat at the centre of table, Dare noted that Tully and Kyou were already well into breakfast, if the pile of food on their plates was any indication. Also present this morning was Lord Navarre of Varaen, who chose to wisely retire early the night before, engaged in conversation with his youngest son Adevane. Both nodded at Dare in greeting as he walked past them and took his place.

Navarre ruled Varaen in the Southern Province before the occupation of the kingdom by Balfure. As an elder statesman approaching his seventieth year, Navarre was an able diplomat who had little taste for power, but knew how lightly he needed to tread around Balfure to spare his people. During those dark days, Navarre managed to reach an accord of sorts with Balfure, allowing him some control over his city.

When Dare staked his claim upon Carleon, it was Navarre who was his strongest ally after Ronen. He knew Dare's father, and played intermediary between the would-be-king and the other leaders of the fragmented kingdom to rally the support needed to launch an assault against Balfure. During that time, Navarre earned Dare's respect by his wise counsel, and a real friendship was forged between the two.

The first thing Dare noted, when he sat down, was Ronen. The Bân seemed preoccupied and barely acknowledged the king next to him, not that Dare was concerned by this. No, it was the look on the man's face that prompted him to speak, even as he was being fussed over by one of the servers.

"You seem troubled," Dare remarked quietly, once his meal was laid out before him.

Ronen glanced at him, slightly startled at having not noticed Dare had sat down.

"It is nothing," Ronen said quickly, trying to shrug off his distracted state.

"Come now, Ronen," Dare insisted. "It doesn't appear to be nothing. We are friends, tell me what bothers you. I know with Aeron it is clearly too much drink." He threw a teasing smirk at the elf, who had taken the seat beside him.

Aeron glared at Dare through narrowed eyes and then muttered something in elvish that was not at all appropriate for repeating. Dare chuckled inwardly; he didn't think elves knew such words.

"Ronan managed a smile at Dare's attempt to lighten the mood, exhaling deeply and expelling his reservations. Dare was correct. They were friends, and he would only work himself into a state if he did not voice his concerns. "I cannot find Celene," he admitted.

"That is hardly a cause to worry," Dare said smoothly. He learned a long time ago Celene was not like most women. Being of Angarad, she was accustomed to going where she pleased, and any man who married her needed to accept it or be prepared for a most tumultuous union. While she took to married life well enough, Dare suspected there would always remain in Celene the free spirit who once travelled with him across Avalyne.

"She is probably somewhere with Arianne. I have not seen the queen this morning either," Dare confessed.

"Under most circumstances, I wouldn't be concerned," Ronen explained, because he too knew the woman he'd married. Part of why he had fallen in love with her was because of her strong, independent nature. He would no sooner try to tether her spirit then he would try to pin a cloud in the sky. "But..." His words faltered.

"But?" Dare stared at him, and by now, even Aeron was paying attention.

"She took her sword and her travelling clothes."

At that, he understood Ronen's concern. Celene would not take her sword with her unless she was fully intending to use it, and the absence of her travelling clothes meant Celene planned to do it somewhere other than Sandrine. What could possibly warrant such a departure from the city without at least giving her husband some word of it? It was unlike Celene to behave so thoughtlessly.

As he pondered this, Dare was suddenly revisited by the uneasiness he felt this morning when he awoke to find Arianne gone. Of course, he'd told himself there were a dozen explanations, and now he knew Celene was gone, it was highly likely the two were together. Suddenly Ronen's comment about Celene's sword made him anxious.

"Ronen, have you see Arianne at all this morning?" he ventured to ask. It was entirely possible the duo chose to leave the walls of Sandrine for a day of exploration. After all, the countryside beyond Sandrine was quite breathtaking, to say nothing of the spectacular waters of Lake Tijon sitting within sight of the city.

The Lord of Gislaine's eyes widened, realising perhaps his situation was not unique, and shook his head in reply, "No, I have not."

Still refusing to think the worst, Dare rose to his feet and addressed not only his guests, but the servants in the Great Hall.

"Has *anyone* seen Queen Arianne or Lady Celene this morning?" he asked out loud, silencing everyone in the room with the question.

Tully stopped eating in mid-chew when Dare spoke because, until that moment, he assumed Keira had gone off with the queen and Celene. He didn't expect to her wait around their chambers until he woke up this morning, especially after drinking himself silly the night before. In fact, he hadn't thought twice about where Keira might actually be. It made him feel a little guilty now Dare was asking after the Arianne and Celene.

There was a long pause as Dare waited for someone to answer, and he was not comforted by the blank stares he received in return. No one could give him an answer. The lack of response was not merely confined to the guests, but also the serving staff. The servers, compromised of young men and women, whispered amongst themselves as they tried to remember when each of them might have seen the queen. Finally, it was Esau who stepped forward and spoke on their behalf.

"Sire, no one has seen Queen Arianne at all," Esau declared.

"Dare, I haven't seen Keira all morning either," Tully spoke up, now convinced all three women were together.

"I'm sure it's nothing to worry about," Kyou declared, seeing no reason for concern in any of this. "They're probably at the market or something."

Aeron shot the dwarf a look, wondering if he had been deaf, dumb and blind during the years Celene was a part of their circle. "When have you ever known Celene to go to a *market*?"

"My wife would not simply leave without telling me," Ronen pointed out, and was in full agreement with Aeron. Such pursuits would have bored Celene to tears. "Besides, she took her blade. What need should she have of it?"

"I have an idea," Tamsyn's voice sailed across the room, and drew all eyes to him, as he and Lylea appeared at the threshold into the hall.

Their arrival immediately brought an air of dignified stillness to the room. As Dare watched Tamsyn and Lylea enter, their expressions gave him immediate cause for concern. Their manner appeared grave, and the gnawing sensation pursuing him much of the morning had finally ensnared him in its jaws. Lowering himself into his chair, he awaited for them to tell him what they knew about Arianne and the others.

"What is it?" Dare demanded, his tone cold and hard. "I would know what has happened to my wife."

"As would I," Ronen added his voice to the conversation. "If there is reason for concern, we all have the right to hear it." He glanced at Tully, whose brow was furrowed with increasing anxiety.

"Arianne has embarked upon a quest of her own," Tamsyn explained, aware the tempers in the room were already frayed and these words would offer no relief.

"A *quest*?" Dare jumped to his feet, his hands knuckled against the table. "She is with child! She is in no condition to embark on any kind of quest!"

"She *must* go on this one," Lylea answered, trying to subdue Dare's ire. "It involves your child."

"My child?" This was getting worse by the moment and Dare's patience was almost at an end. "Why? If there is a quest or some danger to our babe, I should be the one to embark upon it. Not her! How could you keep this from me, either of you?" he demanded, his eyes filled with accusation.

"Please understand it is not our wish to see Arianne harmed," Lylea's calm town was a stark contrast to Dare's growing outrage. She shared his anguish at being forced to allow her only daughter to go forth alone to fight an evil so ancient, but Lylea had thousands of years to become accustomed to sending people she loved into battle. That it was her own daughter now changed nothing. "The quest has to be fulfilled by her. She alone can fight the evil threatening us all."

"And what part does Celene have in all this?" Ronen asked, forced to watch his tone as he addressed the elven queen. Unlike Dare, he was not her son-in-law.

"She pledged her sword, and her life, to her queen," Lylea answered, "as did your wife, Master Tully."

"Keira!" Tully stared at her in shock. "Keira's not a soldier! She's a farmer's wife. She doesn't know how to defend herself! Hasn't she already suffered enough? How could you let her go?" he shouted, and he didn't care who he was speaking to. "She's not strong enough to go out there by herself."

"There is more to your wife than we know, Master Tully," Tamsyn explained calmly. "She chose to go without any prompt from us. As you said, she has indeed suffered at the hands of the Disciples, and lest we forget, she did prevail against them when most would have not. She has talents none of us suspect."

"What is this danger they face?" Dare asked, his head spinning, as he fought to restrain the urge to storm out of Sandrine and go after Arianne.

Tamsyn and Lylea exchanged glances, knowing there would be no peace with Dare, or anyone else present, until they learnt the reason for Arianne's departure from Sandrine. Neither could blame those assembled for their anger, especially Dare's, for it was not only his wife at risk, but his child as well. As a king, husband, and soon-to-be father, it was his natural instinct to protect them both. He had to be made to understand why it could not be him, even though Lylea suspected it would do little to hold him back."

Lylea braced herself, and answered, "An agent of Mael."

An audible gasp rippled through the room a split second before Dare's sputtered in fury. "MAEL! You allowed my wife to ride out with a company of two to face someone who is ally to Mael?"

Mael.

For an instant, Dare was filled with such outrage he could barely think. He knew who Mael was, and he knew the legends of the dark god who took physical form in the Age of Awakening to wage war against Celestials for the conquest of Avalyne. Did Lylea expect Dare to believe sending Arianne with only Keira and Celene to face such horror a credible way to handle the situation?

"Yes," Lylea continued to explain. "His agent has chosen to resurrect Mael by using your unborn child as its vessel. The enemy seeks to bring Mael's essence from the Verse and infuse it into your son's body, displacing his soul for Mael's own and then giving him *your* kingdom to rule."

"By the Gods," Dare heard Aeron whisper in shock, while Ronen had dropped to his seat in horror.

"And you sent her to fight him?" Dare managed to speak, his voice nothing like a low growl.

"She is the only one who *can* fight him Dare," Tamsyn answered for Lylea. "While your child slumbers in her womb, the enemy cannot harm her. It requires your wife and child for his plans come to fruition. Had you gone to face the enemy, he would have killed you outright and anyone else with you. It must be Arianne that goes because she can use the enemy's need for her safety as a weapon."

"And what of Celene and Keira?" Ronen demanded coldly of the wizard. "What of them? How safe are they?"

"Celene pledged herself to her queen," Lylea stared at him. "She is not safe, but she is a good warrior and will acquit herself well. Your wife insisted on accompanying them with no prompt from us."

Tully didn't appear convinced, but could think of nothing to say to refute the queen's words if that was what had happened. He was still in shock at the fact Keira agreed to go on this quest at all. It was so unlike her to behave in such a way. Over the last few years, she hardly wanted to leave home at all. For her to suddenly decide to ride off into the unknown like this left Tully reeling.

"Where did they go?" Dare demanded in a tone of voice that would not tolerate evasion.

"They ride towards the Frozen Mountains," Tamsyn answered.

This was getting worse by the minute, Dare thought. The Frozen Mountains! They were leagues away, and reputed to be filled with ancient dangers. Even he never ventured so far in his travels, and now Arianne was going there? With only Celene and Keira for company? The enormity of it was almost too much for him to endure.

"That's almost the other side of Avalyne!" Tully gasped, unable to imagine Keira being so far away from him, and agreeing to cross that distance without even telling him. *Probably because she knows you'll stop her*, an inner voice in his heard spoke with surprising sharpness.

"Yes," the queen nodded. "They must cross the mountains and descend into Mael's Pit."

"Then, that is where I will go," Dare stated firmly, pushing himself away from the table.

"Dare, you must let Arianne complete this task!" Lylea implored. "You are vulnerable. She is not."

"You do not understand, do you?" He glared at her sharply. "You assume she cannot be harmed, but if she refuses to submit to the enemy, what assurance do you have that he won't capture her and keep her until she is no longer needed? As with all dark magic, I assume this spell to bring about Mael's resurrection requires no permission from her? Just the use of her body and the presence of a vessel? If she does not defeat him, he'll take her alive and that may be even worse than death. If Arianne even allows it to get so far. She knows the necessity of sacrifice. She's learned it by choosing to be my wife. Do you not think that if she believes for one moment she could be overcome she wouldn't kill her herself and the baby to save Avalyne? To save me?"

"She would not do that," Lylea retaliated, refusing to believe that any elf would return the gift of immortality granted by the Celestial Gods so recklessly.

Yet even as the thought crossed her mind, Lylea knew Arianne was always something of an aberration. She took too much after the human who helped to conceiver her, and nothing she had done since birth was according to plan.

"Yes, she would," Aeron spoke up for the first time in this matter. "If she for one minute thought her child could harm either Dare or Avalyne, she would not hesitate to make such a decision."

"Lord Navarre," Dare turned to his trusted comrade, no longer looking upon the troubled visage of Lylea. He was too angered by what he had learned, and although he had no wish to disrespect Arianne's mother, she sorely deserved it in his opinion. "I would request you remain in Sandrine and oversee the kingdom for the duration of my absence."

"Of course, Sire," Navarre nodded obediently.

"I will go with you, Dare," Tamsyn offered, wishing to be present to counsel Dare when the time came.

Dare was still angry at Tamsyn for keeping his secrets with Lylea, but their long friendship stilled his fury, and Tamsyn's knowledge of the events transpiring was needed for the journey ahead. "I will be grateful for your counsel in this mission," he said tautly.

"My wife rides with yours," Ronen stared at Dare. "So I will ride with you. I pledge my sword to my king, as my wife has done for her queen."

Dare smiled gratefully, and could not refuse his aid Celene was his wife, and he would not refuse Ronen's desire to protect her any more than his own. "Thank you, my friend."

"You will need my sharp eyes and senses, such as they are at the moment," Aeron added his voice into the mix. "When my head stops hurting, I am certain I will be of use to you."

"Well you cannot go out there with so much danger armed with an elf who can hardly hold his drink," Kyou's loud voice snorted in Dare's ear.

Aeron frowned at the dwarf, wondering again why it was he considered the master builder a good friend.

"I would be glad to have your company, Kyou" Dare said, grateful to be surrounded by his Circle once more.

"And mine," Tully declared hotly. "You're not going after them without me. Keira's my wife."

"Of course," Dare answered without hesitation.

He sat down again, needing to catch his breath. The night before replayed in his mind, how she felt when he kissed her, how she whispered his name in his ear when their bodies were one. He closed his eyes and in a split second, all that she was since the day he met her, tugged at his heart. He loved her so, his beautiful Arianne, and the thought she was beyond the safety of her home, preparing to fight a battle she may not win, not only for him, but for their child, was more than he could stand.

In this life, meeting her was his happiest hour, and if he had to die to keep her and the baby safe, he was willing to make the sacrifice. Being king without her was being less than nothing.

Chapter Six

The Children of Syphi

As planned, Arianne, Celene and Keira left Sandrine and rode towards Naiad. The own earned its livelihood from the trade taking place when the Yantra forked into the Orean and Riselle tributaries Once there, they could secure a boat to take them north, and pay the local livery to return the horses to Sandrine.

Arianne chose to remain out of sight. Naiad was a small trading post that welcomed newcomers, and the presence of the queen certainly would not go unnoticed. If the enemy did have designs on her baby, then he must surely be watching closely now the announcement of the impending royal birth was made. Lylea was unable to tell if the enemy had Sight of his own or if he was compelled to use agents who spied on her movements. If she was being watched, Arianne knew keeping the enemy in the dark about her plans for as long as possible was key.

So while Celene acquired their transport up river and Keira took charge of buying supplies for the journey, Arianne found a quiet corner at an inn and waited with her hood of her cloak drawn to hide her recognisable features.

Arianne was eager to depart, even though Naiad offered the promise of a warm bed for the night. By now, Dare most surely knew she was gone, and probably the reason for her unexpected departure. If the truth was kept from him, he might believe the three of them were taking a tour of the countryside together. If he did know why she left Sandrine, then he would surely be on his way to find her.

Inviting as it was for her to let him catch up and take charge of leading this quest, Arianne knew she could not allow that. The king's party travelling across Carleon would draw even more attention than she would, and this was an advantage she could ill-afford to exploit. If the enemy was aware of Dare's departure, Arianne hoped it was because he believed Dare knew his plans for the baby and was riding out to confront him in Sanhael.

While Arianne did not like the idea of Dare playing decoy because of Lylea's warning at how easily the enemy could kill him, it would allow her the chance to get to Sanhael without being noticed until it was too late.

* * *

It was late in the afternoon when they left Naiad on a single-masted boat with lateen sails and sailed up the Yantra River. With the gentle slopes of the Iolan Hills flanking them on either side, Arianne watched the setting sun pull long shadows across the land from the bow of the small craft, lost in thought as she considered the quest ahead with some melancholy. Celene was manning the sails while Keira, after some instruction, was guiding the boat up river with the rudder. They indulged in idle chatter for a while after leaving Naiad, but as the day grew short, all three had lapsed into a thoughtful silence as each reflected on their situation.

With her hands resting on her belly, as if she could feel the life within slumbering, Arianne found her thoughts fixed on what would happened if she failed in this quest. She wished she possessed Celene's strength and Keira's courage. Ironically, she was older than both of them, and yet, they endured greater trials in both their short existences than she had in most of her sheltered life.

The only time she was truly been tested was when she had ridden away from Barrenjuck Green, ferrying a sick and blind Keira to Eden Taryn after the Disciples were done with her. She remembered how angry Lylea had been because she went after Dare herself instead of sending one of their soldiers. Love had driven her then to overcome her fear and she prayed it would do the same now.

Glancing at Celene, who was tying down a corner of the sail, and admiring how the blue canvas billowed against the wind, Arianne wished she had her courage. Celene did not shrink from danger, indeed she rode out to face it. How many times had Arianne heard the tales of Celene's bravery in battle, how she had fought alongside of Dare and his circle? Refusing to believe she was any less than a man earned her undying respect from her companions. At times, Arianne wonder if Dare wished she possessed the same steel.

Keira's courage was not as overt as Celene's, but Arianne and Dare owed her a debt nonetheless. The Disciples were Balfure's most trusted servants. It was claimed they were spawned from the Dreaded Mother of All during the Primordial Wars. Though they were able to transform into the guise of man or elf, their true visage was so terrible men could go mad upon seeing it. A twisted amalgamation of three different animals, their bodies were shaped like a great cat while their tails were pointed and sharp like a wasp's stinger. Instead of cat's paws, their feet were the talons of a bird, and, finalising this grotesque shape, was the head of the last human it assumed.

As hunters, they were relentless, and were known to always get their prey once they caught its scent. They stalked Dare across the Northern Province, after he took counsel at Cereine, chasing him across the Baffin Range and finally into Barrenjuck Green. Like a glaring of cats, they tried to run him to ground, and they would have captured him if not for the distraction costing Dare's friend, Braedan, his life. It was only until after Dare entered the Green, with the ancient wood possessing its own guardian spirits, he was able to find refuge with Tully and Keira.

Unfortunately, after Dare had left with Tully, the Disciples found their way to Furnsby Farm, and Keira.

Keira never told them if the Disciples showed her their true forms before they inflicted their torture of the burrowers upon her. In fact, the woman never spoke of any of it. Somehow, she endured the scars of their brutality, and spared everyone around her the terrible details that would only make them feel guilt. Arianne knew Tully worried constantly for her because he did not know the full extent of her ordeal, only the after effects. Arianne wondered if Keira knew how brave she was, being able to hold in the terror that drove lesser men mad.

Yet, here she was, embarking on this quest. Keira thought she was weak, when she was actually the strongest person Arianne knew.

* * *

"You are silent," Keira joined the Queen at the bow. The wind was blowing northwards, allowing the sail to do most of the work and carry them up river. Celene took charge of the rudder, directing the boat to move against the current by weaving it from side to side along the river bank. It allowed Keira the freedom to join the queen, who was sitting alone.

Both she and Celene noticed the queen's melancholy, though neither brought attention to it. It was understandable, of course. Arianne should feel overwhelmed by everything taking place in the last day. Only yesterday, she was celebrating the impending arrival of her child, and today, she was off to face an enemy who had struck at the most intimate of places.

"I am thinking," Arianne looked up at Keira as the other woman sat down beside her.

"Of what's ahead?"

"Of what could happen if I fail," Arianne confessed with a sigh.

"You mustn't think like that," Keira reached for her hand and squeezed it gently. "I know it seems grim, but we will stop this."

Arianne was trying not to let despair overtake her, but it was difficult when she considered the consequences for failure. "I do not know if I have it in me to stop this evil from taking my child. My mother thinks I can stop Mael's agent, but I wonder if she only thinks it because she has little faith in the ability to men to prevail. She forgets until I met Dare, I spent my life sheltered behind the Veil. He was the one who encouraged me to explore the world outside, to see what lay beyond. The time when I came to take you to Eden Taryn was probably the first time I really travelled alone."

"I remember. You saved my life."

"You saved Dare's," Arianne countered, just as promptly.

Arianne knew how much pain Keira experienced with the burrowers burning through her veins, and how much of her journey to Eden Taryn was seen through a stupor of pain and darkness. At Dare's summons, Arianne ridden to the edge of the Green and escorted Keira to Eden Taryn, while he, Aeron, and Tully led the Disciples away.

"It was the right thing to do. As this is the right thing to do," she said firmly. "We can do this Arianne, and if we fail, at least we tried to stop the evil from returning to our world. Sometimes, we have to suffer for the good things. Maybe that's what makes it all worthwhile."

"You don't understand," Arianne whispered, caressing her belly protectively, as if will alone would shield the babe within from all harm. "If I fail, and the enemy is successful, I will have only two choices left to me. The first is to take my own life, because I will not give birth to a monster. I will not raise a vessel of Mael to watch him bring to ruin everyone I love. If I am not given the choice and somehow, the enemy sees to it that I *do* give birth to the child, then neither Dare nor I can allow him to live long enough to reach adulthood. If he does, he will be king. Imagine, if you will, what that means."

Lylea's vision coming to pass, Keira thought. *A bloodthirsty king with an army of beserkers, with the potential to be even worse than Balfure ever was.*

"Don't you see?" Arianne said, with tears running down her cheeks. "If he is born, then we will have no recourse but to put him to the sword, or risk the destruction of Avalyne. I know Dare would do it. For the good of his people, he would make the sacrifice, and I know as surely as I breathe, it will destroy him."

"It is not the failure I fear Keira," Arianne whispered, "It's what we may have to do *after*."

And, to that, Keira said nothing.

* * *

Making camp for the night, they forgot the subject of the quest for the moment. Engaging in idle chatter, as if they were taking a leisurely trip up river instead of the dark journey that could see them all dead before it was done. After Arianne's real fear had been voiced, Keira advised Celene not to speak too frequently about the enemy, because Arianne was painfully aware of him already.

At sunrise, they resumed their journey up the river, reminiscing of past journeys and the days when life was not as complicated as it was now. It would take three days to reach the Winter Keep, where they could be resupplied for their journey to the Falls of Iolan. Arianne wanted only a brief delay before continuing northward. According to Lylea, the enemy would be ready to carry out his spell of restoration in two full moons, and

Arianne had to reach him before that. It was a long journey to the Frozen Mountains and they had no time to waste.

* * *

Upon arriving at the Winter Keep, Celene kept Arianne's presence a secret until she could be properly revealed to Galain the Caretaker. Galain fought alongside of Celene at the Battle of Astaroth, and the former comrades possessed a healthy respect for each other. Once Galain knew the queen was travelling alone with two friends, he understood the need for discretion, and welcomed Arianne into the Keep with the strictest of secrecy.

They shared his table that evening, and Arianne had to admit, the company of Galain and his lovely family was a pleasant distraction from the grim nature of their quest. His wife, a friendly, warm woman named Mika, was thrilled to receive the queen and her friends in the caretaker's wing of the Keep.

Meanwhile, Galain gave Arianne an account of all the news in the region. Working in concert with the elves of Eden Halas and the newly returned dwarves of Iridia, they were driving Balfure's goblins back into the Wilds. Since the dwarves reclaimed their cities beneath the Starfall Mountains, the goblins were being forced to return to their former enclaves in the Cinder Mountains.

When asked why she was travelling, Arianne explained with the impending birth of her child, she wished to see the places of her childhood before it became too difficult to travel. Hence, she was taking the opportunity to see Eden Halas, Barrenjuck Green, and Eden Taryn before the swell of her baby's growth kept her bound to Sandrine indefinitely. Mika, who gave Galain a houseful of children, was sympathetic, and her husband was more than happy provide his queen with whatever she needed to continue her journey.

They left the Winter Keep the next morning, and although he invited them to stay longer, Galain understood Arianne's need to depart. He provided them with a trio of fine palfreys to make the overland trip past the Iolan Falls, since it could not be crossed by river.

A boat ferried them from the Keep to the Eastern Shore. Celene was mindful of everything the instant they set foot on dry land again. Although Galain assured them the goblins were no more a plague in this region, Celene was not anxious to see him proven wrong, with Arianne in such a delicate state.

Upon reaching Eastern Shore, they followed the flow of the Yantra on horseback, letting it rush past them speedily towards the falls. Even from the land, they could see the currents moving swiftly away, and the turbulent cascade that spawned it. In far quicker time than they thought it possible, they soon sighted the cloud like spray that arose from its churning waters.

They saw little of the great cascade, because to see it in its entirety would take them off their course, and theirs was not a mission of leisure. It was one of urgency, and sensibly, they turned their horses to an easier path in the woods to take them beyond its fury.

* * *

The first thing Arianne noticed when they arrived at Caras Anara was the silence.

Caras Anara was the only remaining human settlement along the river before entering the woods of Eden Halas. Before the occupation, there were many such small communities along the Yantra, until Balfure's goblins grew to be such a menace that many of the river folk abandoned their villages for safer territory. Caras Anara was the only one still remaining due to its proximity to Eden Halas. King Halion, father of Aeron, had little tolerance for goblins, and took great relish in driving them from his territory.

It was after dark when they arrived in Caras Anara, and Arianne thought perhaps the hour was too late for these folk and they were all in bed. However, as they rode down dirt track into the small community, their horses seemed troubled, and it took some urging for them to behave as they should. There were no lantern lights beckoning the trio through windows nor was there smoke rising out of chimneys. There was not even the sound of livestock in the barns or the sound of life in the surrounding woods.

There was only silence.

They rode past the local tavern, usually the most popular place in such villages, and saw that it was devoid of any folk. The sign hanging over the entrance swayed back and forth aimlessly in the wind and the door lay wide open, like a mouth agape in shock.

"Where is everybody?" Keira asked, quietly feeling a sense of dread come over her as she looked over the place. This community looked no different from her village in the Green. There should have been lights in every window, smoke from lit hearths, and people chattering away.

"There is something evil here," Arianne said immediately, feeling the malevolence emanating from the empty streets like something tangible against the skin. "I do not like the look of this, Celene. We should leave." It was not a warning Celene took lightly. Her hand was already resting against the hilt of her sword because she could feel it herself, even without the heightened senses of an elf to guide her.

"Yes," Celene agreed readily. "We should."

"Maybe we should go by the river," Keira suggested. "I hate to think we'd be sharing the same ground as whatever caused this."

"Keira is right," Celene turned to Arianne. "If this is the work of goblins, they will not follow us if we are on the river and they will not risk entering Halas."

It was a good plan. Arianne hated to linger in this dead village any longer than necessary. "Agreed, the river is the safest course," she admitted searching the darkened streets once more, trying to see any sign of life in the shadows.

There was not.

"We must find a vessel to take us then," Celene replied, nudging her mount down the sloping road towards the river. She could see the faint outline of a wooden dock and the tops of boathouse by the shore. She supposed a community like this would also supplement their livelihood by fishing.

The sense of foreboding was not dispelled when they reached the river bank and dismounted. The boathouses were in the same state as the houses they passed—silent and dark. Only the lapping of water against the shore gave any indication of life. The horses were still uneasy, and it required Arianne's elven powers to soothe the beasts' anxiety lest they bolt, and leave them stranded in this eerie village if they could not find a boat.

There was no doubt in their minds the people of Caras Anara were dead. How this had come about was a mystery, but it was a certainty to all of them. Even if they saw no bodies giving absolute proof, the stench of doom was unmistakable. Something terrible happened here and none of them were certain where the danger was.

Further along the shore, they saw a forgotten collection of boats varying in size and use. Some were large fishing boats constructed to catch an abundance of fish, and others were smaller for use as transport. Like the rest of Caras Anara, the area was deserted and reinforced Arianne's warning to leave as quickly as possible.

"You two seek out a boat and make it ready for our use," Celene instructed, as she stepped onto the wooden dock. "I shall unpack our things from the horses and lead them on the road away from here."

Both women stared at Celene, not liking the idea that she was going off on her own.

"Are you certain that is wise?" Arianne asked, her brow furrowing with concern.

"I will not stray far," Celene assured her. "I shall only go as far as the road and release the horses. We have no need of them once we leave, and I do not like to think they might fall prey to whatever happened here. Keira, keep an eye on Arianne."

"I will," Keira said firmly, retrieving the blade Celene gave her from the halter across her back. Holding it in her hands made her feel a little safer. Celene was right about that.

"Do not be long, Celene," Arianne declared as she swept her gaze across the shoreline, and felt the hollowness in her stomach at the sight of the darkened boathouses, derelict like the rest of Caras Anara.

"I will not," Celene answered, and she went to unpack the horses while Arianne and Keira went to find them a means of leaving this place, before whatever darkness engulfed this village found them too.

* * *

Celene was mindful of every sound as she walked cautiously from the shore into the main road. She had just unloaded their belongings from the saddles of all three horses. She still heard nothing except the clopping of their hooves, and it chilled her to the bone there was not even the sound of an owl hooting in the night. The woods beyond the village seemed more ominous than ever, with the trees looming over her like long fingers about to close in.

She took a deep breath, forcing away the churning in her stomach to some faraway place because she had no patience to deal with fear when she needed to be alert. The horses were jittery enough without her anxiety increasing their agitation. It would not take much to send them running, and although she was reluctant to let them go, Celene knew they would find their way to Winter Keep on their own.

"Safe journey." She wished them finally, before slapping her mount hard against the rump, startling the mare into a sudden gallop, prompting the others to follow. The horses snorted their indignation at such an abrupt dismissal, but were soon breaking into full gallops down the dirt road leading them out of the town. In a matter of minutes, she was unable to hear their thundering hooves against the hard ground.

Once they were gone, she turned back to the dock, intending to join Arianne and Keira so they could complete their own departure from this place. She made a note to remind herself upon reaching Eden Halas, they should send word to Galain at Winter Keep to discover what happened here. There was no doubt in her mind the folk of this village had come to a terrible end, but she could not imagine any violence which could wipe all traces of them so completely.

Even goblins left bodies behind.

Celene was walking past a boat house with a ramp extending from its wide open doors to the river when she heard something move within its shadowy interior. She froze in her tracks on the path leading to the dock and waited for a few seconds to see if she heard it again. The sound was repeated almost instantly, and Celene frowned, trying to place it. It was a strange, like the flapping of a bird's wings, except it was too fast for any bird in flight.

First, she considered ignoring it, because she suspected there were things in the darkness she did not really wish to discover. When she heard the sound again, this time laced with something she could only call desperation, Celene was unable to ignore the peril, and followed the ramp into the open doorway.

The interior of the boathouse was bathed in darkness, and within her first few seconds inside, she heard it again. The flapping was now accompanied by a desperate but soft chirping, like that of a bird, though extremely weak. Through the window, the glow of the crescent moon illuminated the darkness slightly, though not much, and as she followed the noise to its source, Celene instinctively unsheathed her sword.

She had not taken more than a few steps when she caught sight of a lamp. Deciding a little more light would aid this foolish investigation, she liberated it from its place on a tool bench and lit it. The illumination it provided gave her only a bit of clarity, for the wick was almost gone. If anything, it made the shadows inside the place flicker across the walls like demons dancing in the dark.

She found the bird a few paces ahead of her and saw that it was trapped in mid-air. It took no more than an instant for her to register what she was seeing before she stumbled back, her mouth open in shock and a scream was trying to find its way out of her throat. Looking up at the ceiling, she realised the helpless bird was one of *many* things trapped in this place. As Celene stared with eyes widening in horror, she knew at last what had befallen the people of Caras Anara.

Spiders. She saw at least a dozen poor souls trapped on the silk of a giant spider's web, their bodies now dried husks drained of blood. Celene was barely able to contain her revulsion as she saw corpses of men, women, and children alike, suspended above her head. If not for their clothes, she would not have been able to recognise them as human at all. Reaching out, her fingers trembled as she saw a child within silken threads of the web, hoping against hope that there was still some life left for her to save.

She but only grazed the child's body before the contact proved too much and the corpse broke free of its trappings, landing heavily at her feet. She uttered an involuntary scream when the husk came apart, dropping the lamp on the floor as the glass shattered and spread oil and flames in all directions. Her hand flew to her mouth, trying to contain the retch that wanted to come when she saw what remained of a little boy staring at her with dead eyes. That image came with an even more frightful realisation.

They had probably heard the commotion.

Her preoccupation with the corpse almost made her miss the approach of the creature behind her. Despite its size—and it was large—it knew how to move stealthily. She saw it in the corner of her eye. With a flurry of movement, quick and abrupt, she turned and found herself staring into the compound eyes of a giant spider of Syphi.

The Syphi spiders, named after the Dreaded Mother, originated from the Syphi Chasm in the Wilds. Balfure brought them to Eden Halas after an unsuccessful attempt to destroy the elven city. King Halion and his elves fought bravely and repelled the invaders. Enraged, Balfure unleashed the spiders into woods of Halas to ensure the elves were too busy fighting this menace to aid Queen Lylea he moved on to Eden Ardhen. For years, the battle to drive the creatures out occupied much of Eden Halas' time, but it was thought they were all destroyed by the time Balfure's rule ended. Now, it appeared they had simply found a new home.

Celene wondered how many of the villages they thought abandoned because of goblins had in fact, suffered this fate.

It did not matter Celene decided, because a single creature could not have overtaken Caras Anara so completely that not one person escaped to tell the tale. As the beast closed in on her, she knew this spider was not alone, and the whole of Caras Anara was infested with them. With a surge of panic, she re-alised Arianne and Keira were out there alone, unaware of what lurked in the darkness. She had to warn them!

Unfortunately, Celene's ability to act was hindered by the spider moving in for the kill. She saw its mandibles snapping in hungry anticipation of her blood, and brandished her sword in readiness to attack. She knew she could not spend too much time dealing with this beast when Arianne and Keira might be deadly danger.

Its legs skittered forward as it rushed at her, spitting poison as it leapt with powerful legs. Celene jumped out of the way, thankful there was space available to do so. Although it was larger, it moved with terrifying speed and was soon resuming its attack. This time, there was no way for her to avoid it. Celene lashed out fiercely, her blade tearing through its darkened flesh and eliciting an unearthly shriek of pain. In retaliation, it stabbed one of its spindly legs in her direction, and although she tried to evade it, nothing could keep the barbed limb from penetrating the flesh of her shoulder.

She uttered a sharp cry of pain and was enraged by the injury. Striking out viciously, the blade sunk into the spider's crimson eye and she retracted it with similar vehemence. A screech of agony followed when Celene retrieved her blade, dripping with black blood. Despite being partially blinded, the spider lunged again, trying to tackle her to the ground. Celene saw its intent and jumped herself, diving beneath it as it landed in the place she was standing in seconds earlier. Rolling onto her knees, she swung around and braced herself for its next attack.

Blood was flowing freely down her shoulder and she knew its scent could bring others. Grunting in pain, she was conscious of how much time she was wasting trying to fight this creature when she realised her lungs were burning from the smoke of the fire she had inadvertently started. So preoccupied with the spider, she had not noticed the fire spreading across the roof and down some walls. The rising heat prickled her skin and caused sweat to run down her forehead. With the flames growing taller around her, she came up with a plan.

Instead of running, she stood her ground defiantly, challenging the beast to do its worst. For an instant, the spider paused, recognising the intent of its would-be meal to fight. In the end, pain and hunger overrode its caution and it scampered forward, preparing to devour her. Its fangs snapped in readiness for fresh blood, tired of morsels since exhausting the supply of people in Caras Anara.

Celene saw it approaching and braced herself, ignoring the fear in her heart and reminding herself resolutely this would only succeed if she held her ground. The creature closed the gap between them swiftly and, as Celene saw herself in the reflection of its uninjured eye, her nerve almost gave out. There was an instant of terror when the spider's jaw opened, and Celene could almost smell its fetid breath upon her skin as it rushed her, too quick to stop.

She leapt out of the way at the last minute, and the spider could do nothing but utter a terrified screech of desperation as it ran straight into the fire raging behind her. The flames quickly overcame it and Celene grimaced at the sight of it writhing in agony as it burned alive. Its legs kicked wildly as it tumbled unto its back, continuing to struggle. She could no longer stand to look at it.

When she heard the creak of a wooden banister burning away over her head, Celene knew it was time to leave. Grabbing a piece of timber, she used it as a torch and ran out of the boathouse now blazing, before it collapsed in on itself and her.

* * *

After Celene left them, Arianne and Keira went in search of an appropriate vessel to take them into Eden Halas. They decided on a long canoe resting near one of the ramps and would take the three of them easily. After she and Keira carried it to the shore, they returned to the spot where Celene left their belongings and began loading the craft now awaiting patiently near the water's edge. Neither of them spoke as they did this work, too fearful that if they made any noise, they would give themselves away to whatever menace ruined this village.

A scream tear through the night.

"Was that Celene?" Keira straightened up, staring at Arianne with worry.

"It is!" Arianne declared, and without thinking better of it, took up her sword and ran up the beach, not waiting to see if Keira was behind her.

"Arianne! Wait!" Keira shouted, but the elf did not stop. Uttering a curse and Keira followed, picking up her own weapon as she did so.

It didn't take long for them to see that one of the boathouses was ablaze. Fire and smoke was billowing out of the door and through the windows. Arianne needed no clairvoyance to know this was where they would find Celene. The thought no sooner crossed her mind when she realised the building on fire was not the one to watch. It was the ones near it. Black bodies were emerging into the night—bodies with too many legs and large, blood red eyes.

"Oh, spit!" she heard Keira curse next to her, as they saw the spiders climbing out of the previously silent boathouses.

Two of them skittered onto the path, barring their way towards the burning building.

"Let me pass or you shall feel the sting of my blade!" Arianne hissed as she slashed the air before one of them, showing them that she would cut them to pieces if they tried to stand in her way.

Keira unsheathed her sword, never imaging she would have to use it so soon, and certainly not against *spiders*. They should have run, but Arianne was determined to reach Celene. Keira promised the warrior of Angarad to stay with the queen, who now needed her help. She couldn't leave. Remaining at Arianne's side, Keira prepared to fight, if the creatures rushed them.

The one on Arianne's left lunged, and the queen dropped to her knees, seeing the power in its legs and knowing it would fly over her head. She raised her sword as it flew above her, its tip biting into the beast's plump abdomen and ripping it open as it passed overhead. Black blood spilled out. Arianne felt it splash on her clothes, almost choking in disgust.

The second spider, taking advantage of Arianne's distraction, skittered towards the queen, prompting Keira into action.

"Get away from her!" she shouted, swinging her sword wildly, uncertain if any of the wide, clumsy swipes was doing anything to deter the thing. The spider hesitated at this new attack and then sprang forward again, once it gauged the threat appropriately. Keira stumbled backwards, losing her footing. She fell on her rump just as the creature landed on her, tripping her body with its legs on either side. She let out a sharp scream of terror as she shrank away from its dripping fangs.

No sooner had the sound left her throat did Keira hear the spider shriek in agony and roll off her. She scrambled away and saw a thick piece of flaming timber protruding from its round body.

"Keira, are you hurt?"She became aware of Arianne demanding frantically.

"No," Keira answered, shaking her head as she turned. She saw the spider struggling to rid itself of the spike upon which it was impaled as the fire spread across its body.

Arianne let out a gasp of surprise and relief when she realised Celene had come to their rescue. She moved swiftly, far swifter than Arianne ever thought possible, slashing her blade in a wide arch, ending the flaming creature's agony when she took its head. Arianne was forced to look away in revulsion as the foul creature's head tumbled from the rest of its body and rolled down the beach.

"Celene!" Arianne noted the blood on the Angarad's shoulder. "You are bleeding!"

"I am fine," Celene said, exhausted. She glanced back at the town to see more dark shapes emerging. "We have to go! This entire village is infested. We must be away to tell Halion what transpires here!"

"Well, come on then!" Keira shouted, already running down the sand towards their boat.

Neither Arianne nor Celene could disagree, when they saw more spiders crawling out from their hiding places, having picked up the scene of fresh blood. Running towards the boat, the river was the only thing that could save them now.

"Get in!" Arianne ordered Celene as she helped Keira pushed the boat further into the water.

"But…" Celene started to protest.

"NOW, CELENE!" Arianne roared, stopping her from saying anything else. Celene's blood was drawing the spiders to them like a beacon, causing them to swarm in a frenzy of hunger.

Keira and Celine pushed the canoe into the water until it was floating on its own. Neither looked behind them to see what was happening, the chilling screeches and sound of skittering telling them there was nothing they wanted to see.

"That's enough," Celene barked. "Climb in!"

Both women climbed into the large canoe, quickly picking up the oars so that they could row beyond the reach of the swarm. Only when they started to paddle did Arianne and Keira realise just how many of the things there were, and they were grateful that the river halted their advance. Some of the spiders were pacing up and down in frustration at being unable to reach the prey they could still see. The fire Celene set was now moving from house to house, claiming each building until the whole village was soon ablaze.

"We must get you to Eden Halas," Arianne declared, once they were far enough away from Caras Anara to stop paddling.

Though they could still see the glow of the fire, they were now far enough away to be safe. "You're hurt."

"It is nothing," Celene grunted as Arianne examined her.

"Oh right," Keira rolled her eyes as she continued rowing. "You can as stubborn as a man about such things, Celene. I would have thought that as a woman, you'd have better sense."

"Don't be stubborn," Arianne retorted as she undid the buttons of Celene's jerkin. "I have yet to encounter a spider that did not have some poison in its bite, so you will let me see to your injuries. As your queen I demand it," Arianne stared at her imperiously.

"I think it is exceedingly unfair you should use *rank* to force me to obey," she grumbled

"I know. Do I not do it well?" the elf smiled, a twinkle of mischief in her eye.

Celene rolled her eyes and muttered under her breath, "*Elves.*"

Chapter Seven

The Caracal

The irony of the situation was not lost on Dare, as he pursued Arianne and her companions down the Yantra.

Until now, Dare did not know what torture it was to be the one left behind when loved ones departed to face untold dangers. How had Arianne bore it every time he left Eden Taryn to take on yet another battle with Balfure? It was always a woman's lot to wait and pray her loved ones would be delivered back to her safely because it was the accepted way of things. Today he realised now why she was always so distressed to see him go.

The wait was simply maddening.

Ronen, who was sharing a boat with Tully and Tamsyn, appeared just as anxious about his wife, although he tried hard not to show it. The Lord of Gislaine told himself his wife was a brave woman and a cunning warrior. If there was one person who could acquit herself in any kind of peril, it was certainly Celene of Angarad.

Celene believed it was in the time after the Battle of Astaroth where their love first bloomed. If she had asked, he would have told her she was mistaken. He knew the exact moment he fell in love with her. It was on the battlefield of Astaroth.

Even in the midst of fighting the worst of Balfure's army, he caught sight of this woman, clad in armour, fighting more fiercely than even the most seasoned soldier under his command. She was simply the most magnificent woman he had ever seen. Fearless and determined, she fought that ogre with all the skill at her disposal, when a lesser man would have fallen well before the moment Ronen was forced to intervene on her behalf. He had not even been thinking when he rushed into the fray and speared the beast.

All that was on his mind was the possibility the creature could kill her before they met.

Like his king, Ronen was all too aware this time, it was no ogre Celene was facing. An enemy capable of resurrecting Mael was no ordinary foe, but it would not matter to Celene, if she was defending her queen. She would lay down her life just the same. He was afraid for her, and no matter how much he tried to tell himself she was capable of protecting herself, he feared skill wouldn't be enough.

In the same vessel as Dare, Aeron was silent.

Aeron had in fact been silent for some time now, but this was not unusual behaviour for him. He was prone to quiet reflection when others about him were losing their heads over whatever trial they were facing. On this occasion, his silence had a reason. His heightened senses were on full alert, because he could feel something tugging the edge of his perception, and the sensation produced by that unknown was ominous.

As he rowed the boat in tandem with Dare, he scanned the shoreline running parallel with the Yantra, trying to learn what shape this danger coming upon them would take. It had been growing in intensity for some time now, but Aeron had not spoken of it. He was uncertain if the danger was in the lands they were passing or was it something stalking them.

"What is it?" Dare asked, when he paused in his rowing and noticed the look on Aeron's face.

Aeron did not answer immediately. "I do not know," he replied, and that was the whole truth. He did not know what it was, he only *felt* it.

Dare knew to trust the elf's senses. On too many occasions, Aeron's perception resulted in saving their lives. He tensed, disliking this feeling of not knowing from where danger was coming. "What do you feel?" he asked quietly, for there was no need to alarm everyone just yet.

"It is close," Aeron answered, and his words made Kyou, who was listening in, wary.

"Is it the enemy?" Dare asked.

"No," Aeron shook his head. "It if were the enemy, I would know it instantly. Darkness of such magnitude is not easily missed. This is smaller, but dangerous—I am certain of it."

"The foolishness of it," Kyou snorted in annoyance. "What could they be thinking? Rushing of like that to the peril of all their lives to face who knows what, without telling us! This should be a quest handled by all of us, not the three of them alone."

Aeron shot Kyou a look of annoyance, because this type of rant served no one. Dare was already worried for his wife, and such words would only deepen his fears for Arianne and their child. "These are hardly unskilled women Kyou, Arianne is the daughter of Lylea, and she has been alive a great deal longer than you. Celene fought with us at Astaroth, and Keira—well I do not need to tell you what she faced with far more courage than most men."

"You know I have only the greatest respect for all three," Kyou answered, realising now what effect his words were having on Dare. "Queen Lylea is wise, but this quest upon which she has sent Arianne is ill thought. Arianne is with child and should be guarded, not traipsing about the countryside to face who knows what."

From where he was sitting, Aeron could see Dare's spine stiffen.

He knew that Kyou's feelings about what the three women had embarked upon were mostly tempered by his affection for both. Aeron felt the same way. Arianne was like a sister to him, and he loved her dearly, and Celene was a comrade in battle as well as friend. While he did not know Keira as well as he should, he respected what she suffered for his best friend. He feared for their safety, not merely for himself, but also for their husbands."

Overhead the sun was starting to set, and although Dare wanted to travel further, he knew his companions needed to rest. They had been journeying up river for almost a day, and if the weariness was starting to seep into his limbs then they must surely feel the same. It would be no good to Arianne when they finally reached her, if they pressed themselves into exhaustion.

Besides, he suspected the women might seek shelter themselves. After all, Arianne was unaccustomed to travelling at such an arduous pace, and he knew his wife well enough to suspect she would take care not to harm the babe by straining herself.

The Circle aimed their boats in the direction of land and stepped onto the Eastern Shore. By the time the sun disappeared into the horizon, they were gathered around a campfire watching the dance of flames. They feasted upon some rabbits Aeron and Ronen managed to snare, while Tully did the honours of cooking. The conversation around the fire as they ate was not at all as lively as it had been during the celebration in Sandrine.

"What route do you think they would take to the north?" Kyou asked, in an effort to dispel the awful silence around the campfire.

Dare looked up from his cup of mead as if he had been a thousand miles away and shook the distraction from his mind as he addressed the dwarf. "I think they would journey up the Yantra to the Winter Keep."

"Yes," Ronen agreed with that assessment. "Celene knows the Caretaker there. I believe they fought together at Astaroth."

"Galain is his name," Dare volunteered, having met the man once. "He would offer them shelter for the night, and perhaps horses."

"Horses?" Tully asked.

"Yes," Tamsyn replied before Dare could. "They will need to travel by land to avoid the Falls of Iolan. I believe they are bound for your father's kingdom, Aeron."

"That would be sensible," Aeron agreed. "Mother and Father would certainly give them shelter, and a means to travel west."

While it would be nice to see Syanne again, Dare wished the circumstances of his return to Eden Halas were better. Despite having been given the best of an elven upbringing thanks to the queen of Eden Halas, his relationship with King Halion was never warm. Halion looked upon him as an indulgence his wife was allowed for too long. His lack of interest in the human child brought into his home was part of the reason why Aeron grew so close to Dare in the first place. Unlike his father, Aeron possessed a compassionate nature Halion, sadly, did not share.

"It would be faster to reach the Frozen Mountains by crossing the Baffin Range," Kyou remarked in between chewing his food.

"That would require crossing the Northern Province and then, the mountains," Ronen spoke up. "The route by river is the safest, and the one I think Celene would choose to ease the burden of the journey on Arianne."

"I thought we got rid of all the beserkers," Tully frowned, unaware that the creatures were still roaming about in the Northern Provinces.

"Not all of them," Tamsyn rumbled. "They are like insects. They merely go to ground until they are needed by some dark malevolence to guide them. Until then, they scavenge for what they can."

"Balfure's forces were many," Dare sighed, wishing he had spent more time these past two years ridding Avalyne of that particular threat. Unfortunately, there was so much rebuilding to do after the occupation and the war that the beserkers and ogres—powerless without their master—were less of a priority.

"We vanquished many during the war, but some fled after Balfure was destroyed. With all we had suffered to defeat him, there are simply too few resources to spend on seeking them out and finishing them once and for all. We had to address our wounds, rebuild what was destroyed, and bury our dead. Once we replenish our forces, we will resume the hunt for them."

"Still, what is left of them seems to have grown bolder of late," Ronen pointed out, recalling the focus of their attention prior to the announcement of Arianne's pregnancy. "They have been emerging from their places, attacking the border lands, and fleeing before the Watch Guards can deal with them. It is as if they are preparing."

"They are readying themselves to ally with the enemy," Tamsyn announced, his eyes lifting from the pipe he was smoking.

"Who is this enemy?" Tully asked.

"I cannot say," Tamsyn responded and saw the anger flare in Dare's eyes. The king was still fuming over Tamsyn's silence regarding the danger to Arianne. "It is not that I do not wish for you to know Dare, it is because I am not certain what we are dealing with. I have a sense of him, but little more than that. Not even Lylea was able to look into his mind and that speaks to his strength. All I know is he is very old and strong, and is able to keep us out."

Dare swallowed thickly and saw Tamsyn was speaking earnestly. The mage was a true friend, and although the ways of wizards could be maddening at times, he also knew Tamsyn would not intentionally keep the identity of the enemy hidden, unless there was a good reason for it.

"We have been through much together old friend." He cast his eye upon Tamsyn, realising his ire was largely due to the situation and not because of the mage's actions, "I will trust your counsel in this."

"Thank you," Tamsyn bowed his head slightly in gratitude of the faith Dare was placing in him.

"If you cannot tell us what he is, can you tell us something of his powers?" Aeron asked in an effort to give Dare something more than just riddles.

"Once again, I am uncertain," Tamsyn answered honestly. "I have a sense of him, but it is clouded. I believe he may be able to cloak himself with a spell of glamour that makes people see what he wishes."

"Glamour?" Ronen asked, not liking the sound of that at all.

"Yes." The mage blew another puff of smoke from his pipe. "He can make them believe a thing with such fierce determination, there is nothing else but the illusion."

"That's quite a trick," Tully exclaimed. "How can we fight something like that?"

"By not trusting our eyes," Dare answered automatically. "What we see can be just as deceiving as what we hear."

"So, we must look closer then," Kyou started to say when Aeron jumped to his feet abruptly, picking up his bow.

"Dare! Something is coming!" the elf warned as he stared into the darkness, searching.

"Can you tell what it is?" Dare demanded, getting to his feet with the rest of the circle. They reached for their weapons as they stood up and began searching the darkness, more aware of the shadows than ever.

"No," Aeron shook his head in frustration. He knew there was danger coming, but he could not tell in what form. It was still not close enough.

"I sense it as well," Tamsyn spoke up after a time, his staff clutched firmly in his hands as he too scanned the darkness for the danger that approached.

The circle rose to their feet, brandishing their weapons in anticipation of what was coming for them. They could hear nothing so far, but Aeron remained tense, telling them that whatever it was, it would soon be here.

"Where are they?" Ronen hissed, revealing his impatience. "I wish they would just come!"

"They are close," Kyou warned, his acute hearing picking up the sounds of many feet running towards them. "Be ready, there are many of them."

"Watch each other's backs," Dare ordered firmly.

"They are upon us!" Aeron cried out, pulling out an arrow from his collection and arming his bow in readiness.

Red eyes flashed at them as soon as those words escaped him, and they were followed by a low snarl all of them recognised immediately. The peace of the campfire was shattered by the sudden emergence of large bodies of fur moving towards them at rapid speed, led by snapping jaws and ferociously sharp teeth. They exploded out of the woods, covered in dark fur, with yellowed eyes fixing quickly upon their intended prey. Their savagery was evidenced by their snarls and growl, converging into a tremendous roar that soon brought everything about them to chaos.

"Caracal!" Dare shouted as one of the creatures launched themselves at him. He reacted without thinking, thrusting his blade through its ribs, earning a powerful howl of pain as the weapon tore through the flesh of its back.

They swarmed through the camp, their numbers so many it was hard to count, and their growls draining the world of all other sound. The caracal were another obscenity created by Balfure. Outwardly, they resembled cats, but they were the size of bears. At Astorath, the beserkers used them as mounts, and often these beasts were used to run down helpless prey. When he and Aeron had gone to find the dwarves in Angarad, they encountered many such creatures.

Dare saw one about to attack Tully, and moved to intervene, but he was soon beset by a duo of the heinous creatures who charged him. Thinking quickly, he dropped to his knees and grabbed a log from the fire, jabbing it at them to give them pause. As they hissed in black fury at being held back by fire, Dare saw the farmer was more than adept at protecting himself.

With the short dagger Dare had given him years ago, he saw Tully hack away at the beast attempting to harm him and drive it back. In its attempt to evade the blade, the beast stepped into the fire and uttered a roar of pain before fleeing to douse its wound.

Dare saw a shadowy movement in the corner of his eye and turned, just as a caracal jumped at him. He had no room to move and fell heavily to the ground. Sliding his blade between himself and the creature's snapping jaws; he could feel its powerful claws digging into his skin as it tried to reach his neck. Another was closing in on them, when an arrow suddenly flew through the air and struck the second beast in the neck. The arrowhead protruded through flesh and bone and pierced to the other side.

"Help Dare!" Aeron shouted, unable to go to his king's aid, when more of the cats closed in on the elf, ready to pounce.

A second beast was almost upon him when Dare threw the creature he was wrestling over his head, slamming it into the other's abdomen, and sending them both tumbling. He rolled onto his knees and extracted the dagger concealed within his boot. He flung it with a marksman's aim. The blade struck one of the cats in the breast, and it screamed in pain before collapsing on the dirt, black blood oozing across the ground. Now one was dead, Dare rushed forward to deal with the other.

The cat glared at him with sinister eyes, its teeth dripping with saliva as it circled him, waiting to pounce. It ran forward and leapt with Dare watching closely, waiting for the moment to strike. He swung his sword in a wide arc. The blade sliced through the creature's flesh, tearing open its insides in one gruesome blow. The beast had barely enough time to howl before it dropped in mid-air, its body making a heavy thud upon the earth.

Dare turned around to see the progress of his friends and saw Tully managing to mount one of the creatures as if he were riding a pony. He remained steadfastly attached upon the caracal's back, his hand clutching the beast's pelt, as he steadied his blade for attack. Then, he plunged it into the creature's neck and buried the dagger to the hilt.

Ronen was battling just as vigorously, surrounded by the carcasses of the creatures he already slaughtered. Tamsyn had also produced his sword and was making short work of the creatures foolish enough to attack him. Although the mage had great powers capable of making make short work of all these beasts, Dare knew it was Tamsyn's habit not to rely so much on his magic, when he could perform tasks without it. Meanwhile, with his twin blades, Kyou used his size to his advantage, and was able to gut several of the beasts by getting under them.

When it was all said and done, the campsite resembled an uncovered grave of caracal. Their black blood seeped into the dirt and would soon attract the attention of carrion feeders, who would feast upon their lifeless bodies. Dare immediately ordered their departure, wishing to be away in case any other foul creature chose to make its appearance. They returned to the shore where their boats were waiting and sailed further upstream, away from the carnage.

For the most part, they came away from the melee with only minor injuries. Ronen suffered a bite, but his vambraces took the worst of it. The skin was broken, but it was not a serious wound. Tully and Kyou acquired some minor scratches, all of which Tamsyn was able to attend.

"We rid ourselves of all the caracal," Dare stated, as they gathered around the fire of their new campsite. "I was sure we did."

"I thought so too," Aeron shook his head. "At Astaroth, I was certain we saw the end of them." The archer was cleaning the arrows he retrieved from the dead creatures, appearing none too happy about the grisly task.

"There seems to be a greater frequency of dark things emerging in recent months," Dare replied. "First, the appearance of berserkers and goblin tribes, and now we have caracal—all of whom we were certain were killed at Astaroth—coming out nowhere."

"It's like they're all emerging from their hiding places," Ronen remarked, attempting to see under the swathing of bandage around his arm, and frowning when Tully swatted his hand for making the attempt.

"They hear the call of their new master," Tamsyn mused softly. "This evil Arianne is facing is drawing them to him, just like Balfure."

"Astaroth is empty," Dare said firmly. "Since Balfure's defeat, we have maintained close control of it. They have nowhere else to go."

"Yes," Tamsyn agreed. "They have been bred to be followers, and the enemy knows that. He takes advantage of that weakness. We must wipe them out, or else they will follow anyone with the will to command them."

Dare stiffened, not liking to be reminded of that. It was hard enough trying to remain focused on finding Arianne safely, to think nothing of the child inside her belly, whose fate hung in the balance. If she failed, then it would most likely be his son commanding Balfure's army in the future. The thought made him sick to the stomach.

"I know that all too well, Tamsyn," he said softly.

"I did not mean to worry you any more than you already are, Dare," Tamsyn apologised, seeing the pain in his eyes. "I just want to say what we face is formidable and we must be on guard."

"We are on our guard," Tully retorted. "We fought those things off."

"Yes, you did," Tamsyn nodded, "but did you not find it odd that they came after us specifically?"

Dare's gaze snapped towards the wizard. "What do you mean?"

Tamsyn drew a deep breath and released it by way of his curved pipe. "The enemy knows we are on the move. He knows we are coming and is attempting to stop us any means he can. The question is, does he know Arianne is on the move too?"

Chapter Eight

Eden Halas

Arianne awoke, and for an instant, she forgot where she was.

Sitting up, she saw she was lying on a bed of elven design, although not the one Dare brought from Eden Taryn for their wedding night in Sandrine. It was an unfamiliar bed in an unfamiliar room, unmistakably elvish. The room was all windows, with sunlight pouring through the thin curtains, giving clarity to the ornate designs carved on the bedposts and the other pieces of furniture. Outside, she could hear the rustle of leaves and the peaceful quiet broken only by the occasionally chirp of a bird.

She could have been forgiven for thinking herself back in Eden Taryn. She quickly realised she wasn't. She took in a deep breath and recognised the scent of the forest, crisp and sweet. It reminded Arianne of childhood when she would run through glens covered with wild flowers—lost in a sea of the golden coloured buds. Lylea used to tell her they were drops of sun. Of course, more recent memories soon returned to her, and Arianne knew she was not home at all, but in a place almost as beautiful:

Eden Halas.

After fleeing Caras Anara, she and Keira rowed all the way to the woods of Eden Halas without a pause. They arrived in the country of Aeron's birth during the small hours of the night and were immediately set upon by King Halion's Forest Guard. Although King Halion was known for his dislike of humans entering his borders, he put aside his natural hostility once he learned the identity of all his guests. Aware his wife considered Dare family, and to some extent so did he, Arianne was welcomed to his court as kin. Even if they were not connected through Dare, Eden Halas would not turn away a daughter of Lylea, High Queen of the elves.

Syanne was thrilled to receive Arianne, despite the circumstances of their arrival.

Upon seeing the exhausted and, in one instance, injured state of their visitors, she immediately called for Celene to be taken to the Hall of Healing. Despite protests to the contrary, Celene was more affected than she liked to admit by the venom of the spider that attacked her. In an effort to placate the Lady of Gislaine, Keira volunteered to accompany her so she did not tax too greatly the patience of the elves attending her. In the end, it was the pointed reminder she would be no good to them in this quest, if she were ill that convinced her.

Arianne made up her mind to go find Keira and Celene when a knock on the door received her invitation to enter, and Queen Syanne stepped into the room.

Arianne had only met her on a few occasions. Although the elves preferred to keep to themselves, the elves of Eden Halas were particularly reclusive, and did not like trespassers within their borders. Arianne knew much of this had to do with Halion's dislike of other races. Lylea once explained to Arianne, his disdain originated from the belief the Celestial Gods used the elves to cleanse Avalyne during the Primordial Wars, only to give it away to lesser races. Halion lost everyone he loved in the conflict, and considered this an affront to all he fought for.

"How do you fare this morning?" Syanne greeted Arianne pleasantly, as she took a seat in the chair next to the bed.

Like most elves, she wore her hair long, although Syanne's was unusual because it was the colour of copper, which stood in sharp contrast to her blue eyes. The queen was tall and slender, with high cheekbones. The shape of her face told Arianne, save for his dark hair, most of Aeron's looks came from his mother. This was of little surprise to Arianne, since Aeron also took after Syanne in manner and disposition, unlike his older brothers Hadros and Syannon, who were very much their father's sons.

"I am well," Arianne answered, smiling at the queen. "I feel as if I have slept for days."

"It is no wonder after fleeing from spiders and travelling across the country. That is not work for a queen, let alone a woman with child," Syanne spoke with a hint of reproach.

Arianne shrugged, not wishing to discuss the reasons for her journey, and decided to make a change of subject instead. "You did not come to our celebration in Sandrine," she remarked.

As soon as the comment left her lips, Arianne felt sorry for doing so, because she saw the guilt stealing across Syanne's face. Clearly, the queen wanted to be there, and the expression of regret made Arianne feel unkind for using it as a means of distraction.

"I was needed here," Syanne said quietly. "The king felt it too dangerous for me to travel south. We did not know about the spiders in Caras Anara, as we have been dealing with the remnants of Balfure's goblins. It has required Halion to cooperate with men of the Winter Keep and the dwarves of Iridia," she explained, as proof of the urgency of the situation. There was no other reason why Halion would deal with them otherwise.

Arianne suspected Syanne did not wish to admit Halion probably disliked the idea of his wife travelling to city ruled by men, when Aeron was already present in Sandrine and capable of representing his court. "Galain did make mention of that," Arianne answered, hoping to move past the moment. "He said that the goblins were being driven back to the Cinder Mountains."

"Yes," Syanne brightened up a little, grateful that Arianne was not dwelling on her absence at Sandrine. "Syanon has taken some our best warriors to help the humans push them back farther, and I think Halion will be sending Hadros to Caras Anara after your report of spiders."

"Tell him to be careful. There were many. I believe the entire village was consumed."

"How terrible," Syanne winced in horror, and it was easy to see how this queen could have defied her husband to give shelter to a helpless human babe left in the care of a dying nurse. Once again, Arianne decided Aeron's compassionate nature was definitely inherited from his mother.

"Yes," Arianne nodded in agreement, and took the opportunity to inquire after her companions, "How is Celene? Do I need to apologise for her?" A flicker of mischief crossed her face as she tried to move away from such grim talk.

Syanne laughed shortly and shook her head. "Perhaps a little. She is exceedingly stubborn. I thought Dare was difficult to treat, she might even exceed *his* obstinacy."

"That would not surprise me," Arianne giggled, picturing in her mind's eyes the consternation Celene was causing amongst the elven physicians in the Hall of Healing. "She is a good friend and has already saved my life once on this quest."

"I do not doubt that," Syanne chuckled "She believed she was ready to travel *last* night."

That sounded like Celene, and Arianne had to admire the Angarad's optimism, even if she was somewhat unrealistic. "She would think that," Arianne shook her head in resignation. Celene's stubbornness could sometimes override her good sense.

"Fortunately, after our healers treated her wounds, they gave her something to sleep, for her benefit as well as theirs." Syanne laughed, and then added, "your other companion is up and about. There is something about her that is most unusual. I am not certain what it is, but I sense darkness and pain."

"It would not surprise me," Arianne admitted, because even Lylea sensed it. One could not survive the torture of the Disciples, and the taint of the desert burrowers, without some scars left behind. "Rest assured, she is someone who can be trusted."

"I know," Syanne smiled. "We were certain any companion of yours had to be worthy of your friendship, and this Green she speaks of seems to be very enchanting."

"It is," Arianne smiled, pleased Keira made a good impression. "The woods of the Green are old. I believe they may be even older than the woods of Eden Ardhen. They say the trees are haunted by ancient spirits from the time of Enphilim, and they protect the folk of the Green."

"How fascinating," Syanne remarked. "She is the same one who protected Dare from the Disciples, is she not?" The queen ventured a guess, having been told the tale by her adopted son years before.

"Dare owes her his life," Arianne confirmed. "It was Keira who refused to give him up to Balfure. She endured the desert burrowers to keep him safe."

"That is what we sensed, then," Syanne mused, before declaring as if she was making a royal proclamation. "She will always be welcomed here. In fact, you all must stay with us for a few days and allow the Lady of Gislaine to heal, before you set off on your journey again."

Arianne hesitated, because she knew as soon as Celene felt able, the Lady of Gislaine would be eager to travel. Indeed, Arianne herself was conscious of time, and knew they needed to leave as soon as possible. As much as Arianne would like to take advantage of Syanne's hospitality, the threat to her child overrode all other considerations. Furthermore, she suspected if King Halion knew of her quest, he would react in just the same manner as Dare. The king of Eden Halas would not let her leave this place without warriors to protect her, and Arianne's mission needed to continue within its shroud of secrecy.

"If I know Celene, she will think herself ready to leave as soon as she awakens," Arianne stated, hoping to avoid giving away anything unnecessarily. "We will stay a day and then we must be off."

"Arianne," Syanne reached for her hand and squeezed it, "I can tell by what you are trying *not* to say there is urgency to this journey of yours. It is your right and I will not press you, but do not be premature in your desire to leave. The venom of the syphi is nothing to take lightly. She *needs* rest."

Arianne was torn because Syanne was right. Celene *did* need to rest, but they had such a long journey ahead of them, and so little time. In the end, she chose to confide in Syanne, because she was not just the queen of Eden Halas, but also Dare's adopted mother. She trusted Syanne would understand her need for secrecy, and her reasons for haste."

"We ride to confront an enemy who seeks to bring forth Mael," Arianne finally revealed.

"Mael!" Syanne gasped, and then fell silent as if speaking his name was liable to summon the dark god into the room with them, there and then. "And Dare sent you out alone to deal with this menace?"

She had the tone of a mother who just discovered her son had done something inordinately stupid against all the tenets of his upbringing.

"Dare does not know, or rather he did not when I left," Arianne quickly explained, before her husband earned himself a cuff the next time his adopted mother saw him. "My lady, you cannot tell the king why we are here. You know your husband as well as I know mine, he will not let us leave here alone, if at all, for such a perilous quest. If I am not allowed to complete it myself, Avalyne will fall into darkness again, and Dare will almost certainly be destroyed by the consequences."

"But why..." Syanne protested, unable to imagine any danger warranting Dare's exclusion at the cost of the wife he loved above all else.

"The enemy seeks to fill the baby with the spirit of Mael. He intends that Mael shall be resurrected as the heir of Carleon."

"By the Gods..." the older woman whispered, unable to imagine a more monstrous plan. "How much time do you have?" she asked, once she recovered her composure.

"I must reach him in two full moons, or his plan will come to pass. My mother has told me while I carry the baby, the enemy cannot harm me. However, if Dare were to confront him, he will be killed without hesitation."

Arianne went on to reveal what she learned from Lylea and Tamsyn about the enemy's designs, and why it was necessary to go on ahead and keep her journey a secret. If Dare rode out after her, the enemy would believe the king had most likely learned of the plan and left his wife at home to deal with the threat himself. Their advantage lay in the fact the enemy did not know it was Arianne herself who was coming to face him.

"This is a dangerous course," Syanne said, after Arianne finished her tale. "I cannot help but fear for you, and I would still prefer you embarked upon this with an escort of warriors, if not Dare himself."

"But he could be killed!" As much as she loved Syanne for thinking so much about her, she wanted Dare to have no part in her quest, not if his life could be lost as a result.

"I know," Syanne sighed heavily. "I am accustomed to seeing him place himself in danger. I cannot say the same for you."

"I will be fine," Arianne assured her. "Once Celene is on her feet, we will continue. She has proven to be an able protector. We have a long way to go to cross the Frozen Mountains."

"The Frozen Mountains?" Syanne's eyes widened in worry. "In your condition?"

"I will manage," Arianne said firmly. "I *have* to."

"Those mountains are cursed," Syanne frowned, her anxiousness for Arianne's welfare compounded now she knew where the young queen of Carleon was headed. "There have been many dark tales spoken of it."

"What sort of tales?" Arianne asked, wondering if she really wanted to know. It was not as if anything Syanne told her would change her mind to go there.

"Stories of travellers crossing those mountains disappearing, never to return," Syanne stated. "Something dwells there that feeds on the flesh of elves and men. Do you really want to risk the danger?"

"I am already in danger, and I grow more so, the longer I am kept from completing my quest. I have no choice, my queen. My son's life hangs in the balance."

Syanne's shoulders slumped and she resolved to say nothing more against Arianne's quest, because it was clear Arianne was not going to be deterred from it In her place, Syanne did not know if she would act any differently. There was nothing she would not do to protect her children, and she could not expect Arianne to do any less.

"The queen of Eden Halas is at your service queen of Carleon," she said finally. "Whatever you need, we will provide it if we are able."

"Thank you," Arianne embraced her warmly, grateful for Syanne's help.

Whether she would think herself capable of facing whatever lay in wait for her at the Frozen Mountains when she finally arrived was another matter entirely.

* * *

Syanne was correct, Celene was eager to leave by the time Arianne finally found her at the Hall of Healing.

"I hear you have endeared yourself to the healers," Arianne chuckled.

They were in a room not too dissimilar to the one Arianne had spent the night in, except this one provided a spectacular vista of the forest, with its tall, wide trees that resembled pillars holding up the sky. The Yantra River seemed to flow with less fury, as if it were meandering past them stealthily for fear of waking up the sleeping giants. The trees revealed the spread of the elven community with platforms and steps constructed at midsection, far from the ground, but not quite reaching the peaks.

"They fret too much" Celene frowned, even though the poultice applied to her shoulder was pleasantly soothing. She would never admit it though. "They have that in common with human healers."

"Human healers would have tossed you out the door by now. Elves, fortunately, have more patience," Keira declared, as she stepped into the room behind them.

"You will be happy to know they consider even you more pig-headed than Dare," Arianne said sweetly.

Keira uttered a short laugh. "Well, that's quite a feat. You should be very proud."

Celene gruffed and eased back into her bed, taking a deep breath of the aromatic air of the Hall of Healing. She was the only occupant at present, which accounted for why the elven healers were all agog with excitement at having a patient to tend to. Still, she was not so stubborn she did not recognise the care they had given her. For someone poisoned by a spider's venom, she slept well from the incense they had burning in her room. It left the scent of cinnamon in the air and lulled her into a pleasant sleep.

"I should be ready to travel in a day," Celene assured them both. "I just need today to let my shoulder recover."

"We will see," Arianne said, committing to nothing.

"We cannot afford to wait," Celene pointed out, not about to be talked into lingering longer.

"No we can't, but you still need your rest," Keira threw in. "You need to protect us, and you're in no fit state to do so at the moment. This is as much for our benefit as it yours."

"Exactly," Arianne said. "Another day will not make any difference. Celene, my need is urgent, but I will not have you kill yourself on my account. Take the time to rest, and we will be off again soon."

The Lady of Gislaine despised being fretted upon by healers, no matter how injured she was. Most of her injuries often took place during combat, and she abhorred being reminded she had been bested in battle by having others fuss over her injuries. The only good thing to ever come out of her visit to one of these places, was Ronen.

What chaffed her even more was the fact after all those years hearing Dare talk of Eden Halas, she was finally within its borders to see for herself, but was unable to do so because she was confined to this bed.

"Fine, fine," Celene conceded defeat. "I will stay here, if there is no other alternative, but I cannot promise to be pleasant."

* * *

"How are you enjoying our city?" Keira heard someone step onto the balcony behind her a short time later.

Keira glanced over her shoulder and saw that it was King Halion, who they met briefly the night before. While he had Aeron's dark hair, his features were more severe than his handsome youngest son. He was very much the king, and he wore a tunic of blue silk and a long coat with a gold trim. A gold band adorned his head.

"It is beautiful, my Lord," Keira answered, reminding herself to mind her words. This was not Dare, who appreciated being addressed as a contemporary. This was an elf, who had been king for thousands of years. "A true marvel," she complimented.

He took up position next to her and stared into his city, a small smile of pride crossing his lips as he surveyed the landscape.

"When I first came there was nothing—just the trees. I had not intended to stay. I was travelling south, and just so happened to stop here for rest, but once I did…" He peered past the railing to a particular spot next to the river, a place that seemed to have more sun than most due to a break in the canopy overhead. The clearing was small, but the extra sunlight allowed the bloom of white flowers across the short grass. "I stood right there, looked out into the forest, and knew this was the place to build a home."

"Intuition is a difficult thing to ignore," Keira commented. "Sometimes, a place feels right, even if there is no sense to it."

"Agreed." He threw her a sidelong glance. "That is why my intuition tells me there is more to you than meets the eye. There is something about you that is unfamiliar and odd. If you were not with Arianne, we would not have allowed you through the Veil."

Keira stiffened, and shot a look at the king, wondering how she ought to respond. "I am sorry for your discomfort. You are not the first elf to react this way. I've been told it's because of the desert burrowers. It left something dark inside me, and seems to bother only you elves."

"Indeed." He eyed her suspiciously, not entirely convinced. "No matter, you are here, and Arianne trusts you. I will put my faith in the queen of Carleon, if not in you. In any case, I would know the reason for Arianne's journey. Dare and I may disagree on many things, but even I know he would not send his wife without an appropriate escort on a journey that has so far yielded peril."

To lie to him seemed extremely discourteous after the hospitality shown to them, but telling him the truth was breaking Arianne's confidence. Arianne's quest needed to continue, for all their sakes. "It is not my place to say why Arianne chooses to travel. If you need an answer, you will need to ask her."

Halion frowned, but did not appear unsurprised by her answer. "You do her a disservice by keeping her secret. It is not safe for an elf woman, especially one who is the queen of Carleon, to be wandering about the wilds with only two women as her companions."

"One of those women fought at Astaroth," Keira reminded, ignoring the derision in his tone. "Surely that's safe enough."

"I mean no offense to the Lady of Gislaine, but I would be remiss in my duty to her mother if I did not inquire why Arianne is so far from home. Balfure was not the only evil in Avalyne. There are far meaner things creeping in the deep places of the earth, and some closer than we think. The destruction of one terrible being can sometime be followed by another eager to take its place."

"Do you know of another?" she probed, wondering if the king had intelligence he was keeping to himself.

Halion smiled faintly, as if he knew what she was about, but admitted nothing, unwilling to part with anything unless there was there was an equal exchange to be made. "Not exactly, but if the queen intends to travel the wilderness alone, she should beware of what lurks in the shadows or," he stared at her pointedly, "in the light."

* * *

Celene never met Aeron's brother, Hadros, but she had heard enough of him to know she would not much like him when they met. She was proven correct when he stepped in her room in the Hall of Healing after Arianne left, and she sent one of the elf maids trying to tend her wounds to fetch her clothes instead.

"I am told you wish your clothes so you can depart," he remarked as he eyed her trying to get out of bed. Upon seeing him, Celene retreated back to bed convinced he would only try to stop her, if she continued her present course.

Like Halion, his hair was dark and it hung about his shoulders loose. His features were not as fine as Aeron's and, to her, he seemed older, though it was difficult to say for certain with elves. His tone however was patronizing, immediately bringing out the worst in Celene.

"Only when I am forced to stay in bed over injuries inconsequential to me," she retorted, waiting impatiently for her clothes to arrive. At the present, she was clad in a simple white shift and felt all the more self-conscious for it.

"You are still injured. You should rest," he pointed out, standing by the door with his arms folded.

His gaze was one of reproach, like she was a child. Upon further thought Celene supposed she was in comparison to him but she did not like being reminded of it. "I *was* injured," she corrected him, "but I am well now and I need no other treatment. What healing I required after Eden Halas will take place en route, I do not need to be in a bed for that."

"You are travelling with Arianne," Hadros stated firmly. "She requires protection from what lies in the wilds of your world. If you are her only protection, then you endanger her by your stubbornness."

Celene bristled at the accusation. She did not like this elf, nor the assumption he made that she would place her own needs above that of Arianne's. "As I am a guest in your father's kingdom, I will try not to take offense by that remark."

Hadros showed no repentance at her statement.

"I merely state the obvious," he said haughtily. "If anything befalls the queen while she indulges in this foolishness, then we will all suffer. Does that not warrant you behaving sensibly?"

"I *am* behaving sensibly," she retorted with some petulance. She knew there was a kernel of truth in his words, but she was not about to admit defeat just yet. "I will leave nothing to chance when it comes to Arianne or her baby's safety. I am injured, yes, but the one to best judge how I will be capable of tolerating those wounds is me—not you."

"This will not do," Hadros looked at her coldly. "She should have a proper escort, not a…" He faltered when he saw he was about to say something unforgivable.

"A *woman*?" she accused, and then realised that was not what he intended to say. Not woman, she thought, eyes narrowing as she understood. *Human*.

"Hadros," Arianne's voice filled the room. They both turned to see the queen of Carleon approaching them with Celene's travelling clothes in her arms." "I think that will be all."

"I was…"

"I am well aware of what you were doing," Arianne replied with such glacial hardness to her voice, it was easy to believe she was a queen. "I thank you for your concern and bid you to leave us. Celene and I have much to discuss."

Hadros appeared as if he wanted to respond, but since much of his conversation with Celene was heard by Arianne, there was little he could do but to withdraw. It was just as well for Arianne, as she did not think Celene would have been able to restrain her displeasure for much longer.

Keira brushed past Hadros at the door as he was leaving. The elf gave her a look of distaste as he passed, it made Keira wonder how Aeron managed to be so different from his father and brother.

"What was that about?" she asked, stepping into the room and noting the tension.

"Just Hadros being a dolt," Celene snorted, flashing them a look of annoyance.

"Somehow, I'm not surprised," Keira shrugged and then declared, "I think we need to leave sooner rather than later. The king wants to know here you're going, and I don't think he much liked it when I refused to tell him."

"They all know Dare would not simply let me leave Carleon when I am with child, at least not without what they consider a proper escort." Arianne replied, recalling Syanne's reaction to her news.

"Well, they're not wrong there, but I have a feeling if they find out what we're really about, they're not going to be too happy to let you leave alone." Keira stated this as a certainty.

It was concern for Celene's welfare keeping them here, and it was unfair burden to put on the Lady of Gislaine. Fear for her babe did not make her forget how Celene saved both their lives, and she did not wish to aggravate Celene's injury by leaving prematurely. "You need at least a further day's rest."

"I shall be fine," Celene assured her, even though Arianne was right. Despite her bravado in front of Hadros, her shoulder ached, and she could not lift her sword until it healed better. "Once we're away from here, we can camp at the foot of the Baffin and I can rest then. Although I do not blame them for their concern, their insistence to know may do more harm than good. We do not know by what means the enemy's agent keeps watch over you. If he does not know we have left Sandrine, then we must press the advantage."

"I know," Arianne nodded in full agreement. "You must forgive Hadros and the king," she explained, as Keira helped Celene dress. "They believe the world is a dangerous place for elves and no place is safe for us except behind the Veil. I sometimes think that if Halion had this way, we would all withdraw behind it and never emerge again."

"I suppose," Celene shrugged, as she sat on the bed and pulled up her breeches with one hand. "I see now why Aeron describes his family so little."

"I don't think they're so bad," Keira retorted, helping Celene remove the shift she was wearing. "I think they're just overprotective. Be fair, they're not behaving any differently than Dare or anyone else at Sandrine would. It is unusual for a queen to be travelling the way you are. It wouldn't be right if they *didn't* ask questions."

To that, Arianne could not disagree. She noted the injury on Celene's shoulder as she slipped on her shirt. "Are you certain that you are fit to continue?"

"I am fine," Celene assured her. "I am not about to singlehandedly fight Balfure or an army of beserkers, but I am certainly fit to ride. I can heal on the way."

"I will trust you on that," Arianne stared at her critically. "With everything else that is happening to me of late, the last thing I would require is for you to drop dead from exhaustion, or some other malaise, because of your stubbornness to aid me in this quest."

"If it soothes you somewhat, I will not drop dead—I will faint gracefully from exhaustion."

Keira rolled her eyes and shook her head at Celene's obvious stubbornness, but gave up trying to argue with the warrior of Angarad.

"Thank you," Arianne shook her head, sharing Keira's resignation as Celene grinned. "That gives me a world of comfort."

* * *

Despite the ambivalence of her husband, Syanne was true to her word, and furnished Arianne and her companions with fresh horses and supplies for their journey northward. At their farewell, both Halion and Hadros were present, voicing their reservations about this mysterious journey Arianne was taking with such scant protection into the wilds of Avalyne. Fortunately, Syanne was able to exert what influence she had over her husband, and the trio were allowed to go on their way without further interference.

Nevertheless, Arianne was sad to say goodbye to Syanne, for she suspected it would be some time before they were able to see each other again. If her quest was successful and the baby was born unmolested by the enemy's machinations, she would be bound to Sandrine indefinitely, and it was unlikely Halion would allow Syanne to visit. Arianne was convinced Syanne would very much like to see her adopted grandchild, even if her husband would never acknowledge the baby.

One day, the elves of Eden Halas would retreat behind the Veil, and Arianne suspected they would never again emerge from it.

Chapter Nine

The Blizzard

After leaving the woods of Eden Halas, they approached the Baffin Range—the great mountain divide running along the eastern border of Angarad—past Barrenjuck Green, before finally coming to an end at Eden Taryn. It took almost a week of continuous travel to reach the mountains, but fortunately for them, it was a journey without incident, and there was ample opportunity to take in the sight of magnificent range as they approached it.

For many thousands of years, the Baffin offered protection to the peoples of Angarad, the Green, and the coastal Lenkworth fishing villages from invaders, who found the mountain too much of a hurdle to overcome. Once they reached the foot of the range, they turned onto the Baffin Road, which flanked the western side of mountain from Cereine to Angarad. Turning southwards, they followed it until they reached the Splinter—a narrow pass used by travellers to avoid the long journey to Angarad by cutting across the mountain.

In the meantime, Celene continued to be mindful of her injuries, and though it was difficult for her to ride during the first hours of their departure from Eden Halas, the lady of Gislaine bore it well. Both Keira and Arianne were aware of her attempts to hide her weariness, and Arianne often feigned needing rest herself so they had an excuse to stop when they saw Celene needed it. Meanwhile, Keira took over the cooking duties when they stopped to make camp, ensuring both women took care of themselves. Arianne rather loved her for this.

It was almost nightfall when they finally reached the Splinter. All three were exhausted from being in a saddle for almost the entire day. No one disagreed when the suggestion was brought forth of making camp that night. They ate around the warm fire, wondering how far they would have to continue tomorrow in order to reach the pass that would take them through the mountains. Little was said of the quest, though all of them were thinking constantly of it.

Arianne was preoccupied with thoughts of Dare, and how he would have taken the news of her departure. Without doubt, Lylea would have explained things once he discovered her gone, but Arianne was certain he would not understand. It did not help that she missed him terribly, and each day apart made her long for her king. It was foolishness, this pining for him. It was not as if they had never been apart before. Prior to their marriage, he was always travelling from place to place, and his time with her only came in between his adventures.

Arianne's melancholy did not only originate from her missing Dare—she wished she could be like any woman, enjoying the experience of impending motherhood. She should have been happily dreaming of all the promise a baby would bring to their lives. Yet all she felt was this terrible weight pressing down on her soul, demanding the completion of her quest, or it would cost her everything she held dear. It was not fair.

Celene's worries differed from Arianne's. She did not worry about what Ronen would think about her abrupt departure. She would find out soon enough when the quest was done. She was too practical to torture herself with how her beloved might behave in this situation. Her concerns were greater than this, especially when the full moon was in the sky when they finally camped at the foot of the Baffin.

It was almost two weeks since they departed Sandrine. It would take another week to reach Angarad, after crossing the Baffin. If they had been on foot, the journey would have taken even longer. As Celene calculated the days, she knew time was against them. She was adamant about leaving Eden Halas because she knew they could not afford to waste even one day if they intended to reach the enemy before it was too late. It was a long journey to the Frozen Mountains, to say nothing about descending into Mael's Pit to reach Sanhael, if it still existed.

Keira worries were not about their journey, but about what Arianne would do if she thought they were going to fail in their quest. As it was, the woman from the Green debated whether or not she should tell Celene what had been discussed while they were travelling the Yantra, The thought of what Arianne herself would do to prevent a second darkness from befalling the land concerned her. Arianne's fierce desire to protect those she loved might force her to act irrationally. Was it possible that might mean ending her life?

And would Celene stop her?

This was a possibility Keira did not wish to entertain at this moment. She was certain even if Arianne never said it to her directly, it was a course the queen would take, if the situation gave her no alternative. Keira knew Arianne might be strong enough to make such a sacrifice, but what she did not know was whether or not Celene would stand by and let her friend do this terrible deed.

* * *

The raging wind in her ears and the sudden chill on her skin awoke Arianne from her sleep.

The night before showed them a canopy of stars—a sure indicator the day following it would be clear and good for travel. When she opened her eyes and stared at the sky, she saw grey clouds allowing no sunshine to penetrate its thick veil. The wind was whistling in her ears, and the trees covering the Baffin swayed to its will with each breath of the gale. Arianne sat up and found Keira and Celene already awake, packing away their things to resume their travels, or at the very least, seek shelter away from the tempest.

Arianne raised her eyes to the top of the mountain and saw the higher reaches of it covered in sheets of snow. The wind was gently chipping away at its volume and she understood in an instant why the others were so determined to get moving. If this storm were to grow any worse, it might conceivably precipitate an avalanche that would bury the passage in snow, and force them to take the longer route. As she rose to her feet to help with their quick departure, Arianne sensed something ominous. It was the same feeling she experienced in Caras Anara, although there, the danger was more overt, and did not require elven senses to detect.

"There's some stew left," Keira motioned to the pot on the fire place as she rolled up a blanket.

"You should have awakened me," Arianne replied as she sat up properly.

"Nonsense, you need your rest more than any of us. Come on, eat up, and then we'll get going."

"That snow is going to come down soon," Celene warned. "We need to make for the Splinter or else we shall have to go around it."

Arianne nodded, but there was something in the air making her uneasy, and as she rolled up her bedding she swept her gaze across the mountain top, feeling a chill running through her that was more than just the cold.

"There is something not right about all this," she declared as she went to the pot and scooped out some of the stew.

"What do you mean?" Celene stopped what she was doing and stared at Arianne.

"I do not know," Arianne explained in between bites. She ate quickly, because once they were travelling, the chance to get a hot meal would be scant.

"It is a storm," Keira declared shifting glances between Arianne and Celene. "It is unfortunate, but they are a part of life. They just happen." She sounded as if she were trying to convince herself more than anyone else.

"I do not mean the storm," Arianne clarified. "I just sense something evil nearby. Trust my word. I do not make this claim lightly."

"I believe you Arianne," Celene replied honestly. "But what is to be done? We must cross that breach."

She was right.

Whatever menace lurked in the mountains, they still had to proceed. There was no faster route through the Baffin. With that unhappy realisation before her, Arianne said no more and finished her meal so they could complete their departure.

By the time they mounted their horses, the storm was quickly becoming a blizzard with a wall of snow blowing around them as they rode towards the pass. The cold seemed to penetrate all their warm clothing, until Arianne could feel her teeth chattering as they approached the narrow corridor through the Splinter. The closer they drew to it, the more Arianne was disturbed by what she was sensing. Something terrible loomed in the passageway—something that was going to harm them. She wanted to turn back, but Celene was right—they needed to make the attempt.

Inside the small canyon that had been carved through years of erosion by water or some other force, Arianne swallowed thickly as they moved deeper and deeper into its confines. The horses grew anxious as dirt and soil disappeared beneath their hooves, to be replaced with thick snow. Celene led the way, aware this leg of their journey was worrying Arianne and she went ahead to show the queen there was nothing to fear, though she did not exactly discount Arianne's warning of danger.

Keira stayed in the rear, trying to remain in the saddle as she was being assailed by almost blinding snowfall and gale force winds. Her face burned from the cold and her fingers felt frozen as she clung to the reins. The palfrey beneath her was grunting his displeasure in snorts of cold air escaping his flared nostrils.

They were less than a quarter of the way through when suddenly Celene heard Arianne cry out behind her. Celene brought her mount to an immediate halt and glanced over her shoulder. The elf's features were contorted in fear and sent tendrils of alarm through the warrior maiden. "What is it?"

"Something is here," Arianne said looking about her, trying to find something that could convince Celene, as well as herself, they should leave here while they still could.

"Where?" Celene demanded, her hand reaching for her sword.

"I don't know," Arianne cried out in frustration, "but I can feel it!"

"I can't see anything," Keira declared, looking about the place, trying to see through and seeing nothing that gave shape to Arianne's claim.

Celene scanned the canyon wall trying to find something to give truth to Arianne's premonitions. There was nothing at first—not until she looked closely and saw that the canyon floor was littered with rocks and boulders of varying sizes. This, in itself, was nothing out of the ordinary, since rock fall was to be expected when one was travelled through a mountain. When she observed the rocks more closely, she saw they were jagged and sharp, not at all smoothed from years of precipitation. The look of them made her dismount the horse, uncertain whether her need to investigate was inspired by Arianne's warning or because she was starting to see something odd.

"What have you found?" Arianne asked, still gripped with this feeling of foreboding.

"These rocks," Celene looked ahead and then behind her on the path they had taken to this very spot. "Why are they only here?"

"Does it matter?" Keira asked. "Let's just get clear."

Keira looked up at the increased snowfall, the blanket of white so thick even the rocks were beginning to disappear under their cover. If it fell any thicker across the ground, the horses were going to have trouble moving through it.

Arianne realised Celene was right. Behind them the path was clear. The collection of stones Celene viewed with such anxiety bore no unity with the terrain. They seemed out of place, and were broken as if split apart by an axe. Staring up the length of the passage, she saw the path was clear, and this odd collection noticed by Celene seemed to be only in one specific place.

She shivered, and it was not because the wind was heavy and blowing across her skin with icy force. Pulling her cloak closer to her body, Arianne lifted her eyes to the uneven top of the canyon wall above their heads and saw the raging blizzard of snow and wind. Yet, every sense she possessed told her that this was not right, and the sudden emergence of this storm was by the design of something other than nature.

"Celene, I think we should take another route."

Celene stared at her sharply. "Arianne, it will cause us significant delay."

"I know," she replied anxiously, "but I do not make this request lightly. We should go now."

"She was right about the spiders," Keira reminded, and truth be told, she had enough experience with elves by now to know their warnings should not be taken lightly.

The fear Celene saw in Arianne's eyes was real, and though she did not wish to waste time by finding another way around the mountain, there was something disquieting about this whole situation. For now, she trusted her friend's instincts. Moving away from the rocks, she stepped on something that crunched easily under her boot. The sound was loud and distinct even through the banshee's wail of the wind.

Arianne and Keira heard it too and looked at each other in confusion as to what it was. Celene dropped to her knees so she could investigate. Beneath the print of her boot in the snow was something with an odd, curved shaped partially buried in the snow. Celene brushed it clean when suddenly she pulled back her hand as if she had been bitten.

It was skull—a dwarven skull.

Celene stumbled back in shock, slipping on the ice and landing heavily on her rear.

"Celene!" Arianne exclaimed, swinging herself out of the saddle and hurrying over to her.

"What is it?"

Celene would have answered, except when she looked at where she landed, she noticed another pile of bones, also partially covered by the snow. She let out a short cry of shock as she scrambled away.

"I think you are correct," Celene said in a hasty breath, as she quickly got to her feet. "I think we should leave now."

"There are bones everywhere!" Arianne gasped when she realised what Celene was gaping at.

"Bones? *Whose* bones?" Keira demanded from atop her horse looking about her, trying to see if the thing leaving those remains behind was still present. Her horse was growing increasingly unsettled by the weather, and its unease corresponded with Arianne and Celene's mounts as well.

At first, Arianne thought she was standing on gravel, but that was not it all. The canyon was a veritable tomb. Suddenly, she remembered Syanne's warning about travellers vanishing while trying to cross the mountains—but she had been speaking of the Frozen Mountains, not this pass. What new evil had taken root here?

"There are too many to say who," Arianne declared, sighting bones belonging to either human or a dwarf.

"I will never question you again," Celene declared as both women hurried to their horses.

They rode out of the Splinter, not looking back, and grateful they had come to their senses before it was too late. No one wanted to confront the creature capable of causing so many to die in that narrow expanse. They galloped hard through the snow filled path, paying little heed to the gale lashing at them or the unearthly howl ripping through their ears when they departed. It could have been the wind, but somehow, Arianne was not so certain of that. As they reached the mouth of the passage and saw the land beyond the Baffin, each felt a surge of relief at having escape so narrowly.

Or so they thought.

Suddenly, something tore Arianne from the saddle of her horse.

She let out a small cry of shock, but it was eclipsed by Celene's own shout of outrage as she encountered the same obstacle. There was little time to think as she saw the ground come up to swallow her. All she could do to protect her child was to curl her body into a ball and hope it would be enough to lessen the impact of her landing. She hit the ground hard, and though she was certain her positioning saved the slumbering babe in her womb, she was helpless to prevent the black fog descending over her, sending her into unconsciousness.

* * *

"My queen," she heard Celene's insistent voice prodding her into consciousness. "Arianne!"

There was a moment of confusion when Arianne opened her eyes and felt the dirt scrapping against her cheek, when she wondered where she was. The voice calling her was familiar, and only when her senses returned to her, did she realize it was Celene.

Starlight flooded her eyes when she opened her eyelids. As her blurred vision sharpened, she saw the night sky filtering through the canopy of trees above her. It was only when she heard the voices, did Arianne snap abruptly back to alertness. She tried to sit up, but was hampered by the fact her hands were tied.

Arianne did not know where they were, but it was clear they were deep within the woods. She had no sense of time, frightening her even more, not knowing how long she was unconscious. She could smell smoke close by and upon investigation, saw it came from the fire of the camp they were in. Sitting above the flames was a cooking pot—its contents simmering with heat and a stench capable of turning her delicate stomach. There were at least a half a dozen beserkers moving about the campsite, she realised with horror. Some were guarding her and Celene, the rest were more interested in picking clean the contents of their saddle bags.

"Are you hurt?" she heard Celene whisper quietly.

"No," Arianne shook her head as she gazed upon the Lady of Gislaine who was seated before her cross-legged, her arms bound behind her. A streak of blood ran down Celene's face, the cause being the angry gash slashed across her forehead. "Are you?"

"It looks worse than it is," Celene replied dismissively, since they had larger concerns at the moment.

"How long have I been unconscious? Arianne asked, as she attempted to shake the disorientation out of her head.

"A few hours," Celene answered, watching their jailers cautiously. Their lives hung on a knife's edge at this moment, and unless she found a way to free them both, neither would survive the night. "I feared that you were injured far worse than appeared."

"My strength is not what it used to be," Arianne explained breathlessly, her eyes following the proceedings in the campsite with as much caution as Celene. "Carrying a babe is tiring work, but I am well enough."

"Good," Celene spoke quietly. "That is something at least. Keira is not here."

"What?" Arianne hissed looking about them. "Where is she?"

"I do not know," Celene answered, keeping watch for their captors. "When I woke, she was not with us."

One of their captors, noticing that Arianne was awake, started towards them, his feet crushing the dead leaves beneath him as he barked the foul speech of beserkers to his brothers. Arianne felt her blood run cold as she saw the foul creature advance upon her—his terrible eyes full of purpose. Keira's absence filled them both with a sense of foreboding, and her despair was compounded by the knowledge there would be no help for either herself or Celene from this ordeal. beserkers fed on man flesh, and what they did to women was too unspeakable to think of. The idea of what could befall them both made Arianne's heart pound even louder.

"They will ask your name. Do not tell them," Celene instructed quickly, before her words entered the hearing of the enemy.

The beserkers paused before Arianne and hissed at her, its jagged teeth covered in filth borne like fangs. Arianne raised her chin in defiance of his attempt to scare her, refusing to allow this creature any more power over her than it already had. She wondered why they were not already dead. beserkers did not waste time with hostages. These were undoubtedly a renegade band left over from war with Balfure.

"You are fine ladies," the beserkers spoke, making the hairs on the back of her neck stand on end at its sinister delivery. "Your men will pay a great deal to retrieve you".

The comment explained a great deal.

So, this was what had become of Balfure's proud beserkers army? Forced to banditry and ransoming? Clearly, they identified Arianne and Celene as nobility and hoped to extort a ransom from their families. However, by Celene's warning, it appeared they did not know they had the queen of Carleon in their power.

"You can find that out yourself," Arianne returned sharply, aware her life depended on her identity remaining secret.

The beserkers bellowed in rage at being refused and raised his hand to strike when another of his party barked at him to stop. His hand paused in mid-air as he snarled at her again in rage, before turning away and returning to the horses. The two beserkers standing near by watched them closely.

"They're preparing to move out," Celene explained.

"What happened?" she asked.

"They ambushed us when we attempted to leave the passage. I believe the storm allowed them to lay a trap to capture us. They tied a rope across the mouth of the pass and we rode straight into it. When I awoke, we were here. I am uncertain, but they may have kept us in their lair until the night came so they might venture out in preparation to depart."

"And Keira? Do you think she might have escaped?" Arianne asked hopefully. The other alternative was too terrible to imagine.

"Possibly," Celene replied. "We have been unconscious for some time, so I cannot say for certain. They probably have a lair here, which they are going to take us to, and keep us so they can extract what they need for their ransom."

Arianne's stomach hollowed at the thought, aware beserkers were not skilled interrogators. Balfure left such cruel and precise work to his Disciples. She had no doubt, in getting their information, she and Celene would be made to suffer.

"Do you think they were responsible for the bodies we found?" Arianne inquired, almost afraid to hear the answer.

"Yes, I think so," Celene replied quietly, mindful nothing she said was being overheard. "I think they kill the travellers who are no use to them after robbing them blind, and the ones who might have value—such as us—they keep alive a little longer. Although, I cannot imagine they would honour any ransom debt paid."

"Then, we must escape," Arianne declared without hesitation. "Somehow, we must find a way."

"I agree, but that is easier said than done," Celene replied, even though she was slowly attempting to free herself of the ropes tied behind her back. It was not hard to do because the fingers of beserkers were far from nimble, and their ability to tie ropes even less so. With time, she might be able to untangle the unruly cluster of knots keeping her bound. It remained to be seen whether or not they would have the time to spare. The beserkers before them were sharing a meal—no doubt the precursor to beginning their journey to their lair. Celene would prefer it if freedom came to herself and Arianne before that.

Or else the beserkers might become hungry and decide a full stomach was more inviting than a ransom.

* * *

The watch guard observed the proceedings through the trees as one of the two women made a furtive attempt to free herself while still under the watchful gaze of their captors. The warrior woman was undoubtedly trying to loosen the ropes around her wrist, because the watch guard could read the subtle movements of her body as she made the attempt.

beserkers were blunt instruments. They were created by Balfure to act with brute force and there was a little subtlety in anything they did. They did not have the intelligence to interpret the secret glances being traded by Arianne and Celene, but then, there was little reason to fear the warrior woman's freedom from her bonds. Why should they? There were many of them and one of her. Even if she should free herself, she was unarmed, and her companion was still tied. It would be an exercise in futility that would get one or both of them killed.

The watch guard considered deeply what was to be done. The beserkers were preparing to leave with their captives, something that could not be good under any circumstances. There had been reports of travellers disappearing, and the watch guard was sent here to learn why. The discovery of the women became the answer to that riddle. This was not customary behaviour for beserkers, but since the fall of Balfure in the Citadel at Astaroth, the creatures served no master and were renegades hiding from the king's forces. Like any creature faced with extinction, they were doing what they could to survive.

Whatever the reason for their unusual behaviour, the watch guard had little choice but to act.

The third member of their party, who was knocked off her horse during the beserkers trick, lay at the watch guard's campsite, recovering from her fall. She took a nasty bump to her head when she fell, and only luck had seen her fall into a ditch and covered with snow when the beserkers came to collect her two companions. The woman, who appeared to be one of the folk of the Green, surprised the watch guard by her presence. The folk of the Green were not prone to wandering and certainly not in the company of two highborn ladies. These were questions the watch guard would ask later. For now, there were more pressing concerns.

There were about six beserkers—not a great many, but certainly enough to give one who was preparing a rescue pause for a moment. Stupid as they may be, they were not to be taken lightly. While the warrior woman could potentially be of use, her companion was still bound. No, the watch guard thought quickly—confronting the beserkers was out of the question. The best to be hoped for was the safe retrieval of both, followed by an extremely hasty flight, hopefully with all their skins intact.

The watch guard took a moment to grumble at the inconvenience of the situation. True, the women had to be helped, but the watch guard was on a mission too. A mission not as urgent as the current quandary the noblewomen found themselves, but it was still important. Nonetheless, being one of the Watch Guard meant ensuring the safety of travellers in the realm. The fate awaiting the two women, if something was not done, would be worse than death.

The watch guard returned to the campsite, because it appeared the captives were going nowhere for now. If this rescue was to take place, help was needed.

It was time to see how resilient the folk of the Green *really* were.

* * *

Celene appeared still as the night while her fingers worked deftly on the final knot behind her back. She closed her eyes in concentration, focussing singularly on the purpose of freeing her hands.

Arianne watched her surreptitiously, appearing anxious for the benefit of their captors and keeping their attention on her by asking questions they were ignoring.

Celene knew she could not keep up the charade indefinitely because beserkers were not known for their patience. While they may not be prepared to kill either of them for fear of losing their ransom, the vile beasts were still capable of inflicting untold horror upon them.

Suddenly, the beserker leader who questioned them earlier stared at Celene, his eyes narrowing in malice when he realised she was up to something. Celene felt her heart sink with disappointment as the knot came apart in her fingers. It would do her little good because she was discovered. He cried out to the rest of his comrades as he strode towards her, and Celene was filled with dismay at the realisation that her hard work was for nothing. If they did not kill her for what she had done, they were certainly going to tie her up again, and she would be right where she began.

"Do nothing," Celene commanded Arianne, forgetting for an instant who was queen and who was not. "Do not interfere with them on my account."

"Do not ask that of me!" Arianne cried out desperately as Celene stood up to face the beserkers coming towards her while the two guarding her, brandished their swords in preparation for the order to run her through.

"Escape," the beserkers sneered malevolently, his voice a throaty rumble. Upon reaching her, he gripped her arm to confirm his suspicions she had been attempting to escape. "Escape is pointless."

He raised his sword, readying himself to deliver a blow that while it might not necessarily kill her, would disable her and ruin any chance she had of making another escape attempt. Celene wanted to run, but she knew the weapons of the other two would end any flight before she even had a chance to take a step. She braced herself for the pain and felt anguish rise from the depths of her soul at failing her queen so utterly. She would not go down easily, and not before making him sorry he ever took them prisoner.

There was little chance for the beserkers to do anything. At that moment a horse burst through the bushes, carrying a rider on its back, landing a hair's breadth beyond the reach of the fire. Once his eyes and that of his minions turned to face this new threat, Celene acted swiftly. The edge of her palm slammed into the creature's face and forced him to drop his sword, which Celene liberated swiftly enough, tearing open his belly with one swipe of the weapon. When the others heard the death cry of their leader, they turned back to her. Celene slashed at one of them while the other was halted in his step by the bolt of a crossbow.

Suddenly, jumping out from behind one of the snow covered bushes was Keira. She was obviously working in concert with the rider, who provided her the distraction she needed to steal into the camp. Carrying the same sword Celene gifted to her, Keira burst into a smile of gratitude at their wellbeing, before taking advantage of the chaos to reach Arianne. The approach of a beserkers prompted Celene into action and she ran forward, intercepting the foul creature before he could accost Keira. Swinging her blade with precision, she tore open the berserker's chest, cutting through his leather tunic and spilling dark blood against the greyed snow.

"Get to the horses!" The rider astride the mare ordered, raising a crossbow to take aim at the beserkers again.

"Come on!" Celene urged Keira, who resumed cutting the ropes binding Arianne as she dispatched another beserkers.

"You don't have to tell me twice!" Keira declared, wincing as she saw Celene cut down the enemy and turned to help Arianne to her feet.

Arianne stood up, shaking away the remnants of the cut ropes from her wrists as she turned around and hugged Keira in relief. "We did not know what happened to you! We thought you were dead!"

"I was lucky. I was thrown from my horse and rolled into a little ditch just deep enough to hide me from the beserkers," she explained as she took Arianne's lead and sought out their horses.

Their mysterious rescuer was still holding the beserkers at bay, continuing to fire bolts from the crossbow and cutting down their numbers. Astride the mare, the watch guard did not remain in one place long enough to be unseated. Nevertheless, the beserkers were beginning to regroup, and even though only a few of the beasts remained, it was time for them to leave.

"We can talk later!" Celene barked and hurried towards the horses. Keira and Arianne did not argue and followed her closely, reaching the horses in good time. Celene waited for them to mount, ensuring they were not intercepted by beserkers as they climbed into the saddle. Once they were safely astride their horses, she did the same since the beserkers were more interested in the watch guard, who continued to be the centre of attention.

"Let's go!" Celene shouted as she dug her heels into her horse and the animal bolted forward.

Arianne did the same and the horse broke into a powerful gallop across the campsite. A beserker attempted to pull her out of the saddle, but Arianne kicked out, smashing the ball of her foot against its mouth and feeling its teeth crumble underneath. The beserker staggered back, and Arianne dug her heels into her horse with even more strength, forcing the mare to move even more quickly. The horse thundered forward, following Celene's mount, as they crossed the camp towards the woods.

Looking over her shoulder, she made sure Keira was following, and was relieved to see the woman keeping pace with her horse. Upon seeing their escape, their mysterious rescuer broke off the engagement with the remaining beserkers and joined them in flight. Leaving the beserkers behind, the women rode into the forest with the swiftness of the wind. Arianne heard the swoosh of an arrow, leaning out of the way as it sailed past her ear and embedded itself into a tree.

Arianne did not know how long they rode through the night. Her only concern was putting as much distance as possible between themselves and the beserkers. The thick trees of the forest shielded them from the snow storm. Upon emerging into the open air, they were once again lashed by the strong winds and snowfall. Fortunately, as beserkers did not ride, it was unlikely they were pursued. Their rescuer took the lead, appearing to know the terrain with some expertness.

Shortly before dawn, they were led to one of the many Watch Guard stations built along the Baffin Road to provide travellers with shelter.

Arianne was grateful when she finally dismounted her horse and led the exhausted animal out of the wind and biting snow. The elements had taken a toll on all of them, and their silence as they settled in for the night revealed their exhaustion.

"We are in your debt," Arianne said to the watch guard, as she helped Keira bring in their bedding while Celene started a fire in the fireplace. She noticed their rescuer wore the same type of leather jerkin favoured by Celene

"Yes," Keira agreed. "You saved us all. Me first, and then the rest of us. I don't know what would have happened if you hadn't come upon us."

Keira had awoken to find herself in the company of this stranger, who had apparently tended the wound on her head and taken her out of the snow when the beserkers had overcome Arianne and Celene. Spit only knew how she had managed to move Keira without being seen by those loathsome creatures, but Keira was grateful she had. After leaving her to recover, the stranger tracked the beserkers back to their campsite, and determined Arianne and Celene were alive. By the time she returned, Keira was awake and anxious to find a way to help her companions.

Fortunately, the watch guard had a plan on how to do this, and upon deciding to play decoy, provided Keira with the opportunity to sneak into the beserkers camp and free the queen and the Lady of Gislaine.

The watch guard, who was rummaging through a satchel, glanced over at Arianne's words of thanks and stood up. Lowering the hood of the cloak, the watch guard faced them for the first time.

Long, black hair spilled forth, framing a face with lightly bronzed skin and brown eyes. Both Celene and Arianne stared at her with surprise, for she was not from a race of men familiar to them. Keira had expressed similar surprise when the Watch Guard revealed herself to the mistress of Furnsby Farm. Like her companions, Keira had never seen anyone who looked like this, either.

It was not simply her skin was dusky, but her features were decidedly exotic. Arianne heard Lylea speak of humans who lived on the other side of the Burning Plain, swearing fealty to Balfure, but the desert kept them from crossing over in Carleon. Was this watch guard one of those folk? In any case, she was a long way from home. Arianne wondered who her people were, and was genuinely curious to learn where she had come from.

"There is no debt my lady," she said to Arianne, head bowed slightly in respect. "It is my duty as one of the Watch Guard to ensure travellers are able to go about their business in safety. Though I must confess this is the first time I have ever had to rescue noblewomen travelling alone. With the beserkers roaming wild after Balfure's defeat, it is not wise to wander alone. Should you not have escorts?"

"We have business requiring stealth," Celene said, bristling with annoyance at everyone thinking they were incapable of fending for themselves because there was no man amongst them.

"Then, I would suggest you exercise some prudence. What happened back there could have been worse, if I had not stumbled upon you."

"We would have found our way out of that predicament," Celene said defensively.

"Yes," the watch guard responded with no small amount of sarcasm. "I saw how well you were finding your way. Another minute more and your problems would have been ended permanently."

"Come on," Keira interjected before tempers flared. "We just escaped beserkers without any of us getting hurt or killed. I'm tired and hungry, and the last thing we need to do is argue about this. Celene is right, we have important business to deal with that requires some discretion, but we're also grateful for what you did for us."

Arianne smiled at Keira's ability diffuse the situation by discarding all the other nonsense coming from the clash of personalities. "And I second that," Arianne said, supporting Keira's efforts to move past the moment. "We are thankful for your assistance. We need to cross the Baffin. If we cannot go through the Splinter, is there another route that we might take?" Arianne asked, since this watch guard seemed to know the area.

Visibly relaxing and shedding the tension of the moment, the watch guard offered a conciliatory nod at Celene who returned it before she answered Arianne. "There is something preying on the travellers in the Splinter. Many have died attempting to cross there. Still there is an old goat herders trail half a day's ride from here that will allow you to across the mountain safely. It's not widely known, but I think your horses will make it through, if you tread carefully."

"Thank you," Celene said, feeling a little less tense now they knew there was an alternate route across. "Do you know what happened to the people in the Splinter?" Celene asked.

"No, but I have seen the bodies, and I did not remain long enough to find out what killed them."

"That is probably wise," Arianne could not disagree with that course. "Can you lead us there then?"

"I can lead you to the trail, but that depends on where you need to go." She looked at them in question, wondering where these noblewomen were headed to risk such danger as travelling alone.

Keira did not bother trying to hide their destination after this stranger had saved their lives. "We are travelling to the Frozen Mountains. We need to get there well before the next full moon."

"Keira!" Celene protested, uncertain whether or not she wanted the woman to know that much about their destination.

"Look, we're already delayed, and if she wanted to kill us, she would have just left me in the snow and you two to those beserkers. We've done all we can alone, and we've almost been killed *twice*. We need to start being smarter about this or none of us are going to get there in one piece."

"I know, but..." Celene started to say when Arianne cut her off.

"You are right, Keira," Arianne said with sigh. "We have almost been killed twice, and we cannot continue to keep stumbling through the dark, hoping we don't stumble into another catastrophe." Turning to the woman, Arianne spoke to her. "Keira has told you where we need to be. Can it be done?"

The woman frowned and replied after a moment's thought. "It is going to take some doing. It is a long journey, and there is very little time in which to make it. Might I ask what the purpose of such a trek is?"

"It is safer if you do not know," Arianne replied before Celene could. "Except that it is a matter of great importance."

"It must be," the watch guard countered, "if the *queen* is making it."

Arianne stared at her. "You know who I am?"

Celene stiffened and reached for her the hilt of her sword, but Keira, who was standing near her, touched Celene's hand, and shook her head. She honestly believed this watch guard was not a danger to them, and may even prove useful to their quest.

"Yes," the stranger nodded. "I was at Sandrine for the king's coronation—I saw you at your wedding."

"Then you will help us?" Arianne asked, her distrust of this watch guard wanning, because a woman who was willing to rescue strangers from the hands of beserkers could not be entirely without honour. Furthermore, this watch guard seemed as capable of defending herself as Celene, and was to Arianne, a resource they should not squander.

"It is my duty to help my queen," the woman bowed in. "You and the Lady of Gislaine."

"Well, I'm here too," Keira snorted in mock hurt, although she was glad to see an accord of some kind being reached between them all so that they could get moving again.

"My apologies, Mistress Furnsby," she apologised with a smirk, aware this was the proper way to refer to the mistress of a household in the Green.

"Call me Keira," Keira corrected, never liking to be addressed so formally.

"And, as you know who I am, I would prefer you call me Arianne," the queen said to the watch guard. "This is Celene, and what do we call you?"

"Melia," she replied finally. "My name is Melia of the Nadira."

"Welcome to our quest, Melia of Nadira," Celene said wryly, her hand no longer on her sword. "Let us hope you do not live to regret it."

Chapter Ten

Melia's Story

Their new companion, Arianne, Keira, and Celene learned, had been a watch guard since the restoration of the kingdom.

They knew she came from beyond the Burning Plains, across the desert where the men who dared to cross the parched land settled after finding fertile ground. Lylea spoke of kingdoms with such exotic names as Rayan and Chaldea, while Melia herself revealed her people were called the Nadira. Unlike the elves or dwarves, men possessed an insatiable need to explore, and Arianne could very well believe they were willing to slip beyond the reach of the known world to conquer new frontiers.

If this Melia came from those faraway lands then she had been travelling for a great many years.

Arianne knew Dare appointed many watch guards to protect the lands surrounding the Green from beserkers or any other danger cable of threatening the gentle folk. Before the war, hardly anyone knew about the existence of the villagers in the Green. Since the defeat of Balfure, the revelation, a couple from the Green gave refuge to the future king, might be cause enough for remnants of the Aeth Lord's army to seek revenge. As a result, Watch Guard towers were established along the borders of the Green, with a cohort of guards, to patrol the area and kept a vigil on its lands.

With the end of the occupation, people were travelling freely from one end of the kingdom to the other. No longer afraid to visit other cities, and free to leave Carleon's borders for other lands, they were embarking on lengthy journeys across the kingdom. Furthermore, with commerce and trade being re-established between Carleon, Angarad and Lenkworth, it seemed the Watch Guard's duties were expanded to include the protection of these travellers.

It may well be in the future, the reach of the Watch Guards could extend over much of Carleon.

What quest brought Melia to this part of the world, was something she felt no inclination to reveal. Shortly before the war against Balfure, Melia joined the defence of Cereine. She served with a commander who would become a captain of the Watch Guard. After the war, he invited her into his ranks, and Melia accepted. Her duties usually found her assigned to the eastern face of the Baffin, but on occasion, she crossed the mountains to attend to business of her own.

It almost seemed like Fate's Arrow had directed her to be where she needed to be to help them escape the beserkers.

* * *

"Are you determined to travel through Wyndfyre?" Melia asked, after they settled in for the night.

Outside the snow abated, and although there was still a frosty bite in the air, it was nowhere as chilling as it had been the previous evening. Keira took charge of the cooking duties once more, and so the small station was warmed by the heat of the fire. Celene and Melia agreed to take watch through the night so they were not caught unawares by anything else that might stumble upon them.

"I had hoped to see my home," Celene admitted honestly. "My family were unable to journey to Sandrine for the king's announcement and I wanted to see how they are."

Of course, being practically minded, Celene had no difficulty sacrificing the visit, if necessary. Still, it would be disappointing.

"I can appreciate that," Melia said sympathetically, "But if you wish to reach your destination within the time allotted to you, it will save a number of days if we travel straight across Angarad and avoid Wyndfyre. There are many villages capable of providing us with supplies on the way across."

Celene knew this herself. After all, Angarad was her home. She was fairly certain she knew a few places Melia wasn't familiar with. Still, it was disappointing not to be able to go home, even for a brief visit.

"We can see them on the way back," Keira suggested, aware despite Celene's tough exterior, sometimes put on for the benefit of those who might think her less of a warrior because she was a woman, she felt things deeply. "I've always wanted to go to Wyndfyre."

"Yes, that's true," Celene replied with a forlorn sigh. She agreed without question Melia's suggestion was expedient. It was also very much in keeping with Keira's nature to look at their quest with such optimism. She was convinced they would all come home unscathed. "You are right. We need to shave some time off the trip. We will abandon the stop at Wyndfyre."

Arianne's heart sank a little for Celene because she knew the Angarad wanted very much to see her family again. If she missed the opportunity to see them during the quest, Arianne did not think another chance would present itself again for some time. Unfortunately, the need to make haste to the Frozen Mountains meant the sacrifice was necessary, and Arianne felt guilty Celene would miss the chance to see her family for the demands of the quest.

"Thank you, Celene," Arianne said to her friend. "We will see Angarad when we return. I promise."

"I will survive not seeing them for a little longer." Celene assured the queen there were no hard feelings on her part. "We have more important things on our minds right now."

"I will take first watch," "Melia offered Keira, spooning hot stew onto her plate.

"Wake me when you're ready for some rest," Celene answered as they sat down eat.

"Tell me," Melia looked up at Arianne after a few minutes of silent dining, "what brings the queen of Carleon to the edge of Avalyne?"

The women exchanged glances with each other, wondering whether or not the queen ought to answer Melia's question. Although they trusted Melia to a point, Arianne was uncertain whether or not the watch guard should be told the purpose of their quest. She knew Keira considered Melia no danger, but Celene was a little more wary, and doubted to some degree the accuracy of elvish senses. Furthermore, Melia was still reticent about her reasons for being on this side of the Baffin when she should have been on patrol near the Green.

"Why were you on this side of the mountain?" Arianne asked, deciding if Melia wanted their trust, she had to afford them the same courtesy.

Conscious of the question being made by the queen of Carleon, Melia felt duty bound to answer. She hesitated a moment as she decided how to respond.

Finally, she spoke after a long pause, "I am searching for my mother."

Judging by the reluctance in which she volunteered the information, Arianne guessed the matter was intensely difficult for her to confide in others. Arianne waited for Melia to elaborate, which she did a few seconds later.

"My father visited these lands in his youth where he met my mother, who apparently lived along the banks of the Yantra River. They were together for a time, but after I was born, my mother grew weary of being wife and mother, so she left us. Eventually, he returned to his people, and I was raised in Nadira with my father's family. He told me little about her, and when he passed on, I felt that I had to find her. I travel between the Baffin and the Yantra every few months, hoping to find her while serving as watch guard."

"Would it be simpler to continue the search instead of moving back and forth from the Baffin?" Keira asked, unable to imagine such a commute to be an efficient way to search.

"I was a stranger when I arrived in these lands. The Captain of the Watch Guard was a soldier of Cereine. He recognised my skill and accepted me as one of his own during the defence of that city in the war. I owe him my loyalty, and when he asked me to serve as one of the Guard after the war, I could not refuse. Besides, it serves my purpose—I often meet travellers who give me valuable intelligence for my search."

"Such men are rare," Celene agreed readily, understanding all too well men who could see past gender were few, and she herself had sworn her allegiance to Dare for that very reason. "But they do exist."

"The Yantra is a great river," Arianne pointed out. "Your search may take years."

"I know," Melia answered, not blinded to the reality of it. "That is where being a part of the Watch Guard is useful. They are the eyes and ears of Avalyne. They can help me in my search."

"And your mother?" Keira asked. "What do you know about her?"

"Very little," Melia confessed with a frown.

Arianne wondered if that was the truth or if Melia had reached the limits of what she was willing to impart to them about her purpose. Arianne could understand her reluctance. It was a deeply personal issue. Melia appeared to have spent many years searching for her mother—a quest no doubt fraught with disappointment and frustration. Such emotional turmoil must have made it difficult for her to make friendships, or confide in others.

"I know she is of a people who used to dwell along the river, and there were not many of them," Melia continued to speak. "Her name was Ninuie."

"I do believe that is an elvish name," Arianne revealed. "The River Elves, to be certain. Have you sought her among the elves dwelling along the Yantra? They may know of her or her people in Eden Halas." Arianne made a note to make inquiries on Melia's behalf when this was all over. Queen Syanne took an interest in the human folk living in the area surrounding Halas, even if her husband disliked the idea of becoming friendly with their neighbours.

"I will be certain to do so now," Melia replied, taking in her suggestion. "For now, however, I would like to know why it is you are journeying so far north."

Now Melia had told them the truth about her origins, and Arianne could sense the sincerity of her words, she could not deny the watch guard the same courtesy. It seemed only fair. Now that Melia was their guide in the northlands, she would share the same risk if the enemy chose to hunt them down.

"I am on a quest," Arianne said finally, and saw the surprise in the woman's eyes.

"A quest?" Melia remarked with some astonishment. "Since when is it the duty of the queen to embark upon quests? Is that not a task for the king, or some other warrior in his service?"

"This is a quest I alone can fulfil," Arianne explained sombrely. "Celene and Keira chose to accompany me for they are too thick-headed to let me do this thing on my own," she threw them a smile.

"And even though one is an elf queen and the other warrior princess, neither can cook so I thought I'd better come along to make sure they don't starve," Keira grinned at Arianne and Celene.

"You are funny," Celene made a face at Keira, who laughed at the tongue pointed in her direction. "My queen requires my sword and she is my friend, how could I do any less?"

Overcome with a wave of emotion for the warrior of Angarad, Arianne extended her hand and was met by Celene's in a quick, affectionate squeeze.

"Besides," Celene faced front again, "how do I explain to her husband I let her ride off on her own?"

"Well, I am a watch guard in the service of the king, your husband," Melia said, turning her attention to Arianne, as she reacted her own conclusions about the queen's quest It could be no small thing if Arianne was willing to ride beyond the safe borders of the kingdom into the peril of the Frozen Mountains. "You have my solemn oath I will not reveal a word of what you tell me, unless you first permit it."

"Thank you," Arianne said appreciatively, believing the sincerity of her promise before explaining the situation. "I am with child. The announcement was made but a few weeks ago, so the rest of the kingdom may not be aware of it. My mother revealed to me an evil presence seeks to harm my child. The enemy desires to infuse my unborn babe with the spirit of Mael."

"Mael?" Melia's exclamation of shock was equal to almost everyone else who had been told this news.

"You know of Mael?" Celene stared at her.

"My people know the legends of the Celestial Gods, and their battles with the dark lord Maelog, who was also called Mael the Destroyer. We know Balfure was once his agents, and the Celestials vanquished him from the Sphere. This is indeed foul work."

"We have until the next full moon to reach the enemy, or else Arianne's babe will suffer the consequences," Celene explained now Arianne had fallen into silence.

"I see the reason for your haste," Melia replied. Thoughts of her own quest could wait for now, because if it was true and Mael's evil was attempting a return to the world, they would *all* suffer. "This enemy is at the Frozen Mountains?"

"We believe so," Keira answered. "I've heard terrible stories about the place. Are they all true?"

Melia shrugged. "I have encountered some who travelled that far north and the reports vary. The mountains are perhaps the oldest in Avalyne. I am told at one time they were the border of Mael's lands."

"I know of that report," Arianne spoke re-joining the conversation. "We believe Sanhael wasn't completely destroyed—it lies beneath Mael's Pit, intact. The enemy has been drawing the remnants of Balfure's army to him, taking his place as their master."

"That might explain some of the activity the Watch Guard has witnessed of late. The beserkers are travelling north for certain. Not just beserkers—there is rumour of shifters on the move too, though these cannot be confirmed," Melia revealed.

"Shifters?" Keira turned to Celene and Arianne in question. "Like the Disciples?"

"No, not like the Disciples," Celene answered. "These are true shifters. They can assume the shape of any person or creature for as long as possible. Even *years.*"

The thought a being could maintain the charade of becoming someone you knew for years chilled Arianne to the bone.

"The enemy is giving Mael an army worthy of him," Arianne replied, glancing at her belly and shuddering at the fate awaiting her baby.

No, she told herself resolutely, *I will save you, little one. No matter what I am forced to do, I will not allow you to be taken.*

"Then it was fortunate I happened along," Melia answered, noticing the subtle shift of Arianne's hand against her belly, and felt for the queen facing such a terrible threat to her child. "Though how much, I did not know until this moment."

"It will get worse the closer to the mountains we get," Celene met Arianne's gaze. "You know that."

"I do," Arianne whispered softly. "But our hope lies in secret. He does not know I am coming. He may still think I am in Sandrine and it is Dare who is riding out to face him."

"The less he knows, the better," Celene added.

"In that case, we should not remain in one place long," Melia added. "We should make for Angarad at first light. The journey is four days away on horseback, but if we stay off the roads and travel by night, we may maintain our anonymity."

"And we need fresh supplies," Keira reminded them. "We lost a bit thanks to those beserkers, and we're going to need winter gear if we're going into the Frozen Mountains."

"That is as good a plan as any," Celene nodded her approval. "What say you Arianne?"

"I am disposed towards it," she smiled at Melia. "And I thank you for joining us in this quest. It cannot have been an easy choice for you to aid us. The risks are great."

"The risks are even greater if this enemy is allowed carry out his scheme," Melia returned Arianne's smile with one of similar warmth. "It was difficult enough vanquishing Balfure from Avalyne. I think preventing a similar darkness from falling across the world is the shared responsibility of all who live in it."

Arianne had not thought of it quite that way, but she was glad to hear Melia's words nonetheless, and felt herself considerably fortunate to have the companianship of such brave women. It gave her hope enough there would be an end to this nightmare, and would see her back with her beloved Dare.

Chapter Eleven

The Splinter

The Circle arrived at the foot of the Baffin Range four days after leaving Eden Halas.

Dare's mood was dark after learning from his mother Arianne, Keira, and Celene barely escaped with their lives from Caras Anara. Ronen had even more reason for worry when told his wife was injured by the sting of one of the spiders infesting the small seaside village. Fortunately, the Lord of Gislaine was able to take comfort in knowing, as always, Celene was more than capable of extricating herself from such situations, and anyone else who happened to be with her at the time.

Of course, their stay did not pass without Hadros worsening Dare's mood by rebuking him about keeping a better eye on his wife, instead of letting her roam the countryside with an inadequate escort. It had taken Aeron to keep the king from physically expressing his displeasure upon Hadros' face. Ronen was none too happy either about hearing Celene described as 'inadequate', and told Hadros he was exceedingly lucky Celene was minding her manners, or else he would have learned what she thought of his prejudice.

In an effort to limit further quarrels between Dare and his oldest son, Halion saw them supplied and sent on their way as quickly as possible. Provided with useful intelligence as to which route Arianne was taking to cross the Baffin, Dare realised the women were approaching Angarad through the Splinter Pass. Angarad was familiar territory for Celene, and despite Syanne's warning of the danger to travellers who crossing the pass, it was still the fastest way to reach her homeland.

"This is intolerable," Aeron complained as they rode along the foothills of the mountain, towards the Splinter. "We were certain all of the great spiders were driven out of Highland Woods when Balfure was destroyed."

The battle with the spiders had been an ongoing concern since Balfure unleashed them into the woods when he failed to breach the Veil and reach Eden Halas. For the next three decades, the elves were in constant battle with the creatures who laid waste to almost all the wildlife in the forest, to say nothing about the human inhabitants in the area.

After the destruction of Balfure, Aeron led his father's men in a sustained effort to drive the foul creatures from of Eden Halas, and believed he was successful to that end. Learning of Caras Anara's fate now meant he was not as thorough as he thought and an entire village was destroyed. He felt responsible for those deaths even though he knew he had done all he could to eradicate them forever.

"It's not your fault, you know," Kyou remarked, as he sat upon the pony he acquired from the Halas. Aeron's silence for most of their journey told the dwarf he was most likely still troubled by what had transpired. Unlike his father, Kyou knew Aeron held great affection for humans, and thinking he might have been responsible for the deaths of so many of them would weigh heavily on him.

"You know me too well," Aeron returned quietly, yet Kyou's words did nothing to assuage his guilt. "I do," he nodded, "and I know for an elf, you have a tendency towards self-recrimination, even when you are not at fault."

"I was in charge of the party to drive the wretched beasts from Halas," he declared hotly. "I should have known they were too easy to kill. Such creatures make it a habit of learning to finding new breeding grounds. I should have anticipated they merely found a new home, not they were vanquished for good."

"It is always easy to make such claims in hindsight. You had no reason to believe they weren't destroyed," Kyou countered. "I have fought with you in battle, my friend, and you seldom leave things to chance. You did all that could have been done to destroy the things. Now, you should focus your attention on ridding Avalyne of them for good instead of moaning about how it could have been stopped."

"As usual, you are too blunt for your own good," Aeron frowned, but could not find fault in Kyou's words. There was too much truth to it. He knew he would not shed his culpability at their deaths, even if Kyou was right. He would avenge Caras Anara. Once this quest to save Arianne was done, he would return home and assemble a group of his father's finest men. They would go to Caras Anara and end the threat of the syphi once and for all.

"But I am right," Kyou crowed.

"You are. How is that possible? You dwarves aren't known for your subtlety."

Kyou laughed, and Aeron would have joined him, except a sudden gust of wind swept out of nowhere, dislodging rocks and dust from their place on the ground to be borne into the air. A great chill fell upon them, and although it was bright and sunny not long ago, the sun suddenly disappeared behind thick, heavy clouds. The change in weather was so swift Aeron barely registered the change in the wind, a thing elves were always the first to notice.

As he looked up the sky, he watched the dark clouds hang pendulously over their heads, and without warning, the snow started to fall. Slowly at first, but as the wind intensified, the precipitation matched its ferocity. As they approached the Splinter, the snowfall continued with such speed it was becoming difficult to see the pass ahead or the terrain they had just crossed. The tall trees of the alpine forest could only be seen as dark pointed silhouettes through the whirling gale of ice and sleet.

"There is something afoot here," Tamsyn cried out, making his voice heard over the wind as he rode to the front and nudged his steed next to Dare's.

"What do you mean?" Dare demanded. While he did find it strange the weather had come upon them so swiftly, it was entirely possible it was a natural occurrence. He had seen a freak storm or two in his time.

"It feels as if someone has produced this storm for our benefit," the mage replied gravely.

"Then we best cross the pass as soon as we can. Once we are on the other side, the mountains shall shield us from its might."

Tamsyn was not so certain. The gale force winds were now bringing down the snow from the top of the mountain, and it was coming down on them in large, heavy balls. He wondered if an avalanche was eminent. The sudden snap of cold made everyone pull their cloaks and their coats to their bodies. Even the horses were uneasy. Spirit, Tamsyn's trusted steed, snorted his displeasure, and the mage placed a hand across the stallion's neck, trying to soothe its anxiety.

"Tamsyn, can you sense it?" Aeron asked him as they neared the pass.

"Yes, I can," the mage nodded.

"I have a bad feeling about this," Tully stated. His livelihood depended on being able to read the weather and nothing about this seemed normal. "This doesn't feel right."

"Are you developing elven senses too?" Kyou teased him a smile, but it was a nervous one. There was something to all this. They could all feel it now.

"Let's hurry," Ronen insisted, digging his heels into the side of his horse. "Maybe we can outrun it."

His horse bolted forward, breaking into a gallop towards the opening in the mountain.

"Ronen, wait!" Dare shouted, but the howl of the wind swept his voice out of Ronen's hearing.

The king swore loudly when he saw his friends disappearing into the sudden blizzard. He could do nothing but follow suit, hoping to save Ronen from himself, before he put too much distance between them. When there was magic afoot, it was best to be cautious, even if the danger did not appear overt. The others followed his stead, keeping the Bân in their sights as they followed him into the breach.

Dare knew that it was Ronen's love for his wife making him behave so irrationally. The king could well understand his fear, but Dare spent too many years rushing in where others feared to tread, and learned the wisdom of caution and patience. Years of evading Balfure and his Disciples taught him that much.

The walls of the canyon soon flanked them. The storm seemed to grow a thousand fold in its ferocity, until it became too hard to see through the blanket of snow. Dare could see Ronen ahead and was gratified his old friend had come to his senses to slow down. Kyou and Tully already brought their mounts to a halt, awaiting the arrival of the king.

"Fools!" Dare snapped as he reached them. "We have no idea what lies ahead!"

"We were riding after him to stop him!" Kyou retorted, somewhat offended Dare would think them foolish enough to act so rashly.

"He can't hear us!" Tully broke into the conversation. "We tried to call him before he got too far ahead of us but the wind is too loud. We wanted to tell him."

"Tell him what?" Dare stared at them in confusion as the others caught up with the trio.

"About that!" Kyou pointed at the ground.

Through the snow, Dare saw what it was bringing them to such a complete standstill. The skull of a man long dead stared at him with through empty eye sockets. The king searched the ground and made the same grisly discovery Celene and Arianne made days before. He saw the irregular formations of rock that travelled along their path and knew nothing he was seeing was caused by natural erosion.

Before he could think to utter another word, he heard burst of sound through the wail of the wind that made him jump. It was like a clap of thunder echoing down the canyon over the wind screaming about them. Dare's heart began to pound as Tamsyn brought his mount to halt beside him. "We need to get out of here!"

"I won't leave Ronen!" Dare said defiantly. "Take the others from here and I will go find him."

"No!" Tamsyn grabbed his arm before he could gallop away. "You are the king! I will go!"

"I *am* the king and it is my choice!"

"LOOK OUT!"

Aeron's sudden shout ensured there was no choice to be made, because the elf's cry was imbued with such panic both men stopped arguing immediately.

Dare and Tamsyn looked up and saw a huge boulder tumbling towards them. Dare dug his heels into his horse and sent it running, but Tamsyn had not the speed for such a hasty departure. Instead, the mage raised his staff and the dark gem embedded in its length glowed before the boulder shattered in mid-air, sending fragments in all directions. No sooner had its debris crumbled across the ground, another crashing sound was heard. This time, the deadly projectile from above landed near Tully's pony, forcing the animal to bolt ahead. Kyou's mount reared up on its hind legs as more rocks started to fall around them.

"Ride!" Dare ordered, unable to think of anything else to save them from the deadly barrage.

He didn't need give the order twice, for the others were already surging ahead. Dare looked upward to see more boulders tumbling off the top of the mountain into the pass. He pulled the reins of his horse as one of the large fragments covered him with its shadow, and dug his heels deeper into the animal's flank to escape it. The horse snorted angrily and bolted forward with enough speed to ensure when the rock came crashing down, it would not be with the king under it.

Dare's relief at escaping certain death was short lived. He saw Kyou's horse rear onto its hind legs in fright after a boulder landed in front of it. The dwarf tried valiantly to remain in the saddle, but he was unseated easily. Dare thought absurdly this experience was not going to improve Kyou's opinion regarding horse riding.

Aeron, who was riding with the dwarf, immediately pulled up the reins of his horse, forcing it to turn around. Leaning down with one hand on the reins, Aeron reached for Kyou who was scrambling to his feet after his unceremonious dismount. Another large boulder landed behind them and began rolling forward, propelled by its momentum to pursue the duo. Aeron proved far too swift to be brought to an untimely end this way as he grabbed Kyou's arm and swept the dwarf onto the back of his horse, before riding out of harm's way.

Dare continued his own efforts to escape the deadly onslaught of rocks raining down on them. He could see Tully struggling to escape the rock fall while Aeron and Kyou seemed to be making good pace. The farmer was weaving expertly through the crashing rocks around them. The king attempted to determine the source of this deadly storm, but could see little through the blizzard of rock and snow. Despite the struggle to avoid the crashing rocks around them, Dare noticed the bombardment was isolated to where the circle was attempting to cross.

"Tamsyn!" Dare shouted for the mage, suspecting the mage might be able to discern what was happening and stop this before any of them were killed.

Dare saw Spirit first. The great steed seemed to know its rider was being hailed and paused in its steps until the king reached them. Dare rode next to Tamsyn, knowing they could not linger long.

"The rocks follow us Tamsyn!" Dare stated as another great boulder crashed alongside of him and he had to struggle to stay his horse from bolting in panic.

"I know," Tamsyn nodded, his eyes climbing upwards to the top of the canyon. "I do believe there is an ice troll is at work here."

"An ice troll?" Kyou's eyes shot up. "There's an ice troll on the mountain?"

"I fear so," Tamsyn retorted. Ice trolls were the offspring of the Mael's Primordials. They were capable of commanding the weather to bring about storms, such as the one they were now experiencing. They were ancient and rare, emerging from the ice caverns deep in the mountains only when they were hungry so they could feed on man flesh. Great hulking beasts covered in white fur, they were powerful enough to bring about sudden ice storms and rain down the hail of rocks the circle was presently trying to avoid.

Boulders continued to crash all around them as their mounts descended further and further into panic from the rocks shattering about them in perilous near misses. The troll's frustration at being unable to crush one of them caused it intensify the assault. Their ability to prevail was making the troll more determined to kill them, and it would not be long before one of them was crushed by the barrage.

"We must keep moving!" Dare insisted, seeing Aeron and Kyou disappear through the snowfall. He knew to remain in place was to invite disaster.

"I'll tend to this," Tamsyn shouted. "You take the others and go!"

Dare stared at him. "You're going to fight it?"

"This is an ice troll, I can deal with it! GO!" Tamsyn boomed, showing the king his patience was finite and he would tolerate no more argument.

The bombardment around them was becoming worse and only the storm prevented the giant from throwing his rocks accurately. It was only a matter of time before one of those deadly boulders met their mark. Dare saw the resolve in Tamsyn's eyes and knew he had to obey. Even kings knew obedience when faced with the wrath of mage, and Dare knew Tamsyn did not give him orders lightly. With reluctance, the king nodded in compliance and quickly averted his gaze to Tully. "Stay close to me you, this will not be easy."

"Tamsyn…" Tully opened his mouth to speak when he saw a large rock looming over them.

"HURRY!" Tamsyn ordered and Tully instinctively broke his pony into a gallop. Following Dare, Tully cast a look over his shoulder and saw the mage escaping the reach of the boulder that crushing the space where they had been. Realising he had to trust Tamsyn to his own devices, Tully returned his attention to Dare before he, too, rode through the canyon without looking back.

Tamsyn felt fragments of rock biting into his skin as the rock shattered into a multitude of smaller pieces, scattering across the snow-covered ground. He squinted as he looked above and saw there was indeed a troll perched at the top. The creature was as he remembered it—tall and hulking, covered in grey white fur with two large teeth protruding past its lip from its lower jaw. It saw Dare and the others riding away, and gave chase by flinging as many rocks at the parting trio as possible. Fortunately, this allowed Tamsyn the time to deal with him before one of those rocks met their mark.

Taking a deep breath, Tamsyn remained steady on Spirit. He raised his arms, clasping his staff on each end as he gazed at the turbulent heavens above. Whether or not the troll saw him, Tamsyn could not say. Often with such creatures, its attention was quick to wander and it was more concerned with killing the riders it could see clearly, than the one alone. Holding his staff up high, Tamsyn did not need to speak the words to make the spell work. Only novice conjurers required such things.

The ice troll was not the only one who knew how to summon storms.

A crack of lightning splintered the sky with a thunderous roar. Spidery tendrils of blue and white struck the top of the mountain, creating a tremendous sound making all the other noises before it pale in comparison. The troll screamed above the howl of the wind and Tamsyn did not need to instruct Spirit to move. The horse, sensing the danger, broke into a gallop as the ledge upon which the troll made its murderous assault crumbled underfoot. Tamsyn looked up and saw an avalanche of earth, rock and snow falling to the ground.

He thought he might have seen the creature itself, but the mage could not be certain, as he was too busy riding out of the pass before it was buried.

As he rode away from the destruction, he heard a scream through the blizzard that was neither wind nor shattering rock, but a voice filled with fury and despair. It sounded like it was falling to the ground from a great height before coming to an abrupt end, as the pass was completely buried in rock. The ground shuddered beneath Spirit's hooves and even Tamsyn could feel the tremors in his bones.

With that cataclysmic end, the storm abated. The wind died like a dying gasp and quickly slipped into a whisper. The gale blew away the clouds and, with the departure of thick gray canopy, the blue sky made its reappearance. Tamsyn felt the sunshine upon his face and knew the danger was passed. He brought Spirit to a halt and looked behind him at what he had wrought. The passageway was now completely sealed by rock, stone and soon to be melting snow. The Splinter was no more.

"Tamsyn!" he heard Dare calling after him.

Facing forward, he saw the king's circle galloping back to him, having turned back when the weather shifted for the better. He could see the relief in all their eyes.

"Is it dead?" Kyou asked, peering over Aeron's shoulder at the mage.

"It will cause no more mischief," Tamsyn confirmed, though he was never pleased to end any creature, even one who deserved death.

"Perhaps next time you shall bear little more caution, Lord of Gislaine," Tamsyn gave Ronen a reproachful glare for having rushed off so recklessly into the pass to begin with.

"I have been properly chastised by my king already," Ronen confessed, terribly embarrassed his impulsiveness almost cost him and his friends their lives. He did not think it was possible to hear the king shout so loudly through a blizzard, but somehow Dare managed it. What was worse, it was to Ronen's shame he could not refute any of Dare's angry words "I promise, you will not see me behave so rashly again."

"Not unless you wants to explain to your wife why you are the Lord of Gislaine in the prison tower when we return to Sandrine," Dare grumbled.

"If you were not my King…" Ronen started to say.

Dare did not let him finish, "I'd do more than just *shouting* at you."

Chapter Twelve

Angarad

Arianne and her companions reached the hills of Angarad three days after leaving the Splinter behind.

Despite being a thousand years old, it was yet another place Arianne was never able to visit. She wondered what it was like for her people in the days when they explored the world extensively, basking in its richness and variety, freed from the limitations of mortality.

Had the war with Mael been so terrible it drove out of them the adventuring spirit for good? What happened during the Primordial Wars to make them decide seclusion behind the Veil was much safer than living in the world? These were questions not even her mother could answer, and Arianne shuddered to think what would happen if she failed in her quest and Mael was returned to the world. What would they do then?

Still, despite never having set foot within its territory, Arianne knew Angarad as the land of the Warrior Caste. Its people became tempered by years of war and hardened by the harsh weather this country endured. During the spring and summer months, Angarad was a beautiful place with rolling hills and grassy plains, home to the magnificent Angarad horses. The rest of the year, the harsh winds from the Jagged Teeth and the Frozen Mountains created a perfect storm of wind and ice, bringing hard winters to Angarad.

The extremes of weather made the people of Angarad hardy and disciplined. They were accustomed to living a rigid existence during the winter months and as a result, were known for their endurance. Until they discovered their propensity as warriors, the people of Angarad were horse masters and animal breeders, who dealt in cattle and goats, driving their herds across the land like migratory birds. They were, for most part, a peaceful folk.

Their army was moderate, formed only because its people were occasionally plagued by the remnants of Mael's army from the Primordial Wars. The evil god created many fell creatures from the depths of his twisted imagination, and not all of them were destroyed when he was captured by the Celestials. From time to time, the beasts would emerge from the Frozen Mountains and descend into Angarad, wreaking fear and destruction on the outlying villages. It was this duty that mostly occupied their time.

Balfure's invasion of Avalyne changed all that for good.

When the forces of Abraxes swept mightily brought an end to two thousand years of rule by House Icara in Carleon, it also ended the peaceful existence of Angarad. Overnight, Angarad found itself facing eminent invasion the same as Carleon. Horrified by the thought of occupation, particularly after witnessing the brutality of Balfure's beserkers and his ruthless Disciples upon Carleon's population, Angarad knew it had little choice but to fight.

For thirty-five years, Angarad would be constantly fighting battles to protect its borders against the relentless efforts of Balfure to add it to his empire. While they escaped the occupation befalling Carleon, the price of freedom was great and bloody. More sons and daughters of Angarad lay dead from its defence than any other land occupied by Balfure. War became a way of life for the Angarad. The result was the creation of a warrior society, second to none in Avalyne.

It was into this world, Celene was born.

By the time of her birth, so many warriors had fallen in battle there were not enough men left to replace the ones lost. Women were left to fend for themselves. It seemed the logical conclusion if women were under the same threat from the enemy as men, they ought to learn how to defend themselves. The decision to allow women into the ranks was born out of desperation, but succeeded in setting apart Angarad from every other kingdom in Avalyne.

Women now found themselves applied with the same expectation to fight as any man. Those who could not fight bore children to become warriors who could. This distinction gave them greater power over their own destiny, as young girls grew learning to defend themselves.

Children of Angarad now began their instruction with the War Masters at the tender age of eight. By the time they reached their fifteenth year, they were proficient in the use of the sword, the bow, and the horse. On their eighteenth year, they were conscripted into the ranks, and would remain so for ten years, until discharged. If they survived, they were released from service and allowed to begin their lives anew. Many found, after a life dedicated to soldiering, they did not know of any other existence, and usually remained in the ranks.

Now there was peace for the foreseeable future, Arianne wondered what came next for this country. What became of warriors when there were no more wars to fight?

* * *

Melia was true to her word when she claimed to know of an alternate route across the Baffin which did not require retracing their steps back to the Splinter. Instead, the path across took only a few hours to reach, after departing the way station they used to spend the night. It involved using a goat track known to some of the Guard, but mostly by shepherds who tended the flocks. While they saw neither goat nor shepherd when they travelled across the narrow and uneven trail, the evidence of their presence was left behind by the spoors in the dirt.

They reached Angarad at dusk. It became difficult for the company to see much of the land, except for the silhouette of the Eirian Hills in the distance. Once across, their route took them west near the trading post of Horwyck. With the sun surrendering the sky to the night and the crescent moon gazing down upon them, Celene suggested they take shelter in the town. Once they left Angarad behind them, the opportunity to find a place capable of providing them with a warm bed and meal would be far and few between, if there were any at all.

In truth, once they left Angarad and entered what was known as the Torn Lands, they had no idea what awaited them.

As much as Arianne wished to keep going, she knew she needed the respite from travel. Elven fortitude could only withstand so much, and after weeks in the saddle and sleeping on the ground, she wanted a little creature comfort, even if it was to sleep in a comfortable bed with a roof above her head.

Horwyck was protected behind high walls constructed by the logs of thick alpine trees, shaved to a point at the top. The entrance was barred by a set of equally formidable wooden gates that could only be opened from the inside by the watchman on duty. Above the points of the tall fence, Arianne saw the roofs of merchant buildings, with only a few windows flickering with light. Considering the late hour in which they were arriving, she was not surprised.

Celene dismounted and took the lead, approaching the gate, and tugging at the chord ringing the bell mounted on a pole near it. A short time elapsed before a dour and grimy looking man peered through the small peephole and glared suspiciously at the four strangers coming to Horwyck at this time at night. For a moment it appeared as if he might not let them in, until he realised he was facing four women. His manner softened considerably and he opened the door to welcome them in.

Once safely inside its walls, Horwyck appeared much larger than its fortifications would have visitors believe. Although it was difficult to tell because they arrived in town so late and most of its inhabitants were still in bed, there were more than enough homes and merchant houses to show this was a thriving community. Arianne was quite amused when the inn they happened upon for their lodgings that night was called *The Mysterious Elf.* She wondered if its proprietor had ever actually met one of her kind.

It appeared not, because the round faced matron who owned the establishment was quite chuffed to meet Arianne. The lady knew she was an elf but had no idea she was playing host to the queen of Carleon. Mistress Dora was more than capable of providing her four new guests with rooms to suit their needs, and a warm supper before bed. This suited Keira greatly as she was happy to relinquish the cooking duties for the night.

It was almost dawn when they finally slipped into their comfortable beds, sated by a hearty repast that had them all falling quickly into a fitful slumber.

* * *

It was mid-afternoon when Celene and Melia awoke. They were accustomed to riding for days, and so they were faster on their feet than Arianne and Keira, who were not accustomed to the life at all. Instead of waking their two sleeping companions, Celene and Melia went into the town, attending to their horses and also looking to purchasing food supplies and warmer clothes for their journey north.

As they moved through the market square perusing the wares, Celene took the opportunity to speak of something preying on her mind since leaving Sandrine. She said nothing to Arianne for fear of worrying her, and Keira had reservation enough about her part in this quest. Melia, however, was a watch guard who fought in battle the same as her. Together, they share enough common ground for Celene to bring Melia into her confidence.

"What do you know of the Torn Lands?" Celene asked, as they walked back to *The Mysterious Elf*, saddle bags filled with supplies slung over their shoulders.

Melia threw her a sidelong glance and shrugged. "Very little," she confessed. "I know because of the Primordial Wars, the land is scarred. There are tales of folk who have attempted to settle there, but whether they survived or not remain unknown. They did not return to tell the tale."

"My knowledge of the place is the same," Celene admitted with a frown. "While we were in the market, I thought I might consult a map maker, but there are none to be found of that land."

"There is rumour one has to pass an ancient wood to reach the mountains of ice, but those woods are cursed. Something lives there, something that feasts on the flesh of men," Melia said, reluctant to pass on that bit of information because there was no real proof of this. Men in taverns often told each other fanciful stories to make themselves look knowledgeable to their friends. "But it is just a rumour," she emphasised.

"It may have some truth," Celene returned. "Dare's mother, Queen Syanne, gave us a similar warning about the Frozen Mountains when we were in Eden Halas."

"The elves are long lived," Melia commented. "Her information might come from a source that was actually there."

"Perhaps," Celene frowned, as they turned up the street and saw the lodging house in the distance. "There is more about this quest that bothers me."

"Such as?" Melia raised a brow and waited for an answer. The Lady of Gislaine commanded respect and what concerned her, concerned Melia. Celene's reputation was strengthened by the fact she was one of the king's trusted companions. She had travelled with him across Avalyne as he rallied support to fight Balfure. She, herself, battled at Astaroth.

"The enemy," Celene stated flatly. "He has been watching Arianne all this time, waiting for the baby to come. He must know she is on the move."

"I thought you were hoping he would think she is cloistered away in Sandrine, and it is the king he thinks is coming for him."

"I assumed the ruse would only last for a few days at best, and eventually he would know something is happening. So far, we have no indication he is even aware she is not where she should be, and if so, we have heard no news of anything hunting us. What peril we have encountered is due to chance, with creatures left over from Balfure's forces, not anything directed at us specifically."

"Perhaps he waits for her to come to him," Melia suggested, but she saw Celene's point.

"If all his plans are dependent on Arianne delivering her baby, would he allow her free reign across Avalyne, where any number of threats might kill her?"

"He might believe we are capable of protecting her," she pointed out, but that was assuming a great deal, Melia thought, understanding Celene's fears.

"Something capable of freeing Mael and placing it in an unborn child must have same way of keeping track of his prey. That we have not seen any trace of it, worries me," Celene said, as they finally reached the inn and stepped inside.

"Perhaps he is not as clever as he thinks," Melia pointed out, stepping inside.

"Or maybe," Celene said glumly, "he is exceedingly patient."

Arianne was none too impressed Celene and Melia allowed her to spend almost a day in bed, but understood their reasons. The fact she slept well into the afternoon spoke to her state of exhaustion and she supposed Keira needed the rest too. As the sun began to set on their first day in Horwyck, she felt more rested than she had felt in weeks, and the ache in her limbs subsided somewhat. She stood in front of the mirror in her room and examined herself, taking note of the slight swell in her abdomen, showing her little prince was growing steadily.

His growth was another reminder why they had to leave. The next full moon was weeks away and they had much ground to cover. It was agreed they would eat one last meal in Horwyck and be on their way again. There was the whole of Angarad to cross. Then, they would reach the Torn Lands, a place as mysterious as it was supposedly full of peril.

Arianne tried not to think about Dare, about what he must think of her for embarking on such a quest without telling him. She knew in her heart he was most likely in pursuit. If she lingered in Horwyck long enough he would find her.

But she would not do that. His safety was everything to her, and Arianne could not bear to sacrifice the life of the father for the son. For a thousand years, she had awaited someone with whom she could give her heart completely. The cruelty of fate had seen to it he was human. One lifetime was all they had together, when they should have all the ages of this world. Now this quest could break them apart even sooner.

No—she would not risk his life. She would deal with the enemy. She would save their child.

There was no room for all four of them to eat together in their room, but fortunately the tavern was not terribly busy. They were able to share a table without much scrutiny from the men in the place. Four women alone would not go unnoticed by the male patrons, especially when all were young and fair. Their mission was carried out so far on the strength of its secrecy, and Arianne did not wish that to change.

"So, where to from here?" Keira asked, as she sat at the long wooden table situated in the farthest end of the tavern, away from the bulk of the inn's patrons. The evening was starting to draw the working men into the establishment for their night's drinking and Keira ignored the sound of their raucous conversation several tables away. Below her, the meal of meat shanks was almost gone, and Keira gave her compliment to Mistress Dora, who certainly knew how to provide a good meal.

"Do not look at me," Melia commented when she saw Keira's eyes on her. "This is Celene's country," she said to the Lady of Gislaine. "I only brought you across the Baffin. From here on, it's her job to guide us."

Celene lowered her glass of draught and wiped her lip daintily before replying with a chuckle. "I am up to task, I assure you," she lifted her glass at Melia, who did the same. Although not usually a drinker, she could not resist drinking at least one mug of Angarad brew while she was home. "We will head across the Safrie Plains towards the river."

The Safrie was the main waterway of Angarad. It began its life at Lake Twyn and ended at the mouth of the Brittle Sea. Parts of it were deep enough to sail, and some ships travelled up its length to the second largest city of Angarad—Korrigan.

"We will keep our direction easterly," Celene continued. "I would prefer we stick to the plains. At this time of year with the weather turning cold, there will be few people about, and we can maintain our anonymity."

"Good," Arianne agreed, finishing the last of her meal and pushing away her plate. In truth, the meal was not sitting well with her and she suspected she was going to start experiencing some of the less charming aspects of pregnancy, in particular the morning sickness. "The second full moon approaches and I do not want to waste any time if we can avoid it."

"I agree," Celene replied, when she noted Melia's eyes were staring intently past them "What is it?"

Melia dropped her gaze to her glass, as if caught doing something she should not be doing, and then spoke in a quiet tone. "There's a man in the corner table. He watches us intently."

"Well, we're four women unescorted." Keira glanced back and saw the man staring at them. "He's probably just ogling. I don't think he means any harm."

"Perhaps," Celene said, not liking the attention. "But maybe we should consider leaving nonetheless." She swept her gaze across the table and saw they had all finished eating. Melia and Celene had brought the horses to the hitching rail outside the tavern so they could leave immediately after their meal.

Arianne had no argument with this, and was glad her hair covered her ears. She stood up from the table and slid her hood over her head, concealing her face even more. Keeping her eyes fixed on her companions, she did not turn her attention to the man at all, wanting to give him no sign she noticed him. Melia took the lead, keeping Arianne behind her, with Keira following the queen.

Celene allowed all three of her friends to go before she cast a final look at the man. He was old, with a scar running over a milky eye that was obviously blind. He looked like a trapper, for he wore the furs of various small animal pelts against the leather of his clothes. When their eyes met, she nodded in a gesture of politeness, seeing no reason to be rude or behave as if she and her companions had anything to hide.

They left the inn, rumbling with chatter of people, into the relative quiet of the evening outside. When Celene emerged through the doors, she saw Arianne, Keira, and Melia already at the horses, preparing to leave.

"Perhaps he recognised one of us," Celene shrugged, trying to dispel the worry she could see in Arianne's face.

"You, perhaps," Arianne pointed out, "but he could have seen me at Dare's coronation."

"You might be just a face he found pretty to look at," Keira declared, trying to dispel the tension. They would soon be away from here and on route across Angarad. The man was of little importance.

Until the door to the inn opened behind them and he stepped out into the night.

"I know what you are," he said pointing at them.

Celene stepped forward, placing herself between the man and the queen, "Arianne, mount on your horse and get going."

Arianne did not argue and quickly climbed onto saddle, though she disliked the idea of leaving Celene to deal with this man when it was clearly she he had issue with.

"She's a monster!" the man bellowed louder, this time attracting the attention of the few people on the street. They stopped to stare at what was happening.

"Go!" Celene ordered, taking a step backwards towards her own horse. "Melia, get them away from here. I will follow shortly."

Melia nodded and mounted her horse quickly, even as Arianne and Keira were starting to trot away. She cast a gaze back at Celene, reluctant to leave the Lady of Gislaine, but duty bound to stay close to the queen. "We will wait for you beyond the gates."

The man lurched forward when he saw Arianne and Keira riding away. Celene raced forward brandishing her sword, jabbing its point at him to halt him in his steps. She held the blade, poised before his neck. The action made Melia pause momentarily, but when Keira and Arianne continued down the street, she dug her heels into her horse's flank and trotted after them.

"You're letting it get away!" the man cursed her. "You need to kill it before it escapes!"

"No one is killing anyone!" Celene barked, pressing the blade against his throat with enough pressure to let him know she would use if he pushed her to it

"You don't know what you've done!" he spat. "I know their stink. They look like us, but they're not!" He tried to convince her, a hint of desperation intermingled with the fury in his eyes.

"I know well what they are," Celene retorted. "Or what she is, and she has never been anything but kind. I do not know where this hatred comes from, but that is your own affair. I give you one warning, old soldier, come after us again, and this conversation will not end so calmly. Understood?"

By now, they had drawn a crowd, which made Celene even more frustrated by the situation. She had hoped to keep their presence a secret. Without knowing what means the enemy was using to keep Arianne under observation, she had no idea if this episode would give them away.

"You can't trust them!" The man tried to convince her. "They're not like us! They have no allegiance to anyone but their own. If they're kind, it's because they're trying to trick us!"

"I have no time to bandy words with you, old soldier," Celene lowered her blade, conscious of her audience as she retreated to her horse. It was safe to leave now she could no longer hear the hoof beats of Arianne and the others' horses. "Do not follow us," she warned.

Celene turned around and quickly mounted her horse, grateful the old man had not decided to put up a fight once she sheathed her sword. Instead, he stood rooted to the spot, staring at her with an unsettling look of desperation.

"You're a fool! I have dealt with them before. You think she's your friend, but she's *not*! She'll turn on your like a rabid bitch dog and tear our your throat while you sleep. It's what her kind do! They pretend to be one of you, but they're really not!"

What possible experience could this man have with the elves to make him hate them with such vehemence? Celene thought of Arianne and Aeron, of the friendship and trust between them. She could never imagine either of them behaving the way this man was describing.

"I do not know where this hatred comes from, but it has nothing to do with me or my friends," Celene declared as she stared down at him from her saddle. "But we are done here. Follow us at your own peril."

With that, she tugged the reins of her horse and rode away into the night.

Chapter Thirteen

Shifters

Ever since they encountered the ice troll at the Splinter, a feeling of dread had begun to occupy the thoughts of the king, though he spoke of it to no one.

Whether or not his companions suspected the fear he was starting to feel, he could not say. He only knew it had taken root in his heart and was not letting go. With the passage of the Splinter now buried so completely it was impossible to search it, he thought of the bones he saw on the ground, the remains of travellers who did not have the benefit of a mage to see them through safely.

There was no telling how long the creature had been waylaying travellers with its deadly barrage of rock and stone. The snowfall concealed the true extent of its feasting, but the bones were obviously so many it was hard to distinguish where one ended and another began. The urgency of the situation kept Dare from examining the bones closely, and now they were away from the place, he had to wonder if Arianne, Keira, and Celene passed through the same passage, had they survived?

Tamsyn said nothing about them being dead, but the mage did not always give him the truth he ought to hear, only what was needed. What if it was required he kill the enemy, even if Arianne was dead? *No, she wasn't.* He told himself defiantly. *She wasn't dead.* He would feel it. Somehow, even without the power of Sight Lylea possessed, he would know if Arianne was not in this world.

Because he would not know how to go on without her, if she was.

Once they crossed the Splinter, they would ride towards the Eirian Hills, because Dare knew Celene would be too practical to add so many miles to their journey by going to Wyndfyre and sheltering with her folk. With the second moon approaching, their aim would be to make best speed towards the Frozen Mountains by taking the most direct route there. If they had indeed passed through the Splinter unhindered, they would be bound for River Safrie to the take Bedvyn Crossing into the Torn Lands.

As he entered Angarad, Dare could not help but think of the last time he had entered these lands, and under what cloud he had made that journey. His arrival in Angarad followed one of the worst periods of his life with both, he and Aeron in mourning for the loss of a dear friend. Until then, their company was a triumvirate. Celene and Kyou had yet to join their number. The third member of their set was a man of Sandrine, and Dare's oldest friend after Aeron—Braedan.

Dare met Braedan in his nineteenth year. He left Eden Halas the year before, having decided at the age of eighteen he imposed long enough on the House of Halion. Although Syanne did not wish him to leave, Dare knew it was time. Halion was never happy his queen defied him to raise a human baby. While he never treated Dare badly, his dislike was obvious by his cold demeanour. This indifference was mirrored in Halion's two sons, Hadros and Syannon, though Syannon was a little kinder. Only Aeron was a friend to him, but the young prince spent most of Dare's youth defending the woods of Halas against Balfure with his older brothers and so they saw each other infrequently.

Upon leaving Eden Halas, Dare travelled along the Yantra, with the intention of eventually arriving at the city of his birth—Sandrine.

For years, Syanne warned him against going there, fearful Balfure's agents might recognise him. In his mind, those agents were seeking an infant, and Dare could not imagine how anyone would recognise him as the lost heir of Icara, eighteen years later.

As an experienced woodsman and hunter thanks to his elven upbringing, Dare was able to travel up river, plying his skills at trade, without drawing attention. In this way, Dare lived for the first time in his life among his own race, and quickly discovered there was little difference between men and elves. Each race wanted the same things, dreamed the same dreams, and wished for the same freedom. The prejudice keeping them apart was wafer thin, and he wondered what it would take to break it.

It was also the first time he was able to see what effect the occupation of Balfure had upon his country.

He learned while Balfure ruled from Abraxes, his left his Disciples in Carleon to work his will. When Eden Ardhen was breached, and the elves of that realm chased away, the Disciples built a tower in its woods to celebrate of their victory. They called it Tor Ardhen as a final insult to Queen Lylea. From there, they maintained the occupation of the Southern Province while Tor Iolan was built to guard the Northern Province. Meanwhile, Tor Iridia stood watch over the dwarven homeland.

While Navarre managed to maintain control of Varaen to rule under the watchful eye of the Disciples, the supposed annihilation of House Icara left a void in the rule of Sandrine. With Balfure's continued assaults on Angarad and his designs beyond the Baffin, Balfure chose not to install a Disciple in Sandrine. Instead, he charged the rule of Carleon's former capital city to Braelan, oldest son of House Kelamon, who swore allegiance to Balfure when Carleon fell.

Braelan ruled as best he could, even though he was considered a traitor for taking up a position in Sandrine Keep. Through Braelan, Balfure's iron grip of Sandrine continued with beserkers troops enforcing terrible penalties on those who disobeyed or still resisted the rule of Abraxes. An ambitious man, Braelan knew pleasing the Aeth Lord would only strengthen his position, and while Selkirk and Navarre attempted to ease the oppression of their people during the occupation, Braelan did the complete opposite.

Determined to build a dynasty under Balfure's protection, Braelan eliminated all those in Sandrine capable of leading others in rebellion. Midnight raids by the beserkers resulted in large open graves being dug outside the city walls in the dead of night. Those same walls were used by Braelan to make examples of the particularly defiant.

Falla, Braelan's wife, whose family was killed in the purges following the fall of House Icara, watched in horror as the husband she loved turned into a monster. Determined to save her son from this corruption, Falla took charge of Braedan's education herself. She guided him as best she could to ensure he remained uninfluenced by his father's cruelty. As a result, Braedan grew up painfully aware of how despised his father was.

Dare and Braedan met purely by chance.

Braedan had taken to leaving Sandrine Keep, and frequenting taverns and inns in order to avoid being in his father's presence any longer than he had to. Showing his father he was a useless wastrel only good for drink, Braelan's disgust ensured Braedan was left to his own devices. They met at a tavern, two young men of the same age, drinking and talking about the world they'd lived in. During the entire time, Braedan tried to place why this new friend seemed so familiar. Only when he chanced upon one of few remaining portraits of House Icara not destroyed, did he recognise Dare's resemblance to his grandfather and realise who he befriended.

What should have been a mistake of monumental consequences became instead one of the most fortuitous moments
of Dare's life.

Braedan did not give him up to Braelan. Instead, he told Dare
Carleon needed its true king, and pledged himself to Dare's service. Dare, who at the time only had the makings of an idea in
his head about how to defeat Balfure, refused initially. Explaining to Braedan he was on a journey to learn about the occupied
lands and meet the races that might be of help to them, Dare
was touched when Braedan asked to accompany him.

They left Sandrine together and travelled the length and
breadth of Carleon. For the next five years, they created friendships amongst the peoples of the kingdom and learned how
many yearned to cast off Balfure's rule. They learnt of the desperate plight of the dwarves, hunted across the occupied ter-
ritories, finding refuge only in places far beyond the reach of
Abraxes. Braedan returned with him to Eden Halas when Dare
unveiled for the first time, his idea of an alliance with all the
races, followed by outright rejection from Halion.

Only Aeron saw the vision of Dare's proposal, and he advised
if Eden Halas would not listen then, it was time to seek a higher
authority who commanded all the elves. Leaving Eden Halas,
Aeron took him and Braedan, instead, to meet with High Queen
Lylea of Eden Taryn.

During this time, word had finally reached Balfure the lost
prince of Carleon was still alive.

The Aeth Lord's reaction was swift—Balfure wasted no time
sending out his Disciples—and for the next two years, they
hunted the trio with ruthless determination. It was outside the
woods of Barrenjuck where they were almost caught. In an effort to save Dare's life Braedan sacrificed himself by impersonat-
ing the exiled prince, and leading the Disciples away. The ruse
was simple and succeeded long enough for Dare to reach the
Green, but it came at a devastating cost.

Dare did not know when Braedan died or how much he suffered before the end, he only knew days after Tully led him out of the old wood, they were able to retrieve his broken body. They buried him in the Green, but after the war, Dare returned Braedan to Sandrine, where he was interred in the royal mausoleum.

Others would join his company, such as Celene, Kyou, and Tamsyn, but it would never feel the same as when he was nineteen, travelling the world, feeling free and invincible with his two best friends.

* * *

The company made camp at a ruined sentry post at the edge of the Eirian Hills when the sun started to set on the horizon.

"Aeron," Dare called out to the archer, who had taken position at the highest part of the still standing rock wall, maintaining a vigil on the surrounding area. "Kyou and I are going to scout the area, so keep your eyes sharp."

"Try not to wander too far," Aeron remarked with a little smile. "You know how easily you get lost."

"As easily as you can hold drink," Dare said sweetly before he headed off.

Even though Angarad was friendly territory, Dare was not so foolish as to think the enemy would not repeat the attempt on their lives with a new menace. The snow troll attack came out of nowhere, and now only Angarad lay between them and the Frozen Mountains, Dare expected some form of attack to ambush them on route.

Aeron nodded, watching Dare and the dwarf leaving the campsite to head towards the Mountain Wood, a moderately sized forest of tall trees deserving of a quick survey before they settled in for the night. The forest began on the slopes of the Baffin looming over them and spilled onto the base near the Splinter. To the west, the Eirian Hills were less imposing than the Baffin, and even in the darkness, Aeron imagined the beauty of the rolling hills resembling waves of green across the landscape.

As he observed and kept watch, he imagined the numerous battles taken place in this land, as Angarad fought to keep Balfure out. The sentry tower was destroyed only in the last twenty years, but enough moss and lichens had grown over the remaining stone walls to ensure it blended seamlessly into the landscape—so much so it was difficult to tell where it ended and the hills began.

As he kept watch, he felt the weight of something ominous pressing against his chest, but he did not voice it yet, because the warning could be premature. If the enemy was watching them, then it was possible Aeron was feeling that scrutiny, and there was nothing that screamed danger, just foreboding. There was so much darkness afoot in this quest he tried not to confuse immediate with prevalent.

In any case, the elf's keen vision kept all his companions within sight. Each of their group was engaged in their own undertakings as they settled down to rest from the day's journeying. Aeron could still see Dare walking alongside of Kyou away from their camp, while on the far side of the tower, Ronen was seeing to their horses. Like most knights, his squiring days taught him how to tend to horses, and a small stream near the tower allowed Ronen to water them appropriately before feeding and tethering them for the night.

Tully appeared to be putting the finishing touches to their evening meal, hunched over the simmering pot, while Tamsyn sat by and enjoyed the warmth of the fire. The mage's dark eyes were staring into the horizon as he smoked his pipe, and as he observed the farmer, who over the last few days, had grown more and more distant.

Aeron knotted his brow in sympathy, realising the farmer must surely be worried about his wife. The elf was never married, so he could not fully appreciate the bond that Dare, Tully, and Ronen shared with their wives. He knew each man suffered greatly by their absence and was equally worried about their fates. Aeron never shared an attachment to warrant the anguish he saw in these men, although he knew that Kyou shared a long-standing relationship with a maid called Hanae, who lived in the Jagged Teeth with the rest of his father's clan. Remove Even Tamsyn was rumoured to have some history with the high queen, but Aeron thought that was merely gossip.

Aeron supposed his thoughts on the subject were influenced by his parents.

As the youngest child of House Halion, he was never impressed by the union between his parents, which he thought to be a bad match. They loved each other, but he was uncertain if they *liked* each other. Once an elf decided on a soul mate, it was a bond unbreakable even by death, and elves were immortal. Perhaps his own reluctance for marriage had to do with the possibility he could end up being with someone he might not be able to tolerate for all of eternity.

Certainly it was not the case with Dare, Ronen, and Tully, who viewed every moment with their spouses as precious. In this respect, Aeron appreciated why Tully would be so distracted. After all this time, Keira still suffered the effects of the desert burrowers in her blood. Although Tully never spoken of it in depth, Aeron suspected even with the help of the elves, they were unable to fully expel the venom of the burrowers from her body. It tainted her so completely its vile magic could still be felt by every elf encountering her.

Aeron had not spoken of it to Tully, for it would only upset him.

Like Aeron, Tamsyn also noticed the darkness in Keira and kept silent. The desert burrowers were vicious creatures when the Dreaded Mother birthed them, but after Balfure infused them with dark magic to create the Blinding Curse, it left a stain upon the soul that appeared to be permanent. For the elves, it made Keira extremely difficult to read, and even Tamsyn could not be entirely sure of her reasons when she agreed to undertake the quest.

He did know it had nothing to do with Arianne's baby.

Still, Arianne needed a company of her own for this quest, and so he did not object because Keira proved herself to be a friend to Arianne and Dare since her ordeal at the hands of the Disciples, and the blight of the desert burrowers upon her soul was through no fault of her own.

"Tully," Tamsyn called out to him, when it appeared the man was done with his cooking, as he covered the pot with a lid. "Come join me."

Tully lifted the pot away from the fire and allowed it to cool for the eating, before he took a seat next to Tamsyn on still intact set of steps. When the aromatic smoke from Tamsyn's pipe reached his nose, it prompted Tully to retrieve his own pipe from his coat pocket and light it.

Both men lapsed into a quiet moment of reflection as they gazed at the horizon through a broken wall, and for a moment, Tully thought if he stared hard enough, he might be able to see the Green from here.

"You're thinking of home?" Tamsyn ventured a guess.

Tully exhaled a lung full of smoke and watched it dissipate into air before he answered the mage.

"Yes," he admitted readily, "I miss it. I miss the quiet. I used to think that I was different from the other folk in the Green, I needed adventure and exploration, but now I think I was being frivolous and selfish. I'm not sorry I helped Dare, but I regret Keira paid the price for my foolishness."

"There was nothing foolish in what you did. You were exceedingly brave as your wife was exceedingly brave. What tragedy came about because of that courage is not your fault, but that of Balfure and the cruelty of his agents."

Tully couldn't accept the compliment as much as he wished to believe Tamsyn's words. "Keira married a man of the Green. At least she thought she did. I feel sometimes she's angry with me for lying to her about the man I am. She expected an ordinary life, with a houseful of children. I promised to give her those things when we married. I didn't tell her I wished to wander the world, to see things and go places. For some reason, I had this desire in me. I should have told her."

"Do you think it would have made a difference?" Tamsyn asked.

"I don't know but there is something between us now neither can get past. When I found her after the Disciples had gone, almost dead, I thought I'd lost her forever. But then Arianne took her to Eden Taryn and I thought, if she lives, I'll make it up to her for the rest of our lives, but it's never been the same. She's never been the same. I know it's not her fault, but it's true, and now she's gone off to prove something to me, or herself, and I just don't know what to do."

Tamsyn's squeezed Tully's shoulder gently, empathising with the man's guilt and sorrow. "Perhaps you and Keira should leave the Green for a while. Remain in Sandrine and heal. If both of you have changed, perhaps trying to be the people you were, in the lives you had, is not making things better but worse. Your guilt is deep, but you are a victim of this as much as she. If you don't mind the advice of an old bachelor, that is."

"Leave?" Tully stared at him in shock. The idea of leaving the Green and their farm was so overwhelming he had difficulty trying to imagine it.

Aware this was a tremendously big change from the provincial life of a farmer from the Green, Tamsyn continued to make his case. "If not Sandrine, then perhaps even Eden Taryn. I am certain Queen Lylea would have no difficulty playing hostess to the people who saved her son-in-law's life. Even if they are somewhat reclusive, the elves can be excellent hosts when the mood takes them, and it will give you the chance to get to know each other again."

"But what about the farm...?" Tully started to say in protest when suddenly, it occurred to him the farm wasn't nearly as important to him as Keira. It could become overgrown and swallowed up by the Old Forest for all he cared if it meant rekindling his wife's spirit once more. Right now, Tully wanted Keira back. He wanted the happy, hopeful woman she'd been before the Disciples destroyed her. So what if she had to find herself again in a different place than the farm? They could always go back when she was ready.

"I must think on this," Tully answered. "I can't make any decisions until we find them, and I talk to Keira." Still, there was hope in his eyes, and he gave Tamsyn a look of appreciation for giving him a solution he would never have dared to imagine:

To live a life outside of the Green.

* * *

As they left the light of the campfire behind and scouted the slopes of the hills to ensure they were the only ones present in the immediate area, Kyou noticed Dare was uncommonly silent. He was accustomed to stillness from the elf, but Dare was always more animated, and they often had lively chats about things. Of course, Kyou understood since leaving Sandrine, Dare's sombre mood had to do with his missing wife, but the worry across his brow seemed constant, and ran deeper than his fears for Arianne.

"We will find her," Kyou broke the silence of the descending night, as they made their way across the open ground to the Mountain Wood ahead.

Dare glanced up at Kyou and smiled faintly, grateful for the dwarf's attempt to make him feel better. In their company, it was usually Kyou who was the sombre one.

The dwarf spent most of his adult life ensuring his Clan stayed one step ahead of Abraxes. Chasing the dwarves out of Iridia was not enough. Balfure wanted their expertise and he needed them enslaved for that. In Carleon, they could find no shelter, and most were driven to the very edges of Avalyne to remain free. Kyou was but an adolescent when Balfure descended upon the Starfall Mountains. He became the leader of his Clan when his father Atrayo was killed, his childhood stolen away by murder.

"I know," Dare answered, but he didn't sound convincing, even to his own ears. Despite telling himself he would feel it if she were dead, Dare had no idea if Arianne escaped the Splinter alive. Those bones scattered throughout the pass were burned into his memory. There were so many, and since they were forced to avoid the barraged lobbed by the ice troll, there was no time to conduct a search to satisfy his fear that hers was not there.

"Do you really?" Kyou countered knowingly. "Something has been preying on your mind since we left the Splinter. What is it? The elf's too polite to ask, but I'm not."

"It's nothing," Dare shrugged, not wishing to say because he had no reason to believe it to be possible, and every reason to discount it.

"Not so nothing that we've all been able to see it, well, all except Ronen and Tully of course, but like you they're worried about their wives. It's something more with you. Out with it or do I have to beat it out of you?"

Dare paused and looked at Kyou with amusement. "I would like to see you try."

"Well, you don't have your royal guards or your elven army here," the dwarf teased back. "I can hit you without losing my head."

"You couldn't hit me with your head," Dare snorted. "In fact, I remember a number of tavern brawls where I had to rescue *you*."

To be fair, most of the time, it was Aeron and Celene who rescued them both. During the occupation, they visited many taverns in many small towns on the way to build their alliances and drum up support for the campaign. While Aeron had little patience for drinking, mostly because he was rather lousy at it, and with Celene refusing to indulge in what she called 'the stupidity only men can indulge in,' Kyou and Dare often found themselves enjoying the local libations.

"I don't remember that at all," Kyou replied haughtily, when he saw something appear among the trees ahead. A flash of white disappearing as soon as it appeared.

"There's something down there!" he exclaimed and started running towards it.

"What did you see?" Dare hurried after him, scanning the tree line and seeing nothing in it that gave him caution.

"I'm not sure," Kyou answered, tossing a sidelong glance at Dare as the King caught up with him. "It could be just a trick of light, but I want to be sure."

"Let us look then," Dare fell into stride with him, reaching for Narthaine, the ancient sword Lylea gifted to him. It had belonged to her son, and was a gift to show her blessing of his and Arianne's love.

"Thank you," Kyou said to Dare, grateful that the king was taking him on his word.

Dare's best talent, Kyou thought silently as they approached the wood, was his belief in people.

While he was no fool to be manipulated, his faith in everyone's ability to put aside their differences to work as one was what held the campaign together. As part of his company, Kyou travelled with Dare as he spoke to kings, queens, chieftains and village elders, convincing them to forget the old prejudices so they could be strong. There was a great future to be built for all of them, no matter what part they played in its making.

The woods they approached were made up of tall pine trees that stretched high into the sky. The ground was covered in brown, withered pine needles and cones. Disappearing into the forest, they remained within each other's line of sight, but far enough away to get a good view of what was ahead. There was still enough light left for them to see but it would not be long before they were shrouded in darkness. Kyou would see far better than Dare because dwarves had highly developed nocturnal vision due to the years spend underground.

Dare was about to ask Kyou what exactly he thought he saw, when he too saw something shimmering through the darkness of the trees

"There it is!" Kyou exclaimed as the shimmering form stopped and did not move.

It seemed almost like a wraith as the two men approached it, and Dare unsheathed Narthaine, holding it up in front of him as they closed in. Only when they neared it did they realise their mysterious wraith was, in fact, a woman. For a moment, Dare swore he was looking at Arianne, because she glowed with ethereal beauty. After blinking furiously, he dispelled the notion, realising it was his own wishful thinking.

"Be careful, Kyou," Dare warned. "This reeks of dark magic."

"I hear you," Kyou whispered, his two swords similarly brandished as they saw she had slipped into a small clearing and stood in the middle of a dirt mound, her white dress dragging across the ground, the hem covered with dirt. As Dare approached her, he realized why he had mistaken her for Arianne, because she, too, wore her dark hair long. Her skin was luminescent and flawless, and her lips full and red. She stared at them with the colour of sea in her eyes and smiled at them. For a moment, he felt a fog settle over his mind and he almost forgot he was on a quest to find his wife.

"How do you come to be here, lady?" Kyou asked, closing his eyes when he breathed in the sweet scent of her perfume, which was intoxicating to say the least.

"A friend beseeched us to find you," she whispered softly, and hearing her voice was like being in the presence of the Celestial Gods as they sang the song awakening the world.

"Us?" Dare asked, fixating on that one word and trying to shake away the fugue that was trying to encroach upon his mind.

"My sisters and I," she replied and gestured around them.

Dare and Kyou were surrounded by others like her, stepping out from behind the tall trees as if they had been there all along. There were at least a dozen of them, all beautiful and glowing like she was, filling the forest with that scent, making it hard to focus. Some had hair of gold, while others carried manes of russet and mahogany. All were beautiful, and they were smiling at the two men as they closed in.

"We have been hiding here for so long waiting for our master. Since the world was young. In the trees, we have waited for the call, and it came this night to find you."

"I feel honoured," Kyou grumbled, trying to stay focussed, but the scent was everywhere now and he could not draw breath without it stealing into his lungs. Yet, beneath the sweetness, there was something old and musty, like decay.

"You should feel honoured, Master Dwarf," she smiled. "We do not show ourselves for just anyone. You and your friend must be special indeed."

"Does your master have a name?" Dare asked, realising now, this time, the attack would not come at the hands of the caracal, but something more inviting and no less lethal.

"None that would interest you," she smiled and held her ground as he took another step closer.

"I beg to differ," he answered, aware something was amiss but the power to stop her from approaching was elusive. "What is your name?" he asked instead, hoping to keep her talking, because he suspected when these creatures stopped, that would be when he and Kyou were really in trouble.

"I would tell you my name, but I do not remember," she explained, her brow knotting in confusion. "No one has spoken to us in so long. Not even to each other do we speak."

"That's seems to be a very lonely way to be," Kyou remarked. "Dare, we need to get out of here," he hissed at the king.

The women were closing in on them now, and Dare was fighting with everything ounce of strength he possessed to break free of the shackles keeping his mind from moving his feet. In desperation, he forced his lips to work, plying her with questions.

"Who are you, lady?" he asked again.

She was standing very near to him now, and the scent that was so intoxicating a brief moment ago, had changed to something less pleasing. He thought of rotting leaves and drying mud. Like the scent of a burial ground.

MOVE! ARIANNE NEEDS YOU, he screamed inside his mind.

Something in his brain shifted, not tremendously but enough for him to take a step back from her. If anything could penetrate the fugue in his mind, it was his fear for Arianne. She needed him to help her with this quest. If she failed, she would kill herself, before allowing their child to become Mael's vessel, and that Dare could not let happen.

At his retreat, those beautiful sea blue eyes flashed red like a blood moon, and she lowered her head, spreading her arms. A cloud cast a shadow over her form, and when it disappeared, her body burst into a swarm of insects, spreading out around him before soaring into the sky, creating a mist above his head. Dare raised his sword to fight, it was a useless gesture against an enemy so small, when he realized it was not the swarm he had to worry about.

"DARE! BEHIND YOU!" he heard not Kyou, but Aeron shouting at him.

Dare swung away from the demon swarm to see one of the women closing in on him, but before she could reach him, she uttered a terrible scream of pain as the sharp point of arrow ripped through her flesh and out of her chest. Dare glanced over her shoulder and saw Aeron and the others hurrying through the woods.

Kyou! He remembered the dwarf still trapped in the glamour projected by these creatures. Now fully in control of himself, Dare rushed forward and swung his blade, passing right over Kyou's head to slash at the creature he no longer thought of as a woman. Narthaine cut the white linen of her dress but instead of red, black blood splattered across Kyou who stood in front of her. Her face turned into a terrible visage of pale white skin, and those lips that had seemed so inviting before pulled back to reveal razor like teeth. Her hands became claws and she uttered a screeching howl of pain as she looked down at Kyou, ready to take his head off his neck.

Dare beat her to it, delivering a blow with his sword before she could make the attempt. Taking her head, it flipped in mid-air, hair flailing about before it landed in the ground. The other creatures screamed in outrage at the death of one of their sisters and rushed at him. He heard the whoosh of Aeron's arrows flying through the air and saw another one piercing the shifter through the back, her white gowned body tumbling to the ground.

By now, Kyou had regained control and raised his sword to fight. He swung his twin blades simultaneously, slashing through flesh and bone, and causing the creature to scream. Her agony made her sisters more frenzied and Kyou saw the advance of another creature, seconds before he felt claws tearing across his back, as she jumped on him. Her weight drove Kyou to his hands and knees, and there was a moment of clarity when he knew he would not throw her off in time. Jaws clamped shut and Kyou let out a groan of pain as razor sharp teeth sank into his shoulder and pierced his flesh.

"Get away from him, monster!" Ronen shouted when he reached the dwarf, sending a kick that landed in her abdomen, making her spin in mid-air. She whirled, a tangle of hair and cloth, before landing on the ground next to Kyou. She sat up just in time for Ronen to drive his sword through her throat, until the blade touched the ground behind her and she was coughing up black spurts of blood.

"Are you alright?" Tully rushed in, leaving the others to fight as he side stepped the creatures and went to help Kyou, who was struggling to his feet.

"Yes," Kyou grunted, his pride more injured than his flesh. Upon standing, the pain coursed through him more acutely and he found himself accepting the hand Tully offered.

Seeing that Kyou was being attended to, Ronen began searching for the king, when he saw a blur of white moving through the air at the edge of his vision. He turned around in time to see one of the creatures coming at him, and quickly raised his sword to meet it. A spray of black followed the arc of his sword and he was splattered with it. The fluid stung his eyes, robbing him of his sight briefly enough for the creature to gain the advantage and topple him over.

Ronen landed hard, but managed to keep his sword between himself and the creature trying to tear out his throat. Deciding he had not survived an ogre to be killed by a woman in a dress, he summoned up his strength and threw her over his head. She landed on the grass not far from him, but remained unhurt.

Scrambling to her feet, she began running again, a mass of rage and madness led by gnashing teeth and sharp claws. Ronen stood up quickly and held his ground, waiting until she jumped at him before he used his sword as a spear and impaled her on the point. She screamed in agony, her blood running down the length of the weapon and soaking his gauntlets.

Even with the loss of their sisters, the creatures did not give up, and converged upon Dare, preparing to attack the king simultaneously. Dare positioned himself, trying to find the best defence to keep himself from being torn to pieces. It seemed the stench of blood was making their attack frenzied, and while uncoordinated, the sheer fury behind them was difficult to fight.

The two women lunged at him and he dropped to his knees, crawling along the dirt when they collided with each other in mid-air. He crawled away from them on his hands and knees until he looked ahead and found himself staring into the face of a large black wolf, with silver in its pelt, inches away from him with fangs ready to snap close.

"We do not always look so fair," the thing spoke to him, and he knew instinctively, she was the one who led them here.

He would never use his sword in time, not before the beast tore the flesh from his skull. Nonetheless, Dare was not about to surrender, and prepared to defend himself, however futile the effort was. The beast lunged forward and Dare retreated, struggling in his awkward position to raise his sword to protect himself when the creature screamed abruptly and dropped faced down into the dirt. Protruding from her back, was the shaft of an elven arrow.

It was little more than a second later he saw Aeron appearing over the top of the creature's pelt, halting long enough to pull another arrow from behind him to shoot again. Another sharp scream drew his attention from the elven archer. Dare looked over his shoulder to see Tamsyn despatching another of the women with his sword while Ronen helped Aeron finished the last of the creatures.

Dare sat upright but remained seated on the ground, panting hard as he tried to catch his breath. He felt Tamsyn's hand upon his shoulder a second later and saw the mage staring down at him with concern.

"I am not hurt," Dare assured him, searching the forest floor for Kyou. "Where is Kyou?"

"I'm fine," Kyou grumbled distantly. "I'm alive."

"I'm taking him back to the camp, Dare," Tully declared, helping Kyou across the wood towards their campsite.

"What were you thinking coming in here alone?" Aeron demanded. The elven prince appeared both worried and angered at the same time. "Scout means look and come back if you see something! Did you remember nothing I taught you in Halas!"

"Kyou saw a woman," Dare retorted, embarrassed, because they should have alerted the others before wandering into the woods alone. He should have known better. In Aeron's position, he would have been similarly furious if someone under his care had acted so foolishly.

"A woman?" Tamsyn asked, glancing in the direction of the departing dwarf. "Really?"

"She looked like she was lost!" Kyou barked back defensively.

"It was a trap," Dare explained. "I am not certain, but I think they are shifters. Though the one who led us into the wood was different than the others." He gestured to the wolf Aeron had slain. "She said they were hiding in the trees for a long time and their master called to her."

"That is possible," Tamsyn replied, examining the bodies. "Shifters were birthed by Mael's Primordials. Some of them are little more than vampyrs who craved flesh and blood, but others—like this one." The mage dropped to his feet and ran his hand over the pelt of the dead wolf. "These are of the higher orders. They could change into any shape, and maintain it indefinitely."

"They disguised themselves as trees," Dare realised suddenly, because the clearing in which they had fought seemed much larger now. "Lying dormant until awakened, and sent on this mission to ambush us."

"And it worked splendidly," Ronen grumbled. "They knew what shape to take to trick us."

"Indeed they did," Dare remarked, and noted the blood splattered across his Ban's clothes. "Are you hurt?"

"No," Ronen answered. "Just aches from landing badly. I will be fine."

"We've lingered here long enough," Tamsyn declared. "We should return to camp. For future reference, I suggest none of us wander alone. We see now know how formidable our enemy is, and what powers he has to draw upon to waylay us. We must be vigilant."

"I suppose," Dare sighed as he accepted Aeron's hand to get to his feet, "After all this, I will finally be able to sleep."

Aeron rolled his eyes and snorted, "I admire your ability to see the good in any situation."

Chapter Fourteen

The Edge of the World

It was expected when they approached the Frozen Mountains, the temperature would drop. What Arianne was not prepared for was how sharply.

As they crossed the Torn Lands, named so because of the great chasms in the ground created during the Primordial Wars, the iciness in the air continued to grow the deeper into it they travelled. Leaving Angarad behind after crossing the Safrie River, the lush green of the land was soon replaced by brown grasslands, and the forests of full, leafy trees had vanished in place of tall, well-spaced conifers.

Even with the warmer clothes Celene and Melia had bought in Horwyck, the biting cold invaded the warmth of their cloaks and pierced their skins, as the ground became harder with frost. Despite it being autumn, the weather took on a decidedly wintery turn, and Arianne wondered if it had to do with just their proximity to the mountains or if something else was at work.

Arianne also noticed something more sinister the deeper they went into the Torn Lands: the scarcity of any wildlife. She supposed the harsh terrain could have driven them south, but even so, there would be at least some animals left here. The air was still, with only the sounds of their voices and the horses to break the silence. There was no singing of birds and no chirping of insects, and at night, even the owls remained silence. The whole landscape seemed abandoned.

Eventually, the others noticed the silence too, and although they did not speak of it, Arianne knew they, too, were uneasy. Their rest periods became shorter, since none of them were overly eager to close their eyes. When sleep did come, it was under one of their watchful gazes.

Through this ominous atmosphere, Arianne watched the path of the moon in the sky with growing alarm the time between its reaching fullness was dwindling rapidly. The journey here took almost three weeks, and Arianne knew they would reach the enemy with barely enough time to spare or formulate the strategy to kill him.

They saw no evidence of the threat Syanne warned them against, but there was no doubt it existed. The woods they crossed reeked of death and desolation. Something unnatural seized the land and was unrelenting in its deathly grip. Arianne could feel its tendrils clawing up her back, cold to the touch. The babe inside her stirred as well, perhaps feeling the threat to its existence she was trying so desperately to prevent.

No one spoke of their fears, but Arianne sensed their anxiety, for Celene and Melia's guard was almost always up now, with the two soldiers watching constantly for danger. Keira did her best to keep things light, but the fear they felt was becoming palpable with every step they took towards the mountains.

The situation did not improve when they came across the ruin of a settlement appearing dwarven in origin. Due to Balfure hunting them across Avalyne, the dwarves were forced to find new homes beyond the reach of Abraxes. Some settled in Angarad, while others sought refuge in the Jagged Teeth. It made sense others might choose to travel even further than that to escape the Aeth Lord. With its infamous reputation, the Torn Lands may have appeared to the perfect place for them to rebuild their lives without interference from anyone.

The town they happened upon experienced some form of calamity, but it was of a kind none of them had ever seen before. Whatever the dwarves chose to name this settlement, they would never know. What they found when they rode through the settlement along the frost-covered ground was the entire town was buried ice. To look at it, one would be forgiven in thinking some mad artist had embarked upon the laborious task of sculpturing a representation of the town in ice. Every structure was encased in ice, just as the dwarves who lived in it.

"What in the name of the Celestial Gods happened here?" Celene asked rhetorically, as she gaped at what was in front of them.

They dismounted their horses, leading the animals through the town so they could investigate what took place here in the hopes of avoiding the same fate, not buried in ice was brittle to the touch. Melia's efforts to kick away a doll lying on the ground resulted in the complete disintegration of the object. It crumbled around her boot as if a blast of cold turned it into glass. The watch guard's shock was obvious, and after that, no one was terribly eager to touch anything not covered in ice.

"A sudden blizzard perhaps?" Melia asked her three companions. She came from a land that did not experience winter, and though she had some experience with it after years of living in the west, this was beyond her understanding.

"I could believe a snow storm could cause some ice, but nothing natural could have done this," Arianne declared as she paused at a seemingly unaffected bush and touched one of the leaves on its branches. The leaf crumbled in her hands as easily as the toy disintegrated beneath Melia's foot. The fragment of green in her hand felt like sand or ash—she could not tell which for sure, only that it frightened her. It was no small thing to destroy life in this fashion, and she shuddered at the thought of meeting the thing to have done it.

It was a sentiment mirrored by Celene, who stated, "We should keep going. I have no wish to encounter what did this while we are here. We have more important matters to attend."

"Yes," Keira nodded in agreement, her eyes scanning the dead town. "We're not accomplishing anything by remaining here. I say we just keep riding through, and not look back. Besides, we don't have time to waste," she reminded.

Melia gripped the reins of her horse tight. Her nails were digging into her palm, but she hardly noticed it. This place frightened her more than beserkers, or any other evil she encountered since leaving her home in Nadira. She wanted to run away from this place, to ride back to the safety of the woods the Baffin, but knew she would not. She had made a pledge to the queen and she would see it through.

Besides, it was more than just obligation keeping her at Arianne's side. During the course of their travels, she had come to know all three women, and felt the bond of friendship between them all. Here were women with whom she shared a great deal. Like her, they waited for no man to decide their fate and remained true to themselves instead of complying with what was expected of them. It spoke to Melia's own choices in life.

"I, too, wish to ride away from here and not look back," Melia admitted. "But what did this awaits us ahead on our journey. The only thing we will accomplish, if we ride hastily, forward is run headlong into what did this."

"You are right, of course," Celene frowned, despising the logic of Melia's words, because she felt similar anxiety at being in this icy graveyard. "I do not think there is anything to find. What levelled this place has moved on, assuming some manner of evil did this."

"This is no aberration of weather," Arianne countered. "Something, or someone, wrought this destruction. I am certain the way is being cleared for the enemy."

"Cleared?" Keira exclaimed, staring at her puzzled.

"Yes," Arianne nodded, taking another long look at the town because it was only the prelude to what was coming. "This is the work of the enemy—I am certain of it. He seeks to ensure no one knows of his existence, and this means destroying those who might be able to carry word of him to the rest of Avalyne."

"To ensure when he does emerge, he will do so to the complete surprise of those who might be able to stop him," Celene concluded.

"Your child might be the first step," Melia pointed out. "If what you tell me is true, about the enemy attempting to infuse your child with Mael's spirit, then it is possible he intends to take Avalyne, to prepare it for Mael, when your babe grows to manhood."

Arianne closed her eyes at the horrific plan, and knew both Melia and Celene were right about their suppositions. The enemy would create a kingdom worthy of Mael, and when her son grew up to be king, he would inherit this dark empire. It would also mean that the enemy would have to eliminate all those she cared about, who were still left within his reach, in order to achieve his plan.

"We won't let that happen," Keira assured her. "We'll get there in time and stop this."

"We have to," Arianne declared, after she was able to look at them again. "We must keep going. Our best hope of averting this terrible thing from happening again is to find the enemy, and defeat him."

The others seemed to agree with her and as they mounted their horses, preparing to leave the town behind. Arianne prayed hope would be enough, because failure was unimaginable.

* * *

As Celene had discovered in Horwyck, much of the Torn Lands remained uncharted, save for a few geographical land-marks passed down from the elves during the Primordial Wars. After the elves retreated into the Veil, it was not known if the realm was peopled. With rumours many of the creatures created by Mael survived him to continue their existence in this land, it seemed unlikely anyone would wish to live in here.

As they approached the Frozen Mountains and the blizzard conditions assailing them at the Splinter returned with even more intensity, they learned the dwarf town was not the only village in the Torn Lands. Throughout their journey, they saw other settlements overtaken in similar fashion, and even the alpine woods they travelled through to reach the mountains, were completely encased in ice. It was almost impossible to make a fire when they camped at the night, owing to the wood being too damp or too frozen to burn.

The mountains themselves were stretched across the horizon. Their peaks were covered in white, and seemed perpetually shrouded in a fog of swirling arctic winds. The frosted ground turned into a glacial plain, broken by the dead trees scattered across its expanse. They would have to cross these mountains to reach the chasm known as Mael's Pit. The Pit was created when the Celestials drove Sanhael deep the earth, ridding Avalyne of the city where Mael created an entire host of vile creatures to plague the world.

Creatures that might still be lying in wait for them.

* * *

At nightfall, Celene stared at the moon above her head and was barely able to see through the falling snow its crescent shape was wanning. The sight of it filled Celene with an ap-prehension she took pains to keep hidden from her compan-ions. Their time was growing short, and she estimated they had only days left for them to reach the enemy. Worse yet, what destroyed the settlements and turned the lands around it into an icy wasteland, had yet to show itself.

Celene did not know whether or not this was a good thing.

Once again, as she took the first watch, Celene finally let down the walls she had erected around her heart to see the quest through. She was the strong one, the one who would drive them onward despite all calamity and reservations. Only when the others could not see did she allow herself to feel, and what she felt was a deep yearning for home and her husband.

She missed Ronen so much it almost hurt.

Although she spoke nothing of her need for him because a warrior needed to remain focussed when embarking on a mission such as this, she missed him, terribly. When she indulged them, her thoughts drifted to his wry smile and the manner in which he would soothe her when she was raging at one injustice or another. Between of the two of them, he was the thoughtful one. He took everything in stride, because by Ronen's reckoning, if they could survive Balfure, they could survive anything.

Everything after that, he often said, disarming her with that damned smile of his, is easy.

Until now, Celene had not realised how terrible it would be to die without seeing him again. Now, on eve of reaching their destination, Celene knew it was very likely not all of them may survive this quest. She drew in her breath to dispel such thoughts, because losing hope before reaching the enemy helped no one. Celene had to believe they would survive, or else, they were doomed before they even started.

A warrior who believed she would die would often find a way to make it happen.

Through the howl of the wind lashing at her partially exposed face, she was still thinking on Ronen when she heard something moving.

At first, she thought it might be one of the sleepers tossing and turning. She, Keira, and Arianne had come to learn during this journey Melia did not sleep well. The watch guard was often plagued with nightmares forcing her awake, wide-eyed, and panting in fear. She did not explain what frightened her so, and they respected her silence on the matter. When they drew closer to the mountain, Melia was not the only one to experience nightmares. Arianne, too, seemed to be entertaining a few demons herself in her sleep. In this case, they all knew the cause of Arianne's nightmares, and did not pursue the matter.

At least Keira slept well.

When she heard the sound again, Celene knew it was neither the wind, nor her companions, seemed alien against the night and did not feel natural. As it drew closer, Celene still had difficulty identifying it. If she did not know better, she would have thought someone was dragging something across the ground. Without clarity of vision thanks to the snow falling about them, Celene stood up slowly, unsheathing her sword, as she scanned the dark woods surrounding them.

They did not leave the campfire burning because firewood was scarce and they were attempting to conserve what wood they could find. Now that she heard the horses neigh their disquiet at the edge of their encampment, Celene regretted the decision, for they needed the light.

"Everyone! On your feet now!" Celene barked, waking them all with that one sharp demand.

Melia awoke first, her watch guard discipline bringing her swiftly out of her slumber as she reached for the crossbow lying within easy reach of her sleeping place. Rolling onto her feet, she stood up ready to face whatever danger Celene discovered to raise the alarm. Not far from her, Arianne reached for the hilt of her sword, her eyes watchful of the danger now she was aware of it. Keira was the last to rouse, and her eyes darted about in fear as she tried to see what was coming at them.

"What is that?" Keira demanded, trying to see through the darkness and snowfall.

"I don't know," Celene answered with a frown. She did not know what was out there, but it was closing in on them.

Arianne listened closely. Now she was awake, she could feel the peril closing in on her. "They are near," she said, to no one's surprise.

"They?" Keira asked, her voice cracking in fear. "There's more than one of them?"

"They're all around us," Celene stated because she could hear it without the benefit of Arianne's elven senses. "Arianne, light the fire and remain close to it."

Arianne did not protest. Celene's orders kept her alive this far, and she knew her limitations with her pregnancy entering its fourth month. She could feel her son acutely now, as such was with the way with elves, and her fears for his life made her pay heed to Celene's need to protect her.

"Keira, go to the horses. If you have to get on and lead them away from here, do it. We cannot afford to lose them," Melia said.

Keira nodded and hurried towards the animals, now stamping their hooves in desperate need to be free of the place. Meanwhile, Arianne hurried to the centre of their campsite to light the fire, Celene demanded. The queen worked quickly and felt the first hint of warmth from the newborn fire when the radiating glow of amber spread throughout the campsite. It lit just as the first of their attackers came into view.

It was almost the size of a horse and it moved with as much agility. All three knew exactly what they were dealing with the moment they laid eyes on the creature. Its long body was covered in scales that glimmered with iridescent colours while its head was decidedly serpentine. It slithered across the snow covered ground and glared at them with ruby red eyes. When it opened its mouth, two large fangs stood out from the smaller serrated teeth. It reached Celene first.

"It's a wyrm!" Melia shouted as she took aim with her crossbow and fired.

The bolt from the weapon struck the creature below the jaw and it turned sharply in her direction, hissing furiously at Melia in pain. The angry screech tearing through the air, prompted Celene into action. She dashed forward, struggling not to slip on the snow as she rushed at it from the rear. Celene's unsheathed sword led her charge, and she came up along the side of the beast and swung. The blade sliced through the air before striking flesh. It took every ounce of her strength to penetrate its skin even with the force of the blow, because wyrms were the young of dragons. Had she faced it fully grown, there would be no way to penetrate its thick hide.

Nevertheless, this beast was young, and Celene saw its blood spraying in all directions when she took its head from its body. The creature's cry of pain was cut short as its large body tumbled to the snow, blood pouring from the severed neck.

Unfortunately, its death cry brought the others.

Melia turned around to see another wyrm emerging behind her and she could hear a third approaching as well. Firing her crossbow, the bolt struck the oncoming beast in the face, and forced it to rear up in pain as steel tore through its muscle. In the rear of her vision, she saw Arianne being stalked by the wyrm she heard but not seen. The queen showed herself to be no novice in defending herself, and she quickly took the offensive, stabbing at the creature with her sword while moving with elven agility to avoid the snapping of its jaws. Her blade struck flesh. Although the wyrm howled in pain, it did not retreat and held its ground, preparing to lunge at her.

"Get out of its way!" Melia shouted, prompted by a sudden flash of inspiration.

Arianne reacted to her warning by attempting to do just that, when the wyrm reared its head and widened it jaw to spit something at her. Arianne retreated, assuming the ejecta would be fire or even venom, but what escaped the beast's mouth was a blast of icy cold air. She jumped out of its path and saw that it not only extinguished the fire, but it froze the fire solid like a sculpture.

At least now they knew what became of those settlements.

Celene rushed forward, attempting to help, slashing her sword about wildly to clear a path to Arianne. The wyrms were encircling them, trapping them in the middle of the campsite as they unleashed their icy breath upon the three women, like they were casting a net. Celene dropped down to her knees, trying to keep out of the path of the creatures' frozen breath, but even without being assaulted directly she was feeling its effects. The cold pierced her skin like needles and she was shivering beneath her cloak. Her fingers stiffened around the hilt of her sword.

One of the wyrms slithered forward, lowering its head so it could envelop her in cold. Using the sleet on the ground, Celene threw herself forward, sliding past it and driving her blade into its side as she moved. Ripping open its flesh, its hot blood hissed against the snow as it bellowed in agony and tumbled to the ground, its elongated body going slack.

Arianne saw Celene's efforts to reach her, and soon realised that the Lady of Gislaine was busy enough trying saving her own skin without coming to her aid. Recovering her balance after she avoided the attack of the wyrm nearest her, she remained on her feet without slipping across the sleet, thanks to her elven nature. The creature lunged at her and missed, but was determined to have her. Twisting around on its slithering belly, it sidled toward her, leaving circular groves in the snow. When it neared her, it flicked its massive tail like a whip, trying to knock her off her feet. Instead, Arianne jumped up, allowing it to pass beneath her.

Before she could land, the beast lunged again, and Arianne found herself retreating to escape its fangs when something snagged her foot. She fell heavily on her behind and saw the wyrm closing in on her. Scrambling backwards desperately, she raised her sword just in time to see its jaws widening for the kill. Forcing her weapon between them, she held her blade poised between its jaw and her body.

She could see down its gullet and knew all it had to do was blast her with its icy breath, and she would die just as the other poor unfortunates in those frozen villages. The wyrm regarded her for a second, its eyes glaring at her malevolently, when something drew its attention from her. It retracted its head from before her and screeched angrily.

It was Keira! The mistress of Furnsby Farm was waving a flaming piece of branch before her. In the darkness of the night, the light from the amber flames seemed to fill the whole world, and Arianne let out a sigh of relief as she recovered her senses. Taking advantage of the distraction provided, Celene came out of nowhere, jumping on a small boulder in the middle of the campsite to make a running leap onto the wyrm's back.

Once astride the beast, Celene's legs coiled around its serpentine body to keep it from throwing her off. Like any unbroken horse, the wyrm bucked hard to dislodge her, but Celene remained seated. Raising her sword above her head, she gave the creature no quarter as she drove the blade into its skull. It uttered a short scream of agony before it went limp and fell lifeless to the ground.

Arianne would have thanked Celene, except she was running towards Melia.

Melia's skill with the crossbow almost rivalled Aeron with the long bow, Arianne thought, as she saw the Easterling fire bolt upon bolt at the wyrms stalking them. She managed to keep two of them at bay, but she was fast running out of projectiles. Arianne could see the worry in her face as she continued to strike near fatal wounds in the wyrms coming at them. Soon, she would be forced to rely upon her sword, and Arianne remembered Melia saying she was nowhere as proficient as Celene in its use.

While one of the wyrms writhed in pain from numerous wounds, the other was determined to have the watch guard. The wyrm blew its deadly breath at Melia who barely avoided it, and while a rock served Celene well, another behind Melia gave her no advantage. It bore the full brunt of the wyrm's breath, freezing so quickly it shattered, sending jagged shards in all directions. Fragments of tiny shards sprayed over her and Melia fell, landing on her side trying to avoid the worst of the barrage.

Her crossbow tumbled from her hands as she fell and Melia scrambled quickly towards the sword within reach to defend herself. The wyrm prepared to make its kill as it slithered towards Melia. Arianne had only a second to act before it took her life. Throwing her sword like a spear, Arianne watched the blade fly through the air and pierce the beast in what would have been its neck. Driven by the force of her throw, the sword did not stop travelling until it was buried to the hilt in wyrm flesh.

The wyrm attempted to screech, but could not manage it, since what passed for its vocal chords, were severed. By this time, Melia had recovered enough to thrust her own sword into the belly of the beast, and it spilt its innards onto the permafrost-covered ground when she retracted it.

For a few seconds, no one spoke as they stood amongst the carcasses of the creatures that had almost killed them. All were still stunned by the fact they survived the onslaught. Celene dispatched the wounded beast attempting to retreat while Arianne was saving Melia's life. Just as Keira returned, after securing the horses some distance away, to save Arianne's life in turn. Somehow, they repelled this latest attack, and they did it together.

For the moment, at least, Arianne sensed the danger was over, even though it was not entirely gone. It still loomed over them, but she knew it emanated from the darkened mountain range they would soon be required to enter.

"Are they all dead over there?" Celene asked Melia, as the duty of ensuring the wyrms were dead, not merely wounded, was concluded.

"Yes," Melia answered as she retrieved her crossbow bolts from the dead carcasses. It was grisly work and she had no wish to be any closer to the fledgling dragons, but there was no other way for her to replace them. She needed them, now they were nearing the end of this quest. "They will trouble us no more."

"I heard of dragons when I was a child," Celene declared, grimacing as she scanned the grisly scene in front of her. Already the snow was starting to cover the bodies and, in an hour or two, they would be little more than buried mounds of white.

"The last time these creatures were seen was during the Primordial Wars," Arianne explained. Now the danger was over, she was just as astonished by the presence of these wyrms. "They were thought to be destroyed with Mael!"

"How ever they have come to be here," Celene declared, "these wyrms are young. We should not have been able to penetrate their hides with our weapons. If what I remember of dragon is true, their scales are harder than iron. The only way to kill a dragon is to pierce its belly, because it is the only place it is vulnerable."

"The enemy is responsible for this," Arianne said softly. "He is drawing out these creatures from the deepest depths of the ancient world."

"Well, at least we know what became of those towns," Keira sighed as she went to a shrub, treated to the wyrm's deadly breath, and crushed a branch in her hand. It broke as if it were a dry leaf, turning to powder in her hands. The mistress of Furnsby Farm dusted her palms of the fragments, clear disgust in her face as she did so.

"I suppose," Arianne replied, before coming to Keira and giving her a hug. "I have you to thank for my life. If you had not intervened…"

"We all saved each other," Keira said, accepting her thanks and hugging her back. "I could not simply leave you all behind. The horses are safe so we will be able to leave this place."

"Let us move now," Celene suggested, having no desire to remain here. "I do not know what else is out there, but it certainly knows where we are."

"It is trying to stop us," Arianne announced.

"Stop us?" Keira looked at her puzzled. "Why would it do that? Does it not need you for this plan to resurrect it?"

Arianne took a deep breath and revealed the only thing Lylea told her not to reveal to anyone in her company. Her mother believed secrecy was paramount. Although Arianne trusted her friends, she feared the knowledge might put them in jeopardy. But now that they were in the final leg of their journey, it was important to tell them what came next.

"There is something in the Frozen Mountains I, alone, can retrieve. It has been waiting for me since this quest began, and if we are to defeat the enemy, I must claim it first. My mother showed it to me when we were in Carleon. She ordered me not tell anyone of it because to do so would expose you all to danger."

"What is it?" Melia asked, wiping blood from one of the bolts and looking none too happy about it. She assumed if the queen was telling this to them now, she must be ready to confide in them.

"Because the enemy knows this thing is here in the mountains and it knows only I can retrieve it. He is guarding its resting place to keep us away from it, because if I find it, I will be able to defeat him once and for all. I believe this is why the wyrms attacked tonight. They wish to keep this beyond my reach."

"Beyond our reach," Celene corrected her, making sure Arianne knew she was going nowhere without them, particularly to retrieve this mysterious weapon that could save them all. "Do not tell us Arianne what this thing is. If Queen Lylea feels it is necessary for silence, then we will escort you to its location. Do you know how to get there?"

"Yes," she nodded. "I do."

"Then we better get a move on," Keira smiled.

Chapter Fifteen

The Legacy of Antion

For the first time since departing Carleon, they had a plan.

At first light, they awoke and prepared their horses for travel with Melia leading the way, even though she was as new to the Torn Lands as the rest of them. She displayed an almost elven level of skill in being able to find the best path to the mountains, despite not possessing any special insight that allowed her to do so. What she knew was taught to her by her father and she further honed her craft as a member of the Watch Guard.

The snowfall ceased sometime in the middle of the night, and the white glacial plains glared at them as they approached the Frozen Mountains. As they reached the first rocky slopes leading up to the mountainside, they could see the black, igneous rock gleaming slickly under the melting snow. The elevation of the rocky foothills steepened abruptly the higher up its slopes they progressed, and it became apparent the rest of the journey would have to be made on foot. The terrain was simply too difficult to navigate with horses.

"Are you certain of this?" Melia asked, staring at the jagged terrain they would be required to cross. She spotted at least a dozen places where wyrms or any other menace could lie in wait to ambush them. The mountain itself seemed imposing.

They knew once across it, more dangers awaited them when they descended into Mael's Pit where the enemy awaited.

"It is on this mountain. We must find it before we go any further," Arianne stated firmly, dismounting her horse. Here, they would release the horses, allowing them to graze on what scant vegetation they could find. Elven magic would allow her to call them back later.

Her mother told her the weapon was in the Frozen Mountains, and she had to retrieve it before she and the others entered the Pit. Its importance could not be ignored. Arianne found it a tremendous coincidence the wyrms should attack, only after weeks in the Torn Lands. No doubt the enemy set these creatures against anyone who tried to claim the prize she sought.

Melia exchanged a glance with Celene, who merely shrugged in response. The Lady of Gislaine trusted Arianne's instincts. Her warnings saved their lives on more than one occasion during this journey, and she was not about doubt it now. Keira climbed off her horse to join Arianne on the ground, appearing almost eager to forge ahead. If anything, this entire quest proved without a doubt Keira's worries about losing her courage seemed unwarranted. If anything, it reminded everyone of how much of it she possessed.

While Celene was confident about Arianne's insistence on seeking out this mysterious weapon capable of killing their enemy, she was less so about what might be lying in wait in the mountains to protect it. Last night, they were attacked by wyrms and survived. Those creatures, though, were the offspring of something far older and infinitely more powerful than any weapon they possessed to fight it. Somewhere in the heart of these mountains, more than likely where Arianne's prize was, Celene knew they would find the dragon that sired this nest of wyrms.

A dragon, undoubtedly eager to greet the murderers of her children.

"We've managed to get this far through. I didn't think we'd survive half the things we have, but we've seemed to manage. We can do this," Keira said confidently to the others.

Melia had no argument to make in opposition to this, and as the newest member the group, did not feel she had standing to voice any objections. She reminded herself she was here to protect the queen, and no matter where Arianne would go, Melia would follow her to do just that, but her heart ached at having to leave her horse, Serinda, behind.

"I have told them to find shelter," Arianne revealed, aware Melia's mare was a trusted companion and the watch guard had difficulty leaving her to fend for herself.

"You can talk to horses?" Melia stared at her with surprise. She knew elves possessed keen senses and better agility than men, but she did not know they could speak to animals too.

"Not in the way we speak, but they can sense what we wish for them and the like," the queen explained.

With a little smile, Melia leaned close to Serinda and whispered, "Tell her *nothing*."

Arianne chuckled, "They will find some place to shelter until we have need of them. They will be safe—I promise."

Melia sighed, running her fingers along the ridge of Serinda's nose. She hoped the mare understood this abandonment was for her own good. She wrapped the bridle around the pommel of the saddle and turned the animal's head away from her gently, hoping Serinda would understand the reason for this action. The horse trotted away to join the small herd moving away from them at Arianne's instruction.

"She will find you again," Arianne assured Melia, her hand brushing the watch guard's shoulder in sympathy, when Melia returned to them. "I am certain of it."

"I have no doubt she will find me," Melia whispered. "I just hope she does not wait too long if I am dead. She has been my faithful companion for many years, I would not rest easy even in death to know she was languishing in wait for my return."

As much as Celene wanted to say words of similar kindness to Melia, they could not afford to remain in one place too long. Perhaps the wyrms preferred to move by night, explaining the lack of sighting throughout the day, or perhaps they were being lead into a trap. Whatever the explanation, Celene did not wish to find out the hard way.

The mountain and the enemy awaited them.

Still, something in the pit of her stomach told her the enemy was close. Closer than any of them imagined.

* * *

By the time the afternoon was in the sky, they spent most of the day climbing the steep mountainside, sometimes on their hands and knees and other times helping each other over shelves of rock and across narrow ledges. Their limbs ached, and their palms were cut and scratched from the craggy terrain, where they were forced to find hand holds. Tempers began to shorten as their exhaustion started to set in. The only consolation was the cold did not allow them to swelter beneath their cloaks.

Meanwhile, Melia and Celene kept watch for danger whenever they reached level terrain wide enough for a wyrm of size to emerge. So far, they had seen nothing of the creatures attacking the night before, but it was possible they did not emerge in the day and would reappear when the sun went down. Keira continued her good cheer, and attempted to lift the spirits of her companions. Her unwavering belief they could succeed in their quest gave heart to all present and once again, Arianne was grateful she chose to join them. While Keira was not a great warrior, her lightness of spirit, particularly after what was done to her by the Disciples, was a boon to them all.

While she did not speak of it, Arianne felt something tugging at her consciousness as they journeyed across the mountain. She could feel its reach pulling her forward, and not just her but also the baby inside her. *My son feels it too* she thought, and the moment of communion between herself and her still forming child almost brought tears to her eyes. Arianne wanted so much to meet the babe inside her, before the enemy had a chance to steal his life away.

"No matter what course I must take," she said herself while caressing her stomach, "I will allow nothing to harm you, little one."

* * *

There was a time when all the dead places of Avalyne teemed with life. Before the Winter Wife rolled the arctic tundra across the landscape to conceal the terrible scars left behind by Mael during the Primordial Wars, the Frozen Mountains was as green as the majestic Baffin. From peak to foothills, she hosted a lusty, green forest known to the elves of that time as the Palmira Woods, because of the magnificent view the forest afforded those who walked its paths.

It bore little resemblance to the place Arianne, Celene, Keira, and Melia now crossed.

Time and war scarred the mountain, and the wood was no more, lost to the ravages of Mael's primordials. Their terrible power scorched the mountain, killing every creature living in the forest, in the caves, and burrowed beneath the dirt. The woods were transformed into a twisted version of itself.

No longer beautiful, the tall, majestic trees had grown wild, instead of standing like stately sentinels overlooking the forest. They became gnarled and twisted, the green leaves having fled sharp, thorny branches that snagged and scratched. Bushes and flowering plants were replaced by brambles and thickets of thorny briars stretching across the pass they had to cross to reach the other side of the mountain.

"I suppose that is our path," Melia remarked as she looked at the wall of thick bramble ahead. Her hand went to her sword, knowing the only way across was to hack away the sharp, twisted thicket before them.

"It is," Arianne nodded, sensing now what she sought was on the other side of this dead wood. The nature of the terrain provided the perfect deterrent for someone trying to hide something precious. "What I need to find is on the other side of this."

"Of course it is," Keira sighed, unable to raise any good humour in the face of this latest obstacle.

"I'll take the lead," Celene stated, after taking a deep breath to strengthen her resolve. Unsheathing her sword, she stepped up to the nearest part of the thicket and swung her sword, slashing away at the thorny barbs in her way, the ice and snow on its dead branches scattering as she did so. "Arianne and Keira, stay behind me and close. Melia, you take the rear."

"I do not always need your protection, Celene," Arianne grumbled, as she fell behind the Lady of Gislaine. It was useless of course. Dare told her when it came to the people she cared for, Celene would defend them to her dying breath. Because of their friendship, Arianne knew Celene would do the same to protect not only her, but her child. Still, the queen hated her condition required others to take up the burden that should have been hers to bear. "I can take the rear," she offered.

"You can," Melia added, taking up position behind Keira, "but you're not going to."

"I thought I was the queen here," Arianne threw the watch guard a look.

"You are," Keira smiled sweetly, "and in all other matters you rule, but not *this* one."

"Exactly," Celene replied, as they began to make slow progress through the briars lying ahead of them. "I have no wish to explain to your husband why I let you get cut to pieces trying to get through this place. So, you will stay behind me."

"And before me," Melia added her voice in. "Because your husband is my king, and he can behead me if he so feels inclined." She was joking, of course, but they travelled together for weeks now, and were comfortable enough with each other to take such liberties. Even if Arianne was queen of Carleon.

"He would never do that!" Arianne exclaimed, almost laughing.

"So you say," Melia teased. "I prefer not to take my chances."

"I am more than nine hundred years older than all three of you," the queen snorted. "What makes you think I cannot protect myself?"

"Nothing," Keira answered, because the tone about the conversation was one of jest, no doubt to add some brevity to the misery of their current endeavour. "We're taught to honour our elders. That is why you're travelling in between us. As the oldest, we've got to protect you."

Both Melia and Celene burst out laughing, and Arianne made a face at Keira. "I suppose you think that is very funny."

"Actually, yes," Celene replied from the front. "Keira's reply was far more diplomatic than what I would have elected to say."

"Which is?" Arianne raised a brow at her best friend.

"That the future king of Carleon is already plagued by too many threats to have to endure the stubbornness of his mother." She glanced over her shoulder and gave Arianne a look of pure sarcasm. "In other words, stop being a pain, Arianne."

Melia bit her lip in an effort not to laugh, especially when she saw the teasing smirk that stole across Celene's face as she winked at the queen.

"With friends like you," Arianne grumbled, "I do not need enemies."

"That is true," Celene replied casually, taking no offense at her remark, since this whole conversation was being carried tongue-in-cheek. "You are fortunate indeed."

"How does Ronen put up with you?" the queen asked, with mock sarcasm.

"Oh, probably in the same manner as Dare does with you," Celene replied promptly.

Melia exchanged a knowing glance with Keira before commenting, "I am starting to feel very sorry for *both* these men."

* * *

Their progress was slow.

As they cut their way through the ancient wood, they continued to be assailed by thorns, branches and rocks that always seemed to find skin to tear, no matter how well they thought they were covered. Celene continued to charge ahead, hacking her way through the barrier until she felt the exhaustion in her bones become almost unbearable. She forced herself to continue, refusing to surrender to the weariness she felt. Blinking away the sweat stinging her eyes, and not acknowledging the multitude of cuts to her skin, she took comfort in the fact she was not alone in her misery.

The others were suffering, and so must she.

Glancing up at the sky, she saw night was descending, and she knew they would have to think about finding camp soon. She saw nothing ahead capable of serving the purpose. It also needed to be defensible because the wyrms came from this mountain and the creatures would be seeking them out this night. With no idea how many of the things they might have to face, Celene was acutely aware of how vulnerable they were at this moment.

She brought down her sword again but the blade sliced through so easily through the bramble she might have been trying to cut parchment. The force of her blow disintegrated the section of her thicket as it completed its arc. It took only a second for Celene to process what she was seeing, and she immediately stopped short.

"Everyone be still!" she ordered.

As they froze in their tracks, Celene scanned the terrain before them, and could only see petrified trees, the thicket ahead of them partially covered in ice, and the jagged mountains flanking them on either side. The only way to run was back they came. The bramble itself, seemed different—less alive, if such a thing were possible, and Celene stepped forward again, tapping her sword against the briar only to see it crumble further.

Like brittle glass.

Almost on cue, she heard Arianne speak. "We are in danger, something is here."

"The thicket is brittle," Celene announced, ignoring Arianne's portent of doom, because she already knew what was coming.

"We're in their nest, aren't we?" Melia said, recognising the characteristics of the ruined towns they had seen earlier.

"Or very close to it. Draw your swords, if you have not done so already."

She heard the slide of metal behind her as swords were unsheathed. They had to escape the confinement of this thicket, if they were going to survive an ambush. Moving through the briar with renewed purpose, this time she was able to shatter them easily because of their frostbitten state.

Celene worked tirelessly, aware behind her, both Arianne and Keira were grasping their weapons tight, in readiness for attack, should it come before left the thicket. Melia was undoubtedly scanning the hills, seeking out any signs of movement, so Celene could concentrate on what was ahead. Above, the blanket of twilight descended, and Celene knew from the tension in Arianne's face the creatures were coming. She simply could not bring herself to say it.

Very soon they reached the other side of the thicket, and although they were grateful to have crossed the wood, the shadows stretching over the hills provided no relief. There were too many places for the wyrms to suddenly come upon them. Then, without warning, she heard the familiar sound preceding the battle the night before, the loud, continuous scraping against the dirt of something dragging itself across the ground.

"Take my shield," Celene said, as she handed Arianne the shield she found no use for, until the appearance of the wyrms the night before. Before setting their horses free, she had taken the gift from her father, Yalen, for this very purpose. ,

"You will need it," Arianne muttered, as Celene thrust the object into her arms. "Not as much as you," Celene replied, and turned her eyes to the direction of the sound closing in on them. "Use it, Arianne," she said firmly. "Use it to protect yourself. You carry all our futures within your body. You must protect the child, even at cost to us."

"Do not ask that of me!" Arianne cried out in dismay. "I would do anything for my child—even give up my life—but I won't allow any of you to die for me!"

"That choice is not yours to make," Celene stated firmly, needing Arianne to understand whatever feelings she had towards her friends, they were a necessary sacrifice if the greater good was to be accomplished. "This is for the good of Avalyne."

"Can this wait?" Keira snapped, as she looked about her apprehensively at the source of the slithering sound she could hear.

"There!" Melia barked, pointing to a crack in the rock concealed by shadows, much wider than it appeared on first sight.

She had no sooner said those words than the first wyrm made its appearance, its cold breath chilling her face as it slithered quickly towards her, displaying amazing agility for a creature without limbs. She leapt out of its way and landed on the ground to avoid being frozen to death, the jagged rocks on the ground biting painfully into her elbows and her knees. Trading her sword for her crossbow, she held onto the weapon through the painful manoeuvre, and though she was certain she lost more skin in the process, rolled onto her knee and took aim. The bolt from her crossbow struck the creature's belly and it uttered a gurgling sound of pain.

The creature's cry attracted the others out of their hiding places, and the women soon found themselves surrounded. Melia fired another bolt at the wyrm, for it was far from dead. It sidled towards her to exact its revenge. Running forward instead of retreating, she swerved at the last minute and leapt towards a protruding rock. Using her foot to bounce off it, she carried out a minor feat of acrobatics to land behind the beast. Taking advantage of its momentary confusion, she loaded her crossbow and fired another bolt deep into his body, stopping it for good. Unfortunately, just as Melia had taken advantage of the creature's confusion, the other wyrms took advantage of her own distraction and closed in.

"Melia!" Celene cried out at seeing the watch guard's predicament, and was already running to her defence. Narrowly avoiding being sideswiped by the tail of another wyrm of a tail, she jumped up and let it pass beneath her, meeting it head on when she touched the ground once more. The creature hissed at her, its fangs bared.

"Celene! Drop!" Arianne ordered.

Celene dropped to her haunches without question, and looked up just in time to see her shield flying over her head and towards the wyrm. It spun through the air until it met flesh and bone, and then still kept going. The wyrm did not even have time to cry out when the shield hit the rock wall behind it with a loud, metallic clang. The wyrm's reared head tumbled away from its body, spurting blood that Celene scrambled away to avoid.

Getting to her feet, she saw Arianne giving her a brief glance of acknowledgement, before they turned their attention to Melia, who was attempting to fend off the two remaining wyrms. Arianne came up from behind the two creatures and swung her blade in a wide arch over her shoulder, bringing the sword down upon the midsection of the wyrm. She put all her strength into it, and drove the blade through its flesh until it came to a halt against the ground. The wyrm writhed in agony, its frantic hissing reaching fever pitch when she split it in half. A blast of cold suddenly enveloped her body, and Arianne felt her senses overload with the biting sensation of ice.

The cold was paralysing, and for a moment, she was rooted to the spot, unable to move. It penetrated the layers of clothes she wore, making her feel as if the points of a thousand knives were raking across her skin. She felt her bones turn to ice beneath her flesh and her lips began to quiver as the rest of her shook uncontrollably. Through the fog of pain, Arianne heard Celene's frantic voice calling after her.

"Arianne!"

She felt Keira's hand around her arm, dragging off the ground to her feet. The woman of the Green ushered her away from the fight, leading Arianne behind some rocks away from the view of the wyrms so she could recover from the cold. Once they were crouched out of sight, Keira started rubbing her arms rigorously to generate heat through friction.

"I am unhurt," Arianne managed to say, through her chattering teeth. The cold was unpleasant, and her body was racked with shivers, but it was not permanent. Even now, she could feel the warmth returning to her limbs, as Keira continued to rub her arm. She could feel the blood flowing through her body, as the biting sting against her skin faded away thanks to Keira's ministrations.

"Did I not tell you should have kept the shield?" Celene joked, when as she and Melia found them a short time later.

Around them, the remains of dead wyrms lay against the ground. Arianne knew they prevailed against the assault because these wyrms were young and driven by instinct and inexperience. Had any of them encountered the creatures when they were fully grown, none of the women would have been fortunate enough to escape the experience alive. Nevertheless, these wyrms destroyed whole communities, and Arianne did not take the achievement of defeating them lightly.

"If I had not used it, *you* would not be here to be so smug," Arianne retorted with a grateful smile that her friends were unhurt. Mostly.

Celene was about to respond when the ground beneath trembled with a shudder silencing them all. Around them, grains of dirt were shaking loose from the rocks and pebbles skittered down the mountainside, clacking loudly against the rocky ground. A low rumble corresponded with each new rock fall, like the approach of thunderstorm. The sensation of imminent danger came so quickly upon Arianne, it almost choked her. Any ill effect she had suffered from the wyrm earlier was forgotten because she knew what was coming.

"Run!" Arianne cried out.

But they had run out of time.

The creature emerging from the cracks in mountain was no wyrm. In comparison to this, the wyrms were small and insignificant, this beast was not. This was a dragon, fully grown, with claws and teeth, and powerful muscles rippling beneath the iridescent scales. It was almost beautiful to watch, if you were not the source of its fury. The dragon's red eyes swept across the terrain, taking in the sight of its dead children. Then, she turned her serpentine head towards those responsible for their slaughter.

For an instant, none of them could do anything but stare at the massive beast with their mouths agape in frozen horror. Only when it took a step towards them were they forced into motion. Melia raised her crossbow and began firing at the creature. The first bolt that flew through the air struck the creature in its side had little effect. Even a formidable piece of steel was not going to penetrate a dragon's scales. The dragon shrugged off the bolt as if it was rainwater, and Melia watched with growing fear as the metal bolt clattered impotently to the ground.

"Aim for its belly!" Celene shouted, and wished she had a bow and arrow, which was a weapon more useful for an enemy such as this.

Melia nodded mutely and resumed her efforts. Taking careful aim with one of the few bolts she had left, she let it fly at the dragon. The projectile flew through the air, and this time it was not as easily discarded. The bolt struck its belly, and though it was not enough to bring down the beast, it was successful in provoking the beast's fury and it opened its mouth, preparing to vent the full torrent of its rage.

"GET BEHIND ME!" Celene ordered the others, as she held up the shield between them and the dragon. Celene had no idea if it would hold. The shield was made of dwarf iron mined from Iridia, the hardest known substance. Whether or not it would survive the dragon's cold breath was a mystery she wished she did not have to find out this way. As Keira and Arianne took refuge behind her, Melia jumped out of its path. A blast of ice spewed behind her from the creature's widened jaws.

The steel iced up in her hands and became so cold it was almost impossible for Celene to maintain her grip, but it did not brittle or shatter, giving her the determination to continue. A sharp scream from Keira made Celene peer over the shield to see the dragon's enormous head looming towards them, its jaws wide open. The Lady of Gislaine was having none of it. Instead, she swung the shield wide, slamming the iron edge into the side of the dragon's head. She expected it to be disorientated enough to allow them time to escape.

The action won them no more than seconds, giving Keira time to pull Arianne into a gap between the mountain and another tall boulder, providing them with a temporary hiding place.

"We've got to run for it!" Keira exclaimed. "Did you see where Melia went?"

"No," Arianne said frantically. "We cannot run. We will never make it down the mountain. We need to spear it!" Arianne cried out when Celene joined them in their place of safety between the rocks. The dragon was breathing its cold breath against the large boulder with relentless determination, turning the rock cold, cracks beginning to form in its surface. Eventually, it would make it cold enough for even their brief refuge to crumble.

"I am open to any suggestions you might have…" she started to say, when her words drifted a moment as if she had an idea. Until the dragon smashed its tail against the boulder and forced the words out of her. "We need a distraction!" Celene shouted, as she felt the dragon resume its effort to freeze them out. "Melia, can you hear us?"

"I hear you!" Melia cried back, as she worked feverishly to retrieve the bolts she had used on the worms. The dragon's attention was still fixated on Celene, Arianne, and Keira, allowing her to move without notice for a few seconds. Without them, she was powerless to be of any help to her friends.

"We need you to face it head on!" Celene called out.

"What?" Melia stopped short, and stared in their direction past the enormous bulk of the creature, disbelief etched upon her face.

"We need it distracted so we can strike!" Celene returned, over the dragon's roar.

The creature turned towards Melia, upon realising there was prey out in the open.

Melia grasped what Celene intended, and knew the tactic was dangerous, to say the least. All of them could be killed in one foul swoop, if they erred in its execution. Unfortunately, it was also their only chance. For it to work, Melia had to move now. Taking a deep breath, she raced forward, avoiding a deadly swipe by the dragon's claws when it attempted to strike her as she ran. Upon missing, it used it tail instead, attempting to swat her away like an insect. Melia managed to elude it, leaping onto the boulder Celene and the others were hidden behind.

"I hope you are right about this!" Melia cried out, swallowing thickly when she saw the dragon coming towards her.

She stood her ground, and perhaps it was her defiance, daring to face it in the open with her crossbow aimed boldly, that stayed the creature's desire to turn her to ice. The dragon wanted to feed upon her bones, to taste her marrow upon its tongue. It rumbled forward as Melia began shooting bolts at it, taking precise aim so as to strike its soft underbelly.

The beast roared in outrage and rose up to its full height when its skin was broken, preparing to avenge the pain by snapping its jaws around her skull. Melia's fingers trembled as she continued to shoot, her fear threatening to override her senses. She forced away her terror, because it was imperative she hold her ground. In a matter of seconds, she emptied all her bolts into the beast's belly and heard its deafening roar in her ears. In its fury, it chose to abandon the desire to feed upon her, deciding on the quicker path of simply freezing her.

Melia saw the dragon's mouth widen and knew what was coming. She jumped as the cold blast came at her, landing badly on the shoulder that popped loudly when she hit the ground. The pain was beyond belief, like white heat searing through her body. It forced a cry of pain from her lips and for a few seconds, she could not move. She was almost prepared to let the dragon have her, when Celene appeared, making a running leap onto the rock, her sword brandished high above her head as she ran towards the dragon.

The dragon was reared up on its back legs, its belly exposed as Celene lunged at it. It had little time to react as her sword slid deep into the creature's sternum. Hanging on tight, she let the weight of her body pull her downwards; the blade cutting through the dragon's soft underbelly and ripping open its stomach in a bloody trail. It writhed in excruciating pain and flayed its head from side to side as it screamed a bloodcurdling cry that seemed to fill the world with its pain. The dragon's entire body quaked as the weapon did its worst, tearing out its insides, and spilling blood and innards through the fissure of torn tissue.

As it struggled in agony, Celene was thrown away from the dragon like a rag doll. She landed in the dirt just in time to see the dragon staggering away. The beast was heaving and straining against the agony of movement. Its spilled organs were dragging across the dirt in a gruesome display, before it rolled heavily onto its side, its breath ragged and thready.

Celene picked herself up, glad to have suffered only scrapes and bruises, but her gaze still fixed upon the wounded animal whose life's blood had turned the ground into a pool of dark blood. She saw her sword still protruding from its belly, and knew by its terrible wounds the creature was not long for the world.

A part of her felt sorrow for killing these beasts for they were rare, and would soon be a thing of legend. However it was still one of the enemy's agents, who would have spared no such compassion for them in the places were reversed. With that in mind, Celene's heart hardened to its plight. The dragon's breathing soon shallowed. Soon, the glow of its red eyes dimmed forever, and it moved no more.

Only when she was certain of its demise was Arianne able to release the breath caught in her throat as she emerged from their hiding place. She hated to be protected, but the little prince inside her was fragile, and she understood why Celene wanted her to stay back. If she failed in her quest, all of Avalyne would be lost. She had to keep the terrible vision she had seen in Lylea's pool from coming through.

"Are they okay?" Keira hurried past her, going to see how Celene and Melia fared.

"I do not know," Arianne said honestly, as she saw Celene standing up wearily, an angry gash across the side of her face. Blood stained Celene's cheek and matted the gold of her hair, but other than that small injury, she appeared unhurt. Melia, however, did not move from where she had fallen, alarming all of them immediately.

Keira and Celene hurried to the watch guard who was lying on her back, her face contorted in a grimace of pain.

"Melia, are you alright?" Keira asked, immediately realizing it was a foolish question, since she was still lying on the ground.

Celene, who had grown accustomed to dealing with injuries after years of travel as one of the king's company, immediately knelt down next to her as Melia to examine her injury. "Where does it hurt?" she asked promptly.

"My shoulder," the watch guard admitted with a grimace, as Celene helped her to sit upright. Even the slightest movement sent icicles of pain through her body.

"You saved us," Keira stated, as she knelt down next to Melia as well. "Thank you."

"We saved ourselves," Melia pointed out through her gritted teeth, as Celene made an exploratory examination of her injury. "I merely furnished the opportunity."

"I did not think it would work," Celene answered honestly. "It was a gamble."

Melia shot her a look of astonishment. "What do you mean you didn't think that would work? Are you telling me I stood in front of that beast and dared it on a *gamble*?"

"Would you have done it, if I said so?" Celene retorted, snickering mischievously.

"Well, no!" Melia sputtered indignantly, and then exhaled loudly, knowing she would have done it, even if it was a hazardous plan. They did not have much choice at the time. "I hope to return the favour someday." She made a face at Celene, who winked at her.

"You were very brave," Keira pointed out, giving Melia her hand to hold.

"You certainly were," Celene agreed, concluding her quick examination of her wounded comrade. "If you had not done it, we would never have been able to defeat that creature."

"I hope that is the last of them," Keira sighed, having had just enough of wyrms and dragons for the rest of the day. "At least for awhile."

"I hope so too, after this, I could use a rest," Melia grunted, as Celene placed her hands on the Watch Guard's shoulder and prepared to pop the bone into place. She knew what was coming and tensed even before Celene's warning.

"Brace yourself," the Lady of Gislaine said, and Melia nodded, closing her eyes.

Celene's action was swift, in order to lessen the length of the pain, but not its intensity. The sharp, bone-jarring sensation rose up in Melia's throat and escaped her mouth in an agonized cry as the bone was put back in place. Her hand clenched spasmodically around Keira's, and, for a few seconds, it appeared as if she might pass out from the pain. Admirably, she remained conscious though her pain showed by the tears welling in her eyes.

"I am sorry," Celene apologised for causing her pain, but there was no way around it, if the shoulder was to recover.

"It's alright," Melia whispered. "It had to be done." She panted, trying to come to grips with the pain, when suddenly she realised something. "Where is Arianne?"

Both Keira and Celene exchanged glances, as they realised they had forgotten the queen entirely. Arianne was right behind them when they had gone to Melia, after the dragon was killed. Now that Melia had pointed it out, they looked over their shoulders and saw that she was not among them.

In fact, as Celene stood up and swept her gaze across the terrain, there was no sign of Arianne at all.

When Keira and Celene went to Melia, Arianne fully intended to join them, until something familiar tugged at her senses, drawing her away from them. Instead, she was drawn towards the large crack in the mountain allowing the dragon to come upon them so suddenly.

Prudence demanded she call attention to what she was doing, but so transfixed was she by the sensation, she simply went ahead, thinking nothing of the consequences. Only when she was shrouded by its darkness and assailed by the stench of decay and dung, did she hesitate. Still, the hook upon her was firmly imbedded, and she had no choice but to proceed. A piece of broken briar lay within reach and Arianne reached down and picked it up, using it to create a makeshift torch to illuminate the cavern she entered.

The first thing she saw, of course, were the bones.

They were scattered across the floor, cracked, and none were part of a skeleton. Arianne's stomach clenched when she saw some of them were human, elf, and dwarf, while others were of animals. They were a grisly testament to the many who fell to the savagery of the creature outside. As magnificent as it was, one had to remember it was deadly too. She held her sleeve over her mouth as she entered deeper inside and noted the crushed shells of the wyrms this dragon mother had given birth to. She felt a hint of regret she and her companions were forced to kill them all to survive.

The cavern was the long-time den of the predator, with little else in it other than the remains of its past meals and its droppings. Still, something else in here was drawing Arianne deeper to it. Only when she reached the far wall, did she understand. There was a faint glow beckoning her from the opening of a smaller cavern, one too small for the dragon or its progeny, but the right size for a man or elf.

As she reached it, she understood at last why only *she* sensed it. The same spell keeping the world of men and elf separate was at work here. This was the enchantment allowing the elves to enter the Veil.

Attracted to the light like a moth to the flame, Arianne entered the safety of the Veil and found herself in the small cave shimmering with unearthly light. The glow emanated from a rock pool in the middle of the cavern, with the reflection of the luminescent water dancing across the walls. The aquamarine hues washing over her were calming in the face of the ugly darkness she so recently left behind. Arianne felt the safety of home reach around her shoulders and envelop her in a comforting embrace.

This was what it was like to be in the Veil, to know it protected them from all the evils in the world.

"And what blinds us to it as well," Arianne whispered the unspoken thought for the first time.

The glow came from the centre of the pool. When she neared the edge of it and stared into the clear, bluish-green water, she saw what she had come here to find.

The legacy of Antion.

The sword belonging to her grandfather, the first High King of the elves, Antion, lay in the middle of the pool. The weapon was forged with the stars themselves and presented to Antion when he led the elves against Mael and the primordials. He fell in the middle of the conflict, leaving her mother to take up the mantle of high queen and finish what he began. Arianne's eldest brother, Lylea's firstborn, who left Eden Ardhen centuries before her birth was named after their grandfather.

Lylea explained to her it was impossible to give Antion a proper burial at the time. Instead, they kept him in the mountains, his body hidden away to ensure it was not desecrated by Mael and his agents if found first. A spell of enchantment into the Veil was created and he was placed here, along with his sword, until such time as they could return to reclaim it.

Until *she* could reclaim it, Arianne realised.

She reached for it, her fingers breaking the tension of the pool. The glow seemed brighter and rising from the bottom of the pool, Arianne saw the swirling water take shape. For a moment, she thought it was her eyes playing tricks on her, but then the reflections and shimmers began to take form. She retracted her hand and found herself kneeling and staring as something rose slowly out of the water.

It was the shape of an elf.

He resembled a sculpture made of water as he walked towards the edge of the pool, carrying the sword. He wore the armour of the high king and a helmet with wings. She imagined from the portraits she had seen, he had dark hair and her blue eyes, though none of that was discernible now. He did not speak when he reached her, merely kneeling down and holding out his hands to present her with his sword.

The sword was beautifully ornate. From pommel, grip, hilt, and finally, to the blade itself, it was etched with intricate elven designs. The pommel had the image of a star, indicating the House of Antion. Arianne stared at it, mesmerized, and when she looked up at the water image of her grandfather, she was certain he was smiling.

Taking the weapon in her hand, he bowed his head once in approval and then completely fell apart. The water he was composed of fell back into the pool with a splash. As Arianne sat back to keep from being caught in its splatter, she felt a breath of fresh, crisp air rushed over her face. With a wave of gratitude, she knew then the spirit waiting for someone to come, was finally been released from its duty.

When it was gone, the water still glowed, but Arianne noticed its light was diminishing. Soon, the magic keeping this place secured would be gone and the cave would return to the world again. She wiped a tear from her eye as she wrapped her hand around the hilt of the weapon unknown to anyone's touch for thousands of years.

This weapon fought Mael and slew his most deadly consort, the Primordial Queen Syphia, the Dreaded Mother of All. Their battle was so savage, and Antion's wounds so grievous, he succumbed to them not long after Syphia herself crawled away and troubled the world no more. It was said that Mael's tears was so great at her demise, his grief caused the ice giving the Frozen Mountains its name He took her to be buried in the heart of Mael's Pit.

"Arianne!"

Celene's cry snapped Arianne out of her thoughts. She stood up and went to the entrance of the small cave. Stepping through the Veil, she saw the Lady of Gislaine searching the interior of the dragon's lair.

"Celene!" Arianne called out, causing Celene's eyes to shift to the rear of the cave.

"Arianne, thank goodness!" Celene exclaimed with obviously relief. "Where did you go? One minute you were there, and the next, you were gone! We thought some new menace had come for you!"

"I am sorry," Arianne apologised, reaching her. "I was drawn here, and I found what we sought. Look." She presented her grandfather's sword.

Celene's annoyance was temporarily diffused as she stared at the weapon presented. "Oh Arianne, it's beautiful," she spoke, her voice filled with wonder.

"Did you find her?" Keira called out from the mouth of the cavern.

"Yes! She is here and she's found the weapon."

"Oh," Keira stepped into the cavern, as Arianne and Celene went to meet her half way. "Where is it?" she asked.

Arianne showed her the sword of Antion, and Keira stared at it for a long while. "After all this time, we have come a long way to find a sword. Will it do what you think it will?" she asked, appearing somewhat sceptical.

"My mother believes so," Arianne replied. "This will strike a blow that saves my child's life."

"Then it is good we have finally found it," Keira smiled tautly, showing her doubt had not been dismissed entirely. "We need to attend Melia, she's been hurt."

Arianne felt immediately ashamed because she'd forgotten the fourth member of their company. "How is she?"She asked.

"She will live," Celene answered. "But she can travel no more tonight, and, to be fair, neither can we. It has been a long day fraught with danger, we need to rest and set out again tomorrow."

"Agreed," Arianne nodded. "There is still enchantment left in the cave where I found the sword. Let us move Melia in there, and we can rest without the fear something else will attack us this night."

"That," Keira said with a smile, "is the best idea I've heard all day."

Chapter Sixteen

The Mistress of Furnsby Farm

Taking refuge in the cave for the night, Arianne used her elvish healing skills to complete the treatment Celene began on Melia's shoulder. When she was finished, Melia's pain was lessened somewhat after its painful resetting by Celene. Although it would still ache from the dislocation, at least Melia would have, more or less, full use of it. This relieved Melia to no end since they needed resume their quest. There were other injuries too, while not as severe as Melia's, some requiring attention and others requiring rest.

After moving into the small cave with Arianne's help to pass through the Veil, Keira favoured them with a hot meal, after Celene built a fire, and Arianne ensured Melia was settled for the night. They sat around the pool with their meals, forgetting the bloody business of the day and talked of home, their husbands and all the gossip that seemed trivial in light of their purpose the next day. They avoided the subject of the quest for the evening.

That subject was in abeyance for the night. Still, with the sword of Antion retrieved, spirits were higher.

As usual, Celene took first watch while the others slept, with Keira offering to relieve her during the night. Although they were guarded behind the Veil, Celene was conscious of its diminishing power now the sword lost its ancient protector. Arianne wanted to contribute to the watch, but neither the Lady of Gislaine nor the Mistress of Furnsby Farm would have any of it. She was a woman pregnant, and needed as much rest as could be afforded during this journey. Tomorrow, they would be approaching Mael's Pit, and she needed all her strength for what might lay in wait for them.

As much as Arianne wanted to refute their words, she knew they were right. The second full moon was almost upon them, and she could feel the swell in her belly indicating her son's growth. Her elven endurance brought her this far, but even she could not deny she tired more easily than before. She had no idea what she would face when she reached the enemy, but she needed to be at her best when that encounter took place.

When dawn broke the next morning, they wasted no time in preparing to resume their journey down the icy mountain. Celene emerged first from the cavern, and went to retrieve all the weapons left behind following their battle with the wyrms and its formidable mother. Swords, knives and bolts were reclaimed from the dead carcasses and returned to their owners.

They ate another meal at breakfast to sustain their descent while Melia and Arianne packed up their campsite. The watch guard was on her feet, the night's sleep, and the combination of elven and Angarad healings skills, did much for her condition. She was eager to resume their journey.

As they descended the Frozen Mountains, they were faced with a series of canyons that abutted Mael's Pit. From a distance, they could see the wide chasm leading into the depths of the earth. It snowed the night before, so the tops of the canyons were covered with icicles, frost, and snow. The downward slopes of the mountain would take them through the many corridors and canyons, leading them to Mael's Pit. There was something daunting in knowing its high walls would give them little room to manoeuvre, if ambushed. Unfortunately, there was no other way forward.

The canyons, known only as Mael's Tears, were the result of the dark god's fury at the death of his consort, Syphia. It was said he ripped the earth apart in grief at her death. It was also the final battle ground between Mael and the Celestial Gods. As they finally reached the foot of the Frozen Mountains, and took one of the corridors through the canyons, it was easy to imagine that terrible conflict. Even covered with ice, the violence to the land was evident, like the scars worn by the earth itself.

"I do not know if I am happy to be off that mountain," Melia confessed, as they began the trek through the canyon, her eyes looking about her, and trying not to feel overwhelmed by the high walls around them.

Arianne, who was experiencing the same emotions, agreed immediately. "I share your concern. At least on the mountains, we could see what was approaching us. Here, we are almost blind."

"At least we're almost at the Pit," Keira reminded, attempting to lighten the ominous mood. "The full moon is two days away, and we will be there well before the time needed. That is something to take comfort in."

"That is true," Arianne agreed, but was unable to laud the effort too greatly. "We are still no closer to learning who this enemy is, and how Antion's sword will be of use to us. I suppose one way or another, I will soon know my fate and that of my child."

"And, on that happy thought," Celene grumbled at how much doom was in Arianne's voice at that admission, "we shall continue."

"I wonder what lies beyond Mael's Pit," Melia wondered out loud, trying to move past the subject as they continued along, surrounded by frosted walls and snow beneath their feet. Overhead, the sun was hidden beneath the clouds, and there were too many shadows in the canyon for her liking. "I know there lies a vast sea, but little more than that."

"My people used to call it the Quandiara Sea, which means 'Edge of the World'," Arianne explained, keeping her eyes aloft so the sky was within sight. "Before the Primordial Wars, it was as far as they ever explored. Of course, in those days, ice did not cover this land."

"Maybe there's nothing," Keira suggested. "Maybe, it's the end of Avalyne and if you cross the sea, you'll end up falling into the Aeth."

"Well, that's a grim thought," Celene cast the woman of the Green a look. "I like to think there are new lands yet to explored, that might even have their own races. The Celestials do not always reveal themselves to us and perhaps the folk there have their own trials and victories. Perhaps someday in the distant future, we will encounter each other."

"Some of my people have attempted to sail those seas," Arianne offered. "Of course, they never returned, or they were killed long before they ever reached them. Elves can be convinced to carry out all kinds of foolishness, if enough lather has been placed upon their egos."

"That is not a trait exclusive to elves," Celene pointed out with a smile.

"Absolutely," Melia agreed. "My people are no better. I am from the East, and because of our proximity to Abraxes, many of our tribes fell under Balfure's sway, even before he made his move towards Carleon. The Nadira, who lay in the outermost region of the Eastern Lands, remained unaffected, only because of distance. Of course, we suffered the price for that. The other kingdoms, such as Raya, chose to fight for Balfure, and considered it an affront when we refused him. As a result, we have spent years at war with them."

"There has been little effort made to reconcile with the people of those lands," Arianne admitted from her knowledge of Dare's efforts in that regard. "At present, we are too busy trying to rebuild after the occupation."

"Some people may not be changed," Keira declared. "It may be too much in their nature to be anything other than what they are."

"Perhaps you are right," Melia said glumly. "The world is a large place, and there will always be darkness, as well as those who will exploit it to their own ends."

"I must agree with Melia on this," Celene replied. "I thought we were done fighting, but now it seems the lesser enemies, who remained hidden during Balfure's reign, have chosen his demise to appear. I fear we have a long way to go before there is truly peace in Avalyne."

"Some enemies may not be lesser," Keira pointed out. "Some may have chosen not to ally themselves with Balfure for reasons of their own. They may have grander schemes in mind, and chose to wait until he was..."

"Be still!" Arianne ordered suddenly, silencing them immediately, as her voice echoed down the passage.

For a few seconds, Arianne did not speak, but her sword was drawn, prompting the others into doing the same. Even though the sun was above them, there were many shadows, thanks to the high canyon walls. The formations of icicles here and there, did not help the situation any better. Minutes elapsed, and only their breathing could be heard.

Celene began to get impatient with the anticipation, and though her heart told her to trust Arianne's senses, her mind, relying more on thing she could see, began to falter. "What is it?" Celene asked finally.

"I can hear them," Arianne whispered softly.

"Hear who?" Melia asked, her own patience dwindling. She armed her crossbow.

"I don't know," Arianne replied, wishing there was an answer she could give them. She could only sense something was near.

Their proximity was so close she could feel their breath upon her skin, but she could not see them. She knew they were there, she could feel them!

"Let's get out of here then," Celene prompted, not wishing to discount Arianne's senses, but not at all eager to remain, if there was danger close by.

"I don't know if that's wise, Celene," Arianne stared at her.

"We should not remain to be targets," Melia added her voice. "If they are here, and we cannot see them, we will be far more difficult to overcome if we are moving."

"Melia is right," Celene replied, and saw Keira drifting away from them, falling back. "Keira, the way back is no better than going forward. Stay close."

Keira held her ground and raised her chin to stare at them.

"I am afraid I cannot," she answered.

"What do you mean, you cannot?" Celene started to say when suddenly, the mounds of snow and the stalagmites of ice around them began to change shape. Until now Celene had not paid attention to how many they were, but as they transformed before her eyes, she realised with a sickening sensation they were many.

"This was not the place I would have preferred we had our first meeting, queen of Carleon," Keira said to Arianne. "Although I suppose it could hardly be called a first meeting, since we have known each other for so many years." There was cruel mocking in her tone and her eyes, which had been soft and understanding as long as Arianne knew her, became as hard as flint.

As she issued her cruel words, her red hair began to lengthen, growing past her shoulders, taking on a life of its own. It swirled around her head, like serpents, unrestrained for the first time in too long. Keira's eyes turned blood red, and Arianne's heart turned cold.

"This cannot be," Arianne gasped as the full horror of their situation dawned on her. All this time? The enemy had been among them all this time and they had not known? Not even had the slightest suspicion? Arianne's shame was equalled to her utter astonishment.

"But it *can* be," Keira's words were like a jab from a sword. "Think about all the events leading us here."

Now, her body also began to change shape. While the top half of her remained mostly Keira, everything beneath her skirt was changing into something terrible and grotesque. They could only watch as her limbs were replaced by the unmistakably powerful legs of a lizard. And there were six of them. Her lower half, or rather her abdomen, took on the shape of an insect, growing so large she now towered over them. It was swollen and pulsed obscenely with veins crisscrossing it dark flesh.

Celene maintained her poise, even though, like Arianne, she felt as if all the air was driven from her lungs. The revelation of Keira's deception had stuck like a blow to the stomach. With a sudden start, she realised the man in Horwyck wasn't warning her about Arianne, he had been warning about Keira! Somehow, he had seen through Keira's glamour to know she was not human. How had he seen it and she, who had been at Dare's side fighting all manner of darkness, not realised what Keira was?

"What is happening to her?" Melia demanded. Her crossbow was raised to fire, but her mind was still struggling to reconcile herself with what she was seeing. This was Keira, who had cooked their meals and insisted they maintain their strength and spirits. She saved them from the beserkers at the Splinter and until now, was a friend to them all.

"Who are you?" Celene demanded, realising how thoroughly they were duped, and trying to learn as much as she could to escape this trap with their lives.

"She is not Keira, she never *was*," Arianne managed to say, now starting to accept what was in front of them all this time. "How… how… long have you played this part, monster?"

"Monster?" Keira glared at her, swivelling her fat, turgid body in Arianne's direction. It filled Arianne with revulsion, seeing this beast wearing the face of her friend.

Arianne tried to decipher what she was beholding; this thing that had been Keira. There were parts of her resembling one creature, but there were other parts were similar to another. Her dark flesh looked like leather hide, her legs had brittle, coarse fur. Her hands had now become claws and her lips widened across her face, turning blood red to reveal teeth, serrated and sharp. It struck Arianne in a blinding flash of clarity, who she was or rather *what* she was. Once understanding filled her mind, it made all the other pieces of the puzzle fit seamlessly into place.

"You are Syphia," Arianne stated, without question. "The Dreaded Mother of All."

Oh the irony of it, Arianne thought, fleetingly, as she descended into despair. All this time, they thought the enemy was a man, and how foolish they had been to never consider she might be female, and among them. That was why her mother could not tell her for certain how the enemy would watch her—because the enemy was a primordial, and not even an elf was able to fight them, without the help of the Celestials.

"Oh Gods," Celene exclaimed, her face turning white. "This is Mael's consort?"

"I WAS HIS QUEEN!" Keira, or rather Syphia, roared and her hair swirled about her, as if they were the physical manifestation of her emotions. "I gave him his army! The dragons, the trolls, the caracals, the spiders, and the shifters! Every foul thing inhabiting your nightmares, I gave birth to them!"

"What have you done with Keira?" Celene demanded, refusing to feed her posturing, although inwardly, she was terrified at how quickly things spiralled out of their control. "The *real* Keira?"

Celene's instincts told her there was no hope. Keira was dead. She had to ask, though. She could not abandon Keira to that reality, if there were even the slightest chance their friend was alive, *somewhere.*

"The real Keira?" Keira, or rather Syphia, laughed. "The real Keira is buried somewhere in the Green. I cannot remember where exactly I interred her, but she is there, nonetheless, since no one has yet found her."

"The Green...? You killed her before going to Carleon?" Celene's heart sank at knowing it was too late. It was always too late for poor Keira.

"I did not kill her," Syphia replied, which actually sounded like an attempt at sincerity. "I did not *have* to. When I happened upon the poor mistress of Furnsby Farm, she was already dead. Balfure's Disciples were extremely thorough when they used the desert burrowers on her. It removed the need for me to do the deed myself."

Arianne's eyes widened when she realised what the creature meant. How long had she played the part of Keira Furnsby? "But I..." her voice withered in her throat, because the truth was now revealed, in all its monstrous horror.

"It was not Keira I took to Eden Taryn, it was *you.*"

"You elves," Syphia snorted with derision. "Did you think you had the skill to save anyone from the burrowers? The Disciples used it for good reason—there is no cure for them. The desert burrowers were my children, and I did not birth them to leave survivors. Keira died before her husband returned home to find her and I, who was watching your beloved Dare since the revelation the exiled heir was found, saw my chance and took it."

"You have been playing the part of Keira for all these years?" Melia asked what Arianne had already guessed.

"Why not? I have lain with a god and with other primordials to create perfection. It was easy to play the part of the wounded wife, needing the attention and care of a husband so wrought with guilt, he would explain away any change in her behaviour as the result of her torture. It was remarkably easy to play the role required, and not entirely unpleasant. These humans are far more interesting than the elves ever were," she said snidely at Arianne.

This was the darkness she and the other elves sensed in Keira, Arianne realised. What they had thought to be a blight upon her soul, because of the desert burrower's poison in her veins, was only a ruse to hide the fact that she was a primordial. The greatest one of them all. Arianne wondered if she had really been able to trick Lylea and Tamsyn, too? After all, her mother did send her to find the Sword of Antion, the weapon that had supposedly slain Syphia, all those ages ago.

"Why?" Celene demanded, because like Arianne, she was furious at being duped, but also saddened that the friendship they shared during this quest was a lie. The realisation was a hammer blow to their spirit, which she supposed, was precisely what Syphia had intended. "Why would you do this?"

"Why not? What better way to keep an eye on the happenings in Avalyne, once I had the undying gratitude of the king? I will not explain my reasons, only to say after your warmongering grandfather," she shot an icy glare at Arianne, "wounded me, I needed to heal and retreated from the world. So I slept, for all the ages following the war. Imagine my disbelief when I awoke to find Mael imprisoned by the Celestial Gods, and Balfure of all people, seeking to usurp him? I could not let that happen."

"And so what, you seek to steal Arianne's child to bring him back?" Melia asked.

"Of course," Syphia answered, as if this was no great mystery. "When the Gods punish you, they destroy your body and leave you formless. Balfure created the resurrection spell for Mael but his own ambitions prevented him from using it. I knew I simply needed a receptacle in which Mael's soul could be contained but it could not be just *any* receptacle, it had to be something special. What better vessel could there be than the crowned prince of the newly freed kingdom of Carleon? With its resources and the army I will birth him, he will build an empire covering all of Avalyne. All I had to do was wait for the blessed announcement."

Arianne let out a strangled cry and sunk to her knees, her hand on her mouth as she comprehended the intricate web Syphia weaved. The web she was caught in.

Like a spider, she thought, like a spider Syphia had been, watching and waiting for Dare to appear to claim his kingdom, uniting them all and driving out Balfure, saving her the effort of doing it herself.

Now, all Syphia had to do was take their child, and she would win without a single battle being fought.

"I will not let you touch my child! I will kill myself first!" She raised her grandfather's sword to fight.

A shape emerged out of the snow behind her with such speed, she barely had time to turn around. She saw Celene attempting to intervene, but the Lady of Gislaine was quickly overcome by the snow creatures evolving out of mounds and stalagmites. The size of men, but covered with dark, grey fur, they bared their teeth as they overpowered Celene with sheer numbers, grabbing her arms and legs to wrestle her to the ground.

"Celene!" Arianne screamed, and went for her weapon, but the beast behind her was too quick. Her arms were pinned to keep her from using her sword to any effect.

"Let go of me!" Arianne heard an indignant cry, but realised Syphia's creature would not release his iron grip.

Melia saw Celene being attacked, and snapped out of her shock long enough to shoot a bolt at the attackers surrounding the Lady of Gislaine. One bolt struck its mark, spreading crimson over grey fur as one of these creatures, shifters she suspected, howled in pain, trying to claw at its back to remove the hated projectile.

"That is enough from you!" Syphia hissed, and Melia turned just in time to see the primordial closing in on her. Her hair long serpentine hair wrapped itself around Melia's throat and lifted her off the ground, making her gasp, as she tried to free herself. Then, as if she were a horse flicking away a fly with its tail, Melia was flung across the corridor. She landed hard, and did not move once her face hit the snow.

"MELIA!" Arianne cried out helplessly, watching her friends fight to save her, and fail. "Enough of this," Syphia said to her minions, now the three were subdued. "Take the queen to San-hael. I feel our future master quickening inside her. The full moon is almost here."

"Please," Arianne wept desperately. "You have me, let them go! They are no use to us!"

"I do not think so," Syphia gave her a look of disgust. "These two will not go on their merry way, if I release them. They will try to save you, no matter how futile the effort may be. Besides, you are wrong," she smiled cruelly at Arianne. "I do have a use for them. They are for my beserkers."

Arianne's eyes widened, as she understood. "No!"

Unfortunately, as she was dragged kicking and screaming away from Celene and Melia, it appeared there was very little she could do to stop them or save herself.

Chapter Seventeen

Escape

A great feeling of dread overcame Aeron when he and the circle were following the path, apparently cleared by Arianne and the others during their journey towards the Pit.

In an effort to close the distance between themselves and the queen, it was Tamsyn who decided a faster method of travel needed to be found, after their encounter with the shifters in the forest. Although sceptical at first, largely because he had never seen the creatures described by the mage, Dare grew more and more concerned with what his wife was facing, and finally acquiesced to Tamsyn's suggestion.

It was said the griffins dwelling in the high peaks of the Jagged Teeth were created by Mael during the Primordial Wars, and enslaved to service of the dark god. The Celestial Enphilim freed them, allowing the creatures to fly free for the first time in their existence. In gratitude to the Celestial who gave them their freedom, the griffins swore allegiance to Enphilim and his servants.

When the griffins arrived, they were a sight to behold. Their wings spanned fifteen metres across, and their bodies were that of a great cat, with powerful back and fore legs. Their amber pelts rippled like gold silk, fluttering in the wind and their heads were that of majestic birds of prey, with beaks capable of rending flesh with frightening ease. They came within a day of Tamsyn's summons, and when they arrived, they were more than willing to ferry the group to the Frozen Mountains, upon learning that plans were underfoot to restore their old captor to power.

Thanks to the beasts, they were able to cross Angarad in faster time than it would take if the journey were carried out on horseback. In a matter of days, they traversed lands that would have otherwise taken weeks. The griffins set them down at the top of the Frozen Mountains, and it did not take them long to descend its heights and find the trail that Arianne, Keira, Celene, and apparently one other took to reach Mael's Pit.

Aeron could sense the evil emanating from the canyons beyond the mountains, even before they took to the hewn path created by Celene to the lair of the wyrms and the dragon. The elf had no doubt whoever this enemy was, they were close. Who knew what terrible things lingered in the depths of the world since Mael's capture by the Celestials?

"We must hurry," Tamsyn spoke up, his eyes misting over, as if he knew something they all did not.

"Why?" Dare asked first. "What has happened?"

"I am not sure," Tamsyn replied, lying. He knew precisely what had taken place. He could sense it, even from this distance. Telling Dare would serve no purpose other than to send panic through the heart of the king and the lord of Gislaine. To Tully, he had no idea what to say. There were some things that needed to be seen to be believed. "We must hasten our pace."

"I agree," Aeron commented, and broke into a jog to make his point. He could see the edge of the patch, but what lay beyond the thorny barrier, caused his mouth to fall open from shock. "By the Gods!" he exclaimed.

All these surprises were starting to bother Dare greatly, and his anxiety was increasing by the minute. "What is it now?" he demanded, not knowing how much more of these cryptic exclamations he was going to take.

"Look!" Aeron pointed out, as they stepped into what could only be described as a field of slaughter. Dead wyrms laid strewn about the bloody field, bodies cleaved in half, speared and slashed. It was a grisly scene of death and, if that was not shocking enough to the senses, the dragon lying in the middle of a drying pool of blood was. The creature was buzzing with flies and other insects, its entrails exposed from its split belly. The smell produced made someone gag, Dare thought it might have been Tully.

"It's a dragon!" Kyou exclaimed. "I did not think there were any left! I thought they were destroyed during the Primordial War."

"They were," Tamsyn answered, his expression grave. "These are not ancient creatures, these are *young*. This dragon is not from the war."

"My wife was definitely here then," Ronen studied the slaughter around him, and did not know whether or not he ought to be proud of her efforts or furious she was placed in such terrible danger. "I recognise her handiwork."

"Celene has many talents," Dare frowned, as he examined the beast and was grateful to say, it was definitely dead. Now, on top of all the other reasons, he wanted to find Arianne safe and sound, Dare wanted to hear all about how they had managed to slay a dragon of this considerable size. He was proud of all three women, while at the same time, terrified for them as well. "I had no idea dragon slaying was one of them."

"It seems they are more resourceful than we gave them credit for," Kyou replied, rethinking his views on the lady's ability to defend herself.

"Celene we already knew, but Arianne has her own strength," Aeron replied, recalling how Arianne rode to Eden Taryn with Keira.

"The tracks are confusing to read," Aeron remarked, as he turned his attention to the ground not smeared in blood. "Nevertheless, all three survived the encounter. There are prints leading to that cave." The elf walked on ahead, and started climbing the rocks into the cavern.

"I believe your wife and her friends have acquired the Sword of Antion," Tamsyn explained, climbing into the cavern behind Aeron. The jewel poised on the edge of his staff began to glow, and light filled the cavern to show the sight greeting the women who took their rest within its walls.

"It was here?" Aeron asked, surveying the place with clear revulsion, after seeing the bones of animals and men who met their end as the meal of the dragon inhabiting this cave.

"For almost three millennia," Tamsyn answered casually, as Dare and Aeron went to the far end, where they found further signs of their loved ones.

"They rested here for a while," Aeron explained, his fingers gauging time by the cooling embers of the campfire.

"Well, killing a whole bunch of wyrms and dragons can do that," Tully found himself saying to no one in particular, still unable to believe that Keira took part in all this carnage.

"Someone was hurt." The elf picked up the crushed remains of vegetation and took a breath of it.

"I know this weed," Dare stated, as he took some from Aeron and breathed in its unique scent. "It is used for minor ailments."

"That's good to know," Ronen declared, breathing easier, after the elf's initial pronouncement of someone being hurt. "So they found the Sword of Antion and kept going?"

"Towards Mael's Pit," Dare said with a nod. "Towards the enemy."

* * *

She dreamed of Ronen.

She dreamed he was near and he was seeking her through the mist. It was good to see him, even if he only existed within the boundaries of the dreamscape. She gazed at him with love and pride, noting he was dressed for battle, sword hung proudly at his hip, braces on his arms, and a shield emblazoned with the Dragon of Carleon slung across his shoulder. Watching him as he drew nearer to her reminded Celene why she loved him so. They were two warriors who spent their entire lives fighting one battle after another.

As the divide between them dwindled, Celene began walking towards her husband, wanting to feel his strong arms about her, and to hear him tell her that he was with her and whatever came after this, they would face it together.

When he said those words to her, Celene believed they could defeat anything.

"Celene!" A sharp prodding in her side making the mist around them dissolve, taking Ronen with it.Instead, she woke up against cold, wet, and slimy rock scraping against her cheek and the stench of a stable assaulting her nostrils.

She sat up abruptly as her most recent memories flooded into her mind, and she saw she was in a small room that appeared to a dungeon of some description. The room was in a serious state of disrepair. Its walls were marred with mighty cracks, and the ceiling was half missing. Beyond it, there was no sky, merely darkness devoid of starlight.

Her head throbbed, and her effort to reach for it brought forth the discovery her hands were bound behind her back. Celene attempted to stave off panic at this discovery, especially when she looked around and saw the room, save herself and Melia, was empty. Arianne was not with them.

"Where is she?" Celene demanded, once she managed to sit up to face the Watch Guard.

"Syphia took Arianne with her," Melia announced shortly. "The shifters brought us here."

"I have heard of these creatures capable of changing shape," Celene muttered, as she shook away the disorientation from being rendered unconscious. "But I thought they were legend."

"They're real enough," Melia retorted bitterly. "They are probably more of Syphia's children."

Syphia. Celene closed her eyes, still unable to believe they had been duped for so long. All this time the enemy they had travelled so far to confront, had been amongst them. It made Celene want to kill something, but at the moment her rage was impotently trapped within their prison.

"They were waiting for us," Celene hissed under her breath. "She must have told them which way we were coming."

"Probably," the watch guard nodded, finding no reason to disagree.

She did not know Keira long enough to feel the anguish and betrayal Arianne and Celene no doubt felt. She wanted to offer Celene her sympathy at the loss of the friend who was never really a friend, but there was too much to do right now.

"So, where is this place?" Celene took the opportunity to study her surroundings more carefully.

Through the crack in the ceiling, Celene saw the outline of a city. Its spires and columns were broken, and it was clear some terrible catastrophe befell it, to be in such a state of dilapidation. Some of the buildings crumbled away completely, exposing suites and rooms, covered within with mosaics and withering tapestries. Moss and lichens grew over the grey stone, with vines and cobwebs overhanging balconies and other high places. It did not require Celene to see much more to understand they were presently being held in one of the ancient cities of the elves.

"This is Sanhael," Melia responded, attempting to loosen the bonds around her wrists, but to little avail. As it was, the outcome of her efforts made her skin feel raw and tender, forcing her to stop, before she was further injured.

Sanhael. This was the birth place of the elves. From here, they were given life by Cera who appointed the Celestial as their shepherds, to guide and nurture her children. Here, the elves built the first great city before war and loss drove them to hide behind the Veil. The first blood Mael drew in declaring his war against the Celestials, was to take this city, and slaughter all who lived within its walls. Once he claimed it for his own, he made Sanhael the seat of his power, and from here, he launched his offensive against all of Avalyne.

"Sanhael?" Celene nodded, unsurprised they were brought here. If Syphia intended to resurrect Mael, it stood to reason she would do it at the former seat of his power. She strained to see through the small hole in the door of their cell. Beyond it, she could hear the movement of their captors with no effort made to conceal their identity. "Her heart clenched inside her chest as she recognised the meat of their conversation, because while the substance of their language eluded her, she knew the tongue being spoken.

The brutish speech of beserkers.

As if aware of her realisation, Melia answered coolly, "We've been given to them."

"Given?" Celene's eyes widened, as she stared sharply at the watch guard. She knew what that meant of course, but a part of her was still refusing to believe it.

"Apparently, the beserkers are in need of distraction," Melia swallowed, her face showing her clear revulsion of their intended fates. "The enemy has given us to them to *entertain* them."

"I would die first!" Celene spat in horror. She could not even begin to imagine such a gross violation of her body, and for the first time since this all began, started to feel currents of real terror surging through her.

"You will die anyway," Melia pointed out wearily. There was a brief pause and she spoke again, this time her voice was lowered almost to a whisper, "We may be able to use it to our advantage."

"Use it?" Celene asked, almost afraid to ask what she meant.

"You do not need to know," the Watch Guard replied, appearing somewhat uncomfortable with the question.

"Do not tell me I do not *need* to know," Celene hissed with exasperation. "This is not the time for riddles."

"And I give you none, except to say you must trust me," she repeated herself, still hesitant to tell Celene, for she might balk outright at the suggestion or worse yet, attempt to stop her from attempting it. "If we are to get out of here, we must apply all our resources to escaping so we can help Arianne. They know you as the Lady of Gislaine and a member of the king's circle. They know you would not debase yourself in trying to seduce them. They do not know me, so they may believe it."

Celene opened her mouth to protest, but caught herself in time. Melia had proven to be a trusted ally during this entire quest. Celene supposed trusting her in this matter was the least she could do to show her faith in the watch guard. Besides, she could fault Melia's logic. She would rather die fighting than raped and despoiled by Balfure's savage creations.

"I trust you, Melia," Celene said after a brief pause. "Can I help in what you plan to do?"

"Unfortunately not," Melia said with a little smile, grateful for the trust, for it was no small thing to earn Celene's respect, especially after the betrayal they suffered from someone so close to them. "I'm afraid this is work not worthy of the daughter of Angarad or, more specifically, the Lady of Gislaine."

Celene did not understand, but then she did not need to. "Alright then, do what you must."

"Thank you," Melia replied, before returning her thoughts to the matter at hand. "Wish me luck."

Celene nodded as Melia turned her attention to the door and called out, attracting the attention of the guards at the door. One of them peered through the opening in the door, and seeing she had caught their interest, asked to see their captain. She spoke in the common tongue, but it was obvious they understood her.

He entered the room a moment later, a sight to scare Celene, who had faced far worse in her lifetime. Tall and muscular, his neck was thick and his face just as fearsome and ferocious as the beserkers she had fought during the battle of Astorath. The two women felt like dwarves next to him. There was no way they could hope to overpower him on equal ground, and yet, if they did not, they would face a nightmare far worse than any death imaginable.

"What is it you want?" he growled, his sharp teeth showing as he made the demand. His voice was like a snarl, and the rest of him was savagery given form.

"I do not wish to die," Melia said simply, her tone was smooth, with a quality to it different from her usual speech, almost husky. Inwardly, the watch guard was fighting her fear because she was damn near terrified of what could happen, if this went wrong.

"You won't die," he laughed wickedly, his eyes glimmering in twisted suggestion. "You two are the only females there are for my men. We will keep you alive for many, many years, or at least until we acquire more."

Celene felt herself blanch at the thought and prayed silently to all the Gods this plan of Melia's worked, because being kept alive for the sole purpose becoming the beserkers' toy was enough to make her long for death. The idea of being violated by this creature was threatening to force any sane thought from her mind.

"I would come to you willingly, if you do not harm us more than necessary," Melia offered seductively, forcing herself to remain true to her course, no matter how much his closeness unnerved her.

Celene had to admire Melia's ability to play the part before this beserkers Captain, because she certainly would not have been able to manage the pretext of going with these creatures willingly, not while there was breath in her body. She almost demanded Melia to stop this insanity, but then remembered her promise to trust the watch guard.

"Willingly?" The beserkers Captain stared at her with uncertainty. "What difference does that make to us? We will take what we want anyway."

"You can do that," Melia agreed, aware of the dangerous game she was playing, but somehow she had to inspire this captain's interest. "Or you can let me show you a world of pleasure beyond your understanding. Why do you think human males are so devoted to their wives? Love? Love is for fools. I am talking about lust, pure, dark and savage, the kind that makes the body scream for more. I can show you so much pleasure your mind will know nothing but hungry craving and when that craving is beyond endurance, I will satisfy it with all the skill at my disposal."

"This is a trick," The captain snorted in disbelief, yet, there was glimmer in his eyes, resembling interest.

"I can show you," Melia suggested, her eyes still fixed upon his own beneath their heavy ridges. "Keep my hands tied, and give us some privacy, and I will show you just how much of this is a trick."

By the Celestial Gods, Celene cried out silently, in the confines of her thoughts. *She was succeeding! This beserkers actually believed her!*

The captain stared at Melia for a second, trying to decide whether or not her offer was genuine. For a few seconds, nothing was said by anyone in the room, although both Melia and Celene were holding their breaths in anticipation of his answer.

After what seemed like an eternity, he reached down and pulled Melia to her feet by the collar of her shirt. The watch guard stood up shakily, uncertain whether or not she was happy he fell for her ruse.

Without speaking, he dragged her out of the cell into the larger room outside. There were three beserkers there already. Two were playing sentry outside their cell, and one who was standing guarding at the door to this room. All turned their attention to Melia and the captain as he dragged her to the centre of the floor and lifted her roughly onto the table.

"Show me," he demanded.

"Tell them to go away," Melia replied, glancing at the other beserkers in the room. "This is not to be done for an audience, just you."

She gave him the same smile she had in the cell, the one promising all sorts of pleasure, if he submitted to her small request. "I do not need to be untied," she added, just to give him reassurance she was powerless against him. "Just a little privacy."

He considered her words for a short time before barking at the others in the room, in words she did not understand, but were clear enough when they started towards the door, sniggering to themselves. Melia braced herself for what she needed to do and hoped it would succeed, because in her experience, men did not take rejection well, and one led as this one was would not hesitate to kill her for the insult.

The first thing he did once they were alone was tear open the buttons of her shirt, exposing her breasts to him. She could tell he liked what he saw by the quickening of his breath. Melia was sitting on the table, her legs spread slightly apart as the captain took position between them. His hand reached for her skin and kneaded the flesh hard.

Melia almost gagged from the sensation but swallowed away her disgust. She smiled at him, pretending his touch produced pleasure and the reaction impacted upon him oddly—he did not know what to think. It was clear this beserkers had never been with a female of any kind, and was trying to satisfy his curiosity with her.

Unfortunately, this was as far as she was going to allow him.

Without any warning, Melia lifted her legs up to either side of the captain's neck. She grabbed hold of his head with her feet. In one swift but brutal show of strength, she twisted sharply once her hold was secure and, before he had any opportunity to push her away, snapped his neck with a terrible crunch of bone.

He fell to the ground without uttering a word and Melia exhaled sharply, relief escaping her held breath. Climbing off the table before the beserkers at the door noticed, she saw their weapons on a table at the far end of the room. It appeared the beserkers were going to divide them as spoils.

Melia found her sword and used it to cut the bonds around her wrists. It took some manoeuvring to accomplish, but once it was done, she gathered their weapons and returned quietly back to Celene's cell.

"I'm back," Melia announced as she entered the cell.

"Where is he?" Celene asked, not wanting to know what Melia did to acquire her freedom, not if her exposed chest was any indication.

"Enjoying my seduction," Melia said wryly, as Celene stood up and faced her bound wrist towards the Watch Guard so she could be freed of them.

"I will not ask," Celene declared, as she took her sword from Melia once she was freed, and Melia was fixing the buttons on her clothes.

"Don't," Melia admitted her disgust without shame. "When this is done, I shall have to bathe for a month."

"We can go up that way," Celene pointed to the hole in the ceiling. Obviously, the beserkers never thought they would be able to use it as an escape route, if their hands were tied.

"Good," Melia replied, glancing past their cell door. "I don't relish facing those beserkers when they find out what I did to their captain."

* * *

Escaping from the hands of the beserkers was not as difficult as it appeared. Finding Arianne was another thing entirely.

The city of Sanhael was largely intact, despite its state. It sank to the bottom of a chasm following the Primordial Wars. Judging by some of the cracks weeping with water, behind the rock was the Brittle Sea. It would only a matter of time before it claimed this city, like the rest of the undersea caverns. How this place survived was a freak of nature, but they supposed the enemy never intended to remain here for long, only until its foul plan reached culmination with the birth of Arianne's child.

Unfortunately, their efforts to find the queen were hampered by the fact their escape raised the alarm throughout the city, forcing them out of it, until they could regroup and consider what was to be done. The underworld beneath the Frozen Mountains seemed to be a series of caves intersecting with the remains of Sanhael. Melia and Celene came to the decision to find someplace to hide until the beserkers stopped searching for them.

Once it was safe to do so, they would continue their search for Arianne, though neither was blind to the difficulty of that. Celene had no idea if it was nearing the full moon, or what the enemy's plans, were now Syphia had Arianne in her power. Celene knew she was still alive, but the closer they approached the ritual they drew to the ritual to supplant her child's soul with Mael's, the greater the possibility Arianne might take her own life to save Avalyne.

Slipping into the passages leading to the city, Melia suggested they retrace their steps, in hopes of finding some clue as to the location of Arianne. They made their way down the meandering cavern of rocks and twisting pathways, when voices were heard from further down the tunnel. Soft tones echoed down the narrow confines of rock. Melia and Celene took cover immediately, not prepared to be discovered, at least not until they went after Arianne.

* * *

"Something draws near," Aeron announced to the circle, as they made their way down a passage of rock they discovered to be full of tracks. Whether or not they belonged to Arianne or Celene was difficult to say, for there were many of them, but at least they were fresh.

With Tamsyn's guidance, they left the Frozen Mountains and crossed the canyons known as Maelog's Tears to reach the Pit. The city of Sanhael, driven into the earth following the Last Battle between Maelog and the Celestials, lay waiting beneath it. Descending into its darkness with ropes, the journey down was perilous, and Tamsyn promised to summon the griffins when they were ready to leave. Dare wanted to approach Sanhael without being seen, and flock of griffins would not go unnoticed.

Once on the ground, they avoided entering the city proper. Instead, they chose to use the tunnels to make a stealthy approach, as well as search for the queen and her companions.

"What?" Dare asked, unsheathing his sword, looking ahead with deadly intent. Since descending into this stygian world, his fears for Arianne had increased a thousand fold. He was eager to find something so he could flay its skin from its body to learn the whereabouts of his wife.

"I am not certain." The elf's brow knotted in confusion, as he replied in a puzzled voice. "I do not sense it as a danger, though."

"Isn't that a good thing?" Kyou quipped.

"Could it be Arianne?" Dare asked hopefully, but he knew it could not be that easy. Not after tracking her all these weeks.

"I do not sense her," Aeron replied, and was rewarded with a disheartened expression from the king.

"How close is it?" Ronen's weapon was drawn and ready for attack.

"Very close," Aeron answered.

"All of you," Dare spoke firmly to the rest of the circle, "stay here. Aeron and I will go investigate."

"But…" Ronen started to protest, when Dare cut him short.

"I need you here to protect our backs," Dare quickly explained. "Aeron does not sense danger, but that does not mean it is not a trap."

"Alright." the Lord of Gislaine was forced to concede that much to his king, and fell back, as Dare and Aeron continued down the passage.

"Take care, you both," Tamsyn warned good-naturedly, as they drew away.

"Care to tell me what I will find?" He stared at the mage with impatience.

Tamsyn said nothing, merely giving him a bemused smile.

Sometimes Dare wished that Tamsyn was not quite so evasive. Then again, what wizard was ever anything less than cryptic?

With Aeron leading the way, Dare followed the prince of Eden Halas further up the tunnel, wondering what perils they would find. He left the others behind because the space within the tunnel was narrow enough without too many bodies trying to fight, if there was an attack of some kind. They entered a slightly larger cavern filled with protruding limestone formations, and saw nothing but more shadows.

Aeron paused in the middle of the main track to the cave and swept his eyes across the terrain. Dare knew the stance well. He had detected something. The elf stepped away from the path, moving stealthily against the gravel toward a particularly large stalactite. He was almost upon it when out of nowhere, a lithe figure stepped out and threw a fist squarely in his face.

"Aeron!" Dare shouted, and moved to intercept as Aeron tumbled into the dirt, landing flat on his back. The stranger's movement was lightning fast, as she took up position over him and aimed her weapon directly at the fallen prince.

Aeron froze as he found himself staring into the sharp end of a crossbow's bolt. The woman who stood before him wore an expression of deadly intent fixed on her lovely face. He lay there for a moment, stunned by the attack, particularly since he sensed no danger. Her intense stare did not waver as she looked upon him dispassionately, bearing the stance of an experienced archer who was waiting for her moment to bring down her target. As an archer himself, Aeron knew the look well.

"Dare?" Celene's astonished voice suddenly filled the cavern.

His attacker looked away at the sound of Celene's voice, and Aeron swiftly took advantage of the situation. Swinging his foot sideways, he swept her feet from under her and sent her tumbling forward. She landed into the dirt next to him and Aaron rolled his body around swiftly, throwing a leg over her. Quickly straddling her hips, with one hand he tore the crossbow out of her hand and flung it aside while the other caught the fist attempting to strike him. He clamped both hands to her wrists and pinned them to the ground. The whole weight of his body ensuring she could not break free.

"Melia!" Celene exclaimed, as she emerged from her hiding place and witnessed the conclusion of the melee. "It is alright! This is the king and Prince Aeron."

"Then tell the prince to unhand me!" Melia snapped angrily, while she glared at the elf, her pride stinging from their sudden change in circumstance.

"If you are finished, Aeron?" Dare stared at the elf momentarily, before turning to Celene.

"It was not I that ambushed us!" Aeron pointed out as he climbed off the woman Celene called Melia. As a gentlemen and a prince of Halas, he offered his hand towards her in order to help the lady to her feet.

She ignored it.

"We were protecting ourselves," Melia grumbled as she stood up on her own, dusting herself off as she glared at Aeron.

"ENOUGH!" Dare boomed, because he could care less about whose fault this was. He had only one thought in mind now Celene was before him. "Where is Arianne?"

"The enemy has taken her," Celene swallowed thickly and answered her king. There was more to tell Dare, but she had no idea how to do it. The truth about Keira was going to affect him almost as badly as it would affect Tully. This was one task Celene would happily face a thousand wyrms to avoid.

"Where?" Dare said tautly, in a tone that demanded immediate compliance.

"In the city, to what is left of Sanhael," Celene replied automatically. She was grateful he was here, because now they could retrieve Arianne with the aid of one of the Carleon's greatest warriors.

"That explains a great deal," Aeron replied. "Sanhael was Mael's stronghold before it was sunk by the Celestials into the earth. At least, before he took it from the elves. All this," he gestured to the caves they had been travelling, "is what is left of them."

"Celene!" Ronen exclaimed exuberantly from the mouth of the cavern. The commotion brought the rest of the Circle. Ronen was greeted with the wondrous sight of his wife, alive and well, though looking rather worse for wear, standing before him.

Celene's face lit up with the delight that always seemed like the sun emerging from the clouds after a rainy day. They ran into each other's arms, their lips meeting in a kiss of passion no sonnet or song could ever do justice. Even Dare and Tully, who should have felt envious at the reunion when their own loves were absent, could not help but feel happy the two had found each other again.

"I thought I would never see you again," Celene whispered as she clung to her beloved.

"I would follow you anywhere. Do you not know that?"

"I suspected," she laughed. "I supposed you were too stubborn to stay at home and wait for me."

"I might say the same about you," he grinned.

When the couple had parted, Celene looked at Dare, trying not to meet Tully's gaze in case her eyes betrayed her, and said to the king. "We need to talk."

* * *

Melia stood at the edge of the cavern they found, far away from the heart of Sanhael, listening in silence as Celene revealed the truth about Keira Furnsby to the king and his circle. More importantly to Tully Furnsby, who had no idea for the past seven years he had been a widower.

"I don't believe it," he whispered. "It *was* Keira."

Tully's face was white. He had sunk into a sitting position on a boulder in the cavern, appearing as if he was about to be sick from the truth he had just been given. Celene's words swirled around his head, but had yet to sink in. *Seven years.* Keira had been gone for seven years, and in her place, in his *bed*, a monster pretended to be his wife. The magnitude of the revelation left him shaking, refusing to believe any of this could be real.

Yet, in the midst of the terrible truth, fragments of memory were coming together, revealing a picture he refused to see. So many things she did and said, he attributed to her ordeal at the hands of the Disciples. From their everyday lives together to the intimacies shared in the bed chamber, all of it had been different, even when it was exactly the same.

"No," Celene shook her head, kneeling in front of him, her eyes moist with tears as she reached for his hand, trying to offer him comfort for a pain too immense for words. "She is dead Tully. She has been dead for a long time. She did not survive the desert burrowers. Syphia told us she found Celene at your farm, dead, and upon doing so, buried her body somewhere in the Green."

"No..." he blinked, and tears ran down his cheeks, as he shook his head in denial. "It's not true, she's alive. We've been together for seven years... she's my wife. I would know it." However, his words were laced with desperation and dwindling resistance.

"She played a part, Tully." Tamsyn approached the man from behind, dropping a hand on his shoulder. "She played it perfectly. She wants a kingdom for Mael, and she had no intention of sharing one with Balfure. She lay in wait, allowing Dare to defeat Balfure and reunify Carleon, until he and Arianne produced an heir. This was never your fault. Syphia was consort to Mael himself, the Dreaded Mother of All. She is cunning and vicious, and older than all of us. Do not blame yourself for what you could not see, I was in her presence and she fooled me too."

It was true. He had sensed something in her he could not define. A darkness he thought was left behind by the Disciples, but never at any time did Tamsyn suspect Keira was, in reality, Syphia. He felt anger at the pain caused to this poor farmer, who stumbled into events larger than himself, and was so thoroughly destroyed by it. Tamsyn could already see his anguish breaking apart his spirit. It would never recover.

Dare didn't speak. He wandered away from the others, but he could not ignore the soft sobs that came from Tully, as his grief ripped him apart. Dare, too, found it difficult not to let the emotion break him, as it was doing to the farmer from the Green.

Seven years ago, Dare sought refuge at the farm of this young, idealistic couple who never had any reason to think of Balfure or Carleon. Despite this, they helped him, saved his life by giving him refuge. Still reeling from Braedan's sacrifice, Dare did not fully considered the consequences, never thought the Disciples would follow him into the Green. When Tully sought him out after the farmer returned home to find Keira, Dare did everything he could to ensure her recovery, even begging Lylea for help.

And it was all for nothing.

Not only was she already dead, but she was buried in an unmarked grave, with no one to mourn her. Dare's fury at this was almost as white hot as his rage at Syphia's plans for Arianne and his child. He wanted revenge for both.

* * *

Melia turned away and walked to the entrance to the cave, using the pretext of checking to see if anyone was coming as an excuse to leave. Even though she did not know Tully, or the rest of the king's circle, she mourned the loss of the woman, Keira. Not the one who died, and was forgotten so many years ago, but the one who made Melia, Celene, and Arianne care for her.

"Does anyone come?" She heard a voice behind her, and glanced over her shoulder to see Prince Aeron.

"No," Melia shook her head. "No one comes."

Aeron stood behind her, intrigued by this woman who came to them out of nowhere, and was now a trusted ally, just after another trusted ally become an enemy overnight.

"I did not know her," Melia said softly. "But in learning the truth, I feel I have a lost a friend, which is ironic since I never knew her in the first place."

"It seemed none of us did," Aeron sighed. "If we could be fooled, and we knew her far longer than you, you have no reason to feel shame."

"Perhaps not," Melia looked over her shoulder at the handsome, dark haired prince. "But I value what friends I have, and I do not suffer the loss of even one lightly."

273

"You have others here," Aeron gestured to Celene. "You have done more than duty demands in assisting Arianne and Celene in this quest. That is true friendship—everyone here recognises it. Everyone except me of course," he said, a small smile of mischief tugging at the corner of his lips. "I still have not forgiven you for marking my jaw," he rubbed his chin as if he still felt the pain of her blow.

Melia laughed despite herself. "Oh, did I mark that pretty face?"

"So you think I am pretty," he returned, heartened by her returning smile.

"I think you are impossible," she shook her head and faced forward once again.

Aeron returned to his friends but not before adding, "I do not think I'm the only one."

Chapter Eighteen

Sanhael

She failed.

She failed to protect her baby by killing the enemy, and she failed to end her life to keep the world safe. Her worst nightmare had come to pass, and there was no way she could keep it from consuming those she loved as well. Kicking and screaming, they took her away from Celene and Melia, whose fate preyed heavily upon her mind, particularly when she knew what Syphia intended for them.

The horror of what they were enduring because of her, was more than Arianne could stand, and it made her wail inwardly with anguish each time she thought of it. This was the very outcome she feared most when she allowed Celene to embark upon this journey with her: that Celene's life would be forfeit because of her. Not only Celene's life was endangered, she had brought another into this and now, Melia too would die because of her.

And as much as it shamed Arianne, that was not even the worst of it.

The worst of it was, at this moment, she was surrounded by beserkers and shape shifters. All awaited the arrival of their mistress to begin the ceremony to rip the soul from her unborn son's body. The shape shifters no longer looked like the snow creatures that ambushed them in the canyons of Maelog's Tears.

Even though their bodies were shaped like men, they were blank templates waiting to be rewritten, and they carried out Syphia's ritual chanting the words through mouths without lips or teeth.

There was nothing Arianne could do to stop it. Not even to take her life, and her son's.

She prayed if all hope was lost, if her efforts to stop the enemy had failed utterly, there would still be the chance of saving Avalyne by taking her own life. Thanks to Syphia's deception as Keira, the primordial queen was prepared for this. Her shape shifters ensured once Arianne was under their power, she was given no opportunity to cheat Mael of his new vessel.

Trapped on a slab of rock, in what was once the main courtyard in the city of Sanhael, Arianne's hands and feet were bound, as the shape shifters prepared her for the ritual. Above her, she could see nothing of the moon, but it did not matter. The magic that would destroy her son did not require the moon's power to come into being. It simply needed her.

They ripped open her dress, leaving her belly exposed for all to see. Strange writings were scrawled upon her fair skin in blood—the language was of the Aeth from where the most potent dark magic came. She squirmed desperately as they placed the fouls words upon her skin and marked her forehead with strange concoctions reeking of blood, paying as much attention to her as a painter would to the empty canvas. She was but the vassal of their future master, and while she was not to be hurt, she was not the most important player in this ceremony. Her babe was.

"Please!" she begged them, knowing it was pointless because they were servants to their mistress's will. "Don't do this! He is an innocent! Don't take his life before he even begins it!"

"Do not weep, little mother," Syphia's voice spoke over her.

Arianne raised her head and looked into the face of her enemy. The sight of her made her scream in naked horror.

No longer required to maintain the guise of Keira Furnsby for anyone's benefit, the primordial queen stood over Arianne in her true form. Having discarded Keira's clothes, she appeared even less human than when she revealed herself to them in the canyons. She appeared even taller than before, as she towered over Arianne standing by the altar. Her skin was now entirely devoid of its human pallor, resembling a mottled greenish hide that made Arianne think of something at home in a marsh or bog. Her living hair was no longer russet but instead, the black of burnt wood. She looked down at Arianne with a neck long like the body of snake, moving of its own accord.

What made it all the worse was her face still bore some similarity to Keira Furnsby.

"Do not weep for him, Arianne," Syphia said, her elongated neck bringing her head right alongside of Arianne's, so she could whisper in the elf queen's ear. "He will be the master of all. I will make him a god, and together we will rule Avalyne, as we were meant to be. If you were not so averse to this whole idea, I would even let you raise him. After all, I am a mother too. I know what it is like to be separated from one's children."

"He will not be my son!" Arianne screamed back at her defiantly. "He will be a monster! I have seen the vision of his reign upon Avalyne, and it is a rule bathed in blood! I won't let you destroy his soul and desecrate his body!" She turned away after her declaration, unable to keep looking at the profane sight of the woman, who had been her friend these past seven years.

"There is very little you can do to prevent it," Syphia retorted, a hint of disappointment on her voice as she raised her head up. She supposed she could not have expected anything else from the queen, who was incapable of anything but an impotent gesture of defiance. "I had hoped you could be reasonable. In truth, I did enjoy the camaraderie I shared with you, Celene, and even Melia. It was very different, and I hoped I could salvage it, despite this necessary unpleasantness."

"Unpleasantness?" Arianne swung her head to look at the primordial in disbelief.

Syphia ignored her outrage, and continued speaking as if she were dealing patiently with a petulant child. "Perhaps we will discuss the matter again once Mael is inside of you. We will have more time to talk then, since you will be remaining here until he is born. If you should die, I shall return your son to Carleon, and he will take his place by his father's side."

"NEVER!" Arianne reacted immediately, the outrage twisting her insides into knots. "His father is no fool! He will know the truth."

"Perhaps he will, but you and I both know Dare would never kill his own son," Syphia returned with a smug smile. "You might have the fortitude to do the deed, but not him. He is too good and kind a soul for such a thing. He could never willingly harm a child, especially one you gave him. Even if he thinks that Mael's soul is in his son, there will always be a part of him that would believe the child is salvageable, and that will stay his hand."

"You are wrong!" Arianne countered vehemently, but even as she spat the words at Syphia, she knew the primordial queen was right. This was what Arianne feared, too. That if she failed, Dare would never be able to kill the child, and if he could, it would destroy him.

"I think you know I am right," Syphia declared triumphantly, seeing the realisation in her eyes. "I think you feared, above all else, Dare would not only be unable to kill the child, but he might even try to stop you from doing it. If I did not think so, I would have killed him myself before he became king."

"This will not succeed!" Arianne spat in impotent fury. "You cannot watch me every second for the next five months. If you destroy my son before he is born, I will ensure your Mael will never know life in his skin! I will kill myself, before I let you blight Avalyne with his evil again!"

"You talk bravely," the Primordial laughed, "but you will not know a moment alone, until that child is freed from your body. If I must, I will tear you open to acquire him, when it is safe to do so. You will not harm my future king." With that, Syphia turned to her minion, and said simply, "*Begin.*"

"No!" Arianne screamed in despair as the shape shifters came to her once more. They began chanting the words to begin the dark ritual and the transmogrification of her son into Mael. She tried desperately to break free, but she was trapped, completely and utterly. Not even the Sword of Antion, resting on a stone bench not far from where she lay, could help her. It might as well have been ten thousand leagues away.

"Please! Don't harm my baby!" she sobbed as she struggled, trying to ignore the chanting taking place around her.

Suddenly, a sharp stabbing pain filled her body with such intensity all she could do was scream. It pierced through her skin and ignited all her nerve endings with fire. Her scream tore through the air, like an ill wind sweeping through the city. Her knees tried to pull up, to brace herself against the pain spreading out from her womb to the rest of her. The chanting grew louder, but Arianne no longer noticed it. Above her, Syphia's eyes gleamed in triumph.

"He is coming!" Syphia exclaimed. "Maelog is coming from the void!"

As she finished that sentence, Arianne felt another agonizing spasm of pain, forcing the air from her lungs in another pitched scream. Her hands gripped the ropes binding her wrist, pulling on them as the pain became more than she could stand. She knew what was happening, she could feel the terror of her babe inside of her and felt her heart shatter because she could do nothing to help either of them. Each scream of pain uttered engendered the rejoicing of the beserkers in attendance of the ceremony.

Blood started seeping out of her nose as she screamed. They continued their damned chanting in her ears, as they invoked dark powers to force Mael into her body. With the rising fervour of their words, her pain increased, until all she could hear were her own screams, half mired in agony, half begging for the life of her child. Desperate pleas earning no compassion from those watching, because their purpose was being served already. Her child meant nothing to them.

"ARIANNE!"

She stopped screaming immediately, forgetting the pain, when she turned her head to see Dare at the far end of the courtyard. He was staring at her across the sea of beserkers and shifters, his face a mask of horror, at the sight of what was happening to her. Gods, it was him. It was really him! She was ready to give up, ready to believe all was lost, but that moment of weakness was over. She would fight with all her strength to save her baby because there was now hope!

"ALASADARE! HELP US!"

The entire courtyard burst into pandemonium as the beserkers scattered to meet the intruders. Through her tears, Arianne saw Dare drawing out his sword and decapitating the first beserker confronting him, without thinking twice. With Narthaine in one grip and an accompanying dagger in the other, she watched him fight his way through the beserkers closing in on him, with skill and ruthless efficiency. Arianne had never seen him in battle, but she doubted she would forget it.

He was magnificent in his fury. He moved far swifter than any warrior, man or elf, a perfect engine of limbs moving with skill and coordination. He laid waste to beserkers coming at him with their brutish weapons, stopping their blows with Narthaine, before thrusting the dagger into their bodies to end the threat of them once and for all.

Another came at him from the right, and Dare dropped low enough to avoid the swing intended to take his head off, before turning around and stabbing his dagger deep into the creature's leg. The beserkers howled in pain, before Dare completed their battle by running him through with his sword. Throwing his fist back, he stopped the beserkers coming at him from behind, causing the creature to stagger slightly. Daren spun around and sliced open the berserker's throat with his dagger.

"Finish it!" Syphia shouted at one of her shape shifter minions, reminding Arianne the ritual was not ended, simply interrupted because Dare had arrived.

"No!" she wailed, refusing to allow this terrible thing to happen—not when they were so close to salvation.

The shape shifters resumed their chanting, and Arianne felt the same terrible pain coursing through her, cutting short any protestations she might have about the ceremony. She threw her head back and uttered another blood curdling scream of exquisite agony as the invasive spirit tried to enter her body.

The panic gripping Dare when he heard her scream was a sensation like nothing he ever knew. It made him forget everything around him, filling him with a cold rage that made the beserkers seem inconsequential. Putting everything he had into reaching her, Dare cut a swathe of blood and bone through the obstacles keeping him from his wife.

"Aeron! Help Arianne!"

No sooner than he had said those words an arrow sliced through the air and ended the shape shifter's chanting, just as Arianne's scream diminished into guttural cries of agony. Blood spurted from the shape shifter's neck as he landed hard on the floor. Another arrow flew over her head and struck the other shape shifters participating in the ritual. The accuracy and swiftness of the delivery could only be the skill of one person.

The pain stopped long enough for Arianne to regain some of her senses, and as the aftershocks of agony subsided, she craned her neck to see Aeron renewing his assault of arrows upon Syphia's minions from the other side of the courtyard. At his side was Melia, and together they made a formidable team as they killed off the shape shifters conducting Syphia's ritual one-by-one.

* * *

In the midst of all this fighting was Tully Furnsby.

The imperative for the others had been to save Arianne, and while Tully was equal to the task, he had another reason for reaching the queen. Where Arianne was, he would find Syphia.

Even after everything Celene told him about Syphia's deception, Tully still could not believe the woman he shared the past seven years of marriage with was a phantom. He knew he needed to see it for himself for it to become real to him. At present, it felt like a nightmare from which he could not awaken, the same one he experienced since returning to the farm all those years ago, to find Keira's broken body after the Disciples were done with her.

He moved through the melee, ignored by beserkers and shape shifters like an unnoticed shadow, because it was exactly how he felt. His insides had been scooped out and what was left was hollow and intangible as he walked through the courtyard. He was beyond the arrows and blades flying, beyond the blood and screams, beyond his friends or the creatures they battled. All he saw was the thing that pretended to be his wife.

"Keira!" he called out when he was near enough, and her head mounted on that serpentine neck swung in his direction. He had no idea what he intended to accomplish by this confrontation, but he knew he had to see her. Before this all came to a terrible, brutal end, he needed to understand why she did this to him.

The queen primordial stared at him for a moment, as if he were some nuisance she had forgotten, and her face revealed something familiar, something he had grown accustomed to seeing these last seven years. Puzzlement. There were times when she looked at him as if she had no idea what he was on about. Tully explained away her confusion as the result of the desert burrowers on her brain. It was only logical she experienced some disorientation after the poison her set her mind on fire.

Now, he understood the real reason for it. Her puzzlement was because it was all new to her, because it was all part of the role she was playing.

As she brought her head within inches of his, he saw her lips pull back into a cruel smile once her surprised withered. His stomach clenched in disgust at the sight of her, at the lovely face he'd looked into, now cut with serrated teeth, with eyes more insect than human. Her hair swam about her like eels swirling about in dark water, and he recoiled when strands of it, caressed his shoulder.

"My husband," she spoke the word like a taunt. "How *nice* to see you."

"Where is my wife's body?" Tully demanded, ignoring her words. He had trouble looking into her face, but forced himself to do so because he needed answers. "Where did you leave her?"

"Is that really so important?" she asked, amused by the request.

"It is to me," he bit back. "I want my wife to at least have a burial. She deserves that after what you took from her."

"What I took from her?" Syphia snorted, staring at him with narrowed eyes. "I did not kill her, and I certainly did not put her at risk to be killed by Balfure's servants. *You* did that," she pointed out, drawing blood by the accusation.

Tully blinked, trying to force away the anguish at knowing she was right. He was the reason for Keira's torture, and now, it seemed, her death.

"That may be so," he said quietly, refusing to give this beast any more amusement then she already had at his expense. "But I want to know where you left her, so that she can be mourned at least."

"Then, you shall be disappointed," she replied, her smile widening with cruelty. "I buried her in the Green, but I could not be certain if I had put her into the ground deep enough. There was so much blood, and any animal with a nose for meat could have found her."

Tully swallowed thickly and his eyes moistened in grief. His poor Keira. How he failed her.

"Was all of it a game to you?" he whispered softly, uncertain if she could hear him over the sound of clanging weapons.

"It was not all terrible," the serpent hair stroked his cheek and he tried not to flinch. "I must admit there were moments when I rather enjoyed playing the housewife. You certainly saw no difference in the bedroom. You know," she said with smile, and her face seemed to shift, her features taking on Keira's with more detail, "you can have her back."

Tully's eyes flew open and he stared at her. "What do you mean?"

Even as he asked, he *knew*. He supposed he should have expected this particular carrot to be dangled before his face. Why not? She had violated every other part of him. Why not this too?

"Swear allegiance to me and you can have her back again," Syphia explained, her hair drawing her closer to him, like arms embracing him. "I can be her again. I can take on any shape I please and, if it pleases you, I can be Keira. We can even live in the Green. You and I can raise our baby," she gestured to Arianne who was struggling against the ropes holding her tied to the altar, fighting the shape shifters restraining her. "Wouldn't you like that, Tully? I can give you so many children we'd be the envy of everyone in the Green."

"And what would I have to do?" Tully asked, his tone flat and lifeless. "What would I have to do to make all this happen?"

"Kill him." She gestured to Dare, who was fighting his way through the beserkers. "Kill him and watch him die, as you should have done when he turned up on your doorstep seven years ago. Give him to his fate, the one you thwarted by giving him refuge. You exchanged his life for Keira's. Why do you give him your allegiance, when he was the one who brought the Disciples down on Keira?"

More tears ran down his cheeks, because he would have done so many things differently that night, if he knew the price he would have to pay for his act of charity. He wiped his eyes with his sleeve and stared into her face. "Because he is my friend and he didn't kill Keira. I did."

Without another word, Tully pulled out the blade hidden in his sleeve and slashed Syphia across the face.

The queen primordial uttered a scream of pain as she reeled back, her cheek marred by a deep cut spilling dark blood over her chin. When she lunged down at him again, her eyes were blazing with red fury and her mouth widened like the maw of a gaping abyss. The teeth had come into view again, sharp and jagged.

Tully closed his eyes and let the end come.

* * *

Tamsyn was fighting alongside of Kyou and Dare, using his sword to dispatch the seemingly endless number of beserkers converging on them, when he saw through the sea of fighting bodies, the sight of Tully Furnsby standing before Syphia. The mage lost track of the young farmer and cursed himself for his distraction. Realising the need to get through quickly, he finally used his magic and flung the beserkers coming at him aside. He had not fought a primordial since the war with Mael, and was reserving his strength to combat Syphia. Until he saw the farmer of the Green confronting his wife and Tamsyn cursed his foolishness at not foreseeing this eventuality.

Of course he'd confront her, Tamsyn told himself. *After seven years, what else could he do?*

His realisation came too late, when he saw Syphia open her jaws. Tamsyn knew what was coming even before she expelled a deadly column of green fire from her throat, consuming Tully where he stood. The farmer did not even scream, but the jet of heat created a roar capturing everyone's attention as they saw one of their own disintegrate before their eyes. Flesh, blood and bone vanished in an instant, and there was nothing left but the charred remains on the courtyard floor.

Time seemed to freeze as every member of the circle stared.

Dare's reaction was an anguished cry of rage, which he used to swing his blade against the neck of a beserkers, taking its head clean off its shoulder. The head spun in the air twice before hitting the floor with a sickly squelch. Meanwhile, Aeron and Melia renewed their attack on the shifters around Arianne, firing arrows and bolts, one after each other to ensure there was no opportunity to resume the ritual to resurrect Mael. Celene and Ronen were making their way across the floor, trying to reach Arianne as, Dare had been, while Kyou guarded the king's back.

Which left Syphia to him.

Tamsyn thought of Tully—the young farmer who had stepped outside of his isolated world to give Carleon its king, when it was most likely they would lose him before he had even the chance to fight Balfure. Tully deserved better than to lose his wife, not just once, but twice in a single lifetime. He deserved better than to become Syphia's final victim, because after his death, Tamsyn was not allowing another to die at her hands.

Allowing emotion to guide his actions for the first time in too long, Tamsyn raised his staff and delivered a blast of power at Syphia. The staff glowed with amber light before exploding outward, moving across the air like a fireball and striking her dead centre. The force of it flung her backwards, lifting her off her clawed feet away from Arianne and the altar upon the elf queen was trapped.

Syphia's enormous bulk crushed the wall upon which she landed. The construction groaned at the impact, and when the primordial was able to move again, streams of loosened mortar rained down upon her from the ceiling. Large fragments came away with her body as she pulled herself free. As she shook away her disorientation, she sought out the source of the attack with thunderous rage.

"WHO DARES?" she screamed, glaring at her opponents and discovering quickly she was facing a mage. She scuttled forward on her six legs, meeting the approaching wizard half way.

"It matters not," Tamsyn declared, hurling another volley of magic at her. "Your time is at an end just the same!"

Syphia reacted by picking up a broken piece of column and hurling it at the oncoming blast. The amber orb of power exploded the thick marble construction, sending chunks of rock and dust in all directions. Her legs bowed slightly as she jumped, closing the distance between herself and the mage, until they were only a few feet apart.

"I suppose not, child of Enphilim," she retorted, and opened her mouth, breathing another jet of greenish flame from her mouth.

Tamsyn leapt out of the way, but the green flame turned the beserkers behind him to ash as completely as Tully met his end.

* * *

With the shape shifters restraining her being felled by Aeron and Melia's arrows and bolts, Arianne had succeeded in working one of her wrists free after her constant struggles. Strapped to the altar and unable to defend herself, she knew if she did not free herself of this predicament, Dare and the others would die trying to reach her. She needed to remove herself as a liability so they could ably defend themselves against Syphia and her minions.

Once her hand was free, she was able to move just a little more, and was able to reach at shape shifter who collapsed on top of her altar after one of Aeron's arrows had killed it. Straining as far as she was able to reach, the queen of Carleon felt the ropes digging into her wrists, and tearing her flesh. Gritting her teeth, she ignored the pain as her fingers extended outward as far as she could manage it, until they finally made contact with the fletching, and she gripped its feathers as tightly as she could.

Pulling it free of the body it was imbedded, she ignored the revulsion at the blood splattering against her cheek. She used the sharp edge of the arrow to cut through the rope binding her other wrist. Arianne worked as quickly as she could, aware while Tamsyn kept Syphia busy, she had a window of opportunity to escape. Once her wrists were free, she sat up and began working on her feet.

Realising the most crucial part of her plan was attempting to flee, Syphia shouted at her minions. "Capture the queen! Do not allow her to escape!"

Arianne freed her feet just as she saw a number of beserkers running in her direction. She rolled off the table and took refuge beneath the marble altar, hoping to remain hidden long enough to make good her escape. Across the courtyard, she saw Dare still battling shape shifters, and for a brief second, his eyes drifted to her and he realised she was trapped.

"Arianne is pinned!" he shouted to anyone who could hear.

Melia, who took up position along a partially collapsed staircase at the far end of the courtyard with Aeron, heard the king's call, and her eyes darted immediately to where Arianne was hiding under the altar, surrounded by beserkers. Everyone else was engaged with their opponents and in no position to reach the queen. Celene, Ronen, Kyou, and Dare were cutting down beserkers and shape shifters while Tamsyn did battle with Syphia herself. If the beserkers were to reach Arianne, Melia had no doubt she would be taken from here, until Syphia could retrieve her again.

"Arianne!" Melia called out, hoping the queen could her through all this noise.

Arianne's eyes widened, and Melia saw her searching for the source of her name. A few seconds later, their gazes met, and Melia knew that Arianne was listening.

"Be prepared to run!" Melia instructed, and raised her crossbow so Arianne would understand what she intended.

When Arianne nodded in answer, Melia turned to Aeron. "Are you as good with that thing as they say?" she asked, knowing full well he was. His reputation as an archer had no equal anywhere in Avalyne.

"I am reasonably proficient," Aeron replied, pulling two arrows from his bow and taking aim at the beserkers. "Are you?" He cast a sidelong glance at her with a brow raised.

"I did not shoot you, did I?" Melia replied sweetly, and did the same with her crossbow.

"I will take that as a yes," he replied.

"Good." She almost smiled and then spoke in a more serious tone. "We need to clear her a path out of there."

"Agreed," Aeron nodded. "You take the left and I will take the right."

"I follow your lead, Prince," Melia answered, and raised her crossbow to take aim.

Working in tandem, they rained down a deadly barrage on the beserkers near the altar, each arrow striking their mark, one after the other. The foul creatures fell to the ground like flies, their corpses joining the already numerous bodies on the ground.

Suddenly, realising her efforts to secure her prisoner were being compromised by the two archers, Syphia blasted another wave of heat at Tamsyn, before turning her head in their direction and glaring at them.

Aeron saw her jaws widened and guessed what was coming at them a split second before she expelled her deadly breath.

"Look out!" he cried out as a blast of flame came rushing at them.

Melia looked up in time to feel Aeron's arms around her waist, pulling her off the staircase as the ball of green fire came surging towards them. They both crashed heavily onto the ground, their fall broken by the dead bodies beneath them. There was little time to recover from their near escape, because Syphia was hurling more flame at them. Once more, Aeron grabbed her and they were running for cover, barely avoiding the cascading waves of burning bile setting the ground on fire, along with any beserkers in the vicinity.

"I think we upset her," Melia said, breathing hard as they took refuge behind a column.

"Arrows do that," Aeron remarked wryly.

"Thank you," Melia swallowed thickly, seeing the flames burning in the place where they had been. "I do not think I would have moved fast enough to escape."

"Does that mean you have finally decided to accept the aid of a prince of Halas?" he asked, scanning the area to see if Syphia was resuming her attack.

"I am considering it," she replied. "If we survive this, I will make proper recompense. For now, did Arianne escape?"

Aeron stole a glance past the column and saw Arianne was no longer cowering under the stone altar. She was hurrying towards Dare, but the danger was far from over.

"Yes, but Syphia's attention does not linger too far from her," he replied, seeing the creature seeking out the queen again. This time, instead of pursuing Arianne, Syphia appeared to have a new target to fix her attention upon.

The king.

* * *

Celene, like Dare and the others, attempted to reach Arianne when the onslaught of beserkers and shape shifters derailed her plan. She found herself fighting back-to-back with her husband, as they had not done since Astorath. Syphia gave the beserkers somewhere to go after the fall of Abraxes, and it appeared now she commanded their loyalty as fiercely as Balfure. They were filing into the courtyard in seemingly endless numbers until the circle was fighting for every inch of ground they made towards Arianne.

Ronen was blocking the blade coming down upon him as he held the beserkers in a deathly grip, before he kicked out his leg, landing the ball of his foot on his opponent's stomach and causing him to buckle. Pulling back his sword, he swung hard, shattering the enemy's blade, and taking the creature's head with it. The beserkers did not scream when it fell. The Lord of Gislaine lashed out with his sword, tearing the weapon away from the foul being's hands, and completed the battle when he ran it through.

Something he saw made him stop abruptly. A group of shape shifters, their black bodies changing shape with each step they took, was closing in on Tamsyn. At this moment, the only reason they had been spared the wrath of the Primordial was because the mage was using every bit of magic he could to fight her. Now, it appeared Syphia's shifters planned to ambush Tamsyn and distract the mage long enough for Syphia to gain the advantage.

"Celene!" he called to his wife. "We must help Tamsyn."

Celene followed his gaze, realising what he was staring at and agreed immediately. Nodding at him in answer, she rushed forward, her sword leading her charged, as her blade drove straight into the body of a beserkers in her path. She did not halt her grisly advance until the blade met air on the other side of his back.

"What are you waiting for?" She glanced at her husband with a little smile. "Do I have to save the mage myself?"

* * *

Dare saw Arianne finally free to leave that damn altar, after the beserkers seeking to recapture her had been put down, and he offered silent thanks to Aeron and the watch guard Melia for allowing her to do it. His own efforts to reach her were hampered by the weight of all the beserkers, determined to slay a king this day. It was a pleasure he was going to deny them, as he fought valiantly the numbers rallied against him. Aware he would become their target almost as soon as they saw him, Dare had sense enough to distribute the forces at hand wisely.

Beside him, Kyou was swinging his own blade—each arch was soon followed by a sharp and agonized scream indicating the dwarf lord had made his mark. Kyou's handling of the weapon was next to superb, and he was able to defend himself against sword and axe. The beserkers he felled lay on the ground unmoving, their black blood running into the dirt around their ruined bodies. The dwarf's size did little to hamper his ability to fight the formidable creatures. Since Balfure's invasion of their homeland, the dwarves not only knew how to make the greatest weapons in Avalyne, but they were thoroughly schooled in how to use them.

A beserkers slammed his thick skull against Dare's forehead, and sent the king stumbling backwards. The savage enemy came at him with a mace, attempting to crush his skull with a single blow. Dare slipped beyond his reach when he prepared to bring down the weapon upon the king. Dare managed to get behind him, and was there to meet the beserkers snarling in outrage at his escape, with the point of his blade when he sent it through the creature's neck. The enemy dropped his weapon and clutched the sword, trying to drag Dare forward. Wasting no time, Dare slid the dagger in his other hand through the monster's flesh and tore open his insides, ending any further effort on his part.

"DARE!"

Dare spun around to the sound of Aeron's frantic cry, and saw Syphia coming straight for him.

The beast opened her mouth and spewed forth a wall of fire the king barely avoided when he jumped clear. Hot flames consumed the beserkers standing near him, and their screams of agony filled the air, as well as the unpalatable stench of roasting flesh. Dare had just landed when he saw a shadow over him, and realized Syphia's spindly, but barbed, leg was about to smash down on him. The king scrambled to his feet and ran forward, trying to escape her reach, when another ball of flame stopped him in his steps. Back tracking, he did not have time to react to the tail that came at him.

Arianne watched in horror as Dare was swept off his feet and was flung half way across the floor. He landed badly, and did not get up again as Syphia approached. Even Aeron and Melia's efforts to hinder her progress towards the king did not affect the Primordial, since she was now standing over Dare. Her jaw widened and her mouth smoked with green fire as she drew breath in readiness for another fiery assault.

"You will do no more harm!" Tamsyn managed to escape the shape shifters intending to distract him, thanks to Ronen and Celene, who were battling them even in the midst of this confrontation between himself and the Primordial.

"And what will you do mage?" Syphia demanded malevolently. "Do you think you are fast enough to stop me from incinerating this mortal? Try me, mage, and see which of us is wrong."

Tamsyn faltered, because it was true. He could fight this creature, but could he act before Syphia exhaled the breath waiting inside her body? He was not sure, and he could not take the chance. Avalyne was now at peace because the races had rallied around *this* king. Without Dare, Avalyne would fall to chaos once more and might never recover.

"This cannot end the way you want," Tamsyn said coldly.

"It will end the way I choose," Syphia hissed, her eyes flashing an ever deeper red. "Give me the woman and I will leave him be."

"No," Tamsyn replied. "Never."

"Then watch as Carleon's king dies. Out of the chaos, I will give them a new king—a king who is not only of him but also of Antion. Not only will the world of men follow him, but when I dispatch Lylea, he will be High King to the elves too."

"NO!" Arianne screamed from where she was. "YOU WILL HARM NO ONE! NOT ANYMORE!"

Arianne saw her beloved Dare lying on the ground, blood running from his forehead, and knew he could be dead, *today*. She surrendered her immortality to be with him, and though she accepted those years would be only as long as a single mortal span of life, she was not prepared to lose him so soon. Not before any of the dreams they shared over the years were given shape.

This foul relic of the Primordial War already destroyed Tully, and for all they knew, might have killed Keira too. She was not going to allow it to destroy any more lives. Not Dare's or her mother's, and certainly not Avalyne. No more was she going to stand by and let this creature take away all she loved, beginning with her baby and now, its father.

Arianne stepped forward, ignoring Celene's cries to desist, and placed herself before Dare and Syphia. Her child, whether or not he knew it, would protect his parents even from the womb.

"This ends now, Syphia," Arianne glared at her with a stare capable of burning her dead, if it were possible. "You will cause no more mischief to any of my kin."

"Empty threats do not become you, elf," Syphia declared shortly. "You will come with me, or I will kill your precious king."

"You will kill no one," she said icily, and closed her eyes before chanting words of her own, words as ancient as the world itself. "Not me, not my husband or my son!"

She was the queen.

She was an also an elf, with human in her past, but there was a Celestial in her lineage and his blood ran through Arianne's veins. She never called upon him for help, because it was not the way of elves to call upon those who made them immortal, to fight their war. This evil before her was one Enphilim knew well, and she needed his aid as she never needed it before. Her mother had told her to reach into herself, to bring forth the power she had inside her when the needs was great.

Your blood is more than just human or elf. Your grandfather was sired by a god and that, too, runs through your veins. You will do well to remember that.

The need was never as great as it was now. She made her demand, feeling something shift inside her mind. For a moment, she could feel the waters of the Brittle Sea pressing against the undersea walls of rock surrounding Sanhael. She called upon Enphilim, who gave his son a sword made from the heavens.

Arianne hoped he was listening to her now.

"What are you doing?" Syphia demanded, as she heard Arianne chanting ancient words, predating even the ones her shifters uttered to resurrect Mael.

Arianne did not listen. She continued to invoke the ancient words of calling, and only when the cavern began to shake, did they know what she was doing. The rock began to heave around her, and the cracks miniscule when she arrived began to widen, allowing more and more water to seep through.

"STOP THIS!" Syphia bellowed, leaving Dare, and approaching Arianne.

"Kill her, if you dare," Tamsyn challenged the primordial viciously. He recognised the words, and he willed his own power into her, giving her the help she needed to reach the Celestial he served, to gain a boon to fight this evil from the ancient times.

Behind him, Dare started to stir. The reverberations in the rock travelled through his skin from the ground and roused him abruptly out of his dark sleep. His head throbbed as he sat up, but whatever disorientation he felt was driven away when he saw his wife standing before Syphia, uttering words so old, even he had difficulty in understanding them.

Their effect was obvious. Chunks of rock were breaking free from the walls the cavern. Water spilled from the ocean in columns of white froth. The beserkers and the shifters starting to see the danger, lowered their swords, trying to decide what to do.

The sword. Take up the sword.

Dare did not know who spoke to him, for the voice was unfamiliar, but the prompt was enough. He looked about and saw the sword left neglected on the floor all this time—the beautiful ornate sword making Narthaine seem plain in comparison. Ignoring the pain to his limbs when he attempted to stand, his body filled with rage and determination. Propelled by a singular purpose, he stood up and ran towards Arianne. Syphia was so busy spouting threats she did not see Dare take up the blade and hurl it like a spear.

When she realised her mistake, Syphia made a desperate attempt to evade the blade that brought her to ruin at Antion's hands. Antion's sword, forged from the stuff of stars, sank deep into the creature's belly. The beast threw back her head and uttered a roar of agony, fire bellowing out of her mouth as she expressed her pain. Dare closed the distance between himself and Syphia, as Arianne continued to chant, oblivious to everything but what she needed to do.

The creature was gripped in pain and attempting to retreat, when Dare skidded beneath its belly and retrieved the sword. He slashed again at Syphia's bleeding torso, and rolled out from underneath the beast, as her weight forced her to the ground, avoiding being crushed. The king stood up and rounded the beast's body, standing before Syphia's elongated neck.

Syphia was mustering all her strength to reduce him to a cinder, when a phalanx of arrows and crossbow bolts struck her hide. While it did not penetrate, it served the purpose of allowing Dare to deliver the final blow. Not since he killed Balfure had a blade been swung with such purpose. The sword slashed through Syphia's neck, severing her head from her body, and silencing her screams of outrage.

Syphia's collapse coincided with an explosion of sound all around them. The cavern began to crumble, with the ocean pouring into the city. What shifters and beserkers remained, were now fleeing in blind panic, seeking refuge in the high ground. Dare, still holding Antion's sword in his hand, turned to his wife. He found her in Tamsyn's arms, having fainted from the invocation of such powerful forces.

"Arianne!"

"She is alright," Tamsyn quickly explained, as the king swept his wife into his arms. "The strain was too much for her."

"We have to get out of here!" Kyou shouted as the deluge rose about them.

"Everyone!" Ronen shouted, leading the others towards the caverns, back to the Frozen Mountains. "Let's go!"

As the company made their way through the city, more and more of the cavern began to crumble. Great chunks of stone smashed against the ground, until it was raining fragments of debris over their heads. Dare clung to Arianne, protecting them both with his body while Tamsyn kept behind them, ensuring the king and queen were safe from any other threat. He watched briefly as the water swirled around Syphia's body, staining it with the dead beast's blood briefly.

This time, there would be no resurrection for the Dreaded Mother of All. Syphia's days of mischief upon the world were finally done.

* * *

The company came to a pause when they were a good distance away from Sanhael. Tamsyn brought down a wall and sealed the rest of the caves from the rising tide behind them. There was no telling how many beserkers or shifters escaped the city. Their fear of the water sent them scurrying to the heights of the city, instead of escaping the cavern, ensuring a good many would drown with Sanhael.

Although it would be a few hours before they reached the outside world again, for the moment, the danger was passed, and so time could be afforded for everyone to catch their breaths. Each of them had journeyed far, fought terrible odds and even worse enemies, to reach this point. Tamsyn felt they deserved a rest while they addressed their wounds, and made themselves fit to resume their journey. Although none were injured badly, there were enough wounds to ensure some measure of healing was required for all members of the company.

"Rian," Dare whispered as he lay Arianne down on the ground beneath his cloak. She had not stirred since they departed Sanhael, and despite assurances from Tamsyn she was well, he had to see it for himself.

Arianne's eyelids fluttered at the sound of her name and her brown eyes rested upon him "Dare," she said softly, her hand resting upon his cheek. "You are alive."

"I would not leave you," he almost cried at the sound of her voice in his ears. Her hand drifted to his cheek and he held it there, his heart swelling from her touch. "I promised you a lifetime and that is what we will have."

"Our baby is safe," she swallowed, unrestrained with her tears. "I kept him safe for us."

"I know." Dare took her into his arms and held her tight. "When he is born, I will tell him of how brave his mother was; of what she did to ensure he was born in the light. I love you Rian." He parted from her and their lips met in a soft and lingering kiss. "I have never loved you more than at this moment."

And they held each other for a long time, forgetting the world and the others, because for this one moment, they were neither king nor queen, elf or man—just two halves of the same heart reunited.

Epilogue

The Little Prince

Despite their escape from the Frozen Mountains and the successful rescue of Arianne and Celene, there was no celebration when they finally headed home.

Even though Arianne and her companions were safe, it was difficult to forget who would not be returning home at all. That Tully Furnsby would be denied a proper burial, like his wife seven years ago, weighed heavily upon Dare's conscience. It would be a regret that would follow him all his days, and remind him how much he owed the couple who had lost everything to help him. Arianne tried to comfort him, but she too felt the same sorrow. She was mourning the loss of a friendship of seven years, an illusion from the start, just a way for Syphia to gain their trust.

The griffin upon which Arianne and Dare rode was willing to return them quickly to Sandrine, and Arianne was grateful for this. After everything she had been through, she wanted to enjoy what was left of her pregnancy in the comfort and safety of her home, with her husband close by. Dare would not deny her that request, and in truth, he would be more at ease once she was within the safety of Carleon once again. They did not know how many beserkers and shifters escaped Sanhael, but if more were about, they may try to avenge Syphia's loss on Arianne.

Celene and Ronen decided not to head directly to Sandrine, choosing instead to visit Angarad on their way home. Yalen had not met Ronen yet and Celene thought it was time he met her family. Furthermore; she had not seen her father since leading Angarad's forces across the Burning Plain towards Astorath. She longed to see him and her brothers again, to spend a few weeks in Wyndfyre, before it was time to return to Gislaine. Ronen was so grateful she was alive and well he would have denied her nothing, and the king was happy to spare him while he visited with his Angarad family.

While the griffin offered to bear the watch guard back to safer lands, Melia declined, for she had no intention of leaving Serinda behind. She offered to take the horses back to safer land for Celene and Arianne, who felt similarly about their mounts. Aeron offered to escort the watch guard back to Angarad, despite the lady's protestations she was more than capable of handling herself.

To ensure both were still alive when they reached their destination, Kyou decided it was probably best he accompanied the two. There was only thing worse than travelling on the back of the horse, in his opinion, and that was travelling upon the back of a griffin. In truth, they would pass close to the Jagged Peaks, and it was an opportunity for the dwarf to spend some time with his lady and his family, before returning to Sandrine to complete work on that city's fortifications.

Before their departure, Dare gave Melia orders to give to the Guard at the Green. They were to begin an immediate search of the old wood for Keira's remains. Although the possibility of finding her body was remote, the king insisted an attempt be made. He owed Tully that much at least, and Melia was happy to take the message back for him. If they could not bury the husband, at least they could do something for the wife.

Tamsyn chose to accept the griffins' offer, and returned to his tower in the Jagged Teeth. Dare suspected Tamsyn was grieving the loss of Tully deeply. The mage become fond of the farmer during this quest, and knowing they were unable to save him, burdened the mage greatly.

Dare understood his pain all too well.

* * *

With the departure of the others, Aeron, Kyou, and Melia began their journey home.

The watch guard said little as they travelled, though Aeron's reason for this journey was providing Kyou amusement to no end, despite the elf's claims otherwise. It was clear Melia was more than capable of taking care of herself and leading the horses back to Angarad alone.

Aeron insistence it was a journey unsafe for a lady, did not earn him her gratitude, but rather her utmost frustration. By the second night of their journey, Kyou was growing accustomed to hearing the two bicker about one thing or another. If he did not know better, he would think they were *married* already.

"I do not see why you insist on following me about everywhere—I have been taking care of myself quite a while before your vaunted presence in my life, prince of Halas," Melia grumbled as she returned to the camp with firewood she had been gathering. For some odd reason, the elf decided to accompany her on this task, and Melia was starting to think he did not believe her capable of doing anything for herself.

"I thought you might like the company," he remarked, with just as much exasperation, wondering if there was something wrong with this particular mortal that made her impossible to please.

"I am a member of the Guard!" She dropped the load of wood in her hands and growled. "I am accustomed to being on my own! In fact, I pride myself being able to endure being out there in the wilds in solitude. It is something of a job requirement."

"Fine, fine," Aeron frowned walking towards Kyou, who had been saddled with the duty of preparing the meal. "Obviously, my concern was unfounded. I thought a lady was not safe travelling alone in the wilderness. It is hardly proper."

"Proper?" She glared at him, hands on her hips. If Aeron had known a little more about women, he would have seen this as a posture taken by the gender when preparing for battle. Kyou wondered if he ought to tell the elf that.

Then he came to his senses. It wouldn't have been nearly as funny to watch.

"I am a lady in every sense of the word, prince of Halas," Melia glowered imperiously. "I simply do not need the assistance of an elf, who seems to think without him holding their hand, every woman in Avalyne would fall to ruin!"

"I have no intention of holding your hand, lady," Aeron retorted.

"Do not make me come over there and separate you two," Kyou warned good-naturedly. Both of them ignored him.

"I'm going to check on Serinda," Melia stormed off beyond the radiance of the campfire.

"Are you sure you do not require company?" Aeron called out after her, just to be annoying.

Kyou rolled his eyes in resignation, wondering how a thousand year old elf could behave like a five-year old.

Melia did not respond, but Kyou swore he heard teeth gnashing.

Aeron sniggered to himself as Kyou thrust a plate of food into the elf's hands, shaking his head with a mixture of reproach and disbelief. "When I remarked you were in sore need of female company, I had no idea you were in *this* bad a state," Kyou remarked, giving Aeron a look.

"Female company?" Aeron stared at him with incredulity. "You think I have feelings for that?" He gestured at the path taken by Melia.

"Obviously not," Kyou replied with a straight face. "That is why you insist of following her around like a puppy."

"I resent the implication," Aeron glared at the dwarf, who until a moment ago, he thought was his friend. "The lady is resourceful to say the least, but I am only keeping an eye on her, as I would anyone, including you."

"Were you to keep an eye on me in that fashion, Aeron, people would *talk*," Kyou teased.

"I am not having this discussion with you," the elf retorted, turning to his meal.

"Just as matter of curiosity," Kyou said, not about to let the subject go, at least without a few more digs at the elf's expense. "How long has it been since you were with a woman?"

"I do not see what that has to do with anything," Aeron muttered, suddenly uncomfortable with this subject.

"*That* long," Kyou muttered under his breath.

"Maybe I ought to see what's keeping her," Aeron put down his place and stood up.

Kyou would have told him that was not entirely the best idea, but the elf was already striding towards the horses. Instead, the dwarf enjoyed his meal and braced himself for the inevitable scream of exasperation that would tear through the night in a matter of seconds.

He did not have long to wait.

* * *

Dare paced.

He paced, and ran into Aeron.

"Sorry." The king apologised blankly, and resumed a little farther away from Aeron, who also did the same.

Ronen was content to occupy his time with a deck of cards, and realised perhaps his mind was not on the game, since he was playing himself and *losing*. Kyou sat patiently at the window, watching the display between king and prince.

Outside, it was raining heavily. The wind lashed at the Keep, and the rain filled the air with a fierce pitter-patter that only served to aggravate the tempers of all those present. Occasionally, a bout of thunder would rumble through the air and the king would pause, curse the fact he was startled, and resumed his pacing all over again.

This had been continuing for better part of six hours now, and the entire castle was going through the time in a state of limbo. The anticipation in the air was so heavy no one could think of anything else. Maids and servants spoke in whispers, while soldiers at their posts glanced periodically at the section of the castle where the queen's chambers were situated. Indeed, Kyou would not be surprised if the whole of Carleon was charged with the same anticipation gripping gripped the occupants of this room.

"How long does it take?" Dare paused finally, unable to endure this endless waiting any further. Not even the battle of Astorath was this hard!

"As long as it's meant to," Kyou shrugged. Although he was never in the position himself, dwarf men knew their place at times like this, and it was as far away from the women as possible. All their presence served to do was to infuriate the women, who would order them away until the event was over.

"How can you be so patient?" Ronen demanded, his own frustration expressed when he tossed the cards in the air and let them flutter around him aimlessly. He was not the one in the centre of this maelstrom, but he was just as caught up by it as the rest of them. Ronen was more than aware he could find himself in this position soon enough. Besides, the king was his friend, he could relate to Dare's anxiety.

"I'm not the one whose wife is in labour," the dwarf grinned mischievously.

"That is it." Dare decided he could not wait anymore. Hours he had waited, hours since Arianne was spirited away from him by midwives and Celene. He had no word from any of them, except to see them scurrying out of her chambers at regular intervals. Why could he not be there for her? He was her husband! "I cannot endure this torment any longer. I am going in there."

"No, you're not." Aeron grabbed his arm, before Dare did anything he would regret. "If you go in there, you will only get in their way."

"I do not care, Aeron," Dare said promptly. "If there is any consolation to being king, it is not having to account for myself, if I chose to enter my wife's chambers. Now, unhand me," he demanded.

"Dare, calm down," Ronen insisted, joining Aeron in trying to prevent the king from barging into the birthing chambers. "The midwives know what they're doing. If you go in there, you will only be hampering their efforts to help Arianne deliver the baby. Have patience."

"Do not tell me to have patience!" Dare hissed in exasperation as he threw his hands up in defeat. "My wife is in there, screaming her head off as if she were being ripped apart. I would be there at her side to endure this agony."

"Yes, I am certain you being there at her side is enduring this agony for her," Kyou snorted.

The king was about to question this when suddenly a plaintive wail of a child filled the air. It was one short cry at first, sharp and piercing, then a longer one that tugged at the hearts of all who heard it. The effect upon them all was immediate, with wide grins and back-slapping moving about the room in quick succession. When the door to the birthing chamber opened, Celene stepped out, and the bundle she was carrying announced itself without any difficulty.

"Would you like to see your son?" Celene smiled radiantly.

Dare swallowed and stared at the babe in her arms. The newborn was all creases and pink flesh. His eyes were open, but they were too new for him to see anything. Dare reached for his son and cradled the infant gently in his arms. Though it was impossible to tell who his son resembled more, his bow shaped mouth was definitely Arianne's, and as Dare looked at him, he felt as if his whole life had been in wait for this moment.

"He's beautiful, Dare," Celene commented as Ronen slipped his arm around his wife, and they shared a little kiss as they watched the king regarding his son.

"Arianne?" Dare looked at the Lady of Gislaine.

"Is waiting for you both," Celene concluded before he could say anything else.

* * *

"He *is* beautiful," Dare agreed softly with Celene's declaration when he stood at the doorway to Arianne's chambers, his smile wide as he regarded his wife who looked terribly exhausted after her labours today. "Almost as beautiful as you."

Arianne turned to him and smiled wearily. There was still perspiration on her face and though she would always be radiant to him, it was clear that she was at the limits of her endurance. She was in need of a good rest. Dare carried their son to her and nestled the child in the crook of her arm. Arianne's eyes filled with tears as she saw her babe again, the child born into the light with no trace of Syphia's evil spell, or Mael's darkness upon his cherubic face.

"Oh, Dare." She tried not to cry, but the emotion of the moment made her weak, and she could not help herself. "He is everything we dreamed he would be."

"Yes," Dare agreed, and he leaned over to plant a soft kiss upon her forehead. "He is, my love, the finest thing we have ever done together."

"He will be the first," Arianne smiled happily. "I intend for him to have a house full of brothers and sisters."

"I do not care how many children we have, Rian," Dare whispered, as he held her in his arms as she held their child. "As long as I have them with you."

"And I with you," she replied before their lips met in a warm kiss.

When they parted, Dare stared at his son's face and remarked, "So, what will your name be, young Prince?"

"I was thinking," Arianne said with a little smile, "Braedan Tully."

Dare's eyes misted over and he nodded. "I think that is perfect."

Coming in January 2016

THE EASTERLING

BOOK TWO IN THE AVALYNE SERIES

In her dreams, Melia hears her mother screaming.

When Watch Guard Melia sets out to find her mother, Ninuie, elf Prince Aeron of Eden Halas joins her as her guide. Together, they journey across his homeland to find Tor Iolan, the abandoned fortress where Disciples of the Aeth Lord tortured and maimed innocents. Within its cruel walls, Melia hopes to find truth about her past, while pondering a future with a prince, who has yet to learn falling for a mortal may cost him more than a broken heart.

This is a tale of darkness, romance, and loss where Melia and Aeron face the reality sometimes love is not be enough, and sacrifice may be the only course left to them.

About the Author

Linda Thackeray works at a publishing company a stone's throw from the Sydney Opera House in Australia, but lives on the coast in a suburb called Woy Woy, which apparently means "big lagoon" with her one cat, Newt. She has been writing for as long as she can remember and has never really stopped, although she has not written seriously for at least a decade. She had an epiphany moment a few months ago that made her decide to take it up again and now she is dusting off all the work she has let languish to take stab at e-publishing.